a DANCE with the FAE PRINCE

a MARRIED TO MAGIC novel

ELISE KOVA

Silver Wing Press

a DANCE with the FAE PRINCE

a MARRIED TO MAGIC novel

ELISE KOVA

Published by Silver Wing Press
Copyright © 2021 by Elise Kova

Cover Artwork by Marcela Medeiros
Developmental Editing by Rebecca Faith Editorial
Line Editing and Proofreading by Melissa Frain

ISBN (paperback): 978-1-949694-33-8
ISBN (hardcover): 978-1-949694-34-5
eISBN: 978-1-949694-29-1

Also by Elise Kova

Married to Magic

A Deal with the Elf King
A Dance with the Fae Prince
A Duel with the Vampire Lord

Air Awakens Universe

AIR AWAKENS SERIES
Air Awakens
Fire Falling
Earth's End
Water's Wrath
Crystal Crowned

GOLDEN GUARD TRILOGY
The Crown's Dog
The Prince's Rogue
The Farmer's War

VORTEX CHRONICLES
Vortex Visions
Chosen Champion
Failed Future
Sovereign Sacrifice
Crystal Caged

A TRIAL OF SORCERERS
A Trial of Sorcerers
A Hunt of Shadows

Loom Saga

The Alchemists of Loom
The Dragons of Nova
The Rebels of Gold

See all books and learn more at:
http://www.EliseKova.com

for everyone who stays up late
reading books about kissing

Table of Contents

Vampir Mountains

Midscape

Quinnar

one

WHEN THE MONEY RAN OUT, JOYCE SOLD THE PAINTINGS,
THEN FATHER'S SILVER, THEN MY MOTHER'S JEWELRY AND
DRESSES, THEN EVERYTHING OF VALUE IN MY CORRIDOR. She
sold and sold to fund her parties and ambitions. She sold to
try and reclaim some of the glory that died with my father.

Now there is nothing left.

So today she will sell my hand in marriage.

It hasn't been said plainly. I just know it to be true. I've
known it for over a year now—I feel it deep in my bones,
in the same way I can feel a storm lingering just beyond the
horizon, the air thick with anticipation. It started with little
comments my sisters made, small things, here and there.
Every time, I was "unreasonable" for reading between the
lines.

But that's where the truth always lies, isn't it? The
unsaid between.

Then, mentions of marriage and "suitable arrangements
for my age" became common around the dinner table. I
eat too much and do too little. Marrying me off makes the
most business sense, and Joyce is a businesswoman before
anything else.

The thoughts are as heavy and inescapable as the fog
drifting across the rolling highlands that stretch from my
father's estate down to the dense forests that cluster at the
foot of the Slate Mountains. These worries have been an

unshakable cloud hanging over my head for weeks. I shift Misty's reins in my hands. She lets out a whinny and shakes her head; I pat her neck in response. She can sense my displeasure.

"It's all right," I reassure her. But I honestly have no idea if anything is all right or not. Today's the day Joyce will meet with the man who will purchase my hand in marriage. Everything hinges on discussions had in a room that I'm not even privy to. "Let's go, one more run to the forest."

Misty is a gray-colored mare, but I didn't name her for her coat. She was born in the late fall months like this three years ago. I stayed up all night in the stables with her mother, waiting to meet her. I wanted to make sure that I was the first person she saw.

She's the last thing my father gave me before his ship went down.

From then on, every morning, we've been inseparable. Misty runs with a speed that makes me feel like my feet have left the earth and I soar with the birds above. She runs because she understands the pain of being trapped and saddled day after day. As we fly over the wet soil, cutting through the mist like an arrow, it crosses my mind not for the first time that maybe we should just keep running.

Maybe I could liberate us both. We would go…and never come back.

The trees come out of nowhere—a solid line of sentinels, more like a wall than a forest. Misty rears back, nearly throwing me. I tug and twist, regaining control. We trot along the doorstop of the dark forest.

My eyes scan between the trees, though there is little to see. Between the mist and the thick canopy, anything beyond a few feet is as dark as pitch. I tug lightly and bring us to a stop to try and get a better look, though I don't know what I'm searching for. The townsfolk say that they see lights in the woods at night. Some brave huntsmen who dare to go past the natural barrier of man and magic claim that they have seen the wild and wicked creatures of the forest—half man, half beast. The fae.

Naturally, I've never been allowed into the woods. My palms are slick with sweat and I rub them on the thick canvas of my riding pants. Just being this close always fills me with a restless anticipation.

Is today the day? If I run into the forest, no one would follow me. People who go into the forest are presumed dead after less than an hour.

The sharp cry of our rooster echoes to me over the slowly sloping hills. I glance back up in the direction of our estate. The sun is beginning to tear through the mist with its obnoxiously bright fingers. My brief moments of freedom have expired... It's time to face my fate.

The ride back takes twice as long as the ride out. Pulling myself away from the brisk twilight dawn, thick mist, and all the great mysteries that lie in that dark wood becomes harder and harder every day. It's made no easier by the fact that the *last place* I want to return to is the manor. The woods are appealing, by comparison.

Halfway back, it strikes me that this is the last time I'll make this ride... But I have no doubt that the freedoms I enjoy here, however limited they are to the brief hours of the early morning, are going to completely disappear when I am married off to some rich lordling to be his broodmare. When I will be forced to suffer whatever abuses he inflicts on me in the name of the most wicked thing in the world: "love."

"Katria, Joyce is going to skin you alive for being out so late," Cordella, the stable hand, chastises me. "She's been out here twice already looking for you."

"Why am I not surprised?" I dismount.

Cordella slaps me lightly on my upper arm and points a finger in my face. "Today you have an opportunity most girls would only dream about. The lady of the house is going to find you a smart, sensible match with a man who is going to care for you the rest of your days and all you have to do is smile and look pretty."

I've had enough people "caring for me" to last a lifetime. But instead, I say, "I know. I merely wish I got to have some kind of say in *who* that man is."

"It doesn't matter who the man is." Cordella begins unfastening the saddle as I take the bridle from Misty's mouth. "All that matters is he's rich."

When Cordella looks at me, she sees a young heiress. She sees the house, the dresses, the parties—all the presentations of wealth that Joyce can't let go of. She sees the glittering facade left over from a time when we genuinely had all of those good things, long before it was all hollowed out from the rot of poor decisions and my father's death.

"I hope for the best," I say finally. Anything else would give off the appearance of being ungrateful. And from where Cordella stands as a woman of modest background and opportunity, I have no reason to be anything less than grateful.

"Katria," my youngest sister calls from the veranda that wraps around the entire manor. The sun has barely woken, and she's already dressed, looking like *she* is the one who will get married today and not me in my old, threadbare, mud-stained clothes. "Mother is looking for you."

"I know." I pass the bridle to Cordella. "Do you mind taking care of the rest?"

"I can make an exception today." She winks. Cordella has made such "exceptions" more than once. Misty was a gift from my father, not from the lady of the house. Not long after he began to be absent more than not on the trade routes, Joyce decreed that we could not spare any more expenses on horses. She was already aflame by the fact that Father wouldn't let her sell the foal off. So, if I was to have a horse, then I would be the one who would take care of it. Never mind that my sisters both have had stallions boarded for years and hardly ever ride them. Their expenses have never been "too much."

"Thank you," I say earnestly and start for the manor.

"You stink," Laura says with a laugh as I approach. For dramatic effect she pinches her nose.

"Are you sure that's not you?" I give her a sly grin. "I don't think you bathed this morning."

"I am as sweet as a rose," Laura proclaims.

"A rose?" I waggle my fingers. "Then what are all these stinky thorns?" I descend on her, tickling at her midsection. She squeals, pushing me away.

"Don't! You—You'll get mud on my skirts!"

"I am the mud monster!"

"No, no, save me!" She roars with laughter.

"That's enough." Helen cuts through the brief moment of levity with a severe note. Even though she's younger than me, she acts like she's the eldest. She's the one really in control between the three of us. Mother's favorite. "Laura, come," she orders our younger sister. Laura looks between Helen and I but relents to Joyce's second-in-command.

"You cannot keep acting like that," Helen scolds Laura.

"But I—"

"These childish notions. Don't you want to be a proper lady?"

"Yes, but—"

"Then you should start acting like one." Helen's short-cropped blonde hair falls over one side of her face. She has been coddled her entire life, and yet she moves like an assassin. She's constantly lurking in the shadows, and in my nightmares.

Someday, Laura will wake up and be just like her. The sweet girl I know will have been finally crushed under Helen and Joyce's heels.

"What do you need, Helen?" I try and bring the attention back to me to spare Laura.

"Oh, I came to deliver a message." Helen's smile is like a snake's. It's the same smile as her mother's. The same smile Laura will learn to make, in time. There are very few things about my father remarrying after my birth mother's death that I consider a blessing. But knowing that I don't share blood—and that horrible smile—with the woman who raised me is one of those few things. "Joyce wants you to go and mop the entry for our guests today."

A sudden and intense aroma of smoke fills my nose. I refrain from rubbing it. Whenever someone tells a lie, the scent of smoke is thick in the air. I tried to explain the sensation before and was locked in my room for speaking nonsense. So I've kept silent about the gift since then. It has become one of my precious few tools of survival.

"You mean I must leave and stop sharing your delightful company? How will I ever survive?" As I go to enter the manor through the door at Laura's right, Helen catches my arm.

"Don't think that just because you're getting married you're suddenly better than us. You're a bastard child, born out of wedlock, and a shame to our family name. You're going to marry the lord of some sad little nowhere plot of land and live out the rest of your days in the obscurity we've prepared you for."

Laura stares at her toes. There was a time she would've stood up for me. But that willingness has been crushed. Such sweetness... such light...fading right before my eyes. And I'm too weak and sad to stop it.

"I don't want to keep Mother waiting." I yank my arm away.

No matter what she says, I can gloat a bit today. *I* am the first to marry. Something that Helen wants desperately. She sees me as getting something before her for the first time in her life. The irony is that it is also the last thing I would ever want.

I enter the manor through a short hallway that deposits me into the main entry. Wilted flowers slump over the edges of cracked vases and perfume the air with the peaty and sickly-sweet scent of the early stages of rot. The delicate paintings of the ceiling are soot-stained from years of burning candles with not enough cleanings between. Before the incident on the roof, Joyce tried to force me up on one of the rickety ladders not long after the first time my father left on one of his ships to try and clean the ceiling. Given how young I was, I'm fairly certain she was trying to kill me. "If you're still burdening our coffers at this age," she said, "Then the least you can do is help with the upkeep. You have the hands of a man but the work ethic of a child."

As if I didn't spend every hour, of every day, already repairing and fixing this run-down remnant of bygone days. That is another thing that makes me darkly happy about this whole situation: They are going to lose their most valuable servant.

But as quickly as the wicked thought enters my mind, it leaves. There are vague memories in the recesses of my mind of this place in its early days, when it was still lovely. Of *her*, my birth mother, the mysterious woman my father met in his journeys as a young merchant and brought home with him, ignoring all expectations of an up-and-coming young lord. I can remember sunlight streaming through the now grime-covered windows that overlook the front of the manor. If I squint...I can almost remember her face, hovering over me. A rainbow of color fanning out behind her. She's beaming with joy and love as she sings one of her songs that are imprinted on my heart. I know laughter and music once filled these halls—filled me. But here and now, it almost seems too impossible to believe.

"What are you doing?" A gasp echoes from the mezzanine. I look up to see the only "mother" I have known, the woman who raised me, sweeping down the stairs in a bloodred, velvet gown. Her pale hair is piled up and harnessed by a tiara, making her look like the princess she's always wanted to be. "Men are going to be arriving any moment and you're standing there looking like you've been rolling in the pigsty all morning."

My clothes aren't *that* bad, but I don't argue. "I was coming in to change now." I ignore Helen's lie about the floor. I wonder if it upsets Joyce that I don't fall for their attempt to trap me into a scolding.

"Good. I have suitors to attend to." She folds her hands over her stomach, her nails painted the same shade as her gown. "Do your best to clean up as well as you possibly can. Otherwise, a man might realize what he's marrying and will run away before the papers are signed."

What, not *who*. I have always been her *little monster*. "I'll do my best."

"Good." Joyce wiggles her shoulders and stands a little taller. Whenever she does this, I can't help but imagine her as a large bird ruffling her feathers. "With any luck you will be married before sundown."

"*Married?* Not engaged?" I knew the discussions were happening…but I thought that I would have a little more time. That maybe I could meet the man before we were wed. That I could ruin this somehow.

"We've spoken about this many times."

"I don't think we have." We never have. I know it. And yet, my certainty is shattered with her heavy sigh.

"You are clearly misremembering again. Don't worry, I am here to help you." Joyce gives me that serpentine smile and settles her hands on my shoulders. I believed this lie of hers once. "So you're going to be good for me and not resort to one of your dramatic outbursts, yes?"

Oversensitive. Dramatic. She treats me like I am constantly on the verge of flying off the handle. As if I have ever done anything of the sort.

At least, I don't think I have...

"I'll be good," I hear myself saying. There's an instinct to the response. It's not me. It's what she's trained me to be.

"Excellent."

We go our separate ways, and I retreat to my room.

The second floor of the manor contains what are traditionally the family quarters. I lived there, once. But when my father began traveling more and more, suddenly Helen needed a whole room for her art studio, and my bedroom had the best light.

Here is where you live now, Joyce's voice echoes back to me as I stand at the threshold of the dark hall that leads to my room. I light a nib of candle—one I took when replacing those in my sisters' rooms. It illuminates the cracking plaster of the halls. The crumbling stone that tells the truth of this manor.

It's too much. There's not enough money to keep it in repair, not really. I do my best for the memory of my mother...and so that if Father ever returns he has a home to come back to. But all Joyce cares about are the common areas and her rooms. There's money enough for those. For the facade. Everything else, I think she would let burn.

My bed takes up the entire back of the room at the end of the hall, filling the space with wall-to-wall blankets and pillows. My old bookshelf, also far too large for this room, is mostly empty and the sparse objects that fill the shelves are practical ones only. My prized possession is the lute leaning against it. I go to pick it up and immediately think better of it. Someone is certain to hear me if I try to play now. I think Helen has trained hearing, like dogs, for the sound of my strumming. She protests whenever she is "forced to endure" a single note.

Once in a while, though, Laura will listen. I will miss the nights she finds the bravery to sneak down here and hum along to my playing. The only one who has heard my music in years.

Sighing, I turn to the wardrobe, surprised to find a new dress within. Well, it's not technically a "new" dress. I recognize it as Helen's from the springtime ball two years ago. It was only worn once, so the satin is still in pristine condition. I run my hands over the buttery smoothness, so different from the regular clothes I wear. The high neckline hides the scars on my back. No doubt intentional. I dare to use the upstairs bathroom. It's a small form of protest. But it feels better than the hot water stinging my skin. Most days I am the one heating and gathering the water for everyone else's bath. At the end of it all I don't have the energy to haul up my own. When I'm finished washing, I even dare to look through Helen's cosmetics, selecting a soft rouge for my cheeks that accents the stormy gray of my eyes and a deep red for my lips that brings out the darker rusty notes of my brown hair.

I emerge a new woman. My hair has been brushed and carefully pinned in a cascade of curls that even Joyce would be proud of. I wonder if I would have looked like this every day had my father never married that woman.

Joyce was a widow before she married my father. It was a smart match on the outside: they both had young daughters in Helen and I, and were of a similar economic background—she had inherited a good deal of wealth from her previous husband in the form of rare silver mines to the north. The same mines that only my father's ships could reach.

I caught on to her game early. But my father never saw it. Not even up until the very end, when he last left. He *loved* her. She had been the one to "save him" from the depths of despair following my mother's death. Then Laura came along, the light in both of their eyes, and the "glue," as they would say, to our dysfunctional little family.

Treading lightly across the squeakier portions of the floors, I sneak into my old room. It overlooks the front of the manor and gives me a view of the drive that connects us to the main road we take to town. Sure enough, there are three carriages parked along the front. I see a man in a top hat emerge from the main entrance of the manor. He exchanges a few words with his driver and speeds off.

I wonder how he feels about marrying a woman he's never even met. Clearly he's fine enough to come here and make an offer.

Then again, maybe we have met. Maybe the man I will marry is someone I've crossed paths with in town or at a ball. I shudder thinking of the lecherous Earl Gravestone and how he would look at me and my sisters in our dresses during our first seasons out among society. I pray that he does not come calling for me, or them when their time comes. There are some evils I can't even wish on Helen.

I creep out of my sister's art room before I can be found. Instead of taking the main stairs I take a side stair wedged between the primary bedroom and the wall. It's a servant's access that takes me back down to the kitchens. From there, I sneak through the house using other such hidden halls. One thing that my mother and sister never realized was that by making me their servant, and demanding I act the part, they also allowed me to learn all of the passages built long ago into this decaying home.

The wall of the sitting room adjacent to my father's study glides open on hidden, silent hinges. I creep across the room, footsteps muffled by the carpet. At the far end, I press my ear against the wall and hold my breath. It's thin enough that I can hear the conversations happening in the other room perfectly clearly.

"...and her dowry will be the north runner ships in the Applegate Trading Company," Joyce says.

I bite my lip. There are no north runner ships, not anymore. Those waters are treacherous, and my father had one of the few captains in the world that could sail them. She was an incredible woman; I met her only once but was utterly enthralled for every second of our brief discussion. She was only a year older than me and had been captaining ships for two years already. Perhaps it was reckless youth that enabled her to chart a course that not even the hardest, most salt-crusted sailors would dare to try across those choppy waters to access a rare vein of silver.

But even her luck had run out, as all of ours does sooner or later. She went down with her ship, my father, too. I didn't realize that Joyce had kept my father's disappearance quiet. *She's trying to fully control the Applegate Trading Company,* I realize. My nails dig into the wall. With my father disappeared—but not declared dead—she can assume control without question.

"That's a very interesting proposition," an old and weathered voice says.

I hope it's not too interesting to whoever this man is. Because if he marries me for ships, and then finds out there are none, *I* am the one who will suffer. I have no doubt that Joyce will concoct a clever lie if she needs to, saying the ships went down just after the wedding. *Calm down, poor fortune happens to everyone*, I can imagine her saying.

"Indeed," Joyce says. "So as you can see, this isn't what one would think of as a normal marriage. I recognize that it is customary for the bride to bring her dowry. But I'm a shrewd businesswoman, and I know the value of my daughter and what I'm offering. As such, I am asking all potential suitors to let me know what they would give me in return for the benefit of her hand."

There is a long pause. "My master has no interest in ships," that weathered, weary voice says. "You can keep them."

Master? Does that mean the man speaking is not my would-be husband? What type of man would send a servant to negotiate for me? I did not want love, but I had dared to hope for dignity. But if the man can't even be bothered to come now, then how will he treat me once I am in his care?

"Then what is it that your master would like as a dowry?" Joyce seems absolutely flummoxed that someone would refuse the ships. Though I can hear the delight at this making her voice tremble.

"My master is a collector of a certain variety of rare goods. It is come to his attention that you are in possession of a particular tome he has long sought."

"A book?" A pause. "Oh, you serve *him*." Joyce's voice sharpens. "I know Covolt always refused to sell it, but you will find me a much more amenable businesswoman."

The book… They couldn't possibly be talking about *that book*, could they?

When Joyce entered into our lives she decreed that all remnants of my birth mother be expunged from the halls. I had tried to object, but my father told me it was a natural thing for a new wife to do. That new love couldn't blossom in the shade of old. One night I went to him, utterly inconsolable. I begged him to save something, anything, just one thing. I had already lost the memories of my mother's face by then. I didn't want to lose more.

It was then that he showed me the book. It was a small, old

thing. Whatever lettering had once been stamped onto its leather had been mostly worn away with time. The only marking that was still discernible was an eight-pointed star at the top of a mountain imprinted on the spine. The writing inside had faded, leaving only illegible ghosts to haunt mostly blank pages.

My father swore to me that it was the one thing my mother had treasured most. The one thing she wanted me to have and keep safe—my birthright. And when I was a woman, he would give it to me. But in the meantime, he swore me to secrecy on the importance of the title. I'm sure to keep Joyce from destroying it like she did everything else of my mother's.

When I was worried most that Joyce would discover the book, I had told Father I did not want to wait. *Let me hide it*, I'd begged. But he said I wasn't ready. So he gave me the lute to ensure I had something of Mother's, claiming it was the one she'd used to sing my lullabies.

"My master had hoped that would be the case," the old man says. "He has empowered me to make the following offer: he will take the young woman's hand in marriage and look after her for the rest of her, or his, days on this mortal plane—whichever ends first. She will never be left wanting. He asks only for the book as a dowry. Furthermore, to show good faith toward your family, he will pay four thousand pieces when the marriage papers are signed."

My fate is sealed. Four thousand pieces is more than this entire manor is worth. That is one year's operations of my father's trading company during the best of times. I slowly slide down the wall as I realize this mysterious man who could not even be bothered to come in person will be my husband.

"That is a very generous offer indeed." Joyce's voice quivers slightly. I can imagine she's frothing at the mouth. "I shall draw the papers to immortalize this agreement, and cement the marriage. Shall we sign them tomorrow when your master can come?"

"There is no need to wait."

"Oh?"

"As I said, my master has empowered me to make such decisions on his behalf. I am able to sign for him and he's given me his seal. He said, should you agree to our terms, to conclude business immediately."

"Very well then."

Somewhere between the mutterings over the best wording for the agreement, and the shuffling of papers, I stop listening. I lean against the wall, hands shaking, fighting for air. The world spins sickly fast. I knew this would happen. I knew it. But now it's real and happening so quickly… I thought… *I thought I'd have more time…*

"There, it is done," Joyce declares as she no doubt finishes signing my name on my behalf.

"Good. Tell your daughter to collect her things as you collect the book." More scraping of chairs. "We will leave within the hour."

Just like that, I am married and am leaving the only home I've ever had…for a man whose name I don't even know.

two

"THE MYSTERIOUS LORD FENWOOD." Laura leans against the doorframe as I pack my meager things. News has traveled fast, expectedly, since there are only about five people at the manor at any given time. "I don't think I've ever seen this particular lord at any events."

"I think he's a recluse." Helen is opposite her sister. She has hardly ever come to my room. Seeing her here is an unwelcome oddity. "I've only ever heard him mentioned. They say he lives up north of town, that his estate is right at the *edge* of the forest."

"Oh, *him*!" Laura claps her hands. "I've heard townsfolk say he is an ancient wizard." She spins to face me as if this prospect is the best news she's heard in months. "If he teaches you magic, promise me you'll show me?"

"He's not going to teach me magic." Still, the optimism of my youngest sister tries to tug a smile onto my face, at least until Helen does her level best at squelching any joy that might exist between us.

"She wouldn't be taught magic. She would be *consumed* for it. I hear wizards exclusively drink the warm blood of freshly killed maidens and dance with horned fae in the moonlight."

"If he drank only the blood of freshly killed maidens there would be no young women left in the village." I roll my eyes and try to conceal the fact that I am actually somewhat alarmed that neither of my sisters know anything concrete about this man. They're so embroiled in the social circles of the greater area that if they don't know him then no one does. I had been hoping for some information on my new circumstances. "And no one dances with fae in the moonlight. If you get that close to a fae, you'd be dead."

"Assuming fae are real at all." Helen doesn't believe the old stories. She's too practical, she grew up farther inland and closer to her mother's mines...farther away from the woods and their tales. She thinks Laura and I are ridiculous for our suspicions. Yet she'll absolutely refuse to go into the woods herself. "It's far more likely that he's some horrible, wrinkly old hermit looking for a young woman to make his own."

"I'm sure he's wonderful," Laura insists. "And we will come and visit you and your new husband within the month. I hear Mother is going to buy a new carriage, hire a driver, and get three new footmen for the manor—*and* that's just the start! You'll have to come back and see the spoils your marriage has bought."

Laura means well, but she doesn't realize the dagger her words are.

I'm no better than a prized hog. But at least I could be of some use to her.

"It will be nice to finally have some real help around here," Helen says with a disapproving glance in my direction.

I did everything I could, and then some, for them. When Helen and Joyce first moved in, I tried to make them my family. I began doing things as they asked, when they asked, because I wanted to be a "good daughter." By the time I realized they were turning me into their personal servant, it had gone on too long for there to be any hope of stopping it. Then Joyce began to encourage Father to spend more time on ships. And after the incident on the roof... I never even dreamed of contradicting them ever again.

"I'm sure you both will be very happy here for years to come," I say.

"Until our own weddings," Laura stresses. She just can't wait to get married off to some charming lord. As the youngest and by far the most beautiful of us, she'll have her pick of men.

"Katria, come along now, you don't want to keep your new husband waiting." Joyce appears behind her daughters, eying the trunk she gave me. "Oh, good. I thought it might all fit in that *small* trunk." Joyce looks around the room with disdain. A small room, filled with a small amount of things, for a woman she tried to make small her entire life.

I vow then that I will never let this new husband or anyone else make me feel small. I will try with all my might to stand tall. I will never live cowering again.

"Let's go." I sling my lute onto my back and hoist my trunk.

We four trudge out to the wide veranda at the front of the manor. It's there that I get my first look at the butler who negotiated for my fate. He's tall despite having a bit of a hunch to his back, wiry, with beady black eyes and slicked-back gray hair. His clothes are fine, not overly adorned but clearly of good make. The kind of wealth that doesn't scream at you but whispers with easy confidence. Joyce could learn a thing or two from him.

"You must be Lady Katria," he says with a bow. He then looks to Joyce and motions to the chest at his side. "Here are the four thousand pieces, as promised."

"As you already observed, this is Katria. And here is her dowry." Joyce holds out a small parcel wrapped in silk. The butler unwraps it, checks its contents, and then reverently re-wraps the tome. My hands shake as I fight the urge to snatch it from his grasp.

"Excellent, all is in order. If you'll follow me, Lady Katria."

It strikes me as I'm halfway down the main stair between the veranda and drive that this might be the last time I walk this path. I don't know if I will want to return to this house, or the people living in it. I look behind me, up at them, and behind farther still to catch a final glimpse of the beautiful, time-worn paintings on the ceiling of the entry.

Mother wasn't meant to live here for very long, my father would say. Maybe, neither was I. Maybe I'm just fulfilling my destiny of leaving this place a bit too late.

I'm almost at the carriage when the clopping of hooves distracts me. Cordella leads Misty around the house from the side stables. She gives a wave.

"Miss, I figured you would not want to be leaving without this one."

I breathe a sigh of relief. Everything is happening so fast I wonder what else I've overlooked. Or what else I assumed would sort itself out.

"Cordella." Joyce's voice is like a whip, cracking through the cool air. "Take that beast back to the stables."

"What? Misty is *mine*."

"I'm sure your husband would delight in giving you a new horse, a better horse, as a wedding present. Don't be a selfish girl and deny him that," Joyce scolds.

"I don't want... I want Misty." I look to the butler. "She's a good horse and has been with me her whole life. It would be no trouble, would it?"

"There is room in my master's stables." The man nods.

Joyce shakes her head and brings a hand to her mouth. "I cannot believe it. I know I raised you better."

I purse my lips. Years of experience has taught me that silence is best when she gets like this.

"To think, you would disrespect your new husband and take from your family unnecessarily at the same time, all over a silly horse."

"Silly? See, none of you even care about that horse!"

"You are a lady, Katria Applegate. It is unbecoming to shout." Joyce has gone quiet. "Cordella, please bring that horse back to the stables."

Cordella glances between Joyce and me. But I know what she'll do before she does it. She can't object to Joyce's demands. Cordella turns.

"No! You can't do this! Please!" I rush to Cordella.

"Katria." My name is like a whip from Joyce's mouth. I flinch and freeze. Halted by the mere sound. "You are upset over nothing and making a fool of yourself."

I want to scream at her. She has the remnants of my father's business for herself. She has her four thousand pieces. They could buy a whole herd of horses. *Let me have Misty,* I want to shout. But I can't. Because like Misty I have been trained, I have been silenced by an invisible bridle that my stepmother shoved between my teeth long ago.

A gentle touch on my shoulder startles me. I look up to see that the butler has closed the gap. His eyes are surprisingly gentle and sympathetic.

"I will see to it that my master gets you a new horse."

She will never be left wanting. He had said that was the promise his master made. I could ask for anything I wanted but it would mean nothing. It would be empty kindness for the sake of fulfilling an obligation from people who care more about a book than me.

I jerk away. "I don't want his horses." I don't want his pitying or compulsory kindness. I don't want anything that could resemble closeness in this marriage.

"It's always something with you, isn't it?" Joyce murmurs, loud enough for everyone to hear. "Calm down and be graceful as you venture into this new stage of your life." She makes it sound as if I have somehow chosen this. As if this was something I *wanted.* I glare up at her before getting into the carriage.

Laura rushes forth as the butler assumes the driver's seat.

"Laura!" Joyce is nearing her breaking point.

"Go back to your mother," I hiss at my sister. I shudder to think of what reprimanding she'll face. Laura ignores me and Joyce, grabbing the door and preventing me from closing it.

"I'm going to miss you," she blurts with tear-filled eyes. My sweet sister. Barely fourteen. The best and most unbroken of us all. "You made this place bearable."

"No, that was all you." I quickly embrace her. The butler doesn't rush us. "Don't lose your kindness, Laura, *please.* Hang onto it with all your might until you can get out."

"You don't either." She pulls away and I refrain from telling her that mine was lost a long, long time ago. "I'll look after Misty, I swear it. Cordella will teach me. So maybe the next time you come back, you can take her then. I'll try and speak to Mother."

"Don't risk her ire on my behalf; you know better." I gently tuck a strand of hair behind Laura's ear. Movement over her shoulder catches my eye. "Now, go, before your mother comes to collect you." I gently push her away and shut the door. Joyce ushers Laura up the stairs with some choice, clipped words.

The carriage lurches forward and I quickly lose sight of them. No matter what Laura says...I doubt I'll ever be coming back.

Helen said that Lord Fenwood lived to the north of town. In my mind, that meant slightly to the north. Kind of like how our manor is *just* south. But it turns out Lord Fenwood lives much farther. It's late in the day when we arrive at what is to be my new home.

A tall stone wall, easily twice my height, is the first signifier that we've arrived. There has been nothing but rolling hills and the ever-present forest at my right for most of the day. An hour ago we took a small branching road, more like wheel ruts between the grasses, that plodded along toward the forest. I saw the wall first, stretching out from the trees, like some crumbling remnant of a long-ago castle.

Vines cling to the scrollwork of the iron gate. Small white flowers bloom, giving off a pleasant scent. The gate closes with a solemn clang behind us. There is no sign as to who or what could've closed it. The sound echoes within me with the same finality as a curtain closing on a performance.

We bumble along a winding road between hedges and small trees. It's like a miniature version of the ancient forests, without that same heavy oppressiveness that the true forest gives off. In the distance, I see a stag raise its mighty, regal head. There are so many points on its antlers that I know most noblemen would literally kill to have it on their wall. What does it say about this Lord Fenwood that he would allow such an animal to live unharmed on his property?

Eventually, the overgrowth gives way to a circular, gravel area and the carriage comes to a stop. The butler opens the door and helps me down. I get my first look at Lord Fenwood's manor.

It arcs around the circular end of the drive with two wings stemming out from a central tower. Here is the castle that the wall promised. The mortar work is old but well-kept. I have an eye for these things now, after repairing my family's manor as best I could so many times. The thatching on the roof looks fresh.

There's nothing that's inherently uninviting and yet the hair on my arms stands up straight. The air here feels charged. The manor is literally at the foot of the woods I swore to my father when I was a girl that I would never enter. So I nearly jump out of my skin when the butler unloads my trunk heavily on the gravel.

Beware the woods, Katria. Never go into them. Swear to me, on your mother's life, you will not. It was her dying wish to spare you from them.

"Apologies, Lady Katria." The butler jostles me from my thoughts.

"No apologies necessary." I force a smile and readjust the lute on my shoulder. My predicament is not this man's fault, and the best thing I can do right now is try and make allies where I can. "And just Katria is fine."

"Katria it is then."

"May I have your name?"

He seems startled I would ask and then thinks about the answer for what I consider to be way too long for such a simple question. "Oren."

"A pleasure to meet you."

"Come along, night is falling and we should see you settled before dinner." He hoists my trunk with surprising ease for a man of his years and leads me up three steps and into the grand entry of the central tower of the castle.

I am instantly struck by the craftsmanship of the place. A wooden stairway, with a scrolling banister of lilies and lifelike vines, arches around to the left of the entry. Windows flank the doors on either side, with colored glass leaded together to form intricate landscapes of fields and mountains. I run my fingers over their dark outlines, feeling the ridges of the metal that connects them.

"Is everything all right?" Oren asks.

"Yes. I've only seen windows like this in the town hall." Glass art is a lost craft. There are a few who keep up the old ways, and they're found mostly in the larger cities. They rarely come out to places this remote. This house must be ancient and it's a wonder these windows have survived at all. Or perhaps the lord can pay to have someone out to his estate for such crafts. Lord Fenwood is rich beyond all imagining from what I can tell so far.

"They are rare indeed."

He leads me into the left wing. Before we enter the arched door I try and glance up the tower. But I can see nothing beyond where the stairway curves behind the first landing. "Does the master of the house live up there?"

"Lord Fenwood comes and goes as he pleases," the butler says obscurely. I wonder where he would go; any semblance of civilization is well over two hours away. Perhaps he is a hunter who came into rare fortune and now seeks thrills by going deep into the woods.

"He has a lovely home," I say instead of pointing out that the remark was not an answer to my question. "I can't imagine why he wouldn't want to spend more time here."

The butler pauses in the middle of the hall. Windows that overlook the circular drive line our left, doors on our right. The silence makes me worried that I somehow offended him with the remark. Though I can't see how.

"There are a few rules you'll need to know," the butler says as he begins walking again. I expected rules to accompany my new situation and brace myself for them. "The first is that, should you need anything, you merely need to tell me. I will be available to you as I am able. However, as I am the only attendant of the home, I am often busy elsewhere maintaining its upkeep. I will come to serve you dinner every night, and should make you breakfast most mornings, so one of those times would be the best opportunity to inform me of anything you require."

"That is most generous of you."

He continues as though I haven't spoken. "The next rule is that you are only permitted on the front half of the estate grounds— along the road we entered on—and under no circumstances are you permitted to go into the woods."

"That's no trouble," I say easily. "That was a rule from my father as well."

"The final rule, and the most important one, is that you are only permitted to leave this wing of the manor during daylight hours, regardless of what you hear or see."

"Excuse me?"

"These rules are for your protection," he says, glancing over his shoulder. "We are far from town and close to the woods. The mists are thicker here and carry the old magicks. It's not safe for humans to be out at night."

I try and channel a bit of Helen's bravery when I say, "You can't be talking about the fae. They are nothing more than old wives' tales."

He chuckles as if I am a foolish girl, as if he has seen the fae with his own eyes and has lived to tell the tale. "Fine. If nothing else, worry about beasts of the wood. As long as you are within these walls you will be protected. But where the walls end, my master's protection ends as well. Do you understand?"

"I do." But I don't know how I feel about it all. I suppose the rules aren't unreasonable. And I have long ago given up the notion of going into the woods. I wonder what Father's reaction would be if he miraculously reappeared to discover that Joyce has married me off and my new home is so close to the dark trees that line the impassable mountain range that edges our corner of the world. Moreover, I expected my freedoms to be reduced once I was married and they seem to have expanded some.

All told, my new arrangement could be far worse.

We come to stop at the last door of the hall. As the butler pushes it open, the hinges catch and squeal loudly. He has to put his shoulder into it.

"Apologies," he mumbles. "This wing of the house never sees much use. I will fix that while you eat dinner."

"Tell me where the tools are and I can fix it myself."

He seems startled I would say such a thing.

"Don't let the dress fool you. I'm more accustomed to work trousers than satin."

"My master made a vow that you will want for nothing; he will take care of everything for you. I will see it fixed while you eat," Oren says somewhat begrudgingly. I wonder if his master would punish him for allowing me to do work. If he would be willing to allow me to do it on my own, but is unable.

I'm left with nothing but speculation still on who my husband really is.

Oren leads us inside, setting my trunk on a tufted bench at the foot of a curtained four-poster bed. It is opposite a large, stone hearth, in which a fire is already crackling. Just like everything else in this castle-like manor, the furnishings are fine and well-kept.

"Dinner will be within the hour. I hope you are amenable to eating earlier so that you can be back in your chambers by sundown."

"It's fine. I'm usually an early to bed, early to rise sort of person." I smile.

Oren only nods and leaves me. It isn't until after he's gone that I realize I've forgotten to ask what attire I should wear to dinner. And…if it is when I will finally get to meet the man I've married.

three

DINNER IS IN A ROOM ATTACHED TO THE BACK OF THE TOWER. The space is more conservatory than dining room. Pointed archways that frame expensively large panes give a view of the darkening woods that surround the back half of the manor. I feel like a butterfly trapped in a glass box and carried into an unnatural environment. I'm safe within these walls, but there is only a thin pane that separates me and whatever monstrosities live in the forest.

I stare out the windows at the very back of the room, peering past my reflection and into the depths of the trees. They feel older here than back home. *No*, I correct myself, *this place is my home now*.

"How do you feel about roasted boar and wild vegetables?" Oren carries in a tray on his shoulder from a side entrance.

"I'm not picky when it comes to what I eat," I say with a smile. I've had too many nights where hunger was the only thing on my plate to complain about any hot meal placed before me.

"Good," he says. "We don't have consistent food out here." He pauses as he sets the dish at the head of the table. "That isn't to say we don't have food. We have all we need. But the menu is whatever the forest provides and what needs to be eaten from the pantry."

"I'd be happy to help you forage," I say as I sit.

He looks aghast at the suggestion. "We are not scavengers rooting through the mud for food."

"Of course not." I laugh as if I have never been that person before. The need to scavenge was what prompted me to search my father's library for books on the local terrain. It's how I can tell a safe mushroom from a poisonous one. "I merely think wild mushrooms are delicious. And finding them is an activity I enjoy."

He pours me water and wine from two separate carafes. "It has been noted." *But nothing will come of it.* I can hear as much in his voice.

"Will the master of the house be joining me for dinner?" I ask.

"No, he takes dinner in his quarters."

I purse my lips. "Will I meet him after dinner?"

"It will be close to sundown then."

"He can come and visit me in my chambers if it is late."

"That is not appropriate."

I cough up wine into my glass. "Not appropriate? Am I not his wife?"

"On paper by the laws of this land, yes."

"Then I think it is fine if he sees me in my quarters." I put down the glass slowly, grateful that my hand doesn't tremble enough that it clatters on the table or spills.

"The master is very busy."

With what? I want to demand to know. I've tried for hours to handle this whole situation as graciously as possible. But I still have no idea who the man I married is. I have no idea how he came into his fortune, where he came from, what he wants, and why he needed a book enough to agree to pay for a wife just to have it.

"Could you please pass along to him that his *wife* would be very grateful if he could spend a few minutes with her before sundown?" I look the butler in his beady, black eyes as I make my demand.

"I will pass word along." He promptly leaves.

I eat dinner alone. It might be uncomfortable to some, but I'm used to solitude and time with just myself. In fact, in some ways, it's preferred. Silence is consistent and solitude is safe. There is no one trying to take my food from me. No one demanding that I engage

with them. No one about to push me from my place at the table so
that I can go start on dishes.

The plate is empty before I know it and my stomach slightly
uncomfortable. I ate too fast. The food is also richer than I'm
accustomed to. I lean back in my chair, unladylike, and pat the bulge
of my abdomen. It's been a long time since I felt this full.

This could be worse; I return to my earlier thought. My husband
seems to have no real interest in me. It's better than a man expecting
me to come to his bed tonight so that I can begin work on my "duty"
of giving him an heir to his fortunes. And I seem to have the same
amount as—no, *more* freedoms than back home. Plus, no one will
bother me here.

Oren returns, interrupting me from my thoughts once more.

"Are you finished?"

"Yes."

"Was it enough?" He collects my clean plate.

"More than." I sit straighter. "Please tell the cook that it was
delicious."

He gives me a sly smile and nods. "I will."

"Any word from my husband?" I ask.

The butler sighs. Yet again, something that should be a simple
answer has him stewing for far too long. "I believe he can make
time, five or ten minutes, perhaps. I will start a fire in the study of
your wing. You can wait for him there."

The butler leaves quickly, carrying out the dishes. I stand, and
do a lap around the dining table. I suddenly regret asking if I could
see Lord Fenwood. What if he's upset with the demand? What if he
wants nothing to do with me and now I have only tempted his ire? I
come to a halt and shake my head.

No, if I am to live here, and to be wed to this man, then I have
a right to *at least* meet him once. To know his name. If we have
nothing to do with each other day-to-day, that's fine. But we should
at least acknowledge the other's presence.

Courage gathered, I leave the dining room and head right. To
my surprise, the second door is open. A fire crackles in the hearth.
Mostly empty bookcases line the walls. A table has been pushed off

to the right-hand side, one that I imagine was once situated between the two chairs that are now back-to-back before the fire.

I cross and run my fingertips lightly over the leather. *What a strange sitting arrangement...* I muse. It isn't long before I learn why the chairs are arranged in such a manner.

A voice cuts through the silence and my thoughts, resonating deep in my core. It has the same tonal quality as the low growl of a wolf and sparks a prey instinct within me. *Run*, my better sense urges at the sound. *Run far from here, this is not a place for you.*

"Do not turn," he says.

Despite myself, I glance over my shoulder. Instinct, really. When someone speaks, I look. I wasn't intending to disobey... Not *this* time, at least.

"I said don't turn."

My eyes snap forward again. "I only saw a bit of your shoulder. I'm sorry, I didn't mean—"

"Oren has been over the rules, has he not?"

"Yes." The man I'm speaking to is of tall build, judging from where his shoulder came up to on the doorframe. But that's all I can tell about him. He's leaning against the wall to the side of the door, as if he knew I would try and look upon him despite his order.

"This is the final rule that you must know," he says. "Under no circumstances are you to ever lay eyes on me."

"What?" I whisper, fighting every urge to look over my shoulder once more.

"Oren informed me that you wished to meet with me. I am obliging you, as is now my duty. However, I will only do so if you swear to never look at me."

The chairs now make sense. I wonder if he is horribly disfigured. Maybe he's just cripplingly shy. Whatever the reason, I have no want to make him uncomfortable.

"That's fine with me." I take my seat in the wingback that faces the windows, my back to the door. "I'm grateful you took the time to meet with me."

I hear his footsteps across the floor. He has a wide gait, further confirmation that he's as tall as I suspected. His steps are light, almost silent. He walks like I do, as if he's trying to never make a sound. I can't imagine him being a very muscular man, given his footsteps. No...I'm imagining him as a wiry individual. Not much older than me, judging from the strength of his voice. I try and steal a glimpse of him in the watery reflection of the windows but the room is already much too dark for that. He's little more than a blurred shadow moving behind me.

The chair behind me sighs softly under his weight. The tiny hairs on the back of my neck stand on end. I've never been more aware of anyone's presence. I have never been more tempted to do anything than turn and look and see if my every assessment about him is correct.

"Now, what is it that you would like to speak about?" he asks, somewhat curtly.

"I merely wanted to meet you, is all," I say. "It seemed rather odd to be married to someone without ever—" I stop myself from saying "seeing them" and instead say "—speaking to them."

"You married me without speaking to me, why does it matter now?"

I can't tell if the fact wounds him or not. Did he hope that I would beg and plead to meet with him before signing the papers? Does he even realize that my fate was sealed with a stroke of a pen that I wasn't even holding?

"We are going to spend our lives together," I say. "I'd like to make that as pleasant as possible."

"There is nothing pleasant here."

My husband is *very* cheerful, it seems. I roll my eyes, grateful he can't see my expression. "You have a nice enough house, wealth enough to do as you please, no one telling you what to do—"

"Don't presume to know me," he interjects sharply.

"I would be happy to, if given the chance."

"I have no interest in you knowing me, because I have no interest in knowing you. This is an arrangement, nothing more. All you are is a bargain that I have to live up to."

I clutch my dress over my chest, as if physically trying to shield myself from an invisible wound. What did I expect differently? What had I really been hoping for? Some great romance? *Ha.* The type of love in the stories young girls read isn't true. I've seen "love" between my father and Joyce. *That* is the only love that's real, and it is not something to want.

No, I didn't want him to love me. But, maybe, I'd hoped I would not be seen as a burden, for once.

"Fair enough," I say softly.

"Is there anything else? Or are you satisfied?"

"I'm satisfied."

"Good. I expect to have no issues from you while you are here. Heed the rules, and you will want for nothing as long as you, or I, walk this mortal plane. You will never have to cross my path again."

The chair squeaks as he stands; his footsteps fade. I wish I had something else to say, or a clear picture of what I wanted. But the fact is I've never been allowed to want anything in my life. I've been told what I can and can't have for so long that whatever skill a person is born with to make those choices has been lost to me. It has withered and died from never being used.

I sit for almost a full ten minutes after I'm certain he's gone, just staring out into the dark woods. Night has fallen and the moon is waning, so it's almost impossible to make out the dark silhouettes that bar the forest. The longer I stare the more I am filled with a strange sensation that *something* is staring back at me.

Unable to tolerate the uneasiness any longer, I head for my own room. But as I emerge in the hall I hear footsteps in the main entry. My head slowly turns toward the door that serves as the entrance to my wing. Against my better judgment, I creep across and press my ear to the door.

There are muffled voices on the other side, but I cannot make out what they say. The words are strange, and foreign, spoken in a tongue that I don't recognize. I tread lightly over to one of the windows that overlooks the circular drive. It's empty. Not even the carriage that took me here is parked out front any longer.

Who is there? I wonder. *Do others live here?* Oren made it sound like there were only three of us in the manor. Would he lie? If so, why?

Heed the rules and you will want for nothing, Lord Fenwood said. Oren had also made those rules clear: I am not to leave my

Elise Kova

wing at night regardless of the sounds I hear. Whatever the lord gets up to in the late hours is not my business.

Fine. I don't mind being more long-term house guest than wife.

I retreat to my room and ready myself for bed. The mattress and duvet are among the most comfortable I've ever felt and I quickly fall into a dreamless sleep...

Only to be woken within the hour by bloodcurdling screams.

four

I JOLT UPRIGHT, CLUTCHING THE COVERS TO ME AS THOUGH THEY ARE ARMOR. The screams stop as quickly as they started and echo only in my ears. My heart races; my breathing is short and fast. I look to the door wondering if some bandit or worse is about to break through and murder me in my bed.

But nothing happens. The air is still and quiet once more. There's not even a breeze rustling through the trees of the woods outside. I do not hear the songs of nighttime bugs or the soft creaks of an old house.

I don't know how long I sit like that, but it's long enough that the muscles of my back begin to spasm from holding me so tall and rigid. I exhale and try to release some of the tension as I slip from the covers. Throwing a shawl around my shoulders, I lean against the door to my room, listening. I still hear nothing.

Knowing I must certainly be mad to venture forth, I crack open the door. Gray moonlight, little better to see by than a single candle trying to illuminate the whole hall, streams in through the windows. I look around and see no one.

I dash across the hall and lean against the wall by one of the windows that face the drive. I peek outside. The gravel is empty and smooth, as though Oren just raked it. I keep moving forward as though lingering in the moonlight too long will make me a target in this brisk and eerie night.

Finally, at the door at the end of the hall, I press my ear against the wood. There's no talking, no movement, and no screams. My hand falls upon the handle, trembling. I was given four very clear rules. But that was before I heard screaming. What if there's an attack? What if we're in trouble?

I push down on the handle. It doesn't budge. I'm locked in.

My heart is in my throat as I back away from the door. I shake my head, silently pleading to no one. I'm no longer in the hallway. I'm in the long closet underneath the stairs of my family's manor. The door is locked. Helen tells me that Mother has thrown away the key and that I will never see sunlight again.

I rush back to my room and curl up in bed, drawing my knees to my chest. All night, I stare at the windows that overlook the dark woods and remind myself if I needed to escape—truly needed to—I could shatter them. I have a way out.

Even if that way out is into the woods I have sworn to everyone never to venture into.

When morning finally comes, I breathe easier. There were no more sounds. No other strange things happened in the night.

I venture to the bathroom. I only inspected it briefly the night before. It's the third door in the hall, situating it between the study and my bedroom. It's a strange room with water that flows hot and cold from the tap by a magic I don't understand. I test this phenomenon twice during my morning ablutions. Both times the water steams if it runs long enough.

This is a strange place indeed.

Dressed and ready for the day, I stride down the hall. I'm far more confident in the sunlight than I was the night before. The door handle turns effortlessly, granting me access to the rest of the manor. I step out and am drawn to the dining room by the aroma of freshly baked bread.

A plate has been laid out for me. Two eggs have been fried and laid over cooling slabs of toast. Half a sausage is nestled beside them. It's a breakfast fit for a queen and I make quick work of it.

There's no sign of Oren, or Lord Fenwood, however. And I had desperately been hoping to catch one of them. I wonder if there was an accident last night that prompted them to leave early in the morning and take the carriage to town.

The scream still resonates in my ears.

When I'm finished, I collect my dishes and head to the side door I saw Oren step through the night before. Sure enough, it leads to a well-stocked kitchen. I can't fight my instincts; I look through the pantry at the dry and jarred goods. It's enough to feed ten people for two winters, easily. There's another door that leads down to the basement that I presume is cold storage. I'm not brave enough to venture into the dark after last night.

I walk along a preparation table to the back of the room, where there is a large basin sink set into the countertop, and tidy my dishes. The open shelves along the wall opposite the hearth allow me to return them to their proper place with ease. I emerge back into the dining room, half expecting Oren to be there, ready to scold me for daring to lift a finger.

But there's still no one.

The silence is unbearable. Especially since the last sounds I heard in this manor were those screams. I head back to my room with renewed purpose. I can't stay in this building a second longer. I can't live with that noise as my only company.

I change into a far simpler dress, one that only goes down to my knees so it doesn't get caught in brambles and with slits high on the sides to give me mobility. Underneath, I wear a sturdy pair of leggings. I take my lute, sling it over my shoulder, and venture back out to the main hall.

I come to a stop before the front door and repeat the rules Oren told me to myself. I am allowed to leave right now. It's daytime. And I am only venturing out in front of the manor, not behind. It's within their parameters; I'll be safe. I slowly glance over my shoulder. I might even be safer than in here.

The morning is crisp and refreshing. The air, even at the foot of the mountains, feels thinner and lighter. I can smell the dense pine of the forest behind me. The small saplings that make up the woods before me pale in comparison to their ancestors.

Out of curiosity, I follow an offshoot of the drive around the side of the building. Sure enough, it ends at a carriage house and stables. The horses are in their stalls. Carriage parked. So it appears they didn't head into town.

I almost go over to the horses but immediately think better of it. They'll remind me too much of Misty and that wound is still too fresh. Instead I turn on my heel and walk along the drive all the way back out to the main gate. It's closed, and the gravel here shows no sign of the cart being driven out this morning. Then again, I'm no real tracker—if I had been, my family might have eaten better—so it's hard to be sure.

Feeling braver, I walk along the wall among the brush and bramble. My sturdy work boots give me sure footing. Somewhere between the wall, the manor, and the drive, I come to a glade. Arrows of sunlight strike the ground in beams that pierce the thinning canopy above. The coming winter is making these trees shed and they've bled on the ground in shades of orange and red. At the center of the glade is a massive stump. It must have been one of the old trees, felled long ago to stop it from encroaching too far into usable land.

I sit and brace one ankle on the opposite knee, lute in my lap. Holding the neck with one hand, I lightly strum with the other. It's out of tune. Of course it is, it's been weeks since I last played. I make my adjustments and strum again, repeating until I'm pleased.

Pressing down with my fingertips, I pluck a single note and allow it to hold in the air. I hum, adjusting the pitch of my voice until it matches with the resonant sound in the body of the lute. I allow the harmony to fade and take a breath, before my fingers begin to dance atop the strings.

Pluck, pluck, pluck, strum. The introduction rises to a swell before stopping in a sudden silence. Then, the first note. I sing with the second.

"I knew you,
When the trees
Were on fire.

"I saw you,
When you were

Not a liar."

A brief interlude. I rock with the music. Swaying with the trees and breezes that round out my merry troupe. Strumming as we reach the chorus.

"Our song, rode on the mists of mountains high." I close my eyes, feeling the music within me as much as around me. The forest has fallen to a hush, as if listening to me play. It's been ages since I had a space to play *and* sing. *"Our song, lurked in crypts of kings gone by."*

I shift my fingers on the neck, transitioning back to the verse, now playing each note in harmony as I find the melody once more.

"I saw you,
When the—"

"Well aren't you a surprise?"

I've only heard his voice once before and yet I would know it anywhere. That resonance is deeper than a bass string. Richer than dark chocolate. I jerk, startled, and glance over my shoulder on instinct.

"Don't look," he reminds me.

I quickly stare forward again. "I didn't see anything. Well, just your shoulder again." He's hiding behind a tree.

"You're going to make me think you have some kind of obsession with my shoulders."

I let out a soft snort of laughter and play along. "Well, so far as I can tell, they are quite nice shoulders."

It's his turn to laugh. The sound is as bright as sunlight and as sumptuous as velvet. I have to force my hands to stay still so I don't try and harmonize with it on instinct. I know how annoying I am with the lute in my hands.

"I didn't know you can play the lute."

"I suspect there's much about each other we don't know." He

hadn't seemed interested in opening up the night before to discover such things.

"Where did you learn that song?"

"I'm not sure…" The taste of metal explodes in my mouth, like I ate something burnt or bit my tongue and now have blood on the insides of my cheeks. I hate lying. Whenever someone tries to tell a lie to me, I smell smoke. Whenever *I* tell a lie, I taste metal. Either way, lies are unpleasantness I try to avoid at all costs. "I must've heard it somewhere when I was very young. I've known it for a long time." Half-truths are easier.

My mother was the one who taught me that song. It was my lullaby. But as I grew older, and Joyce entered our lives, my father always told me to keep the things she taught me a secret.

"I suppose those sorts of old songs have a way of lingering in places like this."

"I suppose so." I grip the lute protectively. "Is it all right that I was singing it?"

"Why wouldn't it be?"

I think back to Helen, my mother, and their scolding. Laura's encouragement is weak by comparison. "I'm not a very good singer, or player."

"I'm not sure who told you that, but they were lying. You're exceptional."

The air is still crisp and clear; my nose isn't singed. *He's not lying.* He really thinks I'm good. "Thank you."

"Will you finish the song for me? It's been a very long time since I heard that one performed," he says softly. I can hear in his voice how unsure he is of asking. How hesitant. Maybe he feels bad for how he treated me last night.

"Only if you answer a question for me first."

"Yes?"

"Last night… I heard screams. Well, one scream. It ended quickly… Is everything all right?"

His hesitation is horrible. "Is it possible you had a nightmare?"

"I know what I heard."

"I didn't scream last night."

"I never said it was you." I can't stand his evasiveness. The way he's speaking to me right now feels the same as when Joyce would talk down to me, tell me I was mistaken when I knew I wasn't. Looking for any excuse to explain away or belittle how I thought or felt. "I went to investigate but couldn't because the door was locked—"

"You tried to leave your quarters at night?" There's almost a growl at the end of the question. Rage is a palpable thing and I can feel it radiating off of him. "There are *explicit* rules for your well-being."

I want to glare at him. I want to look into his eyes and tell him how unreasonable it is to lock me up like an animal at night. "Maybe I wouldn't have tried to leave if I hadn't heard screams. I thought I was in danger."

"That is precisely why you were told to disregard anything you heard. You are not in danger. The rest isn't a concern to you."

"But —"

"You are *safe* here." Those words should be reassuring but the way he says them, filled with such anger, pain, and frustration... It almost sounds as though the safety he gives me is begrudging. As though it pains him to look after me. I truly am more ward than wife. The same burden I have always been.

"If I am safe then you don't need to lock me in my wing."

"Clearly I do, because you disregard simple instruction."

"I am *not* your prisoner."

"But you are my responsibility!" The outburst silences even the birds. I hear them take wing to avoid this awkward confrontation. "I made an oath to protect you. That is what I'm doing."

I inhale through my nose and let it out as a sigh. My eyes flutter closed. If there's one thing Joyce and my sisters have taught me, it's how to let things go and move on. Bottling up anger only makes matters worse in the long run. Most of the time, I try and listen to my own advice.

"Please," I say as plainly as possible. I try and pour every drop of invisible pain into that singular word. It is as close to begging as I ever would like to be. "I cannot feel like I am trapped. I swear to you, no matter what, I will not leave my quarters at night. So *please* do not lock the door."

"How do I know you will keep your word?" He sounds skeptical. I can't blame him. He did give me just four rules and I admitted to trying to break one last night.

I wish I could look at him. I wish I could see his expression—that I could meet his eyes and show him that I'm being sincere. How do I communicate those things when I can't look upon the face of the person I'm speaking to?

"You'll just have to trust me, I suppose."

He scoffs softly. "Trust... Such a hard thing to give to *your kind.*"

"Has a woman burned you that badly?" I instantly cringe at my wording. For all I know, he's had a wife before. Maybe she *did* burn him. Maybe his face is so horribly scarred that he won't allow anyone to look at him. My back aches and I straighten my posture.

"Maybe that's what I'm trying to protect myself from."

The words still me. I hear the faint whisper of "stay out" and "stay away" dancing among them. I wonder who wounded him. A blow like he has endured—like I have—doesn't need to leave physical scars; it is much deeper than flesh.

"The vow you took was that I would never be left wanting. I *want* the door unlocked." I play my last card and wait, curious to see if it will work.

He lets out a dark chuckle. I can feel him wanting to resist and yet... "*Fine.* But know that the moment you leave those quarters at night I can no longer guarantee your safety."

"Deal." I can hear him move to leave. Leaves crunch under his light feet. I wonder what he was doing out here to begin with. It couldn't be checking on me. "Wait."

"What now?"

"You never heard the rest of the song." I adjust the lute in my lap and still avoid looking at him. "Would you like to?"

"Yes." That word is wrapped up in somber yearning. I wonder what this old folksong means to him as I adjust my grip and begin to play once more.

When the last note has faded among the trees I know he is long gone.

five

THERE ARE STILL NOISES IN THE NIGHT, BUT I'VE GROWN BETTER AT IGNORING THEM. Fortunately, in the week that has passed, there have been no more screams. One night I heard faint music accented by bells right when I was on the edge of sleep, as if drifting to me from a faraway place. Another night I heard heavy thuds and grunting that rumbled the door to the main hall. A different night, I heard laughter echoing from a faraway portion of the manor.

It's funny how quickly you can grow accustomed to something. Now, I hardly wake up anymore at the strange sounds. The first night after Lord Fenwood and I spoke, I checked the door to my quarters. The handle turned. He did as I asked, so I kept my word and did not open it. After that, I've never slept better.

For a week, I find a strange sort of peace to the repetition of my days. It is nice not to be ordered around or have expectations from sunup to sundown. I can walk through the brush and strum in my glade with not a care in the world. Once or twice, I swear I sense the presence of Lord Fenwood listening again. But if he's there, he doesn't make himself known as an audience.

Then, the peace fades into monotony.

Today, on the seventh day since my arrival, I wake up and lie in bed and don't have the energy to do anything more than stare up at the ceiling. What is the point of getting out of bed when there's nothing to do? At least back home I had a goal. Every day there was something to be done, some necessary upkeep that I would busy my hands with and would make me feel accomplished at the end of the day. At the very least, I'd have Misty to tend to and ride.

When I was married off, I expected to find a new purpose. I was apprehensive of whether I would *like* that purpose or not. But building a home and family would be something to work on and toward. Having nothing to do is becoming utterly mind-numbing.

"You didn't go out into the wood today," Oren says to me at dinner as he pours my glass. I'm surprised he's noticed my habits. We only interact at the beginning and end of the day and I've never seen him between.

"No…" I push some potatoes around my plate with a fork. "I didn't feel like it."

"Is everything all right?"

"Yes—I—I'm not sure, honestly."

"Are you uncomfortable?" He seems shocked I would have any reason to be upset or distraught. I can't blame him. I'm surrounded by a comfortable paradise, where all I have to do is say the word and my wish is granted.

"No, not at all." I laugh bitterly. "Maybe that's part of the problem. Maybe I'm so accustomed to being uncomfortable that I have no idea what to do with myself now that the discomfort is gone."

"Is there something I can get for you?"

"Not something to get…but something for you to do. Would you mind asking if Lord Fenwood would be open to a nightcap tonight?"

His fine gray brows scrunch together as he looks down at me with his beady eyes. "I can ask him."

I wonder what that unreadable expression meant for the rest of dinner. Oren doesn't return. I take my plate down to the kitchen, washing it as I have after most meals and returning it to its place. On my way back to my room I notice that the door to my study is open. The two chairs are waiting, sweating glasses filled with a cool drink perched on tables at their sides.

I'm eager to take my seat. I settle in, shifting until I'm comfortable.

Then, I grab the armrests and lean back into my chair, pressing my skull against the leather. Even if the lord startles me, I will not look. I want this meeting to go smoothly. I didn't realize how badly I've needed to make a genuine connection in my new home until I'm in this very moment. I might not want love from the man...but friendship, a shared goal or understanding, I could do with that, I think. Even in the worst moments at the manor I had Laura.

Oh, sweet Laura. I wonder daily how she's doing.

"You asked to see me?" That toe-curling voice startles me from my thoughts. I wonder if he knows that, however hideous he might imagine himself to be, with a voice like that he could have his pick of any man or woman.

"I did. I thought we might share a drink." I lift up my glass, raising it off to the side so that he can see. I hear the whisper of his footsteps drawing near. Without warning, his glass clanks softly against mine. He's close; if I turned my head I could see him. But I don't. Once more, the fire smolders so low that all I can make out of him in the window is a tall shadow. "What are we toasting to?"

"How about the fact that I've managed to keep you alive this long?" He chuckles darkly.

I laugh as well. "I'm not *that* reckless."

"But I have been known to be." The chair behind me shifts as he settles into it.

"Oh?"

"In my younger years, especially." The ice clinks in his glass as he takes a sip. "I have been the cause of many of Oren's headaches throughout his time caring for me."

"Oren has been with you a long time?"

"Yes, he's looked after me since I was a baby."

"Did you know your parents?" I ask softly, fully aware of just how difficult this topic can be.

"I did."

"How long ago did they die?" I stare into the lemon-colored liquid of my glass.

"What makes you think they're dead?"

"I can hear it in your voice. There's a certain tone people have when they've lost a loved one. That loss leaves a void that gives everything a hollow sound whenever they're mentioned." I take a sip, trying to wash away that sound from my own voice. "*Oh*, this is really good. And sweet, like honey."

"It's mead. Not the best bottle I have but certainly not the worst."

I smile faintly at the thought of him picking out a bottle just for this meeting from some dusty storeroom.

"Who did you lose?" he asks. My smile fades.

"Both of them," I say. "My mother died when I was very little. My father said she was not made for this world—that she was too good for it. But that he was lucky that she at least left me behind for him."

"And your father?"

"He runs—ran—the trading company, as you know…" I trail off. His death is fresher. I've tried to shove it away, into the same box my mother's loss occupies, but it's not the same. I had a life with my father. Mother is just faded memories and emotions imprinted on my very soul.

Lord Fenwood is patient, allowing me to wallow in my thoughts for several minutes.

"Joyce, his wife, she demanded he begin taking a more hands-on approach to the business by going on more trading ships. He was gone so often there were weeks I had to fight to remember the details of his face. Then…the ship he was on went down. No one found the bodies, so there was hope, for a while. But it's been so long now…"

"I'm deeply sorry." He means it. In none of our discussions have I ever smelt a lie on his breath. It strikes me that every single thing I've been told in this house has been as true as rain.

"I've survived."

"As we all do."

Even though we're sitting back to back, I imagine what he must look like behind me. Is he leaning back in his chair as I'm leaning back in mine? If you looked at us from the side, would it look as though we're trying to lean on each other, desperate for support? Isolated in a world where we have been cut off from those who should love us most?

"Oren tells me you are distraught. Is it the anniversary of one of their passings?"

I shake my head. Realizing he can't see me, I say, "No, Mother died in the early fall and Father was in the summer."

Saying it aloud makes me realize how close the first anniversary of his death is, and how much my life changed in a year. I should be sadder, I think. But I have felt some emotions so strongly I think they burned up, leaving nothing but charred edges of my heart behind.

"And 'distraught' might be too extreme a word," I force myself to continue. "I suppose I want something to do, some kind of purpose here."

"You don't need to *do* anything, just lounge in the luxury I can provide you."

"That's just it, I'm not made for lounging and luxury."

"You're the eldest daughter of a trader lord." He chuckles. "Oren told me of your estate. I know the luxury you are accustomed to."

"You still know nothing about me," I needlessly remind him with a bit of an edge. "And if Oren thought our estate was luxurious then you should have him check his eyes." His silence prompts me to continue. "The estate was held together by nails, plaster, and prayer. I should know, I was the one responsible for keeping it upright."

"You?"

"I know I don't look it, but I'm actually rather handy, if I do say so myself; I can do a good variety of maintenance and upkeep. None of them exceptionally well, I'm forced to admit. But well enough. I cannot cook you a feast, but I can make sure the food is palatable so that you don't go hungry. I cannot build you a house, or explain the finer points of architecture, but I can tell you when a roof is going to collapse and where you need to shore it up to make it last another winter until there's enough money to hire a proper tradesman." I pass my glass from hand to hand, thinking of all the things I learned from necessity. Part of me is afflicted with the sudden urge to explain Joyce's cruelty as some kind of misguided lesson. I shake my head and take another sip of the mead. Her intention doesn't matter when her execution was so wretched. I'm trying to give her benefits she does not deserve.

"So you are saying you would rather be my servant than my wife?"

"No," I say, so fast and sharp that I hear him shift uncomfortably in his chair. I don't even apologize for my tone. "I will *never* be someone's servant *ever* again."

I hear him inhale softly. "Apologies for my wording. I would never make you one."

Another truth. I release a sigh of relief. "But I would like a purpose, of some kind. I would like to feel useful, at least. I like it when my hands are busy."

"I'll speak with Oren and see if there are any tasks that he thinks you would be well suited for."

"Thank you." I stare up at the ceiling, wishing there was a mirror, wishing I could get a clearer glimpse of him. "What do you do to occupy the hours of your day?"

He chuckles again and I hear him take a sip. "Me? I'm trying to become king."

I laugh along with him. But the odd thing is, there isn't even a hint of smoke in the air. He's telling the truth.

But there hasn't been a king of these lands in years. What does he hope to become king of? I never find the courage to ask throughout the rest of our pleasant conversation.

The next morning Oren is waiting after breakfast. I nearly drop my plates onto the kitchen floor in surprise at the sight of him.

"You nearly made my heart stop." I breathe a heavy sigh, trying to calm my suddenly racing nerves.

Oren continues shoveling the ash from the hearth, tiny embers still smoldering in the back, ready to help reignite the fire. "I have more business being here than you do."

"Yet you never are."

"How do you think your food is made?" He glances at me as I cross the room to the sink. I expect him to tell me not to clean the dishes, but he doesn't. Perhaps it's because I've been doing it for a week now and he knows there's no point stopping me. Or perhaps it's because of something Lord Fenwood said last night to him.

"I don't know," I admit. "I assumed there might be a cook." I shrug and turn on the water, focusing on the dishes over him. I'm dying to know if there are more people in this house or not. But I don't want to pry too obviously. I already know that won't go over well.

"There is not."

"Then you are exceptional with seasonings." I flash him a smile.

Oren chuckles as he finishes dumping the ash into a metal bucket. "You're trying to get on my good side."

"I'm telling the truth." I cross the room to free up the sink so he can wash his hands—he's covered in soot up to his elbows. "Besides, I didn't think I was on your bad side. Do I need to get on your good side?"

"I suppose having you here hasn't been as bad as expected."

"A resounding endorsement," I say dryly.

He ignores the remark, turns off the water, and takes a little too long to dry his hands. I wonder what he's thinking. "The master has certainly become intrigued by you."

A tingling feeling rushes over my body, like the warm flush of a slightly too hot bath. Why does the idea of Lord Fenwood being *intrigued* by me excite me? I try and push away the sensation before it can reach my cheeks.

"What makes you think he's 'intrigued by' me?" Curiosity gets the better of me. I can't stop myself from asking. I have to know.

"He's been asking more and more after you, and I haven't seen him spend so much time with a new person in years."

He's hardly spent any time with me at all. If this is his definition of spending a lot of time with someone then it's a miracle he hasn't gone mad as a recluse out here. "Well, you can pass along that I enjoy spending time with him too. I feel much less lonely whenever he shares a nightcap with me."

"I will let him know." Oren heads for the side door to the kitchen, bucket of ashes in hand. "Now, come along. Despite my protests, the lord has informed me that you have work to do today."

"Really?" I can't hide my excitement as I scamper after him. However, I stop in my tracks on the threshold of the back door. "I thought I wasn't allowed in the back of the house?"

"*This* area is fine." Oren points to the old stone wall that lines the perimeter of the property where it stretches beyond the right wing of the house and back into the wood. In the dim light of the forest I can make out the point where it crumbles to nothing. "You cannot cross where that wall ends under any circumstances. Our protection extends only within its confines. Which means the garden is safe."

The garden is boxed in between the wall at our right, the right wing of the manor behind us, and the conservatory dining room on the left-hand side. I'm surprised I didn't notice this was here before, but maybe that was because calling it a "garden" is a bit of a generous way to describe this area. Overgrown beds spill onto cracked pathways covered in a thick blanket of pine needles. There's a wooden shed in the corner where the wall meets the house that's held together with nothing more than a miracle. Oren heads over to what I assume is the compost bin beside it and dumps the ash.

"You…grow things out here?" I ask.

"There's potatoes in this bed," he says, now walking along the pathway and pointing as he goes. Sure enough, I recognize the pointed flat leaves of a potato plant. "Carrots are over here, mixed in with the parsley. Rosemary is in the back. The basil bush took over the tomatoes last winter, and then…died." He looks a little guilty about that. "So, how are you with gardening?"

"I'm okay, I suppose." It's a bit of a stretch. Joyce rapped my knuckles with a switch more than once over poor yields. Not the worst scars she gave me. You would think her harsh punishment would've made me exceptional. It made me merely passable because it filled me with nothing but resentment for the task. "But I can certainly clean up this place, shore up the shed, redefine the beds. And if you give me instruction on the plants, I won't mess them up."

He looks skeptical. I'm excited for this project and I don't want it to be taken away from me because I have mediocre skills when it comes to gardening. So I add, "I promise I won't let you down, Oren."

"Why don't you start with cleaning up today?" he suggests. "Then we'll see about you tending the plants."

"Sounds great," I say quickly.

Oren leaves me to it. It's a bit of a daunting task, given the state of the garden. But that just means it'll take me several days to complete. My mind is already starting a list of priorities and filling in all the opportunity this garden has. Maybe, if there are enough supplies after I repair everything, I'll make a bench. This could be a lovely place to sit in late spring or summer when the pollinators are happily going about their business.

I dare to open the shed door, and the whole thing nearly collapses when I do. But inside is a rake and that's all I need for now. I start with the pathways, piling up the needles at the back edge of the garden. There's a clear line where the stone pathways end and the forest floor begins. I push the pine needles off onto the forest floor but go no farther.

It's late morning when I take my first break. I lean against the wall and wipe sweat from my brow. My muscles are sore. It's been only a week of lounging and I've already lost some strength. The stiffness in my bones makes me feel even better about keeping busy. Work keeps me moving, which keeps me strong.

The sound of a sniffle summons my attention, followed immediately by soft crying. I look around for the source and my eyes are drawn to the woods. There, in the distance, I see a young girl with hands balled into tiny fists, wiping wet cheeks as she weeps.

"What the—What are you doing out there?" I call out to her. She continues crying as though she can't hear me. "Little girl, are you lost?"

Still no response.

I look around, trying to see if I can spot anyone else around her. There's no one. She carries a satchel slung across her body. Who would bring a child into the dark forest? I know there are men and women who dare to forage within it but I've never heard of anyone being so foolish as to bring a *child*. I push away from the wall and walk to the edge of the stone pathways, cupping my hands around my mouth.

"Little girl, look, come over here."

She stills, hands dropping from her face so she can look at me. She rubs her nose with her knuckles. And then dashes behind a tree.

"No, wait! Don't run!" I step off the pathway and onto the plush piles of pine needles I just finished raking. "You don't have to be afraid; I'm trying to help you. Did you come out here with your parents?"

I see her poke her little face out from around the tree. Her hair is a painfully similar shade to Laura's.

"It's all right," I coo softly. "I'm not going to hurt you." I trail my hand along the wall, walking to the very edge of where it crumbles to nothing, and come to a stop. "Come here."

She retreats behind the tree.

"Please, it's not safe out here for a little one like you. There's chocolate in the kitchens, I can get you a piece if you'd like." I have no idea if there's chocolate, I just know that bribe always worked with Laura when she was this age.

The girl reemerges. I can see now that she's absolutely filthy. I expected the mud and dirt covering her clothes. I didn't expect the blood.

"Are you hurt?" I whisper.

She shakes her head and begins sobbing once more. A picture is forming in my mind of what might have happened here. Someone must have taken her into the woods, either well-meaning or nefarious, and then a horrible misfortune befell them that this girl somehow managed to escape. That also means that somewhere out there the man, or beast, or even fae who did this might still be hunting her. It might be hiding behind any of these trees.

"I need you to listen to me now. Be a good girl, yes?" She's still crying. I scan the woods for danger and then look back to her. "You'll be safe in the little castle behind me. Please, come with me. The lord of this manor is very kind, and generous. He won't hurt you."

The girl sobs harder. I think I see movement in the woods behind her. I creep forward.

"Can you tell me your name?" I ask. She shakes her head. "My name is Katria. The woods are a scary place, aren't they?" More movement in my periphery. My heart is racing. I extend a sweaty palm. "Come on, take my hand." I don't know if Lord Fenwood's protection, whatever it might be, will extend to her as well. But if she takes my hand, with one yank we will be back behind the crumbled edge of the wall. If I run as fast as I can, we'll be in the garden in a breath.

She stops crying and raises her tiny fingers. My hand closes around hers. Her eyes flash a bright yellow, like torchlight hitting a wolf's eyes at night.

The girl smiles wide, and her mouth is full of too many teeth, dagger-sharp. She wrenches with a strength that she should not possess and pulls me past the wall. I topple head over heels, letting out a yelp of surprise. On my knees, I dig my hands into the moist underbrush of rotting leaves and damp earth, and jerk my head back in her direction.

The girl is no more. In her place is a gnarled woman. She has bright yellow eyes with slits for pupils. Gossamer wings unfurl behind her, dragging on the ground as she stalks toward me with bony claws. Around her shoulders is a swirling shawl of shadow.

I open and close my mouth, trying to form words, but there are none. I blink several times, as if she'll go away, as if I'll wake myself up from this nightmare, but she comes closer and closer.

"Please don't hurt me," I squeak, pushing off the ground, crab-walking backward. I should get up and run, but fear has made a fool of me. Her bloodshot eyes look for my death.

"Maybe I won't hurt you." Her voice is garbled and worn—it's as if someone has ripped out her voice box and shoved it back in the wrong direction. In addition, the common tongue doesn't seem to be her first language. "If you promise to do one thing for me."

"What? I'll give you anything you want."

"Open a window of that room." She points a bony claw toward the dining room. "Leave it open this night."

So she can murder me in my bed later? "I—of course," I say quickly. "Anything you want." The metallic taste of lies fills my mouth. There's no way I'm leaving the window open for this creature.

"*Hmmm*, your kind can lie." It's as if she can smell the metal on my breath, and she reconsiders her offer. "Maybe I'll just make you scream loud enough that he has no choice but to come out himself."

I let out a squeak as I back into a tree. *Get up*, my mind screams.

But I'm locked in place. I have to run. I have to fight. *I can't die like this.*

She crouches before me and digs one of the points of her claws into my chest. "He's begun amusing himself with humans, has he? Let's see how long he'll be amused if you don't have an arm."

The crone grabs my left wrist, yanking my arm. Her right hand rears back and upward. Those wicked sharp claws are going to sink into my flesh. I close my eyes and turn away as I see her hand move through the air.

A roar rocks the earth. The sound is part man, part beast, and all primal rage. Air rushes past me, and my arm is pulled painfully until it pops. I let out a scream as I hit the ground. My head strikes a rock.

I blink, dazed. My vision is blurry and all I can see are the woods. But behind me a struggle ensues. I try and push myself up from the ground, but my one arm refuses to work. The world tilts and I upturn the contents of my stomach. I continue blinking, trying to bring things back into focus. The pinpricks of sunlight poking through the dense canopy are far too bright. The noises far too loud. I fear I might be sick again.

These sensations are familiar. The last time I felt them was when I fell off the roof with Helen. Then, my world became hazy, and when I came to—

"Take her." *That's Oren.* "Go back to the manor, I'll hold her off."

"Thank you." I recognize Lord Fenwood's voice, even in my state, even never having laid eyes on the man. I *know* it's him. Just like I can feel his presence behind me, warm and sturdy, undeniable. "Close your eyes," he whispers, surprisingly tender and in stark contrast to the growling and grunting still happening behind us.

I don't want to close my eyes. If I do, when will I wake up? And what will be happening then? But I want to stay out here even less, so I press my eyes closed with a whimper.

Two large hands slip underneath me, one around my shoulders and one under my knees. I'm weightless as the lord hoists me into the air and clutches me against his chest protectively. *I was right, he is tall.* But far more muscular than I was expecting. I can feel that rippling strength beneath the thin shirt he wears. Strength he's using to protect me.

"You're safe now." Yet even as he says those words, a scream erupts from the beast. Nothing feels safe.

"Please don't hurt me." My voice quivers.

"I will never hurt you." *Truth.*

"What's happening?" I press my face into his chest so I don't open my eyes out of temptation. I don't think I *want* to see what's going on. The image of that woman is already seared onto the back of my lids, threatening to haunt me for forever.

"You're safe now," he repeats. "I have you in my arms, so you have nothing to fear."

It's not an answer. But my nose doesn't singe, so it's also not a lie. I exhale with a whimper and put my faith in him as he carries me back to the safety of the manor.

six

HE KICKS IN THE DOOR TO THE KITCHEN, WHERE THE FAMILIAR SCENTS MINGLE WITH HIS OWN COLOGNE OF MOSS AND SAGE. *Safe*, I repeat the word in my head, *these smells mean I'm safe*. I try and imprint the fact on my very soul. My heart is beginning to slow, though his still races against my cheek. I clutch his shirt lightly, though I can't tell if I'm trying to reassure myself or him.

Back in my room, he lays me down on the bed. I keep my eyes pressed shut. I won't disrespect his wishes, especially not after he saved me.

"I need to go and see if Oren is all right. But first... How are you?" he whispers.

I can almost feel his hands hovering over me, like he wants to touch me. The phantom sensation of his fingertips on my cheeks races through my mind. I try to stay focused but everything that's happened has scattered my thoughts to the wind.

"My shoulder hurts some. My head is splitting." As I say that, I feel two fingertips run lightly over my temple. He gives in, his touch so small and gentle it sends a jolt through me. "I'll be fine. Don't leave Oren out there alone with that *thing*."

"'Thing,' indeed," he repeats with a snarl and pulls away. I hear him move through the room.

I almost call out to him. I don't want to be alone. But I

keep my silence. Oren needs him more than I do. And based on what the creature said…there must be some kind of ward, or protection around this house. They just need to hold off the beast long enough that they both can get back behind the wall. It must be safe in here.

It must be…

It's twilight when I open my eyes next. My shoulder is stiff and screams as I try to move it. But I can wriggle all my fingers and bend my elbow. I think it's just a terrible sprain. My head is splitting but my vision is no longer blurry. I sit up, rubbing lightly where my temple met the rock. My fingers come away bloody. I've bled on the pillowcase, too.

I curse under my breath. Fortunately for me, one upside of womanhood is that I'm already well versed in getting blood out of linens. I pull the case off the pillow, swing my legs off the bed, and stand slowly. The world does a little tilt, but nothing too alarming. I'm stable enough to make my way to the washroom. I look a mess, but washing my face is a significant improvement in getting me back to "human" again.

Pillowcase cleaned, I emerge back into the hallway feeling refreshed. I notice a note has been pinned to the door that leads to the main, central tower. I cross over and read the elegant script that I can only presume was made by the strong hand of Lord Fenwood.

K~

There will be an exception to the rules tonight only.

When you wake, if it is before dawn, you may come out and access the dining room and kitchen. Take whatever you need to care for yourself in body and spirit.

My stomach is still too unsettled from the events of the day to be particularly inclined toward food. But my curiosity is far too intense to turn down this opportunity to wander at night. I crack open the door.

The main hall looks…normal.

I don't know what I was expecting. There's been such a fuss made about me not emerging at night that perhaps I thought the entire castle somehow changed. That beyond the door was a portal to another land. I laugh softly at myself.

Dishware clinking in the dining room stills me. My heart races as though I am back in the forest. I take a deep breath. *I am safe here*, I repeat to myself. I've lived here now for over a week. For over a week, that monster had been in the woods. It only attacked me when I ventured too far. *Within these walls, I have nothing to fear.*

The golden glow of candlelight strikes out the frame of the dining room entry on the dark floor. I pause at the side of the door, not looking in. There are two possibilities on who is eating late, and I'd rather be safe than sorry.

"Lord Fenwood?" I say. It's my turn to have my back against the wall, shoulder barely exposed. "Is that you?"

There's a long stretch of silence. "Just a moment and I'll be done."

"Don't rush on my account; I'll come back."

"No, no. Stay." Is that longing that I hear in the unfathomable depths of his voice? I don't move.

"What are you eating?" I ask, before the silence can become awkward.

He chuckles. "Nothing particularly fitting of a lord. A hunk of cheese I cut mold from and a knob of bread that I couldn't let turn stale." He hates wasting food. That similarity between us, however slight, softens my stance. "But at least the mead is good."

"Oren didn't make you dinner?" Dread fills me at what this might mean.

"He's had quite the day so I gave him the night off."

"Is he all right?"

"He is."

"Thank goodness." I heave a sigh of relief.

"Though he very well could not have been." Lord Fenwood's voice shifts into the realm of disappointment.

I pick at a string on my blouse, tugging on it. It's then I notice that the string comes from a gap at the seam of my shoulder. That monster nearly ripped my sleeve clean off.

An idea strikes me. I tug and pull off the sleeve the rest of the way. I continue ripping at the seam down to the cuff. I'm left with a long, rectangular piece of fabric that I tie firmly over my shut eyes.

Fingertips resting lightly on the doorframe, I step into the dining room. At least, I think I do, it's impossible to be sure. The heavy cotton of my blouse over my eyes nearly blots out all light.

"What are you—" His chair scrapes over the floor.

"I can't see anything, I swear it." I hold up both of my hands, trying to calm him. "I just thought it might be easier to talk this way, rather than around a door." He says nothing, which sets my nerves ablaze. I know I must look a right mess in my still-soiled clothes, one sleeve missing. "I wish I could look you in the eyes so you could see how sincere I am when I say I'm sorry. But since I can't do that, I thought this might be the next best thing."

Unless he has figured out a way to leave the room and pass me completely undetected, I can only assume he's still standing there, utterly silent. I wonder what expression he has. Is he upset? Or maybe he's amused, or even *impressed* that I thought of a blindfold as a solution... A harmless fantasy of him being delighted by me runs away with my thoughts for a second. But the memory of Oren fighting that monster in the woods alone so the lord could save me sobers me right up.

"My Lord, I never meant... I didn't intend to go beyond the edge of the wall." I stare in what I hope is his direction. For some reason I imagine him sitting in the same chair as me, at the head of that long table. Made small by this empty room.

"You swore to me you would not. I should have known better than to trust you." Frustration seeps into his voice, bleeding from a wound I never intended to make.

"Please hear me out. I never meant to betray your trust," I say quickly. "I saw a crying girl among the trees. I was afraid that someone had brought her into the forest and something wicked befell that person. She had blood on her. She looked... The girl looked like one of my sisters when she was no older than seven. I was trying to help her and before I knew it she had become that *thing*."

"A fae."

Those two words shake me to my core. I realize I never *really* believed in the fae until now. I spoke about them. I warned my sisters of them. I think I even tried to look for them during those dusky morning rides. But in my heart of hearts, I never believed the old folktales, that the woods were filled with them—the wandering folk of a long-ago war between humans and magical creatures.

"They're real," I whisper, and stagger forward. I hold out my hands, searching for the chair at the opposite end of the table. I hear his footsteps as he rushes to me. My hands don't meet the wood of a chair back. They close around his soft, warm fingers. The lord is before me in an instant, stealing my breath with his presence and preventing me from awkwardly bumping into something. "Are the fae truly real?"

"You doubt your own eyes?"

I shake my head. My knees feel weak. He must sense it because I hear him pull out a chair and he eases me into it. Lord Fenwood sits next to me.

"Yes, that thing you saw in the woods today was a fae." He scoops up both of my hands. There's not a tinge of smoke in my nostrils. He's telling the truth. Or at least he believes it's the truth. But after what I saw and heard... There's no other explanation.

"They are as monstrous as the stories say."

"Fae can be," he agrees. "That's why I told you to never go in the woods behind the manor."

I shake my head as a chill rips through my body. "Fae can shape-shift?"

"Not quite. All fae are born with innate abilities. Most have wings or claws they can summon on command, along with various other inherited traits from the beasts of the forests. But one ability all fae share is the gift of glamour—fae can make themselves appear as anything they like. Mind you, it's just an illusion, a magic trick of the senses, and very hard to continue once they are touched."

I clutch his hands tighter on the word *touch*. They're soft, callus free. The hands of the lord who spends his days in a tower. Not like my hands, rough and scarred. Or like the clawed fingers of that monster.

"Is there any other way to tell a glamour from real? Other than touch?"

"Pure water will wash away the glamour of a fae."

Right as rain. I wonder if the expression is a holdover of some ancient advice for dealing with the fae.

"The creature wanted you." My voice cracks a little as I think of what the woman had initially asked of me.

"I bet it did." He chuckles darkly. "In the end, it got me. It just didn't live to tell the tale."

"Are you a fae hunter?" I dare to ask. A man, alone in the woods, holed up in a house warded from those magic beasts. A man who doesn't let others see him, perhaps out of fear that they could use the information against him. Because if I saw him, I could identify him. I would have knowledge the fae would want and would clearly kill for.

"I do hunt some, from time to time," he finally admits.

I inhale sharply. My fingers tighten around his. I am married to a man who hunts the most dangerous game in this world.

"Do you hunt at night? Is that why I hear the noises?"

"It's better if you don't worry about the noises." He begins to pull his hands from mine. "The less you know, the safer you are. That creature already tried to use you once to get to me."

The idea that I could be used to get anyone continues to startle me. I'm not accustomed to meaning that much to anyone or anything. My feelings are becoming murkier by the minute, clouded with emotions that I've never felt and am ill-equipped to understand. His fingers slip from mine and I'm filled with the insatiable urge to snatch back his hands.

Before I can, he runs a knuckle over my cheek. I feel him tuck a wayward strand of hair behind my ear. My breath catches. How close is he? I imagine his face mere inches from mine, staring at me with all the desire I've hardly ever dared dream someone would look at me with.

"What else should I know about the fae?" I whisper. I only know the warnings my father would give me in the folk stories he told me when I was a girl.

"You don't need to know anything else. With any luck, you will not be cursed with fae in your life for very long." He pulls his hand away.

I try to catch it and grasp nothing but air. No doubt looking a fool in the process. "But the more I know, the more likely I am to be of help to you while they pursue you."

"You've already been help enough. More than you know, really." No smoke, no lies. "Now, you should get some rest. Eat what you can and go back to bed."

He stands and I bite my lip. There's more to be said. I can feel how tired and worried he is. I'm filled with the urge to say something as comforting or as beautiful as the old songs my mother would sing when I was fussy. But I'm not a poet; I can only repeat the words I'm taught. My whole life I've been a vessel, allowing others to fill me with their wants, needs, thoughts… There is so much of everyone else that there is no room left for me. And now, when I need something of my own creation to offer, I come up short.

I hear him leave and can't even muster the words to tell him good night. I realize even later that I never properly thanked him for saving me.

To my surprise, Lord Fenwood gives me a second chance to find my voice the next night.

As I return to my wing from dinner I find the door to the study open, fire lit, chairs at the ready position. I take my seat, eager to speak with him again. I've had a day to recover now. My head is clearer. And my guilt has been lessened some with the opportunity to apologize to Oren over dinner as well.

I hear Lord Fenwood's footsteps the moment he enters the room. Warm heat rushes over me at the sound, pooling in my stomach. My throat is already gummy. Just as I try to squeak out a greeting, a cloth is dropped over my eyes from above. I reach up, my hands grabbing his in surprise.

"What are you—"

"You gave me an idea the other night," he murmurs as he continues tying the blindfold. The silk is cool against my flushing face. "I wanted to try it again, if you don't mind?" His voice comes from above and behind me. He must be kneeling on his chair and reaching over. The sounds of him—his words, his breathing, his movement—fill my ears and are accented by the ghost of his warm breath on the nape of my neck. I try to suppress a shiver and lose.

"It's fine with me," I manage to say.

There's a bunch of movement behind me, the scraping of the chair, the clinking of ice in his glass. I feel the air move as he comes to stand before me, and my nose picks up keenly on the crisp and earthy aroma that follows him. I imagine him looking down at me. There's something vulnerable, in an exciting way, about knowing he can see me when I can't see him. In my mind's eye, he's a mere silhouette, picked out from the darkness by the firelight. His features are hazy voids, waiting to be filled.

"Stand," he commands. I oblige. He takes both my hands in his and guides me a step over. I listen as he moves the chair I was just sitting in, presumably to face his seat. "There, now sit." He guides me back to the chair.

"It's not fair," I blurt, catching his hand as he goes to pull away. "You can see me, but I can't see you."

"The rule—"

"I know the rule; I'm not trying to change the rule." I want to touch his face, to feel the bridge of his nose, to run my fingertips down to his lips and outline them. Are they full or thin? What is the cut of his jaw like? Or the angle of his brow? "May I ask you questions about what you look like? That way I have something to imagine about the man I'm speaking with. All I know right now is that you have very nice shoulders." I grin.

"Very well. I shall grant you this." He chuckles, pulls away, and takes his own seat. I amuse him. I'm shocked to find how much I like that.

Suddenly, the new seating arrangement feels like an interrogation. It's rather thrilling. I've gone from being vulnerable due to my lack of knowledge to having the power. He's going to answer my questions. "Your hair, is it long? Or short?"

"Somewhere in the middle," he answers.

"To your shoulders?"

"Just beyond, only slightly."

I purse my lips to stop myself from grinning like a fool as I begin to paint my mind's portrait of him. "I should warn you up-front, it's impossible to lie to me. So don't even try."

"I wouldn't even dream of attempting it."

"Good." I lean back into my chair. "Is your hair curly? Wavy? Straight?"

"Mostly straight. It does often have a mind of its own, however. Oren is always telling me to cut it shorter as it gets in my eyes constantly."

"Do you pull it away from your face when it gets in your eyes?" I can sympathize with the frustrations of longer hair.

"I've been known to weave in a braid or two from time to time." I can hear the smirk in his voice.

"What color?"

"Dark brown, a bit darker than yours." That gives me a near-exact shade.

"What color are your eyes?"

"Green."

"Like the pine trees?"

"No, more like a lime," he says. I burst out laughing. "What's so funny?"

"Green like a *lime*?" I shake my head. Who would describe their eyes like that? "That's such a bright color."

"I have been told I have piercing eyes."

I scrunch my brow slightly, trying to picture the exact shade. Is it truly as vibrant as he says? Dark brown hair, bright green eyes... It makes for a beautiful combination. "What about your jaw?"

"What about it?" He seems amused I would ask.

"Is it wider? More narrow? Stubbled?"

"I try and keep myself clean-shaven. I admit my success with it can be varied."

"Are you successful right now?"

"No." I can almost hear the smirk in his voice. A light stubble, then.

"And the shape of your jaw?"

"I admit I've never analyzed it." A pause. I imagine him running those smooth fingers of his over the roughness of his stubble. Pausing as he says, "More square? I suppose?"

I let out a low humming.

"You don't seem satisfied with that answer."

"I'm just..."

"Say it," he demands. I think it would be impossible not to heed that firm tone.

"I'm trying to figure out what's wrong with you," I admit and immediately busy my mouth with my glass of mead.

"What's *wrong* with me?" I hear him take a sip as well.

"You sound...stunning," I admit as little more than a whisper. "I thought you might have not wanted me to see you because you were hideous."

His glass clanks softly on the table. I hear him stand. I've offended him. Before I can apologize he's there again in front of me. He hooks my chin with the knuckle of his pointer finger and his thumb. He guides my face up toward where I imagine his to be. I know he's just a breath away. I feel every little bit of aching distance between us, paired with a surprising need to cross it. I'm hot all over, but I can't move to alleviate the tension. He's trapped me with two fingers.

"Maybe," he whispers, "I'm trying to protect you *because* I'm stunning. Because if you were to look at me with those eyes that Oren tells me are like a tempest sea, I could never let you go."

I can smell the sweet liquor on his breath. I wish I could taste it on his mouth. That want is so all-consuming it startles me. My mind pushes away instantly. *No*, whatever is happening between us is the last thing I would want. This is the start of the same road that leads to how my father ended up so entangled with Joyce.

Romance starts well and ends badly. That's how it fools people into attempting the futile effort. Joyce was Father's "light," pulling him out of the despair of my mother's death. And then, once she had him, she showed her true colors.

I won't let Lord Fenwood or anyone else ever ensnare me.

He releases me, as if sensing my hesitation. As if realizing that I've finally reached the same conclusion that he has. The best thing for us to do is avoid each other at all costs. If we can't see each other, then we can't lust after each other, and this heat will ultimately fade.

"Good night, Katria."

Yet even as I make those realizations and vows, just the sound of my name on his lips has my breath catching. He leaves me with the remnants of the fire smoldering in the hearth—smoldering within me. I sit alone in the darkening room, still blindfolded, slowly tweaking the delicious mental portrait of him I've begun to construct.

seven

I PACE THE MAIN HALL FROM THE ENTRANCE OF THE DINING ROOM TO THE LEADED GLASS BY THE DOORS; I PEER OUTSIDE AND SEE THE DRIVE IS STILL EMPTY; I REPEAT. My skirts *swoosh* around my ankles, as agitated as my nerves. I wring my hands.

"This is a terrible idea. A terrible, *horrible* idea." Not that I had any say in it. The letter was waiting for me next to my dinner plate last night, Oren said it arrived by way of carrier pigeon. I was shocked that a carrier pigeon could find its way out here. Even more shocked that my sisters had actually decided to make the journey to come and visit like they promised weeks ago.

Laura sounded properly giddy at the prospect. And she had mentioned making an attempt when I left. But I expected them all to be so enraptured by their four thousand pieces, their new servants to boss around, and their new dresses to try on, that I didn't think they really would come and see me. I bite my thumbnail and curse under my breath.

Part of me is wracked with guilt for thinking so little of Laura. We've always had a positive relationship. Of course she would come to see me. And I can only imagine how her circumstances have changed without what little shielding I could offer from Joyce.

As far as Helen, she's not coming to see me; she's

coming to try and make a mockery of me and no doubt relay her findings back to Joyce.

I can imagine her in the carriage, chatting Laura's ear off about the wretched circumstances I must certainly find myself in. I stop and take a deep breath, smoothing out my skirts. That is why I've worn my best dress today. That is why I must show her the lovely home I now have, the weight I've gained from proper food and care, the luster that has returned to my hair and eyes—and most importantly, that I never think about her or Joyce anymore or their trivial desires. I am fine, no, *better* without those two.

At last I hear the whinny of a horse and the gravel grinding underneath carriage wheels. Gathering every last scrap of composure, I step outside and wait at the top of the three steps. Oren rode out to meet them by the main road and be their guide. He dismounts, casting me a wary look, one I share.

My sisters' new footman opens the door to their carriage and they come bursting out.

"Katria, it's so good to see you." Laura rushes over, arms open wide. The sight of her fair hair reminds me of that creature in the woods. I shake off the memory and descend the stairs to meet her.

"You really didn't have to come all this way," I say, returning her embrace fiercely.

"I couldn't bring Misty," she whispers quickly. Here I was, trying to admit I hadn't been hoping to see Misty pulling their carriage. "I tried."

"Don't fret over that." I keep the words low enough that Helen can't hear, but firm. Laura has more important things to worry about now than my old horse.

"We wanted to see how you are doing." Helen folds her arms in her usual stance. "From the looks of it, you're well."

"No complaints, certainly."

"Will you give us a tour of your lovely new home?" Laura links her arm with mine, and gazes up at the manor in awe. She no doubt sees the same things I did when I first arrived—its castle-like appearance and the well-preserved craftsmanship of bygone days.

"Let's skip the tour," I say, patting her arm. I had rehearsed and planned for how to avoid showing them around since a good two thirds of the manor I am not allowed to enter. "Most of it is drafty, empty, boring rooms anyway, and I would much rather spend time with you, catching up on what has been happening back in town."

This sparks a long-winded explanation from Laura about all of the gossip of high society that I was never really a part of. She carries on as I escort my sisters to the study that the lord and I usually use for our nightly conversations. I've procured a third chair. And, with Oren's help, a bottle of mead to share with them.

"What is this?" Helen asks as I pour the drink.

"It's mead." I hand her a glass. "I certainly had never had it until I came here. My husband is able to import it from far away." I honestly have no idea how easy or hard this mead is to come by. But Helen looks begrudgingly impressed so it's worth opening the bottle. Laura is beaming at the honey liquid. I hold out my glass. "Cheers, to smart, fortuitous matches."

Our glasses clink together and we each take a seat.

"Speaking of, how *is* your match?" Laura asks, voice dropping to whisper. She glances to the door, as if Lord Fenwood might walk in at any moment. "He isn't as horrible as we feared, is he?"

"Not at all, he's positively lovely," I say with a genuine smile. Helen's lips purse slightly, as they do when she's silently fuming. It prompts me to continue. "He's been nothing but generous, kind, and understanding. He enjoys my lute playing, even. He'll sit out in the woods with me while I play." He's done that a few times now over these past weeks. The last time, he trusted me enough not to try to steal a glance that he sat on the stump behind me. Our backs almost touching…which caused me to dream about his skin pressed against mine the following night.

Helen snorts. "Be realistic. No real man is sitting out enjoying your lute playing. Have you not been satisfying him enough in bed that he feels the need to go out of his way and try and woo you with such ridiculous gestures?"

I don't know where to start with that remark. I want to insist that he genuinely likes my lute playing. But my defensiveness will only make Helen double down. Worse, just with those few words, she's made me doubt my instincts. Even though I've never smelled smoke on him. Even though I sit in my new home with my new life…she manages to bring out the old me, the meek parts of myself that I still can't shed around her.

"He has made no demands in that department."

My sisters glance at each other. Laura leans in. "But you *have* fulfilled your duties as a wife, haven't you?"

I purse my lips.

"That's a no." Helen seems amused by this revelation. "So he *is* as hideous as we expected. You couldn't even muster up the courage."

"It's not— He's not."

"Then why did he not greet us? A bit strange for a lord of the manor not to greet his guests."

"He's busy during the days. And you are not normal guests, you're kin. He knew I could handle the formalities." I've been wondering what he thinks of this meeting. My Lord Fenwood doesn't seem like the sort who enjoys unexpected houseguests.

"There is no reason why a man of sound mind and body would not take his new bride to bed, even with as merely passable looking as you are." Helen says it as though the fact should be obvious. As if I am a foolish woman for not realizing it myself.

"Perhaps such things are not his priority." I shift, sitting a little taller. I might have started to wonder if, or when, he would take me to bed…but I rarely let those thoughts out of their vault in the corner of my mind during daylight hours. Those are for enjoyment during the quiet hours of the late night only.

"What is his priority then?" Laura asks.

"His work."

"Oh? Tell us about that?" She smiles as she deftly shifts the conversation, much to my relief. My little ally, even still.

"He's a hunter." And that is all they will know of my husband's true profession.

Helen snorts. "No hunter catches enough game to afford land like this. I'm sure hunting is an excuse and he's sneaking off at night to some other woman. He's made his fortune and now plays the field."

I think of the noises, of the rules, of the mysterious tower and whole other wing of the house that I've never explored or even questioned. What if he does have another woman over there? One woman by day, and one by night? I bite my lip.

Helen reaches forward to pat my knee. I almost kick her in her button nose. "There, there, many women have unfaithful husbands. But you must give him an heir to his fortunes, and quickly, if you wish to stay relevant to him. Otherwise he could put you out on the street without a second thought."

"Don't you think he's hideous? If he's so horrible looking, enough to bargain for a wife, then how could he ever get a lover?" She's trying to break me down. Mess with me. Tear me apart. I don't want to let her, but the frustrating thing is she's had years to hone this skill—Joyce no doubt prepared her for this. She knows exactly what tears me down and what buttons of mine to push.

"His home is so close to the woods. He *must* be a hunter," Laura interjects. "And there must be rare game somewhere the woods are this thick and old." She leans in, eyes shining. "Maybe he hunts the fae."

I nearly spit up my mead and instead force a laugh. "A fae hunter? Don't be ridiculous."

"I could imagine he must look positively dashing, all dressed for the hunt." Laura brings the back of her hand to her forehead and swoons. I busy my mouth with another sip of mead.

Helen tilts her head. She's inspecting me. I hate it when she does this. She's able to put together things that no one else would see.

"You *say* he's handsome…and yet you seem to doubt that. You proffer no proof, no detailed explanations of how fine he is, not even a mention of your favorite feature of him…" She hums. "You haven't even seen him, have you?"

I open my mouth and wordlessly close it, pressing my lips into a scowl. This skill of hers has been my nemesis for ages.

Laura gasps at my silence. "Is that true? Have you even *met* your husband?"

"I have." This is exactly why I didn't want them to come. I knew they would find out the strange truths of my new arrangement. I knew they would use it against me even though I am the one in the lap of luxury. I have the husband they so desired. I have safety,

security, and freedoms. Yet Joyce's specter lingers over them, telling
me that I have nothing.

"Then how could you not know…" Laura seems genuinely
confused.

"We've only spoken when I couldn't lay eyes on him."

Helen sighs and shakes her head sadly. "It is a shame to see your
weaknesses and inferior intellect so taken advantage of. This is why
we had to protect you and keep you so close to home, Katria. If we
ever let you out freely, we knew this would happen."

My blood boils. I'm used to their jabs against me. But now they
disparage the man that saved my life. They try and turn me against
the *one person* who has not brought harm or malice toward me.

"I am not taken advantage of. I don't know how you could
possibly think it." I motion around us. "I want for nothing. Anything
I desire, if I name it, I shall have it. My husband is kind, respectful,
and gentle. You should dream of a man like him." *Because a man
like him would be far better than you deserve*, I wish I could say
aloud to her.

"And yet he refused to give you the decency of looking you in
the eye when he first met you," Helen says.

"Katria, you know I want to find this all deeply romantic…but
this isn't a storybook." Laura grabs my hands. "It is *strange* he will
not let you see him."

"He's not harmful."

"Moreover, you don't know where his wealth comes from." Helen
sighs. "Think about this logically, we're just trying to help. There's
no way he affords all of this from hunting alone. He demanded only
a book as your dowry. What if he's engaged in some strange, illegal,
back-channel markets?"

I know she's not trying to help. Yet…Helen has a point, both of
them do, for all I hate to admit it. If my husband is a fae hunter, as
I suspect, then who does he sell his game to? Who pays him for the
kills? And if he does it purely for the sake of goodness, and ridding
the world of those beasts, how has he or does he make his money?

They're all questions I don't have the answers to. I wish I did.
Because in the void of an explanation, doubt is now taking root.

"I'm worried about you," Helen says.

"You have never been worried about me," I snap. "All my life, you stepped on me." Helen has the audacity to gasp, as if offended. "You turned me into your servant."

"To protect you from the world. To ready you for it by hardening you. And you're deflecting." Helen wields her words like daggers, knowing just where to strike. "This isn't about us anymore. If we were so horrible, then congratulations, you escaped us." Helen wears a thin smile, slightly smug. She knows just how horrible she was, that expression admits it. But she's also right, it doesn't matter how they treated me anymore, I'm free of them. I clutch Laura's hands a little tighter and hope she knows she's exempt from these harsh truths. "If you want to *stay* escaped, you should make sure you're secure in your new home."

"Is that a threat?" I say.

Helen laughs. "I have no control over you, your marriage, or your new life. All I'm saying is, if your husband is engaged in something illegal and is thrown in irons, you could face destitution or be forced to share in his fate as a co-conspirator. If your husband is dallying with another woman, and decides to replace you with her, then you will be out on the street. If your husband throws his wealth around and wastes it, you will find yourself in a similar position as before… and you know what that position will be?"

My stomach churns. I know where she's headed with this. Yet she says it anyway.

"You will have to come crawling right back to us," Helen proclaims as she rises to her feet, lording over me as she always did whenever Joyce wasn't around to do it herself. She's a spitting image of her mother. "So if you don't want that to happen, you should heed my warnings. Make yourself useful to your husband. Know the circumstances you now find yourself in. Be cunning. That's always been your problem; you never think two steps ahead and it makes you so easy to use." Helen looks to Laura. "We're leaving now."

"But we just got here." Laura clings to me. "Can't we at least stay the night?"

"I am *not* staying in this strange place with her strange husband."

"Perhaps Oren could bring you back tomorrow?" I suggest to Laura, ignoring the instant guilt I feel for volunteering Oren without asking. But I've done my level best to impose on him as little as possible. And I will make all my meals for a month in gratitude for this one thing. I wouldn't mind some time alone with Laura—to perhaps discuss ideas to get her out of that house faster, before she's ruined by Joyce and Helen.

"Do not impose yourself," Helen scolds her.

"It would be no imposition," I insist.

"Mother would never want you here."

Ah, Mother, the trump card. The unobjectionable reason. Laura rises reluctantly. Our fingers are still laced together.

"Come and visit soon, yes?" Her eyes are dimmer, duller. I can hear a piece of my heart cracking at her pain. *Be strong*, I want to say. *A little longer and you'll be out of there, one way or another.*

"For you, yes," I say. I will go back to that house for my sister. And maybe, maybe the next time I leave I'll take her with me, too.

"Good." Laura throws her arms around my shoulders and gives a tight squeeze. Helen hardly looks back once as she glides out of the manor. No doubt eager to report her findings back to Joyce.

"Strange that your sisters would travel all this way only to turn around and leave," Oren says as he serves me dinner.

"I'm glad they did. Well, *one* of them," I mutter darkly. "If they ever send word that they are coming again, respond immediately that only Laura may come. Never open the gate for Helen or Joyce ever again. They aren't welcome here."

Oren stills, pitcher in both hands, my wine glass still empty. "It will be up to you from now on to decide who is or is not permitted in these halls."

"What?" The strange phrasing snaps me out of my angry trance.

"Nothing." Oren shakes his head, pours my wine glass. "Oh, the lord of the manor told me to inform you that he will not be able to meet with you this evening." With that, Oren heads back toward the kitchen. Lord Fenwood hasn't missed an evening drink in over a week now. This news only feeds my uneasiness.

"Oren." I stop him. He looks at me with a pitying gaze. He feels sorry for me. *Why?* I have a few guesses. But I have a nagging feeling that look has nothing to do with my family. "You would tell me if there was something wrong, right?"

"Of course. But don't worry, everything is as we intended." He disappears.

All through dinner I replay his strange phrasings and mannerisms in my mind. Something was wrong. Or maybe it wasn't, and my sisters got to me. I'm looking for excuses to find problems when there aren't any.

I ready myself for bed, and tuck in. But sleep eludes me. I keep repeating my sisters' words. Helen's are cruel, certainly. And she no doubt said those things to tear me down. But that doesn't make her *wrong*, either. Even Laura was concerned for me.

Should I be more worried about my situation? What if Helen is right and this freedom and comfort that I've found is so fragile that it can be ripped from my grasp and shattered any second? I clutch the duvet. It's so soft…softer than anything I've ever owned before. I can't give up this bed. I can't give up my freedoms here. *I won't give up this life.*

I'm on my feet. I throw a robe over my sleeping gown and leave my room. It's a full moon tonight and the hallway is bright. I still briefly as I realize it's been almost a month since I arrived.

Halfway to the door I begin to second-guess myself. If Lord Fenwood doesn't want to be seen or for me to know the truth about him, then that's his business. I should leave it be. I'm about to turn around and go back to bed when I hear multiple sets of footsteps in the main hall, thundering down the stairway, and across to the other wing of the manor.

That's when I notice the letter that's been slid under the door to the front hall.

Cool nausea sweeps over me as I pick up the envelope. My name is written on it in Lord Fenwood's handwriting. I flip it over and break the seal. The letter reads like it would in my worst nightmare:

To my wife, Katria,

I have business to attend to of a dangerous sort. In the event I never return to these halls, I leave everything to you: the house, all its contents, and the tidy sum hidden underneath the floorboards of the closet adjacent to my chambers. It should be enough that you can live out the rest of your days in comfort. I bequeath it all to you, wife.

And should I never return, you are a free woman and should enjoy your life as such.

Sincerely,

Lord Fenwood

The way the letter is worded… He has no intention of returning. That much is painfully apparent.

My sisters were right. I go from cold to hot as I crumple the letter my hand. Throwing it on the ground, I grab the door handle and twist. Damn the rules. I'm getting the truth.

eight

THE ATRIUM IS EMPTY. But the door directly across from me is ajar. I've never seen it open before. I glance between it and the stairs that round up the tower.

I take the stairs first, two at a time. Based on the noises, either Lord Fenwood left with a group of people, or that group was here to murder him for some horrible deed he never thought was worth telling me.

I emerge onto a loft, bracing myself to see the lord, or Oren, spread out in a pool of his own blood. But the room is void of anyone else—living or dead. However, it does look as if it has been ransacked. Cabinet doors have been left open. Boxes are on the floor, contents overturned. This room was some kind of workshop. There are paints, splattering the floor and still in jars. There are herbs drying overhead. Their aromas mix with the scent of wood shavings and a metallic, sharp twang of blood that I can't seem to find the source of. I want to spend hours slowly inspecting this personal space of Lord Fenwood's. But there's no time.

Back downstairs, I head through the door to the right wing. It's the opposite setup as my quarters. Though instead of a study, there is another workroom. Nowhere do I see the copious tools a hunter would require. In fact, the only weapons I see are a few bejeweled daggers. One's missing on a row of pegs.

He did say he hunted fae, however. Or was that a clever

lie to a gullible woman he knew wouldn't question? I slam my hands onto one of the countertops, and jars and vessels clank together as I curse under my breath. Fae hunter? I should've known better than to think such a thing was real.

My sisters were right and I abhor it. I don't know *anything* about this man. *But I will before dawn*, I vow to myself.

At the end of the hallway, unlike mine, there's a final door. It leads to a set of stone stairs that wind down into the darkness. A rush of cool air from those mysterious depths reminds me that I'm still just in a robe and nightgown. I shift my weight from foot to foot with restless energy, debating what to do next. Wherever the lord has gone, and whomever he's gone with, whoever might have taken him, they can't be too far ahead. But I've already wasted time looking through the various rooms. If I go back and change, I'll lose them for sure.

I let out a string of curses and rush back into one of the studies to gather a lantern that I light using a nearby tinderbox. Drawing my robe tighter around me, I stand once more on the precipice of the stairs. I give myself a slow count of ten to find every scrap of bravery I have ever possessed then start downward.

The spiral stairway wraps in on itself two, four, twelve times. At the bottom is a long tunnel, cold and damp. My light stretches only a few steps ahead of me. I feel the darkness as though it were a living monstrosity, whispering threats from the unknown. My hand shakes slightly, rattling the lantern. The flame inside flickers. I grab my wrist with my other hand and hold it steady. The last thing I want is for my only light to go out.

The tunnel looks like one of the oldest parts of the castle, based on the stone and mortar, but at no point am I nervous about my safety within it. There are fresh support beams across the ceiling. Someone has been keeping up this ancient passageway. The question is *why*.

In the distance, a silvery archway is illuminated by moonlight—a way out. As I approach, I can hear voices drifting through the woods. I slow my pace and set down my lantern. The passage has slowly sloped upward, so the floor is no longer puddled with water. I notice several sets of footprints. I can't tell how many people came ahead of me because it would be impossible to walk this passageway any way but single file.

But there are enough wet footprints that I'm worried, because I'm definitely outnumbered.

I should turn back. I know I should. But now curiosity has its hold on me and keeps pushing me forward. I came hunting for the truth. I won't leave until I have it.

The tunnel drops me out into the forest. I shiver, though I can't tell if it's from the cold or the immediate feeling of being exposed. Every shadowy tree looks down on me with anticipation, pale moonlight winking like a thousand-eyed beast in the canopy overhead.

Voices prevent me from cowering back into the tunnel and running for the safety of the manor. There's a worn stone pathway that winds through the trees, fighting against the forest undergrowth. The voices are coming from the direction the walkway leads. I follow along on the edge of the path and soon see orange flickering. I crouch low and move with as much stealth as I can muster, getting close enough that I can make out every word the people are saying, but I don't understand any of them. They speak in a strange tongue I don't recognize.

Have these people taken Lord Fenwood? Or, are they his accomplices? His letter sounded like he knew he would do something tonight that would get him killed. That's what keeps pushing me forward. I need the truth from this man, just once.

I come up against a tree and place my back to it. The people are chanting now. I can see shadowy outlines of them dancing in the firelight. I sink onto the blanket of pine needles that cover the forest floor. Crawling as slowly as possible, I creep up to the top of a small ridge.

The pathway that stretched out from the tunnel snakes through the forest and into a basin. Trees are perched on the ridge all around the circular area. In the little valley, there are four people.

No, not people, *monsters*.

One man has horns like a stag sticking up from his head. He keeps running his fingers through the fire, miraculously unburnt, while chanting low and thick. Another man and a woman dance around him. They have both stripped down to their small clothes and their bare skin has been completely covered in bright purple paint, a pattern of swirls, dots, and lines slithering across with an almost hypnotic effect as they move.

The woman has hair a deep red, dark brown skin, and wings like a butterfly. The man is pale, and has rams horns curling on either side of his face, and strong arms that end in bony claws. I shudder violently at the sight. They sing and squeal and cry out to the moon above as it stares down at what I can only describe as some kind of dark ritual.

These creatures are fae. No wonder why Lord Fenwood thought he would die tonight. I'm certainly not safe. I should leave before they spot me. But the fourth person's presence is what keeps me here.

Standing opposite the man chanting and playing with the fire is an old gentleman with beady black eyes and gray, slicked-back hair. Oren is half naked, his chest painted as well. Unfurled from his back are two pale, gossamer wings, like those of a dragonfly. My throat goes dry and gummy. The slight hunch to his back... *I let a fae into my bedroom.*

Lord Fenwood let a fae into his home. He must have found out Oren's true nature and planned on confronting him tonight. I dig my fingers into the dirt and pine needles, resisting the urge to scream in frustration.

Confronting Oren to out him as a fae would be suicide, the lord must have known this. Hence the letter. I think of his strong arms protecting me. What if he's done this to keep me safe? He should have just sent Oren away.

Before I can take any foolish actions, all four people raise their arms and faces to the heavens above and let out a primal scream that comes to an abrupt stop. Slowly, reverently, they all turn to face the ridgeline opposite the pathway. Standing on a boulder, lording over the group, is a man I can only presume is their leader.

He wears a cape trimmed heavily with wildflowers. His broad chest is bare. Little more than a loincloth is draped around his waist and does nothing to hide the bulging muscles of his thighs. Across his body, more lines and symbols have been drawn in luminescent paint. Draped behind him, dragging on the ground as he walks, are tattered, crimson wings.

He exudes an air of power and authority. I am as entranced by him as I am terrified. He's like a poisonous draught that promises to be the most delicious thing in the world...you'd knowingly risk death just for a taste.

The leader lifts up a small item with both hands as he descends toward the bonfire in the center of the glade. I can't make out what he's holding until he's closer to the firelight. My heart drops out of my chest, rolling down to stop at this man's feet. Lord Fenwood is dead. He must be.

Because this fae monster holds my mother's book.

Heart racing, I bend my knees so I can get a better look. *No, it couldn't be, please let it be anything but that.* But sure enough, the book has the all-too-familiar markings on its front and spine.

The four other fae walk slowly around the fire to each touch the man, chanting, whispering. They caress him like lovers, like sycophants, like supplicants who see him as a god. The leader comes to a stop and opens the book. His lips move, but I can't hear the words he says. At the same time, the other individuals begin dancing once more. The pale blond chops off a braid from behind his ram's horn and throws it into the fire. The antlered man rips a piece of his clothing and quickly reduces it to ash. Oren runs a bejeweled dagger down his palm and holds it over the fire to allow his blood to drip into it. The fire changes color, going from a normal orange, to bright white, a deep red, and then an unnatural black streaked with purple and white.

Then, the leader closes the book, and raises it over his head. He's going to throw it into the fire, I realize. Foolish instinct to protect that worn tome takes over. I push up off the ground.

"No," I whisper. "Please don't." The book is all I have as proof of the mother who loved me. It was supposed to be the last gift from my father. None of the fae notice me now standing atop the ridge. They're all too focused on the man and the book.

He begins to move his arms; gravity is now in control.

"No!" I scream and charge forward.

The fae turn toward me. I would be frozen with fear if not for the momentum the slope of the ridge gives me. I run, arms pinwheeling; I'm off-balance. The man's hands leave the book as I close the gap. Everything happens with surreal slowness as the book falls through the air.

The fae with the butterfly wings charges for me, but the others seem too stunned to do anything. I duck around the woman and jump for the book before it can meet the flames, but my foot catches on a root. My ankle crunches, I twist. It's too late, I'm too far off-balance. How did I close so much distance so fast? How did I ever get this close to fae while still breathing?

Not that it matters with the way I'm falling...

The man's eyes widen, a vibrant emerald shade—the same color as spring, as the rebirth of the earth itself—unnatural, stunning. We lock gazes and my breath is stolen from me. His terrifying beauty is the last thing I see before I fall into the flames, and the world explodes with white heat.

nine

I F I'M HONEST, DEATH HURTS A LOT LESS THAN I THOUGHT
IT WOULD.

The fire has turned into sunlight, enveloping me like
a blanket. Nothing hurts. In fact, the opposite. Maybe it's
like the time Misty stepped on my foot and broke several
bones. I didn't realize how bad it was until a few hours
later. Cordella told me about how a body can go into shock
as she bandaged me in the stables so Joyce wouldn't see
and scold me for getting hurt.

I went into shock over a broken foot. Falling into a
raging fire would be a whole different level of numbness.

But I'm not completely gone. There's shouting in the
distance; the garbled words gain a brief moment of clarity
before becoming too far off to hear. I'm drifting in a pale
sea, being taken out to the great Beyond I have no choice
but to submit myself to. I hear new voices, chanting and
singing. This isn't like the feverish words the fae spoke
around the fire. This singing is bright and joyous. I hear
the chords of a thousand lutes playing and somehow know
they're all strumming for me.

I think I hear my mother's voice among the chorus.
She's singing for me to come home. She's singing for me
to return to her. *Finally, finally*, the chorus sings my heart,
reunited finally.

Silence.

Then a woman's voice. "What are we going to do with her?"

"We take her to Vena," a familiar voice decrees. *I know that voice. How do I know that voice?*

"Are you mad?" a man asks. "We can't take her to Vena. Even if she could survive that long here—which she can't—we can't take a *human* to Dreamsong."

"Vena is the only person who will know how to get my magic out of her," the second voice says. It's deep, like the lowest note of a lyre rumbling in harmony with thunder on a distant horizon. Unmistakable. I try and fight for consciousness.

"Hol has a point," another man says. "Even if we wanted to, she'll die before we make it to Dreamsong."

"Then we'll have to move quickly, won't we?" the deep voice says.

"Or, we leave her back in the Natural World; we go to Dreamsong, ask Vena what we should do, and then go back to perform the ritual that will restore the magic to its rightful place," the woman says.

"Unless you plan on tying her to a chair, I doubt she'll stay put. That much has now been made painfully clear to me." That's the deep voice again. He seems to know me.

Do I know him? My head feels so fuzzy and heavy. I crack open my eyes.

"She's waking up," Oren says.

It's midday and the sun is blinding. I blink slowly as the world comes into focus. Oren hovers over me, wearing a shirt this time. However, two slits must be cut in the back to let out the dragonfly wings that swoop on either side of him.

I jerk away from Oren and from the other four people who are behind him.

"It's all right, we're not going to hurt you," Oren says.

"She's not going to believe you," the woman with the butterfly wings says. I recognize each of the individuals now as those who were gathered around the fire.

"Let him coddle the human until he's blue in the face, then we will force her to do what we want." The man with ram's horns folds his arms over his chest, biceps bulging, highlighting faintly shimmering markings that run up them. "I don't care if she has the magic of the kings of Aviness. She's not going to know how to use it. We can overpower her."

"You're not going to force me to do anything," I snap. Likely not the best thing to do. But my head is splitting, I'm surrounded by fae, and I'm tired of being spoken about like I'm not here—that's something Joyce would do to me.

All five of them stare at me in varying degrees of shock. The woman's lips part and she gapes at me. The man with the stag horns exchanges a wary look with Ram's Horns before turning back to me. Their leader furrows his brow slightly, dark brown hair cascading into his face with a tousle of the wind.

"I didn't think you spoke common," the man with stag horns says to the man with ram horns.

"I don't," he replies, still staring at me. "And I bet she doesn't— didn't—shouldn't—speak faeish either."

"Is it the magic?" Oren looks to their leader.

"Likely," he murmurs in that deep voice of his, gaze shifting back to me. His eyes are greener than the sunlight canopy around us. Greener than should be possible. A unique shade, almost like a...

"Lime," I whisper and inhale sharply. "No, no, no, *no*." That single word is on repeat. It can't be. It's not possible.

He crouches down. His tattered wings twitch slightly behind him. There's still remnants of purple paint underneath his nails.

"You've broken *all* the rules, Katria." The words are steeped in frustration.

"It's you," I breathe. "Lord Fenwood."

"I suppose now that you've seen the real me, you should know my real name, too. Davien." He motions behind him. "The gentleman with the antlers is Hol. My other horned friend is Giles."

"You're not even going to attempt a horny joke? Disappointing," Giles mumbles while grinning like a cat.

Lord Fenwood—Davien ignores him. "The lady is Shaye. And of course you know Oren."

I've scooted myself all the way back against a tree in an effort to get as much distance as possible between me and these creatures. As my back presses against the bark I begin to get a better sense of my surroundings, even though it's nearly impossible to tear my eyes off the fae. I expect them to launch at my throat at any second even though they haven't killed me yet.

We're not in the deep pine forest anymore. Ancient oak trees stretch up with a spiderweb of branches to catch the sunlight and cool afternoon breezes. Moss dangles off their limbs, swaying. Small motes of light, a rainbow of fireflies bright enough to be seen in the daytime, drift around us. The moss has an iridescent sheen to it, not unlike the crimson of Davien's wings.

Every color is brighter than I've ever seen it. Every scent is sharper. The air itself feels alive, powerful and fearsome, in an entirely different way than the dark forest. I do not feel threatened here. Yet, at the same time, this feels like a place of great danger.

"Where are we?" I ask.

"We're in the Bleeding Woods, to the northeast of what you know as the Slate Mountains."

"Northeast…" I struggle to process information. "There is *nothing* northeast of the Slate Mountains. They're utterly impassable. The world ends." Every fool who has ever tried to go across them has never returned.

"Impassable for *your kind*." Hol glances in my direction from the corners of his purple eyes before going back to scanning the woods around us. Every muscle in his body is tensed. Like he's ready for a fight…or ready to run. "At least, without the help of people like us."

"The Slate Mountains are a line between worlds," Davien says with forced calmness. There's agitation burning in the backs of his eyes. He's frustrated with me. Fine. Let him be. *He* was the one who kept all of this a secret and who's now dragged me into it. "On the other side of them is the former kingdom of Aviness—where we are now."

"Most people call it the fae wilds these days," Giles says, scanning the forest while he speaks, the wind tousling his blond hair around his horns.

"Why have you not killed me? Why have you taken me here?

What do you want from me?" My questions become hasty and frantic.

"I want the magic you stole." Davien's voice becomes more of a growl. "The magic that was my birthright."

"I didn't take any magic." I shake my head.

He grabs my shoulders with his broad hands and shakes me. "You came into the glen, you disrupted the ritual, *you* stepped into the flame."

I suppose I did do all of those things. "I never intended— Fine, if you want whatever this magic is, then take it back. I truly don't know what you're talking about and I wouldn't want it even if I did."

"If only it were so simple." A shadow crosses over his face. "I spent my entire life, nearly twenty-four years, looking for the pieces I needed to complete that ritual. I waited five years just for the stars to be aligned. And you think you can *give it* to me just because you say so?"

"Enough." Oren presses fingertips lightly on Davien's forearm, interrupting the man's rant. "You're not accomplishing anything with this."

"Maybe he will," Shaye says with a devious grin. "We've never had a human who stole fae magic before. Maybe if he shakes her hard enough it'll burst out of her. Or her head will pop right off."

My eyes go wide.

"None of us are touching her." He must realize he's contradicting himself, because Davien releases me with a frustrated sigh.

"I think you just touched—"

"Silence, Giles." Davien pinches the bridge of his nose. The way he looks at me now reminds me of every measure of disdain Joyce and Helen ever showed me, and then some.

"I didn't mean to—" I begin to say. My instinct to placate at that mere look is brought forth.

He cuts me off. "That much is clear. And yet you've risked ruining everything." Davien begins to walk off through the woods. "We're taking her to Vena."

"Up with you," Oren says gently, helping me to my feet.

"All the way to Dreamsong, through the Bleeding Woods, with a human." Shaye glances back at me before locking eyes with Hol. "I give her three days."

"Generous," Hol says. "I'd be shocked for two."

"Great, now I have to pick between one—which seems too short—and four, which we can all agree is far too generous," Giles mumbles. "I'll take four, if I must. Hear that, human? I'm being optimistic for you."

They're talking about how long I'll manage to stay alive, I realize. I shake my head slowly; it becomes a ripple down my spine that quickly evolves into shudders. I can't move with my bones rattling so violently. My back hits the tree and I slide down it once more, curling up into a ball and clutching my head.

"We have to get moving." Oren tries to pull me up by my elbows. "It's not safe for us out here."

"Of course it's not! I'm not safe with any of you."

"None of us are going to hurt you."

"At least not while you have Davien's magic," Giles says with a singsong voice. His skirt swishes slightly around his thighs as he walks.

A whimper works its way up my throat and escapes as a muted, garbled noise. "I want to go home."

"You can't," Oren says.

"Take me back," I demand. "Take me back now," I repeat, louder. It's enough that I gain Davien's attention. He stops and slowly turns to face me as I push myself off the ground of my own accord. "You—You made a deal when you married me. You took an oath that I would never be left wanting. And I *want* to go home."

Davien slowly stalks over, his muscles rippling with a power that calmly promises that he could tear me apart if he desired. His fae magic is like an aura. I'm shocked that it doesn't ripple the air around him like heat off of stones on a summer day.

"About that," he almost purrs. "First, *home*, where would that even be? Back to that 'decrepit manor' you told me your family lives in? Is that where you consider your 'home'? Or did you make my estate your home?"

"You left it to me, in your letter." I try not to let myself be intimidated, but it's harder and harder the closer he gets. "I want you to take me back there."

"I hear how you keep using that word—*want*. But it's not going to have the effect that you think it will."

"But—"

"Yes, I made you a very generous vow that, I'll point out here and now, I did not have to make. And you're right in that I had to uphold it. However, you're forgetting a rather key part of it." He comes to a stop before me, staring down the bridge of his nose. "My vow only lasted until you, or I, departed that mortal plane. And seeing as we have now crossed the Fade into the land of Midscape... we are no longer on *that* mortal plane. So my vow was fulfilled and is nullified."

He takes a half step closer. My back hits the tree again, preventing further escape. He's so close that I can feel his breath, just on the edge of the brisk air of winter.

"You have no claim over me here."

"I just want to go home," I whisper.

"I will take you back to your pathetic world as soon as I have the magic within you." He grabs my chin, tugging my face upward to make me look him in the eye. "Until then, you are under my command. You listen to me and I might just get you out of this alive."

I try and think of everything I've ever learned about the fae. Monsters? Confirmed. Can't tell lies? I'm pretty sure that's true, since I've never smelled a lie on any of them. Have to uphold their vows? It seems so, since he's so eager to weasel out of the vow he made on marrying me. How can I use any of that to survive? *Think, Katria, think!*

"So if I go with you to this Vena, and give you whatever magic is in me, you'll take me back to the manor?"

"I swear it."

I swallow thickly. That sounded like a vow. And I didn't smell smoke. "Fine. Then lead on."

He releases me and turns away briskly. As he crosses by his companions I see the woman, Shaye, murmur to him. I can barely hear what she says: "Next thing you know, she'll be trying to say that she's still your wife. As if human laws can be upheld here." She looks back at me with a snide grin. She knows I can hear her. I get the sense she wanted me to.

Even though with her red hair and butterfly wings she looks nothing like Helen or Joyce, she reminds me more and more of them by the minute.

I gather my muddy, soiled robe around me, try to walk with dignity that I know I don't possess right now, and trudge forward barefoot into the woods. It's a miracle that my feet didn't get cut up last night—at least the forest floor here is covered in a plush, comfortable moss. The thought gives me pause. I stare down at my feet, wiggling both of my toes.

"What is it?" Oren asks.

"Tell her to hurry up," Hol shouts back at us. "We're giving her four days max before she dies here. No time to dally."

"It's nothing." I shake my head and press onward, breezing past Oren and the ugly sense of betrayal his mere presence fills me with.

Last night, I twisted my ankle on a root badly. I heard the bones crunch and the tendons snap. I shouldn't be able to walk right now. But the joint feels fine. In fact, now that the initial haze has cleared, I feel like I could dance, run, jump, and sing.

If only I had a reason to do any of those things. All that lies before me is a long march through enemy territory.

But at least my ankle is a quiet assurance of one thing—maybe I do really have magic. Otherwise, how would I be walking right now?

ten

NOT QUITE SURE WHY IT'S CALLED THE BLEEDING WOODS. Compared to the forest back home, this place is—*Dare I think it?*—cheerful. My company notwithstanding, of course.

They talk amongst themselves throughout the day, mostly ignoring me. Davien says little; he leads the pack and broods quite dramatically. Oren also stays out of their discussions, lingering back, closer to me. No doubt to make sure I don't run. I make sure I keep my distance from even him. Whatever trust he might have earned from me is now gone.

Inevitably, the conversation drifts back to me along with their eyes. They ask how I'm doing. They say I must be tired. They say my weak, frail human body must be breaking down.

Every time, I assure them that I'm more than capable of carrying on. I can go a little farther.

It's the fourth time they do this that I'm finally worn down. The sun is setting on the other side, the *wrong* side, of the mountains that loom above us—a strange phenomenon for me, and further evidence that I'm very far from home. The sun rises from the mountains...not sets. I come to a halt, crossing my arms and glaring at them.

"Are you ever going to tell me *why* exactly I'm going to die in the next three days?"

"Do you really want to know?" Hol asks.

"Oh, can I tell her?" Giles seems a little too eager for my liking. He grins and it's then that I notice his teeth are just slightly sharper than a normal human's would be.

"I suppose I'll let you deny me the pleasure," Shaye says to Giles.

"Tell her whatever you want," Davien calls back. "But don't stop moving."

We begin our march again. Giles speaks as we do. "Since you're human, I'm going to assume that you know basically nothing about the world you live in." I roll my eyes. He ignores it. "What you need to know is this. There are three worlds: the Beyond—where you go when you die; Midscape—where you are now, and where those of us with magic still reside; and the Natural World—the world humans were given after the ancient wars, and where you're from.

"Between each of these worlds is a barrier. The barrier between Midscape and the Beyond is called the Veil. The barrier between Midscape and the Natural World is called the Fade."

"All right." I think I follow. Though it seems too incredible to be real. "We crossed the Fade to get here?"

"Correct," he says.

"So the people who try and cross the mountains cross the Fade and actually end up here? In Midscape?"

"Not quite."

"Fortunately not, for them." Shaye tilts her head back and barks out a laugh. "Death is kinder to a human than accidentally ending up in the fae wilds."

I cross my arms over my chest and fight a shiver. I'm still in my nightgown and robe. What I wouldn't give for the dignity of a pair of trousers or a proper dress.

"Humans, and the regular creatures of Midscape, aren't supposed to be able to cross the Fade. Only a few of the elves can; it's the Elf King who maintains the barriers between the worlds. By not allowing the majority of people to cross on either side, he keeps his power."

"*Elf* King?" I repeat. "There's more than just fae here?"

"There's elves, mer, lykin, us... There were dryads long ago, but they died off after they made the humans. There's also vampir, but they haven't been seen in centuries. I think they were last heard from a couple hundred years after the Fade was erected. They might have gone the way of the dryads."

Dryads making humans... All the creatures from the old folktales being real... I feel dizzy and pause to brace myself against a tree and catch my breath. "It's impossible."

"What was that?" Giles calls back to me.

"Don't tell me; she's finally giving up for the day?" Shaye asks.

"This can't be real. I have to be dreaming." I shake my head with a laugh. "Magical creatures? Ancient wars? Barriers between worlds? *No*. No, this isn't real."

"Unfortunately for you, it's very real." Giles puts his hands in pockets hidden by the folds of his loose skirt. "Because we haven't even made it to the part that's going to kill you."

"Oh. Good. More things that can kill me other than the villains of all of the stories I was told as a girl." I scowl at him.

"Keep moving," Davien shouts. I frown even deeper and push away from the tree. The march is a fairly brisk pace, and while I wouldn't say I'm tired yet, it's also a lot more than a stroll in the woods. I glance behind me. It's like we're running from something. Whatever would strike fear into the hearts of these people, I know I don't want to meet. My thoughts go back to the woman that attacked me in the woods. Perhaps there are more like her out here, too.

"Humans aren't made for this world," Giles says. "Only one human can survive here—the Human Queen."

"Where does she live?" If there's a Human Queen then maybe I can find my way to her. Surely she would be sympathetic to me, right? I curse inwardly. What am I thinking? Make it to a Human Queen? Even if Giles told me where to find her, I wouldn't know one city from another here. I don't know anything about this world. The sickening feeling of helplessness settles on my shoulders and I want to scream.

"Nowhere you want to go. She's married to the Elf King and lives far to the south."

"May they rot with all elves behind their wall," Hol mutters under his breath.

"Let me get this straight, you're saying that humans can't survive here, so all humans were long ago pushed out into the—" I try and remember what he called my world "—Natural World."

"Look at that, she can be taught. I'm like a proud papa over here." Giles wipes an imaginary tear from the corner of his eye, sniffling dramatically.

I ignore the remark. It's the closest I'm going to get to affirmation so I continue. "And because humans can't survive here...I'm going to die?"

"More or less." Giles shrugs. "Can't say we've ever really tested it. Shaye, you once saw a human dragged to Midscape, right?"

Shaye glares at him for putting her on the spot. But she answers anyway. "I did. It was a horrible idea from a horrible person who did horrible things." Her eyes are distant as she speaks. She doesn't seem to look at anything. "It's the food, the water. In Midscape humans aren't nourished the way they should be. They wither and die alarmingly fast."

I swallow thickly and glance back toward the mountains. I try and ask as casually as possible, "How does someone cross the Fade?"

"Don't even think about trying to do it." Hol sees right through me. He ties his long auburn hair back at the nape of his neck, combing it around his horns. They look more like mother-of-pearl than bone. "The Fade is a dangerous place, even for us. Remember, no one is supposed to be able to cross it. We can only navigate it with magic and broken passageways that are a risk every time we try. If *you* tried to go into it, you would certainly die."

It sounds like I'm going to die either way. But I don't say the remark aloud. They've given me enough food for thought that I chew on the silence for a while. Every now and then I look back up at them. The three talk between themselves. Shaye's shimmering butterfly wings twitch on occasion, proof that they're real.

Or that I'm having the most horrible, vivid dream ever.

I hold out my forearm and give it a firm pinch. It hurts. No, not a dream.

Sighing, I run my fingers through my hair. They catch on a series of knots. I begin tugging and teasing out the tangles. It gives my hands something to do while I think. As if untangling my hair will help untangle me from the mess I'm in.

I don't even notice the group has stopped until I'm a few steps away from them. Jostled from my thoughts, I look around. The ruins of old houses, long forgotten, spread among the trees like a child's toys forgotten and left out. A large oak tree rises up from the remains of one home, boxed in by the crumbling walls.

"We'll stay there tonight." Davien points toward the building I was just looking at.

"Must we?" Giles shivers and wraps his arms around himself. "This is a cursed place."

"It's only cursed if you allow it to be," Hol says firmly, though I can't tell who he's trying to convince, the rest of us or himself.

Oren has come to a stop beside me. I glance over at him and whisper, "Is that how curses work?"

"No, curses are—" he begins to say but is cut off by Davien.

"This place is not actually cursed." His low voice rumbles through me. I hate that it is the same voice I spoke to all those evenings this past month. The same voice that kept me up in my bed late at night, sighing softly and yearning for just a glimpse of the face that went along with it. It would've been kinder if his voice changed when we entered this world. I still don't know how to remedy the difference between the handsome, kind, and *safe* Lord Fenwood I was imagining, and the powerful, deadly fae standing before me. "It is merely a place of brutality and great trauma."

"The sort of trauma not even the trees forget." Shaye looks up at the leafy canopies we walk under, as if trying to commune with those very sentries.

We enter into the ruins through a crumbled archway and work our way over the boulders and rubble, around the central oak, and to the back corner.

Giles picks up a stick from the ground and draws a circle around him. Oren motions to me to stand back with the rest of them. I watch with fascination as he marks four lines on the circle—each pointing in a different cardinal direction. As he makes the markings he murmurs, "North, South, East, and West, anchor me into this world." He digs the stick into the ground at his feet. "Fill my body with magic; allow me to wield all the power of the rock and leaves of the trees."

Lifting the stick, he points it at the tree in the center of the stone walls. The tip of the stick barely touches the bark. "Let us be safe within your boughs; let your bark be our shield, and branches be our walls."

His normally hazel eyes glow a faint emerald at their edges and the tree comes to life with a symphony of groaning and creaking wood.

I stumble backward. Oren catches me with a hand, helping me stay upright. I watch as the bark peels away from the tree and arches overhead. New branches sprout and weave together to form walls that merge with the stone remnants around us. Leaves unfurl to turn a canopy into a roof. When the light fades, there is a hut waiting for us.

"How..." I breathe. I can't form a cohesive sentence. I should be terrified. I should want to run at the sight of that. And yet... It was *stunning*. Magic was one of the most beautiful things I've ever laid eyes on. The feeling of power steeping in the air. The rush as it swirled around us and the tree came to life. The way it moved...

"It's called ritumancy," Oren answers my unfinished question. "Every type of creature in this world has their own form of magic, different from the others. The fae have ritumancy—meaning we use rituals to harness and use our powers. We cannot perform magic feats greater than a simple glamour, or using our physical gifts, without first performing a series of steps to charge and/or store it."

Giles holds up his hands as if on cue. Tensing his fingers, claws shoot out of them. They're the same as I saw last night when he was dancing around the fire. As he relaxes his hands, the claws vanish.

I think back to what Lord Fenwood—Davien, I remind myself firmly; Lord Fenwood never existed—told me the night of the dining table. No wonder he knew so much about fae magic. Here I thought he was a hunter when he was actually one of them himself.

The group settles in for the night. Hol makes the fire while Shaye and Davien go off hunting for dinner. They come back with hare that's promptly carved up and roasted.

Hol hands me a piece and says, "It might not taste like anything, or do anything for you, but it can't hurt to eat it."

My stomach growls, apparently loud enough for them to hear

because Giles lets out a snort. I don't really want to eat their fae food, but I have to try and keep my strength. At the very least, even if it tastes like ash and fails to nourish me, my stomach will hopefully feel full. And that'll be enough to quell its singing.

"Thanks," I mumble and take the thigh he's holding.

As I haven't eaten anything all day, it smells like heaven. Mouth watering, I take a bite, bracing for a mouth of campfire. But instead... it's the most delicious thing I've ever tasted. Had I even eaten food before this? I take another large bite, wiping liquid fat off my chin with the back of my hand.

"At least you're making an effort to eat it," Oren says with a smile.

"It can't hurt," I repeat Hol. I don't want them to know that I can taste the food. Maybe other humans were lying to the fae. *We* can lie, after all, and they can't. Maybe making them believe that the food and water fails to nourish us is a tactic for us to escape and get back home. Perhaps it's the food that will allow me to cross the Fade.

Dinner finished, the group settles in for the night. Hol takes first watch, Giles second, and Oren third. My best shot at running is when he's on duty. If I'm going to escape, it's going to be then.

The forest floor is more comfortable than I expected. The thick carpet of moss cradles my body and I fall into a surprisingly deep slumber. I wake when Oren stirs next to me. I positioned myself close enough that he wouldn't be able to move without me feeling it. Pretending to still be asleep, I sigh softly and roll onto my side. Covering half my face with my hands, I crack one eye open and peek out between my fingers.

Oren and Giles whisper among themselves. The conversation is brief and Giles takes his spot among the group on the ground. I wait until his heavy breathing has become soft snores.

Moving slowly, I roll onto my stomach and put my hands underneath my shoulders. I push myself up on my palms and knees and scan the group, using the smoldering remains of the campfire for light. My eyes snag on Davien. Even in the low light, his amber skin is practically luminescent. The orange embers contour his muscles, the sharp cut of his jaw, and the line of his brow, softened by sleep.

If I look only at his face, he's not too unlike the man I imagined, down to the slight stubble. But then I see the crimson, iridescent wings stretched behind him. *No*, the Lord Fenwood that I knew was an illusion. All along, this fae was manipulating me. When I left my family's home, I swore I would never be used again.

That promise to myself didn't end just because I crossed into their world.

I slowly stand, tiptoeing out through the archway made of branches and bark. Oren leans against the opening of the ruins. His dutiful watch comes to a halt on me.

"You should be asleep," he whispers.

"I have to go to the bathroom," I say sheepishly, ignoring the metal taste in my mouth. "I figured I shouldn't do that where everyone else is resting their head."

"You can do it over there." He points to the other side of the tree, right next to the shelter. "I will look away."

"I can't—that's too…" I sigh in frustration. "I can't do it that close to people."

"They're all asleep."

"I get stage fright." I shift my weight from foot to foot as though the need is urgent. "I'll go just behind that tree. It's far enough away." I point to a large oak tree near another ruin.

Oren purses his lips. "Fine, but hurry up."

"I'll do my best." I press my hands into my lower abdomen. "That food isn't sitting right with me."

He gives me a pitying look, almost enough to make me feel bad for lying and running away. But he was the one who lied to me in the first place. If he cared about me he would've told me what he was or stopped them from taking me here.

I cross over to the tree and step behind it. After a second I glance back. My eyes meet Oren's. I mouth the words, *Don't look.*

He rolls his eyes and looks away. This is my chance. I dart from the tree to behind the crumbling wall of another long-ago-destroyed house and listen to see if he is giving chase. The forest is silent. I don't think he saw me move.

I take a breath, brace myself, and make my escape.

eleven

I WONDER HOW MUCH TIME I BOUGHT MYSELF AS I PUSH
AWAY FROM THE WALL, SPRINTING STRAIGHT BACK BETWEEN
OAK TREES. Eventually, Oren will come looking. When he
doesn't find me, I'm sure he'll alert the others. I have to
assume that they're good at tracking. I've nothing to base
that assumption off of, but I would rather hope for the best
while planning for the worst. Given how my luck has been
this past day, they can no doubt track a beetle across a
mountain range.

Far enough that I know I'm out of view, I begin to cut
left and head in the direction we came from. There was a
creek not too far back. I've heard tales of people crossing
bodies of water while being chased by dogs. Something
about washing off your scent trail. Fae seem to be part
beast, so maybe the premise is the same. It can't hurt.

The small motes of light that illuminated the forest in
the daytime have made their beds upon the dark moss,
turning the forest floor into a sea of stars that ripples away
from me as I run through and closes back in over my
footsteps. The trees shimmer like water—what can only
be described as magic pulsing off their trunks and into the
leaves before falling back down to the earth as luminescent
haze. Everything here feels alive, *awake*, feels like I'm
being watched with every step by ancient beings.

I press my hand into my side. It aches and my lungs

are burning. I catch my breath for only a second and keep running. If I can make it to the creek, then maybe I can throw them. I paid attention to the path we took today. I'll find my way back and then I'll head into the mountains. I'll cross the Fade. If they can do it, so can I. After all, I have this magic of kings, or whatever it is that their ritual was supposed to create. I can do this; I know I can.

The creek comes into view.

I jump down the shallow bank, splash in the water, and leap across. It's as my feet touch down on the other side that I see the blur of movement in my periphery. I spin toward the source on instinct.

A man pummels into me. He came from the sky—a blur of bloodred iridescence and starlight. We hit the ground together. I bring up my knee on instinct, looking for the soft spot between his legs that will surely shake him and instead finding his ribs due to the awkward way we fell. He's half on top of me, pushing off the ground now, trying to catch my wrist as I struggle to free myself.

"Unhand—" A large palm clamps over my mouth.

Davien's bright green eyes meet mine. The only thing keeping his nose from touching mine is his hand. His hair cascades over his shoulders and tickles my cheek.

"Are you trying to get yourself killed?" he snarls.

I try and speak against his hand, the muffled sounds unintelligible until he removes his fingers. "Your friends kept telling me all day how I'm going to die anyway. I might as well hurry it up."

"And yet we're still trying to keep you alive." He has yet to pull away. His body is crushing mine against the creek bed. Water rushes against my side in cool contrast to the heat of his firm muscle.

"You know who else tried to keep me alive? My mother and sisters. You know how they did it? Locking me in rooms, preventing me from having friends, taking anything that brought me even the slightest amount of joy. They treated me like a *thing* more than a person." I blink up at him, my eyes burning.

The words spill from me uninvited. I don't want to be saying these things, not to him, not here, not now. But in this moment, it feels as though there can be nothing hidden between us. He's compressed all the space where secrets could live into dust. It's just *him*, assaulting my senses like he has been for weeks. Except now

I can see him. Now I can stare into those bright green eyes as they expose me. Now it's more than the barest of touches and I can feel his body on mine as his weight crushes my barriers.

"I want to live—more than anything—and because I want that, I refuse to spend my hours as someone's thing. I'm going to live my life, the way I want to live it, or die trying. So help me live or be ready to kill me," I finish, voice quivering.

He opens and closes his mouth. Still undecided on his words, he shifts his weight and presses a hand into the ground by the side of my head. With space between us once more, I can breathe again. I've never felt so laid bare.

"Get up," he says, barely more than a grunt. "You'll catch a cold if you lie in the water."

Davien makes room for me to stand. I brush the dirt and rocks off of my tattered robe. My nightgown is alarmingly translucent on the side where the water flowed over me. I close my robe about me a little tighter. If he noticed the impropriety, he made a point not to look.

"Live your life the way you want to live it..." he echoes and laughs softly with a shake of his head. "What a selfish aspiration."

"Excuse me?" It's my turn to close the gap between us. I rise to my tiptoes to try and stare him in the eye and still come up short. "What did you say?"

"You want to live your life in total disregard for everyone and everything else. It's selfish."

"I made my sacrifices. I earned this." I shake my head, backing away. "I don't have to defend myself to you, or to anyone."

"You're right, you don't, because you clearly don't care for others." He shrugs. "Not that I could understand someone who chose to live their life that way."

"Oh? And how do you live your life? Holed up in a manor in the human world? Finding brides whose families have the things you need for your nighttime rituals? Am I even the first human bride you've taken?" I'm surprised at how much I want him to say that I am. How wounded I would be if I was just one of many.

"You are." He gives me a glare so cold I shiver. "And I did not accept you as my bride lightly. Had I a choice, I wouldn't have. I never wanted to involve you in any of this. If your father had just given me that damn book when I first demanded it years ago, none of this would've happened. I had to wait and prepare an offering I knew your family could not refuse."

"My father's death—"

"I had nothing to do with it," he interrupts firmly, but still somewhat gentle around the delicate subject. "Nor do I or did I find joy in it. I sent Oren expecting him to negotiate with your father, not Joyce. I didn't even know he'd passed to the great Beyond, only that he was away and rumor of your family's hard times."

I heave a small sigh of relief.

He continues, "But last night...when I finally, *finally* had everything I needed in place, years of work all coming to fruition for a cause much bigger than myself—much bigger than you will ever know...I—I..."

"You?" I whisper when the silence stretches on to the point that I'm afraid he won't continue.

"I *still* thought of you. I left you that letter in an attempt to make it easy should anyone claim that you didn't have a right to that land, that home. You would have been taken care of for the rest of your mortal days. And all you had to do was follow the rules I gave you for your own benefit and stay put."

My stomach churns, and not because I ate food from the fae world. I'm sick because I don't smell smoke and fae can't lie. He's telling the truth.

All I had to do was stay put. One final night of heeding the rules and the total freedom I've always craved would have been mine. Davien would've been out of my life and his riches in the Natural World would've been mine.

"And here we are again." He shakes his head. "Another night where you risk *everything* by not staying where you were put."

"If you want me to go along with this, you have to start telling me what is happening. Treat me like an equal. I know I should but I can't follow rules blindly." Joyce has scarred me too deeply in ways I'm only beginning to understand for me to go along with something without question.

"Do you think you deserve that?" He arches his eyebrows.

"If you have any fondness—no, any respect—for me, then you'll do this. I am not a relic that you can store on a shelf until your next ritual. I'm a breathing person. Don't treat me like a thing and I won't have a reason to be out of place because the place I'll be in is the one I've chosen."

Davien sighs heavily. He runs a hand through his hair. Half of it slicks back thanks to the water of the creek. The other half falls into his face. "Do you promise that's all it will take?"

"I swear it."

"Give me one reason why I would think you would keep your word? You swore if I unlocked the door, you wouldn't leave. You lied." There's hurt on his face. Maybe that's why he never wanted me to see him before. The man is an open book of emotion. He spent so much time in physical isolation that he never had to learn how to guard himself.

Whereas me? I learned that skill very quickly thanks to Joyce and Helen.

I shake my head slowly. I can't think of anything I could offer him to prove I'm telling the truth. I could tell him how I taste metal when I lie. But he has no proof of what I can taste or not. Laura never said she could smell metal on my breath, the few times she indulged me with a sniff.

"I guess you don't have any reason." I shrug. "I guess the best thing I can do to prove it to you is to start acting in good faith myself. I'll head back to camp, right now."

His emotion changes. His brow softens slightly and arches upward. His eyes narrow, just a little and for only a second. It's like watching thoughts dance across a person's mind, exposed in a way I've never seen before.

I cross the creek and splash up the bank on the other side. I'm several steps away when I realize he's not following me. "Are you coming?"

"Are you honestly planning on walking?" He chuckles. His mighty wings—all four of them—unfurl on his unspoken command and spread out behind him. So it's true what he told me about the fae being able to summon and dismiss some of their animal features. The wings had vanished after we'd toppled in the stream and now they seem to grow in size. Slightly translucent streaks pick up the light of the forest floor. He's positively radiant. With a mighty flap, he half jumps, half glides over the creek and steps next to me. "There's a much faster way. And if I'm treating you like an equal, then I should extend it to you as well." His arm wraps around my shoulders and pulls me to him. Once more the strong length of his body leaves me breathless. "Do you trust me?"

"I don't know," I whisper.

"What a state we're in, aren't we?" he says with a smile so dashing it should be a crime. "I can't trust you and now you seem to have some reason why you can't trust me."

"Well, you did betray my trust, too," I admit.

He seems genuinely surprised by this. "What? How?"

"You lied to me about who you are."

His brow furrows. "What should I have said?" he asks softly; I'm staggered by the sincerity. "That your new husband was a fae who was destined to leave you? Would that have made you happy?"

I can't meet his eyes anymore. I don't have an answer. "I suppose I just wish things were different," is all I can say. He hooks my chin and guides my face back to him. His eyes are open and inviting.

"I have spent my whole life wishing things were different. And we are on the cusp of it all changing. And once it changes for me, it will change for you too." *Truth. Truth. Truth.* "Once I have the power that's in you, I will see you back to your world. You'll still have that house. You'll still have all the riches I left behind. You will live with every comfort you want and whatever joy you can buy."

"What about the fae in the forest?"

"They were after me, not you. Without me there, no one will come and harm you." His arm tightens once more. "So I will ask you again, an impossible question to a human, from a fae...do you trust me? *Will* you trust me? Can we start over?"

I should say no. Every human instinct in my body screams no. I can't trust this man. His very design as a fae is to be my enemy.

And yet, in a small breath, I defy even myself when I utter, "Yes."

His movements are a blur. In one fluid motion he pulls me to his chest while reaching with his free hand to catch the backs of my knees. He bends forward and sinks low into his legs. Then, he jumps upward with a mighty flap of his wings.

We take to the skies.

The canopy rushes past us. I try and shield myself with a hand, pressing my face into his chest. Davien shifts as well, taking the brunt of tree limbs with his shoulders and neck. The forest becomes a distant memory as we break through its leafy barrier and slow to hover among the stars.

"Look," he whispers.

I peel my face from his chest and shoulder as we begin to descend. We're falling much more slowly than should be naturally possible. Davien stretches out a leg and points his foot. With just the tip of his boot he meets one of the upper branches of an oak tree and then pushes off once more with another flap of his wings. We arc back upward, magic sparking like embers off the wings behind him.

"See, it's not so bad." He looks down at me with a grin. I bite my lip and finally admire the world around us now that I'm at least somewhat confident I'm not about to fall.

Even though I know I should be afraid. Even though my stomach has fallen from my body. My heart is soaring.

"Not so bad…" I repeat, the thought getting lost among the splendor.

From this vantage I can see the entirety of the Bleeding Woods. They spread all along the distant mountain range and thin as they near a vibrant city at the top of a hill in the distance. I can make out the spires of a castle against the dark sky. It's the only significant sign of life that I can see. Above us, the heavens have never been so bright. The stars look more like the sandy shores of an ocean, rather than the tiny specks I've always known them as.

"It's incredible," I whisper. I loose a hand from around his neck and point toward the castle. "What's that?"

Whatever it is, he doesn't like it. I can feel his shoulders tense before a scowl sweeps across his face. Even the brilliance of his eyes seems to dim with the shadows of trauma.

"That is the High Court. It's the hill on which the first kings were crowned, where the glass crown of the fae resides, and where the Fae King lives and rules."

"And you want to kill him." The words are easier to say than I think they should have been. But I have no horse in this race. I hardly care about fae kings and queens.

"How do you know that?" He glances down at me as his toe touches another treetop and he launches us off again.

"You told me you wanted to become king once." I relax more into the safety of his arms.

"You didn't forget." He chuckles. "I thought you would've written that off."

"I would've, if I'd smelled smoke."

"Smelled smoke?" He furrows his brow. I realize I haven't told him about my gift.

"Well, you see…" Every time I try to tell someone about it, things end badly. I tear my eyes from him, looking away. That's how I see the motion in the distance. There's a blur of shadow. I blink and the figure is gone, only to appear from a puff of smoke closer. "Look out!" I shout. But I'm too late.

Davien turns. His eyes widen as he sees what I see. A man has come seemingly from out of nowhere. A shawl of shadow identical to that on the woman in the woods that day is around his shoulders. He condenses darkness and hurls a spear of it right for us. Davien tries to react, but not even he's fast enough.

His cry fills the air as the spear punches through his shoulder, blood pours down on to me, his arm goes limp, and I slip from his grasp as we plummet back down to earth.

twelve

A TREE BRANCH RAKING AGAINST MY BACK IS THE FIRST THING THAT JOLTS ME OUT OF MY HAZE OF SHOCK. I quickly turn myself into a ball, bringing my knees up and shielding my face with my forearms. I want to make myself as small as possible. I know I am going to hit all manner of branch and tree limb on the way down, but the smaller I am, hopefully the fewer I hit.

My strategy works, for the most part. At least until one unlucky limb has me doubled over on my side. All the wind is knocked from me. I wheeze and roll off the branch, narrowly missing another one on my way down. A final branch I allow myself to hit. Prepared this time, I'm able to brace myself and catch it with both hands. My fingers are ripped across the bark, torn up in an instant. But it slows my descent.

Though it doesn't stop me from hitting the ground awkwardly. Luckily, the thick blanket of moss cushions my fall. I'm wheezing and aching all over. My body is covered in bruises and scratches. This is why Joyce forbade me from heights after the roof. Nothing ever goes right when I'm high up.

A heavy thud next to me steals my attention. I get up and rush over to where Davien has landed. He's so very still. It isn't until I'm on my knees at his side that I can see his chest moving.

"Thank the gods," I whisper. I may not know fully where I stand with this man. He might have betrayed my trust in some murky ways. But I know that *he* is the best chance I have of surviving this world and getting home.

The man who launched the spear descends gracefully through the canopy. He moves from branch to branch on his tiptoes, nothing more than a whisper of smoke between. With a *pop* he materializes on the ground not far from me.

"You're alive." He *tsks*. "How utterly disappointing. I expected this to be far simpler. To think I couldn't kill a fae with stinted magic and a human. I'm losing my touch."

"Stay away," I manage to say. "Don't come any closer."

"Or what?" He adjusts the shadowy scarf that swoops across his shoulders and upper chest. I was right, it is the same as the one worn by the woman from the woods who attacked me weeks ago. "I don't know why he dragged you here, human, but let me assure you that you are far out of your depth."

Like I don't know that. He continues approaching. I hold out a hand and repeat, "Don't come any closer."

"I'm waiting to see how you'll stop me." He shakes his head with a sinister smile.

I turn back to Davien. He's my best hope. But the moss around the shoulder the spear tore through is already stained a deep red. I shake his good shoulder lightly and plead, "Get up, please."

"He's not going to get up. He's the last loose end that should have been tied years ago," the man snarls. His white hair shines in the moonlight as he holds his spear aloft. He takes a step forward and adjusts his weight to throw.

"No you don't—" Shaye shouts from a distance. I can see her and the others trying to close the gap. But they won't be fast enough.

I have to stall. I have to do something. "I said don't come any closer!" I scream a final time. My fear and rage grows within me. It's a swell that can't be contained. Emotions and wants that have burned so hot they've become something…tangible.

The power bursts forth from my palm, turning into a wall of light. It rushes toward our attacker with deadly force. In an instant, he's enveloped. Silence fills the air as the man is turned into a reverse silhouette—a solid outline of white that's too blinding to look at. Then, he explodes.

The force of the magic has me knocked onto my back at Davien's side. The shock wave rushes through the woods, violently shaking loose limbs from the trees and shearing the moss from the soil and bedrock underneath. My ears are ringing as the forest goes suddenly dark and eerily silent following the blast.

I sit, realizing the pains from my body are as gone from this earth as our attacker is. I blink at the epicenter of the blast—where he was standing just a moment ago. There's nothing but a singed bit of hard rock. I stare at my hand.

I... I did that? How? A thousand questions swirl in my mind, immediately coming to a stop the second I hear a soft groan next to me.

"Davien?"

His eyes crack open. "What just happened?" he murmurs.

"I think I killed a man." I return to staring at my hand, waiting for the realization that *I just killed a man* to sink in.

"He was a shit stain on this earth. Good riddance." Davien sits, rolling his injured shoulder. He pauses, looking to the wound. Poking his finger through the torn and bloody hole of his shirt, he runs it along unbroken skin and sighs. "It seems you healed me, too."

"You…don't seem happy about that?"

"I'd be happier if I was the one to heal and protect myself." He stands with a scowl and stalks over to the center of the singed earth. Davien digs the toe of his boot into the only remnants of the man, spitting.

"Well, you're welcome." I stand and go to draw my robe around me; my hands hit something wet. Davien might be healed, but his blood is still all over me. I cringe at my own filth.

"I shouldn't need to thank you," he murmurs without looking at me with those distant and unfocused eyes.

"Excuse me? I saved your life, and because of that I now have to live with the fact that *I killed a man*. So maybe a 'thanks' would ease that process a bit?" My hands are shaking. There's the slimy, sick feeling I expected that comes from knowing I ended a life.

"I shouldn't need to thank you because I should have been able to do that myself!" Anger overflows from him, an unbridled, unyielding rage that is far greater than anything I could've created on my own. "You stole the power of our kings—and took it for yourself. Just like your kind took our lands and our songs and stories. You took what should have been *mine*." His hair falls, scraggly, in front of his face. His breathing is ragged.

I can only stare in shock at his misplaced rage. I didn't ask for any of this. I certainly don't want it. But the anger is radiating off of him as waves of power that still my tongue.

"Davien, that's enough." Oren breaks the silence. The group has arrived. "We should keep going. The king's Butchers are on our trail."

"We walk through the night," Davien declares after taking a moment to breathe and collect himself. "We don't stop until we cross the Crystal River and are in Acolyte land." He looks back at me. "I'll carry you myself if I have to."

"I'll be fine." I fold my arms and watch as Oren leads Davien away with a hand on his back. Stern words are being exchanged between them, mostly from Oren. Giles and Hol are close behind. Shaye lingers.

"Are you coming?" she asks.

"Not like I have any other choice," I mutter and drag my feet.

She grabs my arm. I try and yank it away, but she holds fast. This close to her for the first time, I notice faint golden tattoos that swirl up the side of her face. They almost blend in with the brown of her skin.

"Walk with your head held high, human."

"I have a name."

"Walk with your head held high, *Katria*." Her obliging me with the use of my name gives me pause. "You have the power of kings within you. Do us all the courtesy of not shaming it."

"What does that even mean?" I don't know why I ask; she's not going to give me an answer.

Yet, she circumvents my every expectation when she does. "The ritual we performed in the wood last night was to draw out the ancient power of the lost royal family of Aviness from the last living heir."

"Lost?"

"Assassinated would be more apt," she clarifies, voice and expression taking a dark turn. "They ruled for centuries, until Boltov the First killed King Aviness the Sixth. After that...the fae land was torn apart from the inside, the Boltovs usually ending up on top. But the only way they managed to keep control and rule of the fae is by systematically killing every last one of the Aviness bloodline— anyone who could possibly reclaim the mighty power of the first kings to truly rule the fae."

Shaye points to Davien. "*He* is the closest thing our people have to that lost ruler and the power they carried in their veins. That ritual was to restore his power to him as the sole remaining heir of Aviness...the last limb of the family tree that Boltov hasn't severed at the neck."

"His birthright," I whisper.

"Yes. And you *stole* it by stepping into the fire when he was supposed to be the one to. So until we find a way to wring it from your fragile human bones, give our history a modicum of respect and at least act like you walk with the power of ancient royalty." She finally releases me.

I rub my arm and begrudgingly nod. She rolls her eyes and begins trudging along. I follow closely behind.

"May I ask you something?"

She glances at me from the corner of her eye. "Go on."

It's strange. Shaye has been the farthest thing from friendly toward me...but she doesn't strike me as cruel. I've spent years around those who are genuinely cruel. There's a certain manner to a person when they're looking for every possible way to tear you down.

Shaye doesn't seem like she's hunting for ways to be mean for the sake of it. Naturally abrasive? Somewhat, perhaps. Cautious might be more apt. But however those natures of hers seem to manifest, she doesn't appear to *delight* in my misery.

"How does the last living fae heir end up in my world?"

"Because that was the only place he could go that he would be safe." Shaye sighs. "A little more than twenty years ago, the Boltovs and their Butchers—"

"Butchers? Like the man who attacked us tonight?"

"Yes. They're either murderous fae who swear to defend the Blood Court the Boltovs have made, or poor souls who are born into the Butchers and are never given a choice. Butchers relish in bloodshed and engage in its sport." She cringes, an expression I share. "The Boltov Butchers have made it their life's work to eradicate any who would threaten the Boltov claim."

"Can women also be Butchers?"

"Why couldn't they be?" Her answer is guarded, expression unreadable.

"There was a fae that attacked me in the woods...but she seemed like she was really after Davien. She wore the same shadowy cowl as the man tonight."

"Your assessment is right; she was a Butcher." Shaye scrambles up a shallow ridge and then, to my surprise, offers a hand to me. "We tried to patrol those woods as often as we could—on both sides of the Fade—but some of Boltov's men and women would slip through from time to time."

I take Shaye's hand and she hoists me up with ease. Her biceps are wider than the limb I struck on my fall. The woman could likely break me in two if she tried and after years of manual labor, I am not frail.

"So he was hiding in my world to get away from the Boltovs and their Butchers?"

"Oh, right, I never finished." Shaye sighs and shakes her head. "I hate this story."

"You don't have to tell me." Though I do desperately want to know now. Kings, evil knights, runaway royalty, it has all the makings of the storybooks Joyce would read to Helen and Laura. The ones I would hear by pressing my ear to their doors at night before I'd creep back to my bed and tuck myself in.

"You want to know, so I'm going to tell you." Shaye takes a breath and continues the tale. "King Aviness the Sixth's death sparked a seemingly endless cycle of people vying for power. There are three things that give a king control over the fae: the glass crown, the hill on which the first king was crowned—which is also where the glass crown resides—and the magic of the ancient kings. If a man controls all three, he controls the fae."

"I see. So just one of them isn't enough?"

"No, though any of those three things holds immense power. So any family tangentially related to Aviness tried to exert their claim to the glass crown and powers as the true rulers of the fae, but the Boltovs always got to them before they could get anywhere near the crown, much less the hill of the first king on which the High Court sits.

"Most retreated into these woods for protection, some abandoning their bloodline altogether, not that it made any difference. The Boltovs saw that the trees were watered with their blood, systematically hunting out any of the Aviness lineage who could lay claim to the dormant, old magic of kings. Davien was only tangentially related to the bloodline, but it didn't spare him from the hunt."

"Tangentially related? What does that mean?"

"His mother was a widow. She remarried...poor thing didn't even know that her new husband was the last, distant survivor of the Aviness family."

"How could she not know?"

"He was only related through a number of marriages and cousins removed, a rogue twig on the family's branches."

"It sounds like the man Davien's mother married hardly had the blood at all," I say.

"Indeed. The last true Aviness by any significant measure was put to death nearly thirty years ago."

"And if Davien was born before his mother married, he has no blood relation to the family at all, merely marriage."

"Yes, but that's enough of a link to make the Boltovs nervous."

Davien's story is eerily similar to my own in some ways. I can't help but think of Joyce, widowed and with child, marrying with the hopes of security and secret ambition. "Does he have any siblings?"

"No."

At least no one suffered like I did. "So I take it the Butchers killed his father?"

"And mother, even though she had nothing to do with the family other than a marriage band and vows." Shaye pauses as we pass through another town of ruins. The sun is beginning to creep over the horizon and the morning's first light paints the stones in a ghostly hue. "Oren, Davien's butler and nanny from birth, took Davien and retreated back to an old Aviness stronghold on the other side of the Fade. One that still had some of the old wards. It was the best chance for Davien to reach adulthood beyond Boltov's reach—when he would be strong enough to return and fight for us all."

That explains why it looks like a castle. "Why would a fae stronghold be on the human side of the Fade?"

"Because the elves find perverse delight in taking our land and when the world was cut up, some of what was ours went to you humans." She wears a look of disgust. But in a positive display of her character, she doesn't seem to direct it toward me. More at the circumstances…and those long-ago elves.

"So Davien was raised in the human world?"

"Yes. Cut off from our people and the magic of Midscape…he's lived a lonely life of struggle. The only thing that's kept him going is the obligation to free us from Boltov's tyranny. Because their grip becomes tighter on these lands by the day. And if he dies—if the last with a claim to the power of Aviness perishes—then nothing will stand in the way of Boltov finally unlocking the full power of the glass crown. The power of kings will no longer be tied to the Aviness bloodline and will be free for the taking."

thirteen

WHAT ONCE FELT LIKE A FOREST OF MAGIC HAS NOW BECOME A HAUNTED GRAVEYARD. After Shaye's tales, we walk in silence for most of the morning. Every forgotten house, left to ruin and rot, is now a tombstone in my eyes. Every tree is a marker of some fallen fae, butchered in their beds so that this Boltov family could rule unquestioned.

There's a deep ache in me I can't explain. Human. Fae. Suffering is universal. It'd be impossible to look on this barren landscape and not feel sorrow for the horrors that have been wrought.

Maybe it's those stories and their uncomfortable truths that helps me at least compartmentalize what happened with the Butcher. It wasn't as if I meant to kill him. The magic acted on its own. Moreover, if I didn't take his life, he was certain to kill me. And…it doesn't sound like he was someone innocent of atrocities, either. Maybe by ending his life, I saved another? That's a dangerous logic. But I need to keep my sanity together somehow right now.

I don't really have hours in the day to allocate to having an emotional breakdown. Too busy surviving.

As dawn breaks, the little motes of light rise from the moss and begin to dance among the trees once more. They illuminate the air, buzzing around me with a happiness that is now muted by the truth. I wonder if they are actually spirits of murdered fae. But that's one curiosity I won't indulge.

We move without incident throughout the day. Everyone remains on alert, scanning the horizon lines at all points. Giles and Shaye have taken wide sweeps of the woods around us, remaining within view, but far enough that they can see around distant trees and look across ridges that might be too high for the rest of us.

Hol, Oren, Davien, and I remain in a pack. Oren and Davien at the front, Hol and I behind. Though there isn't much conversation happening.

Just like Davien promised, we hike all day through the woods. My stomach is practically roaring by nightfall and my feet are aching. It doesn't matter how soft the moss is, the support of a pair of shoes would make all the difference for my throbbing feet.

"We should break for dinner," Hol says, loud enough that it gets Davien and Oren's attention.

"We need to keep moving." In contrast to his words, Davien stops. "We can't rest until we're in Acolyte territory."

"I'm not saying rest. I'm saying stop for food." Hol glances back in my direction and then back to Davien with a pointed look. "Just a short break."

Davien's eyes settle on me. I purse my lips as I can feel him assessing me from the top of my head to the bottoms of my feet. Shaye's earlier words stick with me and I try to hold my head high, even though I know I currently possess all the dignity of a disheveled raccoon.

"Do you need to stop?" he asks me.

"I can keep going," I force myself to say when all I want is to shout, *Five minutes please!* I'm not going to slow them down. And the faster I help him get this magic out of me, the faster I can go home and get out of this deadly situation that I was never meant to be in.

"Good, we carry on then."

"Davien—"

"Your true king has spoken." Davien cuts off Hol with a glare. "If we keep walking, we should cross the Crystal River by dawn."

"Very well." Hol folds his arms.

"Sire, *true king*, permission to speak freely?" Shaye has perched herself on the top of a rock we're passing by. She's been close enough to overhear the whole conversation.

"Granted," he growls.

"You're being an ass." Shaye smirks. "That is all."

Davien huffs and puts his back to us, storming off. I think I see Oren give the slightest bit of a chuckle. There was no smoke attached with Shaye's comment...which means she was telling the truth about him being an ass—at least as far as she sees it. I bite back a snicker.

But a few hours later, I don't even have the energy for playful amusements. Right foot. Left foot. That's all I have the strength for. *Right foot, left foot*, I echo in my mind as I move. I'm telling my legs to bend while begging my feet to hold me upright. I thought I knew the depths of strength I could draw from—what I was capable of accomplishing when forced to. But this is shattering every previous notion and putting more to the test.

All at once, the trees break and the sound of rushing water assaults my ears. I blink, standing at the edge of a riverbank unlike any I've ever seen. It's lined not with sand, or rock, but *crystal*. Hundreds of thousands of shimmering shards reflect the moonlight like glass. Magic swirls underneath the water, split into a thousand fractals by the stones.

"This must be the Crystal River," I murmur with relief.

"It is," Shaye affirms.

Without warning, she scoops me up into her strong arms. I wrap my arms around her neck like I did with Davien. Even my arms feel tired. Though who knows how... I didn't even use them at all today.

Shaye leaps into the sky, flapping her butterfly wings behind her. Hol is at our side, using a pair of white bat-like wings that he dismisses with a thought on the opposite bank. Shaye's flight is stronger and more sure than Davien's. She had mentioned something about Davien being weakened by being cut off from the magic of this world. Perhaps that's why his wings have that perpetually tattered look to them.

Davien crosses the gap with Giles in his arms. Sure enough, he more leaps and glides than truly flies like Shaye. But my cheeks still warm slightly at the memory of being in his arms—at those first sensations of weightlessness as we drifted through the starry sky. During those brief seconds where things truly seemed like they were starting anew between us.

My landing is far more graceful during my second experience of flight than the first. We touch down onto the bank on the other side. As soon as my feet meet the damp earth a shiver runs through me. Shaye grips my shoulders.

"Give it a moment, it'll pass."

"What..." My teeth chatter so violently I can't finish my question. Luckily Shaye seems to know what I'm going to ask.

"The Crystal River is one of the Acolyte's demarcation lines. You've left the control of the Blood Court and we have heavily warded our lands against them. The magic is feeling you out... making sure you're not foe."

Sure enough, as she's speaking, the feeling of hands rubbing all over my body subsides, leaving gooseflesh in their wake. I force another shiver, trying to shake the sensation.

"What would happen if I'm foe?"

"Wouldn't you like to know?" Shaye grins. Before I can press, she looks to Davien. "There's an outpost not far from here. We can make camp—"

"We continue on to Dreamsong," Davien says, brushing past us.

"Dreamsong is another half-day's walk." Shaye's hands fall from my shoulders and she rushes to be at Davien's side. "You have to stop. *She* has to stop."

Davien looks back at me with the same agitation as before. "You can heal yourself, can't you?"

"I don't know..." I murmur. "I have healed myself... But I'm not sure how—"

"Good. Restore strength to your muscles with the king's magic and carry on with the rest of us."

"My lord, I think Shaye—" Oren tries to say.

"I have spoken!" Davien's voice echoes between the trees, long before the pinched-up agitation in his shoulders does.

"Katria..." Oren starts softly.

"I'm all right." My turn to interrupt him. "Don't worry about me. I can keep going."

Oren regards me skeptically but says nothing. I'm not going to give in. I won't be the weak human they expect, ready to topple over at any second. I can keep going.

If only I could use the power on command, however... I stare at my swollen feet. I noticed a while back they've begun to leave little blood spots on the moss where I walk. It doesn't matter how soft the ground is...my feet have become one large blister that is now ripping open.

I hear the fae talk around me, but I'm too focused on my aching feet to even pay attention to the words being said. *Heal*, I think, *Heal!* But the magic does nothing. I've never even thought magic was real until today, why do I think I can suddenly use it on command? *Yesterday?* I blink up at the dawn. What day is it, anymore?

I've been walking forever...

The world tilts as I begin to sway. Every step is shakier than the last. My knees threaten to lock or give out.

Right foot.

Left foot.

Shaye says something to me but it's muffled. I blink several times. The trees are becoming hazy. There's something wrong with my eyes *and* ears.

"Almost there," I think she says.

Almost...not soon enough.

Right foot.

Left foot.

Dawn has broken. The forest is alive once more. But I enjoy none of it. I'm an automaton. I move to prove it to myself and to the man with the bright green eyes who looks back every now and then just to ensure that I'm still upright.

"Look," Giles says from some distant place. "It's Dreamsong."

We stand at the top of a ridge where the trees have broken. Below us, a city has been erected. I've never seen anything more beautiful. My eyes water as the world goes sideways. The blurry metropolis tilts, spinning as I do.

Everything goes black.

I groan softly, rolling over on my feather mattress. The duvet is heavy on me. It's as soft as it always was, pulled right up to my ears, blocking out the late morning's sunlight.

As I yawn, consciousness slowly returns to me. I had the strangest dream. It was a long dream, too. And so vivid… I dreamed I was in the land of the fae, that I was pulled there following a ritual in the woods.

Laughing softly at myself, I push back the covers, expecting to be met with my room at Lord Fenwood's manor. I stop with a sharp inhale. This is *not* that room.

Sheer curtains waft in the breezes of a late afternoon, teasing me with glimpses of a city sprawling beneath my second-story, arched windows. The bed is a simple platform, as comfortable as anything, but a stark reminder that I am very far from anything remotely familiar. I run my hands over the linens. They're almost identical to the ones Davien used in his estate.

Did he import them from Midscape? I wonder. He must have. It occurs to me I've never felt any material this buttery soft. Of course it was made by magic.

My room is sparse. Whitewashed walls are split by dark beams that support a high ceiling. There's a mirror hung above a dresser to the right of the bed. A chair is situated by the far opening.

But…that's it.

I push back the covers and sit cross-legged to massage my feet. Just like the last time I woke up here, I've been healed. The soles of my feet show no signs of blistering or trauma.

So I have magic. And I can use it. Just not consciously. "Great, simply *fantastic*."

When I stand, I notice that my robe and nightgown are nowhere to be seen. I've been dressed in a simple, silken shift. Delicate embroidery lines the neck—a similar design to the markings Shaye and Giles have on their flesh. I'm too grateful to be out of those soiled clothes to be horrified by the idea that someone stripped me down while I was unconscious.

I inspect myself in the mirror, turning right and left. The usual pallor of my skin has brightened. My hair seems a richer, more vibrant chestnut. This is more than the change I saw from the good food and easy life of Lord Fenwood's manor. I look positively radiant. I should get forbidden, ancient magic more often.

As I twist, though, I notice the low-cut back exposes the upper edge of the gnarled scars that stretch between my shoulder blades. *Whoever dressed me must've seen it.* I feel sick and try to situate my hair over the old wound. It aches at my mere acknowledgment of it so I try and put it from my mind.

Opening the door to my room, I poke my head out into the hallway. There's no one. I start down the hall toward a stairway at one end. The other doors along the hallway are closed—more bedrooms, I presume.

Voices drift up from the bottom of the stairs. They're murmured and soft. But one sticks out.

"Okay, I think Shaye said it clearly enough. But just for emphasis—you were being an ass. Like a donkey. But more… stubborn and frustrating." *Giles.* And I suspect I know just who he's speaking to.

I'm not intending to creep down the stairs, it just sort of works out that way. My footsteps are light enough that no one notices me. And it's not my fault that the table in the great hall is positioned in such a way that no one sitting around it has a clear view of me when I emerge.

"I was trying to keep us safe," Davien insists.

"You were trying to wear her down," Shaye says, shoveling food into her mouth. "Either because you were frustrated with her because she has the magic…or because you were trying to push her to the point of using the magic for you again so you could see it. Regardless, still an ass, and you should get yourself together. It's no way for a king to act."

Davien glares at her. "We were being hunted by the Butchers."

"There was a *single Butcher*, who we killed. Well, *she* killed. Great trick, that, especially to do it without a ritual to prepare the power. Once you get the magic you should learn how to do it, too." Giles tears a piece off a loaf of bread and takes a large bite. He continues talking with his mouth full. "We might be the town screwups about most things. But we can at least make sure no one lives to tell the tale of how badly we mess up."

"Just like that woman in the woods," Hol murmurs over his goblet.

"Exactly like that Butcher in the woods," Giles agrees.

They're talking about the woman who attacked me, I realize. Shaye had mentioned something, too, about patrolling the woods on either side of the Fade. I might owe my life to more than just Davien.

"She *exploded* that man. A magical outburst like that certainly drew the attention of fae near and far," Davien insists.

"Good thing no one lives in the woods, huh?" Giles grins.

"I'm certain King Wotor felt it." Davien leans across the table. His voice becomes heavy and serious. The teasing stops. "Which means he's going to come after me—and her by extension. He knows the old magic has returned to these lands."

"Who's King Wotor?" I ask, drawing their attention to me. "Yes, hello, just woke up. Is he the head Boltov?"

"He is. King Wotor Boltov the…what are we on? Tenth now?" Giles leans back in his chair, looking oddly smug. "Just stick with 'Boltov' because it's easier. Anyway, he's going to try and kill you the first chance he gets."

"Lovely. I'm noticing a trend that, in the fae world, everything is going to kill me sooner or later."

"Our sweet deadly home," Giles muses to Hol, who rolls his eyes in reply.

"So how do we make sure that doesn't happen? Because I very much like breathing."

"Now that you're up, the first step is to talk to Vena." Davien stands. "If anyone will know what to do…it's her."

fourteen

THE LARGE GATHERING SPACE THE STAIRS DEPOSITED ME
INTO IS CONNECTED BY TWO MASSIVE DOORS TO A WAITING
HALL THAT LEADS TO VENA'S AUDIENCE CHAMBERS. She
sits on a golden throne, surrounded by thorny roses and
hummingbirds. Her rich, dark skin is offset against the sea-
foam blue gown she wears and the bright green, bat-like
wings that extend from her back. Her dark hair is piled high
on the top of her head, pinned in place with gold-dipped
flowers.

She's speaking with three individuals when we enter.
But as soon as her gaze lands on Davien and I, she *shoos*
them with a wave of her hand.

"Davien." The way she says his name is with deep
reverence. "Our king has finally returned." Vena stands,
holding out both of her arms as she approaches. "I apologize
I was not here to greet you properly on your arrival."

"You were strengthening our western front. There is no
slight." Davien clasps forearms with her, hands nearly back
at the elbows. They lean forward and when I think they are
about to kiss, they tilt their heads in opposite directions,
giving a peck on each cheek.

"You are gracious." She gives a small curtsy and a
bow of her head before releasing Davien. Then she turns
to me. I can feel her demeanor cool some as she makes
her assessment. "This is the one." It's not a question, so

neither Davien nor I answer. Vena narrows her golden eyes as she approaches me. She grabs my cheeks with her hands, tilting my face right and left. "I can see the power in you…a mighty force that your human body struggles to contain."

"A power that is rightfully mine." Davien steps toward Vena as she releases me. Even though he acts like he is a king to most, he seems more of a follower in Vena's court. "How do I free the magic of kings from her?"

Vena purses her lips, continuing to stare at me. "The power has imprinted on her. I see it coursing through her every vein. It trails her every movement."

"Really?" I lift my arm, watching for magical sparks of light like when Davien flew, or when Giles performed his camp-making ritual. There's nothing, and I find I'm mildly disappointed. If I'm going to be hunted for having magic, I want to reap the benefits of having magic. I want to feel as powerful as these people regard me. Not…myself. Same old Katria as I've always been.

"It's not beyond freeing, is it?" Davien asks.

"Let's hope not." Vena's lips tug into a frown. "This will require research and study before we decide on the best course."

"We don't have time—"

"Our borders are secure," she interrupts Davien with a smile, resting a hand on his shoulder. "I know you have spent your life worrying about decaying barriers and ancient rituals fading with the passage of time. But this is not your ancestral home in the Natural World. We are strong here in Midscape. We are your warriors, future king of the fae. You can entrust us to keep you safe while we deal with the final stage of reclaiming your power. We have all waited this long, we can wait a bit more."

"Even if the borders are safe…won't I die just from being in Midscape?" I ask. Davien's friends made it a point to tell me just how certain my demise was for hours when I first arrived.

Vena looks me up and down once more. "Do you feel like you're dying?"

"Well, no…" I trail off.

"You certainly don't look as other humans have by now. You're not withering away." She approaches me and places her fingertips under my chin, tilting my head left and right. "In fact, you're luminescent. Have you had our food yet?"

"Yes, in the woods."

"And how did it taste?"

"Normal," I say. Emphasizing how delicious it was seems unnecessary.

"Normal?" Davien repeats. "Why didn't you say anything?"

I shrug. "I was starving. I thought I might have been hallucinating." The lie tastes like licking freshly polished cutlery. He suspects the lie, too. His eyes narrow skeptically.

"Eat again," Vena instructs. "And inform Davien or myself immediately should anything change in flavor or nourishment. Though I suspect it won't."

"Why? There has never been a human—other than the Human Queen—who could live in our world. Not since the Fade was erected." Davien folds his arms over his chest.

"I suspect it's because of the magic within her. It's healing her wounds, is it not? Perhaps it is also turning our food into sustenance for her, despite her being human. Or maybe it's because the magic is a part of this world that exists within her. There's no real precedent for what has occurred, so any explanation is viable." Vena shrugs. "She's alive, so that's really all that matters, yes?"

"I definitely prefer being alive," I chime in with the obvious. "But does that mean once the magic is out of me I'll begin…withering?" I can't muster the strength to say "die."

"If my speculations are correct, then yes." Vena nods. "So we will make certain that when we do remove the magic from you, we are also able to return you to your world in short order."

"Could the magic be used up in keeping her alive? She's not of this world. Her connection to it can't strengthen the power." Worry streaks across Davien's face. Worry not for me, but for the magic in me. I press my lips into a bitter smile.

"I doubt the king's magic will be used up by a human so quickly." Vena's words are careful. She doesn't explicitly say no. She says she *doubts*, not a firm yes or no. I have to be mindful about the language of the fae. They can't lie…but that doesn't mean they're always sworn to the truth, either. I think of all the times my father emphasized the tricks of negotiation—those skills will serve me well here.

"You might be right." Davien purses his lips. He no doubt hears the same thing I do. But nothing more can be done. We're all trapped in this unconventional circumstance. "What can I do to assist you?"

"I will let you know as soon as I've discovered something worth sharing. Researching shall be my sole focus. But, in the meantime, restore your bond with this land. Strengthen your own innate magic before you inherit the power of kings." Vena smiles in a fond and almost maternal way. "Relish in our safety and comfort before you go and reclaim your throne with battle and bloodshed."

Davien sighs heavily. For a second, I think he's going to put up a fight. I can see by his expression he wants to. But, to my surprise, he doesn't.

"Very well. I leave this matter, for now, in your care, Vena."

Vena looks to me. "And you, enjoy all Dreamsong has to offer. Places like this of peace and safety are rare in the fae wilds. Seeing it as a human is even rarer. Relish in it to your heart's content."

"I will, thank you." I give a small curtsy to Vena as we leave. She has a twinkle in her eye and nods in reply. I don't know if I should be showing her respect. But it feels right to do so.

With a few quick steps, I catch up with Davien. He glances at me from the corner of his eye. The silence between us is heavy and more awkward than it's ever been.

I clear my throat to break the quiet and say, "For what it's worth, I don't mind a short reprieve here. I haven't really had a chance to catch my breath over the past few days. It'll be nice to feel safe."

"You can feel safe among the fae?" he asks.

We come to a stop in the short antechamber between Vena's audience hall and the gathering room. I bite my lip and run a hand through my hair.

"To be fair, I've always felt safe around you," I admit. *Even when I haven't wanted to.*

"Until you knew I was a fae." He moves to leave.

I catch his hand. It's as warm and soft as it was that night in the manor—the first time I wore a blindfold. "Even after...I never thought you would *hurt* me."

"Yet you tried to run the first chance you got, regardless of what I vowed to you." He hasn't pulled away, not physically at least. Yet I can see I've wounded him. The deep hurt resonates dully within me, echoing from his palm to mine.

"I could trust you but not the others," I point out. "They did spend the first day talking about how I was going to die."

"Didn't I betray you, though?" He steps forward, wings twitching with his agitation. "Didn't you say that how I concealed the truth from you turned into a wound? Can you trust someone who betrayed you?"

"I..."

Davien comes to a stop a hair's breadth away. I can feel every inch of his tall, lean form. He stares down at me with an intensity that no one has ever given me before. He waits for my answer, our hands still locked.

"You can't have it every way, Katria. You tell me one thing. You do another. You trust me, until you don't. You're interested in understanding my predicament but do little once you know it. What is it that you really feel?"

"I don't know," I whisper, admitting to both myself and him. That's likely the root of all our problems. "I don't know *what* I feel about you. I don't know how to reconcile the man standing before me now with the Lord Fenwood I knew back at the manor. Because that man... That man..." *I was beginning to develop real feelings for.* The confession is a quiet, begrudging whisper across my mind. And the second it's heard, every barrier I've ever built is strengthened once more.

I will never let myself fall in love.

To love is pain. Even just the start of it has me aching. Confused. Torn apart at the seams by conflicting interests. Was this how my father felt? Did he know Joyce was terrible for him and yet something...*something* refused to allow him to leave? Even when he knew she was wicked, he called her his light.

Now I'm falling into the same trap. This man began to spark feelings in me I never wanted and I have to stop them now, otherwise I might follow him to my demise in this world that threatens to kill me at every turn. I must, at all costs, ignore the emotions brewing in the depths of my heart.

"I am that man," he says.

"Lord Fenwood was a lie."

"I am fae, I can't lie, no matter how much I might want to. Everything I told you—everything I was then—is who I am now. You cannot pick the parts of me you enjoy and abandon the rest." He releases me. "I am both the Lord Fenwood who enjoys mead as a nightcap with a brilliant conversationalist, and Davien Aviness—fae and rightful ruler of the Kingdom of Aviness, which I have every intention of restoring. You trust me as I am, want me as I am, or don't."

I watch as he leaves, struggling for words. It doesn't matter anyway, does it? He'll get his magic out of me and then we'll be done. I'll go back to my world and live alone in that manor he bequeathed me, far from where anyone could ever harm me. He'll stay here and be king of all the fae and forget I ever existed.

He doesn't look back once.

I hover in the antechamber, not ready to reemerge back in the main hall. I can hear them talking in hushed tones. I wonder what's being said but think better of trying to listen. I don't want to hear it...not really. They're talking about me. No, they're talking about *Davien's magic* within me and how they'll get it back. I'm just an unwanted vessel. An extra step everyone loathes. A burden, yet again.

Hanging my head, I bite back a bitter laugh.

A door opening across the hall startles me. I see a young boy step through. Two tiny horns are perched just above his temples. A small, wiry tail twitches behind him as he heads toward Vena's audience hall, a plump messenger bag slung over his shoulder.

"Excuse me?" I say softly. He jumps, clutching his bag protectively. His chest heaves with the panic of surprise. "I'm sorry, I didn't mean to startle you." I point to the door. "Where does that go?"

"What'll you pay me to know?"

"I have to pay you for an answer to a simple question?"

He puffs his chest and wipes his nose with his thumb. He no doubt looks very tough in his mind's eye. "Nothing is free."

"I'll just walk over and find out myself, then." I push away from the wall.

"Oh, you're no fun, miss." He groans. "Fine, it's just a side access to town. Are you needing something? I can fetch it for you."

"For a price, right?"

"You learn fast, I see." The boy has a snaggletooth grin and soft purple eyes. "I'm little, so I can sneak anywhere and—wait…you're *her*. The human. Aren'tcha?"

I wonder how he knew. I couldn't tell Oren was fae for weeks, until I saw his wings. Without the inhuman features visible, it's impossible to tell the fae are any different from me.

"I have no interest in working with you." I bristle at being discovered.

"Hey, hey, no need for the long face, miss. I'm not gonna hurt you." He laughs. "I've just never met a living, breathing *human* before."

I fold my arms over my chest protectively, rethinking my course of action. He doesn't look older than ten. But maybe his appearance is a glamour. Maybe he's another monster in disguise.

"Sorry, I have to go."

"Wait, didn't you need something?" He dashes in front of me. "I can help you get it. Really. I won't even ask much."

I glance back to the door, biting my lip. "I want to go somewhere with music and song. What will that cost me?"

He thinks about it for a second, puffing out his cheeks while he does. "I'll do you one better. I'll get you a cloak so no one notices how funny you look without claws or tails or horns or wings"— *Oh, I'm the funny looking one?*—"and *then* I'll take you somewhere with music. And all it'll cost you is…"

I brace myself.

"A dance."

"A single dance? That's it?"

"A single dance is my price for everything I just said."

Fae can't lie. Which means he can't go back on his bargain. It seems harmless enough… "Sure."

"Really?" He blinks and then his smile widens. He bounces from foot to foot with restless excitement. "*Excellent.* You just bought yourself the best guide in Dreamsong. There's nowhere Raph the Light-Footed doesn't know how to get to."

His enthusiasm is infectious and I can't stop a smile from cracking my lips. One that widens as the door opens and sunlight hits my face.

fifteen

THE AIR IS SWEET AND TASTES LIKE FREEDOM. I tilt my face toward the sky, relishing in the warm sunlight. As my gaze drops, my heart begins to race as it truly hits me:

I'm in a world of fae and magic.

Men and women wander the street, going about their business as though their unnatural features are utterly un-noteworthy. I see a couple laughing, hooking arms with each other and spinning around a bend. There's a father and his children, dutiful assistants for today's trip to the grocer. A girl flies overhead, chased promptly by two others, shouting something between them that's lost in the sounds of their buzzing wings and magic.

Everyone has something unique—horns and hooves, tails and wings. I see bright pink hair and cat-like eyes. I should be terrified. *Find fear!* my better sense shouts at me from the back of my mind, *these people are your mortal enemy.*

But I'm not afraid. My heart beats with a rhythm that matches their footsteps. My eyes drink in everything about them. And my feet want to run *toward* something utterly indescribable—something that I've no idea who, or what, or where it might be. I want to see and touch everything around me. My drab world has found its color and I want to make it *mine*.

"If you keep gawking, people'll notice." Raph tugs my

hand and jerks his head to the right. I take his cue and we begin to move.

Every building in Dreamsong is more magnificent than the last. They're made of wood and stone, iron and glass. Silken bedsheets hang out to dry on lines strung across the street, perfuming the air with lavender and soap. I stop at one particularly stunning gate to run my fingertips over the ironwork. Thousands of tiny holes have been punched through a thin sheet of metal, turning it into a delicate lace. Ribbons and bows are unfurled along it, so lifelike that I'm shocked they don't blow away in the breeze.

"Come *on*." Raph takes my hand and tugs. "I thought you wanted music, not...what was it that you were doing just now? Human magic?"

"No, humans don't have magic." I chuckle softly. My eyes are still on the gate even as he tugs me away. "I was admiring it. The construction is so beautiful; I've never seen anything like it."

"It looks pretty normal to me." He shrugs. Oh, to grow up in a world where all this is normal. "This way." We round the building with the lacy gate, ducking through a back door and into a small courtyard in the back-left corner of the lot. "You wait here."

"All right." I remain in the shadow of an arbor over the side door as Raph scampers up to a kitchen door and knocks several times. It opens and a red-faced maid pokes out her nose.

"The mistress of the house is going to skin you for certain this time. You can't keep calling like this."

"She doesn't have to know I'm here. Can you get Ralsha?" Raph clasps his hands and holds them up like he's begging. The woman puts a hand on her hip and arches her eyebrows. "Fine, I'll give you a delivery whenever you want it. But you're not getting anything else out of me."

"Good boy. Wait a moment."

Everything has a price here, I remind myself as I watch the interaction. I must remember that and to pay attention to every word people use. Luckily, I have experience from my father in doing so. *It's not just what people say, but how*, he would tell me. *Pay attention to everything.* Before Joyce came around, he even let me sit in on some of his meetings and would ask me for advice after. One of the few times I felt like I could use my senses about lies to be helpful to someone beyond myself.

Ralsha is a young girl, no older than Raph. But where Raph has short auburn hair, Ralsha has long, deep violet curls. She squeals at the sight of Raph, throwing her arms around his neck. There's clearly some young love brewing and I bite back a warning to them both. Maybe the fae are immune to the pitfalls of love we humans must endure. Regardless, their mistakes are not my business.

With some eyelash batting from Raph, Ralsha goes back in the house and returns with a cloak. Raph gives her a peck on the cheek and a wink before returning to me. Ralsha melts into the doorstop... before she's summoned back inside by the maid I saw earlier.

"Here you go. It's actually a good cloak, too. Ralsha's mum is the best tailor in Dreamsong. Ralsha says she's even got an enchanted loom that can weave invisible thread into fabric."

"If it's invisible thread, how would you ever know it's there?" I grin.

Raph considers this for far too long. It only makes me grin more and he sticks out his tongue at me. "If she says it's there, it must be." *Oh, right, they can't lie.* "Now, turn around and let me put this on you." He holds out the cloak.

"What service." I laugh softly and turn.

"Well I told you I'm the best guide—" His words have a distinct halt. I flinch instantly. I know what he's seen. This stupid silken dress and its stupid swooping front and back. I feel a small finger press into my spine between my shoulder blades. "How'dja get this one, miss?"

He's a child. He doesn't know better. He doesn't know that it's rude to ask about people's gnarliest scars so plainly.

"I don't remember," I murmur. As I say the lie, the metallic taste fills my mouth. But it's not just because I'm lying. I tasted blood that day, too. I'd bitten my tongue from the screaming and thrashing. I smell the singed aroma of burning flesh peppering my memory. "I've had it forever. Since I was a little girl. No older than you. It's always been there."

He snickers. "It's wicked looking. You must be one tough human to endure something like that and still be all right."

I shrug the robe onto my shoulders, feeling much less bare. My ugliest secrets are hidden once more beneath the armor of fabric. "I like to think so."

"Good, you have to be tough to survive the fae." He grins again and we're back out in the streets.

After another few minutes of walking, we come to a tavern. I hear the scorching hot strings of a well-played fiddle. Underneath is a feverish drumbeat, setting a lively pace for the other performers. A pan flute soars above them all, stringing together a melody that turns the whole raucous collection of sounds into breathless song.

"What is this place?" I whisper.

"The Screaming Goat." Raph grins. "You wanted music. There's none better in all the fae wilds. Well, don't just stand there. Go in." He gives me a shove and I stumble toward the arched entry.

There's no doors or windows in the Screaming Goat. Just columns and archways that make up the front facade, letting in the sunshine and letting out sound. There are also no chairs—only high tables that men and women stand at, stomping their feet to the music and watering the ground with frothy ale.

My eyes are drawn to the low stage opposite the entry where the band plays. Men and women twirl on a dance floor in front of it.

"Try to look less conspicuous, *gosh*." Raph pulls me to an empty table by one of the archways. He scrambles up onto the half-wall, standing like he owns the place. A barmaid comes over, setting down a flagon in front of me. "Hey, where's mine?" Raph whines.

"Maybe when you're older." She winks and walks away.

"Rude." Raph rolls his eyes.

I almost miss the whole exchange, instead too focused on the music. The lively jig is played in common time. The man with the panpipes leaps across the stage, egging on the dancers with his own fancy footwork. I've only ever seen one performance before... My father brought a traveling band to one of his last parties for the Applegate Trading Company after I had begged and begged. The party happened to be on my birthday and he couldn't refuse, even despite all but banning music following my mother's death as "too painful."

Joyce got to pick the music that night. So of course it was some dull collection of stuffy instrumentals played by men twice my father's senior. Gods forbid we actually had genuine fun at one of those parties. If we had, this is what our manor might have looked like—might have sounded like. I try to imagine it and the thought is accompanied by a comical image of Joyce nearly losing her head from all the stomping across her ridiculously expensive rugs.

A smile cracks my lips. I'm tapping my foot along to the beat. My gaze drifts as the man with the panpipes spins. It's then I see a whole pile of instruments off to stage right. Leaning against them is a lute. It's not nearly as fine as my mother's, I can tell that from here. But the strings are intact and I would bet anything it's in tune.

"What're all those?" I ask Raph and point to the pile of instruments.

"Instruments for performers." He shrugs. "I see people go up and take them whenever the bar is quiet. A silent tavern is a sad tavern," he says as though he's repeating someone else.

Surely I'm misunderstanding. "So anyone can play those?"

"I think so." He shrugs. I wish I knew if he was telling the actual truth, or telling the truth as best he knows it. "I've never seen anyone get in trouble for playing them. Oh, wait, do *you* want to play?"

"No, no…I'm not any good." Yet even as I say that, I'm popping my knuckles. I'm itching for the harmonies to the panpipe's melodies that I know are trapped in the strings of the lute.

"Eh, you're likely right."

"What?" I look at him, the echoes of Joyce and Helen suddenly tangling with his words.

He drops his voice. "You're a human. There's no way you could play well enough to keep up with fae. I'm sure you're just blown away by the quality of our bards."

I am. But that doesn't mean I couldn't keep up. I think I could…

Stop that noise!

Mother, she's doing it again. She's playing the thing!

If you play the lute one more time I will chop off its neck or yours.

Helen's and Joyce's words drown out the music for a dark second. I stare at the soundless instruments from underneath the weight of all the words they filled me with. So much of Joyce and

Helen pressing down on me, making me small. Never enough of me to stand against them. Never…

Laura's temple is against my knee. She tilts her face up toward me. *One more song before bed,* she mouths.

"No," I whisper.

"No, what?" Raph is confused.

Understandably so. He wasn't there the day my hand in marriage was sold for fortune. He wasn't there the day that I vowed to never again let them or anyone else trap me, make me feel small, turn me into a tool instead of a whole person.

"You're wrong. I can keep up." I glare at him. "And I'm going to show you."

"Wha—wait!"

I'm already weaving across the dance floor. I approach the stage with enough intent that the panpipe player gives me a nod with his goat-horned head. I return the gesture and he steps away. It looks almost like permission.

The thumping of the dancers' feet rumbles behind me. The deep resonance of the drum is within me. The music drowns out every word Joyce or Helen ever said for a brief and glorious minute while I step onto the stage and head right for the lute, slinging its strap over my shoulders.

"Hello, friend," I whisper, lightly strumming, soft enough that no one will hear but me. As I suspected, it's in tune. "Shall we?"

I spin and step forward, falling into the melody. My foot taps along with the beat as my fingers begin to move on instinct. The other players regard me with excited glances and encouraging smiles. They nod their heads at me, I nod back at them.

Now a quartet, the music is richer, deeper. I lock eyes with the fiddle player, a woman with a head shaved to display similar tattoos to what Shaye and Giles have. She grins at me and nods. I nod in reply.

We're not speaking with words, or thoughts, or even gestures, really. There's direction in the music that we hear. Little signposts along the way that say, *if I play this, you play that.* And, together, we make music all our own, made for this moment and that will never be heard again.

We turn emotion into song.

Sweat drips down my neck as the tune shifts. The fiddler breaks away from the rest of us, rising to a crescendo, demanding all attention. The rest of us fade until she comes crashing back down in a new melody.

I recognize this, I realize.

"There once was a lass with hair so fine,
I saw her dance and said she's divine.
So I took her down to the mer folk sea,
And said Jilly will you marry me?"

The whole tavern gives a *whoop* in time. Everyone unites in song for the chorus.

"Soon there will be a wedding,
A vow an' a kiss an' a proper bedding.
Soon may the Jilly-lass come,
Down by the mer folk sea."

My hands fly across the lute. There are only short breaks between the chorus and verse. Barely a few notes. I always loved this song for that reason. It was a challenge to play and even harder to sing.

"Now Jilly and I are a family of three,
We live on down by the mer folk sea.
Jilly went to the shore one day,
And looked the mer folk's way."

Another *whoop* before the second chorus.

"Oh no, sweet Jilly girl,
You've gone t'far where the sea ocean whorls,
Jilly was taken away,
For her wishes sh'll have t'pay."

My hands fly across the strings. I've come as far into the song as

I know. I glance over to the drummer. He looks my way. The other man and woman do as well. Expectant.

My fingers seize and halt.

That voice...the person who led the singing... Sick, hot, horror crashes over me. *It was me.* I was the one singing. I wish I could go and curl in a corner and die faster than the song is.

Suddenly, out of nowhere, a deep, masculine voice fills the room with song.

"But Jilly will be coming back,
I'll go out when the ocean's black.
I'll break'er bond wit' the cold, dark sea.
Because the best mer folk is me."

As the tavern *whoop*s a final time, I look to the source of the voice. My fingers continue to play on instinct now that I'm no longer wallowing in the horror of what I've done.

I lock eyes with Davien. He's singing with the rest of them, leading the tavern toward the end of the song.

"Soon there's a beach of three.
Jilly girl, child, and me.
Soon we'll be happy again.
And we'll live to a hundred an' ten."

The musicians continue to play as I duck away from the band and back to the side, returning the lute to where I found it. My face is flushed and I can feel it only get redder as I step off the stage to a small amount of applause. I try and duck my head with shame...but the encouraging smiles people give me, the pats on the shoulders... by the time I reach Davien, I've a smile of my own.

"You look horribly smug." He sounds upset, but his face hasn't received the note, because he wears a grin that seems almost impressed.

"I don't know if smug is the right word." I look back toward the stage, where the band is still playing and people are still dancing and twirling. I only just finished performing, and already want to go back. "I've never done anything like that before, and I'm surprised by how good it felt," I admit to both myself and him.

Davien seems startled by this admission because he promptly changes the topic. "You really shouldn't be wandering by yourself alone."

"I thought it was safe in Dreamsong?"

"It is."

"And Vena told me to go and enjoy the town. That's what I did." I shrug. "Besides, I wasn't completely alone. Had the best guide in all of Dreamsong."

"About that..." Davien's voice gets heavier with frustration and he looks over to the table Raph and I have been standing at. Hol is there now. He stands next to a woman with long black hair and curving ram's horns. The two are giving a proper scolding to Raph.

"Hey—" I push past Davien. "Don't be mean to him, he was only helping me. I asked him to."

Hol gives me a very, *very* tired look. Even though they couldn't have been talking with Raph for more than a few minutes, he looks as if he's had this conversation for hours. "There's a difference between 'being mean' and necessary discipline."

I shudder. He sounds just like Joyce.

"Do you know what you could've done?" the woman snaps at Raph.

"I wasn't gonna harm her!" Raph insists. "I just wanted to see how long she could dance for."

The woman grabs him by the ear and tugs on it lightly, hissing into it, "She's *human*. She breaks far easier than we do."

"I agreed to his terms willingly," I say. I can't stand to see Raph treated this way because of me. I wonder what they'll do to him. I can only imagine fae punishments will be even worse than Joyce's. "I don't mind one dance."

A heavy hand falls on my shoulder. I look up to see Davien. "You need to be more careful about the deals you make here," he says solemnly. "You agreed to a dance without setting any terms, any limitations. Raph could've made you dance until you died from exhaustion. He could've made you dance into a river."

"But…" My voice quivers slightly. Just when I thought I was safe. "He said he wouldn't hurt me."

"He wouldn't have intentionally. But Felda is right, he didn't think through how it might impact you. He's young and foolish."

"Now," Hol says firmly. "You will absolve her of all deals she's made with you."

"Do I have to?" Raph whines.

"Yes, *now*."

Raph looks to me. He kicks dirt off the wall he's still standing on. Hands behind his back, looking guilty, he says, "Your debts are paid, all has been gained, nothing is owed, we stand as equals."

They sound like magic words, so I expect to feel tingling across my body, but I don't. I feel as normal as I did when I made the deal with him. But if what Davien said was true, I unknowingly gave this little boy immense power over me.

"And apologize to her," the woman, Felda, says.

"Sorry," he obliges, barely managing to look me in the eye.

"All is well," I say. "And thank you for releasing me from my debts."

"I really wasn't going to hurt you," Raph insists under his breath.

"That's enough of you for one day." Hol picks up the lad and sets him down on the ground. "I believe you still have business with Vena. You should get to it and not keep her waiting. It's because of her we have a roof over our heads at all. So take your duties to contribute to Dreamsong more seriously."

"Right, right."

"We'll see you at home later," Felda says, her voice softening some. She reaches for Raph. In my mind's eye, she grips the boy with both hands to further shake and scold him. But instead she pulls him to her for a tight hug. "We love you, Raphy."

"*Eww*, Mom, there's people, *ugh*, love you too," Raph mumbles and scampers off. But not before his mother lands a kiss on his forehead.

"We really are so sorry for his actions." Felda straightens and scratches the back of her head, looking guilty on her son's behalf. "He can be a handful at times."

"I'm not upset," I remind them. I'm still confused as to what I just witnessed. In an instant, she showed him more affection than even Joyce showed her own flesh and blood daughters.

"Still, as an apology for our son, we would like to offer you a seat at our table and extend every measure of hospitality to you both," Hol says.

"It would be our honor to dine with you." Felda bows her head toward Davien.

"As it would be ours. Lead on." Davien motions for the door and the couple leads the way to my first meal with the fae.

sixteen

Davien follows behind them, pausing when he notices that I'm not in step with him. "Are you coming?"

I fold my arms and walk up to him. "I would appreciate it if you didn't speak for me."

"Would you have refused them?"

"I don't know." These fae have done very little to endear me to them. I'm not sure if I want to be sitting at their table and breaking bread.

He chuckles and shakes his head. Under his breath I can hear him say, "You really are human."

"What is that supposed to mean?" We start walking.

"You would not only pass up an opportunity for Hol and Felda to be allies by sitting at their table, but offend them as they tried to make amends." Davien laughs. "You don't understand anything about how words can be twisted against you. About deals, rituals, or the laws of hospitality."

"Don't mock me." I glare up at him. Yet, as if he's ever in a competition with himself to see how much he can frustrate me, he smirks. His green eyes sparkle in the sunlight.

"I'm not mocking you; I think it's charming that you've lived a far simpler life."

"I doubt it. But even if you're right, simpler doesn't mean good." I avoid staring at him, instead looking at the joining on a roof.

"How did you know that song?" he asks, seemingly out

of nowhere. I wonder if he can tell I'm uncomfortable and is trying to backtrack to something more harmless.

I glance back up at him. Can he tell I'm uncomfortable?

"Wait, don't tell me, it's yet another one of the old songs you've heard around town?"

"Yes," I lie, and swallow to try to remove the taste of metal from my mouth. It seems like the more I lie around him, the harder it becomes, and the longer that metallic taste lingers at the back of my throat. My mother was the one who taught me almost all the songs I know.

"It really is incredible how much of us is left in that world…" He trails off, eyes filled with longing as he stares ahead. Davien is a good head taller than most people, so he can see down the entire street without issue. But I don't think he's looking at anything in particular. I wonder what he's trying to see, what place…or time.

"It really used to all be one world? I heard the old myths, about the ancient magic wars. I remember what they told me about the Elf King carving up the land. But I thought…" I look around me. "I guess I have to believe it's true, seeing this place, seeing you." My gaze snags on intricate leaded glass that adorns the second floor of a building we pass. "Glass art, did it come from the fae as well?"

"It did." Davien smiles. "The fae are an offshoot from the dryads. They were the old sentinels of the forest, long before the magic wars were even a whisper on people's lips. Unlike the fae—which were a natural evolution of time and magic—the dryads made the humans with their own hands. Initially, the fae looked after the early humans, teaching them how to use their magic to work with nature."

"Humans had magic?" I try to imagine such a world and fail.

"Long ago, before the Fade. Perhaps that's why you are able to be a vessel for the ancient kings' magic."

I curl and relax my fingers, trying to see if I can feel the magic that even Vena said she could sense in me. But I feel absolutely nothing. I know the magic is real, I've seen it. It poured from me in the woods that night. Yet I can't summon it even if I try.

We arrive at a stone house with a clay roof. Hol and Felda lead us inside, down the hall, and to a kitchen that takes up the back half of the house. Davien and I are seated around a table as Felda and

Hol bustle about their kitchen. I notice pegs by the back door—a messenger bag very similar to Raph's hangs on one.

"Please don't punish him…" The soft words slip from my lips unintended as Felda sets down a board with a rustic sourdough loaf and knife.

"What?" She blinks and tilts her head at me.

"Raph. Please don't punish him when he returns home. I wouldn't want him to be hurt because of me."

"Hurt?" She shakes her head and seems aghast at what I am suggesting. Her brows furrow slightly, as though my concern has offended her somehow. "We would never hurt our son."

"But, in the tavern…you seemed so upset."

"I *was* upset." Felda puts her hands on her hips. "I don't know how I managed to have the most precocious child in all of Dreamsong, but I guess that is my honor and burden to bear." She grins as though some part of her really does think it is an honor to be associated with Raph's antics. "But he's been appropriately reprimanded already. As long as he doesn't step out of line again today—which is a challenge sometimes for that boy—there will be no more words on the incident when he gets home."

"Oh, good…" I stare at the bread that Felda begins to cut. Is it really that simple? I've never seen a child be so easily forgiven when they erred. Helen and Laura never made a mistake. And whenever I did, I felt the repercussions for days usually. When I sense the weight of another pair of eyes on me, my gaze is drawn across the table to where Davien sits. He watches me with a slightly furrowed brow, as if he's inspecting or studying me.

"Please help yourself to our bread and wine," Hol says ceremoniously as he pours mead into each of our cups.

I welcome the excuse to look away from Davien. His stare is just too probing. I worry about what he would see if I met his eyes for too long. I never expected to miss the blindfold.

"How are you finding Dreamsong?" Felda asks.

I welcome the change in topic with a smile. "It's a truly magnificent place. The fae are some of the best craftsmen I've ever seen."

"We have a good many who possess old rituals on tradesmanship, long passed down in their families and courts."

"When you say rituals…is it the same as what I saw in the woods that night?" I look to Davien.

"That was a ritual, yes, but so was what Giles did when we made camp in the Bleeding Forest," he says.

I chew on a slab of bread for a moment, considering everything I've learned about fae and their magic so far. The bread is tangy and has the right amount of chew to complement the crisp crust. "So a ritual can be anything? And accomplish anything?"

"There are *some* limitations," Hol says. "For example, we can't bring back the dead, or change someone's heart."

"So as you can see, not many limitations." Davien smirks.

"How is a ritual made?" I think of what Vena said about finding a way to get the magic from me. Is she going to make a ritual herself?

"There are a few who are in tune enough with their magic and the inherent laws of our world to invent new rituals. But most rituals are passed down orally or in written tomes kept within families and courts," Hol explains.

"It's why the nearly complete eradication of the Aviness family crippled the fae and has made us weak for centuries. The glass crown had a ritual performed on it long ago that still stands and demands loyalty from all fae…but it can only be worn by the true heir of Aviness. As long as an Aviness heir is alive, it will heed no other master. And it requires the power of the lost kings to unveil its full potential." Davien looks out a window with a glare, casting his anger toward someone or something far beyond the table.

"So fae can't perform magic with their thoughts?" I think about my actions in the woods. How the magic came to me unbidden, heeding only my subconscious need to survive.

"There are some exceptions, like summoning wings or claws," Hol says. "Or our glamour."

"But otherwise, no," Felda adds. "However, there are some rituals that give us varying control over power for a certain length of time—like what's on the glass crown. What we can do during that time, and how long it lasts, all depends on the ritual."

"You saw one such example in the woods." Davien brings his

attention back to the present and rests it on me. "The way that Butcher moved is a closely guarded ritual, passed down in their ranks; they cast it on the capes they wear. I've heard it's called 'shadow stepping,' where they can move from darkness to darkness. It makes them particularly deadly at night. But the ritual expires quickly. They only have so much movement they can perform in that manner before the charged magic is exhausted."

I'm beginning to frame fae magic in terms I can understand—that I'm familiar with. I think of when I repaired the plaster on the walls of our manor. The "ritual" would be the act of combining the ingredients and mixing them in a bucket. I suppose the bucket—or vessel for the magic—is the fae performing the ritual, though it sounds like the vessel can also be a thing, like the glass crown or the Butchers' capes. Then, they can use the plaster—magic—until it runs out or becomes useless—dries.

With this framework, I say with mild confidence, "I think I understand."

"Really?" Davien arches his eyebrows; he seems impressed. I give him a sly smile.

"I think so. Here, let me see if I have it right…" I explain my analogy to them. "That's about it?"

Hol leans back in his chair and chuckles. "No wonder we could teach ancient humans. For a people who lost their magic overnight, there's definitely traces of understanding there."

If that's true, I might be able to learn how to use the magic within me. I avoid Davien's attentive stare by helping myself to another slice of bread, dipping it in the oil and herbs before popping it into my mouth. It's like he can sense what I'm thinking. I wonder if one night at the manor he bored a hole into my mind with those eyes of his while I was blindfolded and oblivious. Now, he has a window to my innermost thoughts whenever he wants.

I bite my lip. I really hope that I'm wrong about that…because my mind isn't a place that anyone should spend too much time in. It's dangerous enough for me, and I live here.

The rest of the meal goes smoothly. By the time Hol and Felda escort us to the door, I can honestly say I've enjoyed myself. Felda actually gives me a little squeeze before we depart.

"It's been a delight to meet you," she says. "Hol has filled me in on some of your circumstances, more than he likely should, I admit." Her mouth quirks into a mischievous grin. I see where Raph gets it from. "I know that coming here wasn't part of your plan…but I'm glad Davien has you with him."

I glance over to where Davien and Hol are engaged in an intense, hushed conversation. They don't seem to hear Felda's soft words.

"I'm not… I don't know what you think. But—"

"You don't have to explain," she says a little too quickly. Like *I'm* embarrassed and she's doing me a favor. "It's just nice to see someone with him. Hol and his other king's knights have certainly tried their best. But they had their obligations here, keeping Dreamsong safe. They could never stay with him for long, either, because as you can see with Davien, we fae aren't meant to live in your world. I can imagine how lonely it was with only Oren for company. Bless him, he's a good man, but not the greatest conversationalist." She laughs. I smirk as well. "From what Oren has said, it sounds like you two get on well."

Before I can say anything, the two men rejoin us.

"We should return to the main hall," Davien says. "The last thing we want is for Vena to need us for something and us not be available."

"Of course." I nod. We bid our final farewells and return to the streets of Dreamsong.

"I'm glad they're doing so well," he says after we're far away from the house.

"Were they not?" They seemed like an enviably normal family to me. More normal than what I ever thought possible, previously, for a family.

"Their family's ancestral home is in what is now the Bleeding Woods. Their Court of Leaves was led by one of the last blood survivors of Aviness," he says with a somber note. I see his hands clench and the muscles in his jaw bulge. "The Butchers drove them out of their home well before Raph was even born."

Davien slows and shoves hands in the pockets of his loose-fitting trousers. He's wearing a tunic that's open low on his breastbone. The flat expanse of his chest is on display underneath a series of necklaces. He fits in so naturally here. There's something to the air around him that just…belongs.

I suppose that's not what surprises me. What surprises me is how envious I am of it. It's not the fae that I want to be a part of. I just want to *belong*. I want some people, some place, some time to be *mine*. I want to not be a castaway fighting for forgotten scraps on the floors underneath tables I'll never have a seat at.

To have a family. A table.

"If you become king, will they get to go back to their home?" I ask softly. "Will they rebuild the Court of Leaves?"

He meets my eyes, exposing the murky depths of his pain. So many things about this man are still a mystery to me. But rather than being frightened…I find myself more and more intrigued by the endless possibilities of them. I want to ask. I want to know. I want to peel back every layer of him as I feel him doing to me every time we're together.

What's wrong with me?

This endless push and pull between us threatens to rip me apart.

"If—*when* I become king, these lands will once more belong to the people who made them. The courts may return to their ancestral homes or rebuild anew, whichever speaks more to who they are now.

"I will see that the fae are strong again. That we have a seat at the table at Midscape's Council of Kings. I will demand the lands the Elf King stole from us back and I will fight for the fae to return to the prominence we deserve. I will see every court rebuilt to keep the High Court in check, so that no king ever feels so powerful that he can act without accountability. I will use the power that's trapped within the glass crown and the hill of the High Court to help my people however I am able for as long as I draw breath."

I stand in awe of him. The way he speaks is filled with conviction…and not because he's practiced these lines like Laura or Helen did before Father's parties so they had the best chance to woo a suitor. He speaks the truth that he knows, that he has cemented onto his heart above all else.

The need to touch him becomes irresistible. A man with a noble mission is more attractive than I ever expected. I want to hold his hand and caress the soft skin of his palm. I want to press my fingers across the strong muscles of his chest and…and…my mind gutters.

Heat crashes over me, flushing my cheeks and making me shift my weight from foot to foot as it pools uncomfortably in my lower abdomen. This man makes me want dangerous things. Things I've never thought I wanted before and certainly never *needed*.

"We should return to Vena," I say, my voice not sounding as strong as normal.

"We should." Yet his eyes are still locked with mine, head ducked slightly. For the first time since coming to this world, he looks and sounds like the Lord Fenwood I knew in the manor.

The rest of our walk is consumed by an awkward, tense silence. Our shoulders brush seven times. But who's counting?

Yet we both resist closing that dangerous gap between us. Because in that space was the line of no return. And somehow, in broad daylight in the middle of a busy street, we just came dangerously close to crossing it.

seventeen

It's just Giles, Shaye, and me for dinner that night. They're already sitting, food half gone, when I emerge from my room. I indulged in a midday nap after returning from Hol's to try and clear my mind. But I find it's just as murky when I wake. My thoughts, and dreams, all revolve around Davien and this strange new world...even if I don't want them to.

"Where's Oren?" I ask as I swing my legs over the bench at one of the tables in the meeting hall.

"He had some house business to attend to," Shaye says.

"Oh, I see." *Don't ask about Davien. Don't ask about Davien*, I repeat in my mind. Yet, "And Davien?" *Damn it, Katria.*

"Vena wanted him. Likely something to do with the ritual to get the magic out of you." Giles rips off a drumstick from an unrecognizable breed of large, roasted bird and begins viciously chomping with his sharp teeth. "Knowing the two of them, they'll have something figured out by morning. Smart ones, they are."

"Anyone is smart compared to you, Giles." Shaye grins.

"Good thing I keep you around to make up where I lack." Giles chuckles.

Shaye quickly turns her attention on me, shifting uncomfortably in her seat. "I heard you went out for an adventure in town today."

"Hol tell you?" I carve off a hunk of breast meat for myself, grabbing a slice of bread and spoon of vegetables from a serving dish at the same time.

"Among others."

"Others?"

"People are talking about the new singer and lute player on the scene in the Screaming Goat." She grins and picks bird-sized pieces of bread, popping them in her mouth. "You got more fire in you than I thought. I didn't take you for the type to go rogue."

I shrug. "I like music and wanted to hear it."

"Good thing she's got a bit of roguish tendency in her." Giles chuckles. "This is a whole city of rogues. Vigilantes. Ne'er-do-wells. Treasonous scoundrels who don't fit in anywhere else and would slit our current king's neck if we had the chance."

"Everyone has seemed lovely to me," I counter, digging into the food.

"*Everyone?* Even our dear king-to-be when he was throwing a tantrum in the woods?"

"Well…" I always knew the anger wasn't directed at me. Though it was annoying, to put it mildly.

"How about the ten-year-old who was ready to make you dance for his amusement like a puppet?" Shaye raises her eyebrows.

"He wasn't going to hurt me." I come to Raph's defense yet again. Even if the situation could've ended badly, it didn't. And I truly believe he didn't mean me harm.

"Could've ended up the same."

"I believed he wouldn't have."

"Stop sticking up for people when you shouldn't. If someone treats you badly, call them out on it." She shakes her head and glances at me from the corners of her eyes. "Never thought I'd hear a human defending a fae…or saying they're 'all right.' What has the world come to?"

The notion of pointing out when someone treats me badly is strange. I try and find a place to settle it onto my psyche. I like the idea enough to try and implement it. "Maybe I'm not your average human?"

"Not as long as you have the king's magic within you," Shaye agrees.

"I hope Davien can get it soon and bring order to this mad world..." Giles murmurs.

I remember what Davien said in the streets today about Hol. "Did you both live in the Bleeding Woods once?"

They exchange a look that's worth a conversation. Giles is the first one to speak, starting with a shake of his head. "I lived in the Court of Pillars originally."

"Court of Pillars?"

"The Boltovs came through and demanded our axes and rituals. We weren't much in the way of combatants and couldn't put up a resistance. Though we tried. Those ancient crafting tools were all we had..." His eyes and voice become distant. Shaye reaches across the table and rests a hand on his. Their eyes lock and there's another moment of understanding between them that I'm an outsider to. The connection between these two is deeper than I originally gave credit.

Shaye speaks. I can almost sense that she does it so Giles doesn't have to. "I lived in the High Court originally."

"The High Court?" I repeat softly. "The place with the castle? Where the—"

"Boltovs live. Yes." Shaye returns her hands to her lap, staring at her plate a moment before taking a swig of her mead with purpose. "I was born there...and I think from the moment I drew my first breath, I exhaled the promise that I would not let myself die there."

"Shaye..." Giles says softly.

She meets my eyes with an intensity that I can't turn away from. "After my birth, the Boltovs assessed me, determined me worthy, and I began the training to be a Butcher."

I think of that man in the woods who was so intent on killing Davien. I imagine him living a life of blood and battle from birth. Knowing no scrap of kindness in a way far, far worse than I can comprehend. "How did you escape?"

"They turned me into a weapon," Shaye muses over the edge of her glass. "The thing about the Boltovs is they don't realize weapons aren't loyal by default. A sword knows no ruler, only the hand that holds it."

"So you found a better ruler?"

"I found a mind, thought for myself, and became my own ruler," Shaye insists firmly. "I realized I was not a tool to be used by others. But a soldier—a knight, a *person* that any king should delight in having on their retainer. That I was not indispensable as my first king thought me. So, I found my own mission, and that happened to align with a better king."

I pick at my food, and shift in my seat, trying to get more comfortable. Suddenly, I can't find a position where my skin feels right. Something she said has jarred me, tilted my world beyond easy repair.

"How did you find that mind of yours? One where you defined your own worth?" I ask softly. I dare to bring my eyes to her, afraid she'll chastise or mock me. To my surprise, she doesn't. She stares at me, intent and expectant. "How were you able to break away from the king who controlled you? How were you able to tell yourself that he no longer mattered or even—even spite him?"

"It started with a thought," she says softly. As she speaks, my innermost insecurities are dredged up from the murky depths I try and drown them in. "A thought that maybe the reason why he tried to keep me down was because I was better than he could ever be. He was afraid of me—afraid of what I could become if he didn't control me. So he spent every bit of his energy making me feel less. Making me feel worthless. Making me feel like I was nothing without him."

Wretched girl, do as I say and maybe someday you'll find someone who loves you, Joyce's words echo from a history I've tried to blot out.

"I made him feel strong. Ruling over me, telling me what to do, thinking my every breath was dependent on him...that was what gave him power. Which meant *I* had power. He needed me. And I wanted to take that from him. So I did. I found a mind of my own and I kept it. I harbored it in secret until the moment I could get away. And then I vowed to do everything I could to destroy him." Shaye stabs her knife into the table at her side. "I will die happy if I am the one to slit his throat when this is all over. But even if I'm not, knowing I helped the person who dealt the final blow shall be my life's greatest work."

I stare in awe at the woman. I should be afraid, I think. But…
But I admire her fiercely. She's everything I wish I could've been.
Everything I hope I can still yet be. But my villains aren't kings
and their loyalists…they're dressed in layers of silk. They powder
their noses and then turn them up at me. I can dine with fae but the
thought of my mother still makes me cower.

"I think you've stunned her into silence." Giles nudges me as he
speaks to Shaye. "You have to go easy on the poor human. She's not
used to our viciousness."

"Don't go easy on my account." I pick up my fork and knife,
tearing into my meat. "I'm finding things very comfortable here. So
act normal."

Shaye arches her eyebrows at Giles, who snickers. The two are
silenced when the doors to Vena's hall opens. Davien and the leader
of Dreamsong stride out, still engaged in an intense discussion—at
least until Davien's eyes snag on me.

"Good, you're eating," he says.

"What else should I be doing?"

"Nothing else. It's just good you are…because you'll need all
your strength for the ritual come morning."

I barely get a wink of sleep that night. The entire time I toss
and turn. If it's not the thoughts of what the ritual might entail, it's
the sight of Davien, grinning like a fool and casting those bright
green eyes toward me. I even get out of bed at one point, halfway to
the door to hunt him down and demand to know what will happen,
before I think better of it. I'm going to see him in a few short hours,
I remind myself. There's absolutely no need to go sneaking to his
room in the middle of the night, wherever it might be.

As soon as dawn breaks, I'm out of bed and down the stairs to
the main hall. The tables are still being set, candles being lit by taper
and magic alike. A familiar voice calls out to me.

"Oi, miss human!" Raph scurries over. He has a basket half

the size of him filled with fresh loaves of bread. "You need to go anywhere today?" He gives me that snaggletooth grin.

"No... But I could use your help in getting something." I crouch down, eying the bread in his basket. First I will seize the opportunity of Raph's nimble little fingers with a new—more careful—deal. Then I'll nimbly snatch some bread of my own.

"You know I can deliver anything you need. What can I do you for?"

"I need a lute. Any lute. Doesn't have to be a particularly nice one." Last night would've been far more bearable if I'd had something to play to pass the time. "What will that cost me?"

He thinks about it, puffing out his cheeks while he does. "I want to see the Natural World."

I snort, imagining Raph back on the human side of the Fade. Maybe I could employ him at the manor after the magic is out of me. The idea of Raph helping me tend that overgrown garden almost brings forth laughter. I don't hate the image. He could be an apprentice of sorts to me. Or perhaps I to him. Living that close to the Fade...maybe there's some old remnants of human magic I'd find in me. Laura would find amusement in Raph at the very least. I've begun to imagine her living with me, too. She'd get the magic she sought, and I would gain the knowledge that Joyce wouldn't corrupt her.

"I don't think I can give that to you. Try again." I select my warm loaf from the basket. He hums. I suddenly notice he's avoiding my eyes. His cheeks are slightly flushed. "You have something else in mind?"

"I'm thinking."

"I'll wait." I tear of hunks of bread, popping them in my mouth while he works up the courage to ask for whatever it is he wants.

"Iwannahearyousinggain."

"I'm sorry, what was that?"

"I wantta hear y'singagain."

I lean toward him. "One more time."

"I want to hear you sing again." He finally enunciates every word, looking painfully yet adorably shy as he does. "Play me a song with the lute I bring you."

I'm on the verge of agreeing when I think of what Davien said. "What song?"

"Any song of your choosing."

"When?"

"Any time of your choosing."

"For how long?"

"Any song, any time, in any fashion of your choosing. You have free will to decide the circumstances of how you fulfill this deal."

I hum and narrow my eyes. "You know I know your parents now, right? You're not trying to be sneaky, are you?"

His skinny tail twitches with annoyance. "I'll bring you a lute if you play me a song as you want, when you want. But when you play, I have to be able to sit right in the front to listen. That's all I ask. No catches. No tricks."

"Deal." I stand and ruffle his hair. Who knows if he'll actually bring the lute, anyway? "You're not so bad, for a kid."

"And you're halfway decent, for a human." He sticks out his tongue at me.

"Raph." Davien's tone is a warning.

I stick my tongue back at the little fae, making sure Davien sees so he knows our jest is mutual. I glance back at him with a slight grin. "I started it."

"I'm sure you did." He holds out a hand expectantly.

It takes me a moment to realize he wants a hunk of my bread. Maybe I like the man more than I think I do, because I actually pass him a chunk without telling him to get his own.

"You're not quite the docile wife I was expecting as the daughter of a lord. I feel like our time together is punctuated with me finding you in places you shouldn't be, doing things you shouldn't do."

"It's a curse of mine," I mumble, thinking of my childhood. I always ended up in their way, or finding a place Joyce didn't want me to. Like a back entrance to her closet. In Helen's studio.

Or the rooftop...

"I rather find it a delight. If I was going to be married in the Natural World's record to any human, I suppose there are worse ones to be saddled with." He's fighting a grin and losing.

"I'm *shocked* you didn't find a wife before me, with charm like that." I shove bread into my mouth.

"I'm shocked you didn't find a husband before me, with manners like those."

I roll my eyes but crack a smile. It falls as a thought occurs to me. "You said married in the Natural World..."

"Don't worry, we're not married here by any stretch." He starts for Vena's audience chamber. "There are no tricks and no laws of the fae I've used. Rumors of fae stealing women's hands are greatly overexaggerated."

"Of course." I force a smile back on my lips as the sinking feeling that initially pulled it from my cheeks continues down my chest and into my stomach. It settles like disappointment in my gut. Why does this feel like a surprise? He said he'd leave me the manor. He was coming to the fae world and he was never going back. I'd be a widow. Alone in the world.

Alone so no one can hurt me...

Alone...lonely...

"I made sure Oren structured the arrangement so it would dissolve once I left." For once, he's oblivious to my turmoil. He doesn't even look at me. "You will be free to marry whom you please, Katria. And I am free to make a smart match to secure the future of my kingdom."

"You think of everything, don't you?"

He slows his pace and finally looks at me. The world seems to still. My breath snags. There's depth to his expression that, for the first time, I can't read. Is it sorrow? Or worry? I can't tell. His brows are pinched up slightly in the center and I'm fighting the urge to take his hand. I want to touch him. *I want to...* My mind slams against the walls I've built around myself once more. Not allowing me to even think about anything one step further.

"I do try," he says softly. "But even kings are sometimes caught off guard."

The sentiment is as gentle as a feather falling. It lands on a cold, dark part of me that I try desperately to hide from the world. My heart beats in reply, as if it's trying to push blood and warmth back into that unused corner of my soul. The way he's looking at me now...*regret*. That's what it is.

"Is that why you were so harsh to me in the woods after I first arrived?" I ask, trying to honor the promise I made to myself last night, inspired by Shaye. I'm sure she does much better at taking people to task when they have wronged her, but this is the best I can muster. "Because, the way you treated me then... I knew you weren't angry with me but it still wasn't—"

"Fair," he finishes. Davien tips his head to look me in the eyes. I'm aware of just how much it closes the gap between us. His eyes are filled with what I'd call remorse. They drop to my hands, which he scoops up thoughtfully. His thumbs brush over my knuckles, nearly making me forget entirely about what it was we were just discussing. "I know. I should have apologized to you sooner. Shaye was right and I was acting a petulant child, frustrated with the circumstances. So you're right, too, in that it had nothing to do with you. But that's no excuse. I'm sorry, Katria. I won't let it happen again. Will you forgive me?"

"Davien, I..." Have I ever been apologized to this gently or sincerely? My walls crumble under the heat of his presence, so heartbreakingly close.

"Oh, good, you two are already here." Vena breezes past us. Davien drops my hands and steps away, his cheeks a little redder than they were a moment ago. "Finish your breakfast and let's get started. There's no time to waste."

She opens the doors to her audience chamber. But the hall isn't empty. Standing in the middle is a woman wrapped in a familiar black shawl. It's the same as what I saw that night in the Bleeding Forest and that day back home. My breath catches. But Davien isn't so off guard that he can't manage a snarl.

"Butcher of Boltov," he growls and lunges to attack.

eighteen

DAVIEN IS FAST. The Butcher is faster. She's a blur of motion, raising a short sword to block Davien's dagger. They move so fast that my eyes couldn't even keep up to see where he drew the dagger from.

"Davien!" Vena calls. He's already moving again, darting back and lunging with his other hand and a different dagger. The Butcher deflects a second time. "Stop this." Vena rushes over. "This is Allor, and she is an ally to the Acolytes."

"She looks like a Butcher to me." Davien continues to put pressure on Allor's blade. The woman wears a lazy smirk. I can almost see her holding herself back from carving Davien to bits.

"And you look like a spoiled prince to me, so let's not get into the name-calling, *hmm?*" Allor says. Her voice is as soft as her shadow cloak.

"Enough." Vena grabs both of their shoulders, physically trying to push them apart. It's about as successful as trying to move two mountains. "I *asked* Allor to come. She's going to help us figure out the ritual to get your power."

"You're trusting a Butcher?" Davien glances to Vena.

"*You* trusted a Butcher."

"Shaye had already left well before she joined us. This monster—"

"Again with the name-calling." Allor rolls her eyes.

"Will both of you just put down your weapons?" Vena acts like she's speaking to two children.

"Him first." Allor sneers.

"Why you—"

"On my count." Vena sighs. "One. Two. *Three*."

The two slowly ease apart. Davien returns his daggers back to sheathes hidden in the wide belt around his waist. Allor returns the sword to a scabbard on her hip. But her hand doesn't leave the hilt. Which is far more unnerving when her eyes dart over to me.

"The rumors are true, then. You do have a human here."

"I'm Katria." It feels much better to be called by my name than "human."

The woman's grin widens and she nods her head. "Allor. But I suppose you already figured that out."

Wispy strands of short black hair are pulled back at the nape of her neck. A long white streak cuts a wedge out of her hairline along her brow toward her right temple. She's about my height, but twice as muscled as I am...which says something since I've never considered myself to be a particularly frail person.

"Care to explain yourself?" Davien says to Vena.

"Allor is one of our key informants to the inner workings of the High Court. Without her, we would be very much in the dark about what the Boltovs are doing. She was the one who helped get the information for the restoration of the king's magic—the one who told us about the relic we needed in the Natural World to complete it," Vena says.

Davien considers this, eyes darting between Vena and Allor. He's clearly still skeptical. Even if I can't see his face, I can feel it off the man.

"Is this true?" Davien looks to Allor.

"Could she lie even if she wanted to? Better question would be why you doubt her." Allor inspects the pommel of her sword, flicking imaginary dust from it.

The muscles in Davien's cheek twitch but he keeps his voice level when he says, "Then I am in your debt. When I am king you shall be—"

"Spare me." Allor holds up a hand. "I'm helping you because

it suits me. Let's not make more of a fuss than we need. Though I know that's hard for you kingly types." She still wears a little smile, like the world is some big joke and she's the one laughing. It's the look Helen would get when she knew I was in trouble but I didn't know how yet.

I know better than to trust a look like that.

"What are you getting for all this generosity?" I ask.

"I get to sleep better at night knowing I helped my people." The words sound scripted to me and do little to calm my nerves.

"What are you *really* getting?"

Her smile turns slightly sinister. Still like my sister's. Still everything I hate and know to be wary of.

She turns to Vena. "Why does this human care so much for our politics?"

"You didn't answer me," I say. She was vague at best.

"What I get out of this arrangement is my business." Allor folds her arms.

"I admit, I'm curious now," Davien says casually. "What has Vena promised you?"

"Safety here in Dreamsong…and the absolution of my crimes from our next king."

Davien gives Vena a pointed stare. It seems I'm not the only one who knows how to read him, because Vena says, "Everyone needs something, Davien. And many will be like her, looking to free themselves from their past life."

"We will speak on this later," Davien says like a proper king. I can feel his annoyance. If it were me, I would already be giving Vena choice thoughts for speaking on my behalf. But I can also see her point. Thank goodness I'm not the one ruling. I don't know if I could navigate these types of decisions.

"I think that's for the best," Allor says. "They'll begin to wonder where I am if I'm gone for too long."

"So what is it we're doing?" I ask. Hopefully the faster we do whatever it is, the faster Allor leaves. My nerves are still rattling in an entirely unpleasant way.

"I asked Allor to research the ancient records stored away in the High Court for any kind of information on a magical transference.

Since she was the one to find out how to draw out the magic of the ancient kings, I thought she might also be the one to find us a solution to this mess," Vena says.

"And did you?" Davien arches his eyebrows.

"Perhaps..." Allor adjusts her hair, enjoying far too much that she has this secret information and clearly no inclination toward sharing.

"Allor," Vena says sternly.

"Fine, yes, maybe, I can't be sure."

"Incredibly helpful," Davien says dryly.

"Will you let me just tell you what I've found?" She glares and continues. "There are old texts on 'abdication.' It only happened twice in the records of the old kings, but it *did* happen. And when it did, one king would pass on the power to the next through this process. The previous king would draw out their power and store it in the glass crown. Then, when the new king was crowned, the power would flow from the crown to him so long as the previous ruler decreed it.

"Granted, this other person still couldn't *wear* the glass crown—that can only be the true heir of Aviness, so long as there is a living heir. It seemed as though it was more safeguarding the powers in instances of an heir being too young to rule. Someone would stand in and then abdicate *back*." Allor shrugs. "It's a bit murky, as a lot of the ancient rituals and their effects are."

Davien runs a hand through his hair. I can hear him curse softly under his breath. Finally, he says, "Is *that* all? Are you done wasting our time?"

"I've hardly 'wasted your time.'" Allor rolls her eyes. "I'm telling you that it *is* possible to get the magic from her and give it to you. You should be falling over yourself trying to thank me."

"Possible for ancient, powerful kings at the height of their power who possessed the most sacred relic of our people—the glass crown. I still fail to see how that helps us here."

I'm beginning to realize I need to get to the bottom of everything this "glass crown" can do. Shaye said it commanded loyalty from all the fae. But I'm getting the impression that it's a lot more than even that.

"It means there's a ritual designed to move the power," Vena says. "And we don't know if the glass crown must be the container that the power is moved in. Or if it can be something else."

"Of course it must be the glass crown. What else would be mighty enough to contain the magic?"

Vena motions to me. "*She* is not the glass crown, and the power seems to be residing in her just fine."

Davien turns to me and his face lights up. My heart skips a beat. No one has ever looked at me that way—like I'm the most important thing in the world. And then, my heart stops, sinking like a lead weight into the pit of my stomach with the realization that it's not *me* he's looking at…it's the magic in me.

He doesn't care about you, a nasty voice inside me whispers, *not really. When he looks at you he sees the magic*. I bite my lip and wish it wasn't true. But I know it is. Davien's brow furrows slightly and I wonder if he can read me like I can read him. The notion is as comfortable as crawling through thorny bramble. It prickles my arms and rakes up my spine. I look away and break whatever connection was forming between us.

"We should try," I say. "The faster this magic is out of me, the faster I can go home." When I bring my eyes back to Davien's, he wears a slightly confused and wounded look. I barely resist remarking about it. How can he look at me like that when all he wants is this power? When I am otherwise just an inconvenient vessel?

Vena saves me. "Agreed." She crosses to me and rests her hands on my shoulders. Suddenly it feels like she's placed the weight of the world there. "I know none of this will make sense to you as a human. But all I ask is that you continue to open your mind and heart to it. Your ancestors, so very long ago, possessed a magic that was stripped from them when they were left on the other side of the Fade. Perhaps, now that you are here, you can reignite those forgotten powers and let them serve you once more."

"I'll do my best." It's all I can offer. My gaze shifts to Allor. "What do I do?"

"First thing is you'll need something to store the magic in. I thought ahead and brought this." Allor takes out a glass pendant on a silver chain. The glass is cut in such a way that it catches even the faintest of flickers from the chandeliers overhead and breaks down the light into rainbows. *"You're welcome."*

"Another relic?" Davien asks. Even he sounds skeptical of the woman now. Which makes me feel better, if only slightly. I can't shake the feeling that there's something distinctly *off* about her.

"Indeed. It was among the royal jewels...down in the vaults where Boltov keeps the old Aviness treasures. Don't ask me what king or queen it belonged to, I've not the foggiest."

"Taking this was reckless of you." Yet even as Vena says the cautioning words, she's moving toward the necklace.

"I know. But you're glad I did." Allor grins and holds it out.

Vena takes the pendant with both hands, cradling it gently. "Yes, that is the make of the old ones," she whispers and returns to me. "Here."

I accept the necklace. I expected the glass to feel sharp given its many edges, but it feels more like velvet underneath my fingers—warm, soft, almost alive. I inhale softly as a rush surges through me.

"What did you feel?" Vena misses nothing.

"It—It felt familiar," I admit. "Something about it... I've felt this before."

"That's the power within you recognizing this as familiar and calling out." Vena looks back to Allor. "What is the next step for her to abdicate this power?"

"From what I read, the king that abdicated held the glass crown and looked into the eyes of his successor. He said he would impart the magic and throne. And then it would be handed over and the new king would be crowned."

"Seems easy enough." Davien comes to stand before me, walking with purpose. I stare up at him, heart instantly racing once more thanks to his proximity. "Good. Look into my eyes, Katria."

The way he says that...so easy, almost sultry. I bite my lip. I hate what this man does to me against my will. I don't want everything to be ignited by the mere sight of him. But he couldn't be more handsome than in that ethereal way of his.

"What next?" I whisper. Even though they just told me what this ritual entailed, my mind is already blank.

"Wait, first..." Vena says. She's buzzing about in my periphery. Whatever she's doing, though, is lost on me. All I can focus on is Davien's eyes. Perhaps the ritual has already started. They've never looked brighter—never been more all-consuming. My stare wanders, riding down the edge of his nose to land on his lips, a dusky pink that begs to be kissed. It's good my sisters never laid eyes on him. Even though he's a fae, they would be utterly shattered. Maybe him being fae would make them desire him all the more. He's dangerous...*forbidden*.

So what hope do I have? I swallow thickly. I don't have an answer.

"Two separate. One together," Vena murmurs. Her fingers impose on my field of vision as she reaches up to Davien's cheek. She draws swirling lines and dots across his right cheek and then his left in a dark purple ink that slowly fades as it dries. Then I feel her finger on my cheek. "Two separate. One together."

"Two separate," I'm compelled to repeat. The ink seeps into me like the words.

"One together," Davien finishes, sending a rush through me.

Vena moves behind me. I'm trapped between her and Davien. Not that there's any escaping. There never was for me. As soon as Joyce married me off I was destined to be with this man...even if that marriage is no longer valid.

"Now, start," Vena whispers into my ear as I look into Davien's eyes. "Breathe with him." Davien inhales and I do the same, just like the drawings on our cheeks mirror each other. "Exhale. Inhale. Exhale."

The breaths are so slow and deep that I'm lightheaded. I lean closer to him and I think I see him do the same. His soft fingers brush against my calluses as he cups my hands, holding the glass necklace with me between us.

"Gather the power of kings—the power that does not belong to you. Take that foreign magic and cast it to its rightful owner," Vena instructs.

I inhale on Davien's exhale. Everything is thrown off for a second. I quickly get back in sync. This whole ritual is hanging on me and I've no idea what I'm doing. The longer I'm trying the more frustratingly apparent it is.

But I have to try.

I begin to focus on every inch of my body. I focus on the muscles of my feet as they press into the ground, keeping me stable as the rest of me feels like it's trying to fly away. I focus on my stomach, still doing flips at the way Davien continues to stare at me. I focus on my physical body to the point that it fades away. As if once my mind has understood it, then it no longer needs to be considered.

Then…what's left is song. That thrumming beat I heard when I fell into the fire. The music of ancients, all singing together in a chorus that's highlighted by my mother's voice.

That must be the magic. Magic is happiness, warmth, familiarity. Pure power should make someone feel good, after all.

I have to let it go. This wasn't meant for me. And yet, it already feels as though it's one with my blood. As though there's no way I could ever untangle it.

Still, I have to try.

Holding the necklace tighter, I imagine the power flowing down my arms, much like the magic I saw flowing through the trees the first night I tried to escape. Davien's face is illuminated. I dare not break our eye contact. But I can only assume that it's working.

"Now say the words," Vena commands softly.

"I give this magic to you. Take the—" I don't get to finish.

Magic explodes out from me with a sharp *snap*. I'm sent backward, landing awkwardly on Vena. Davien is staggered, brought to his knees. Even Allor is on the ground. The necklace is sent flying, skittering across the floor to land far away from all of us, miraculously unbroken.

Davien curses. "Why didn't it work?" He looks between Vena and Allor with an accusatory stare. Somehow I've avoided his blame and ire.

"It was a first attempt." Vena helps me off of her with a kind smile. At least she's not cross for how we landed. "Rituals rarely go smoothly the first time, especially ones that are adjusted and adapted as they're being performed."

"I need that power," Davien growls.

"You will have it. And we have time to get it." Vena stands and brushes unseen dust and dirt from her flowing clothing. "She is safe here as long as the magic is within her. Our borders are secure." Vena looks to Allor. "Does King Boltov have any inclination of what's happening here?"

"He has no idea what's happening in Dreamsong right now," Allor says a little too easily and smiles a little too widely for my liking.

"Then we have time." Vena extends a hand to me. "How do you feel?"

"I'm fine." I take her hand and stand, swaying slightly. "A little tired, I suppose."

"I imagine that would take it out of you," Vena says thoughtfully. "We should adjourn for the day."

"But—"

"Exhausting her will do nothing." Vena interrupts Davien's objection. "We'll try again tomorrow. And Allor, if you hear anything or find anything that might help, let us know."

"Of course. Now, I should return before any of my fellow Butchers wonder where I've gone off to." She gives a little wave and steps over into the shade of Vena's throne. With a puff of smoke, she's gone. I look around the room, searching for where she could come up next.

"Don't try looking for her; she's likely already out of the city. She has a unique talent for shadow stepping over long distances, which makes her very useful to us," Vena says.

"Butchers," Davien mutters.

"Are you sure we can trust her?" I dare to ask. Vena arches her eyebrows. "What is she giving them?"

"Nothing. They've no idea she's working for us." Vena seems to bristle at the fact that I would accuse her of any ill design when it comes to this arrangement. I suppose I can't blame her. I am an outsider. But I can't shake this feeling...

"She's gone from the High Court for a very long time. Plus, her answers...didn't you hear how she avoided anything direct?" I say.

"You should leave the management of Dreamsong and the

Acolytes to me. You focus on regaining your strength so we can try again tomorrow."

"You mean the management to me, don't you?" Davien says, locking eyes with Vena.

"Of course, Your Majesty. A slip of the tongue. I'm not accustomed to you being here."

"See it doesn't happen again."

"Would you like us to stop working with Allor?" Vena asks Davien and folds her hands before her, clearly confident she already knows the answer.

"No, she's proved her use. And if she ever steps out of line or becomes not useful...then we'll kill her." Davien starts for the door. He pauses, glancing at me. "You, come with me."

"What?"

"I want to speak to you."

I glance to Vena, who just shrugs. Thoroughly confused, I follow Davien out of the audience chamber. We emerge back into the meeting hall, now empty of all except the various attendants and a few unfamiliar faces in a corner.

Davien's arm wraps around my waist, pulling me toward him. His wings unfurl with a shower of sparks.

"Wh—" I don't get to finish.

"I'm going to fly unless you tell me not to." He locks eyes with me once more and our sides melt together.

"Take me away," I whisper. He wraps me in his arms and leaps for an open archway along the top of the gathering hall. In a breath we're out of that oppressive building that reeks of our failure to separate the magic from me and stepping into the open air.

nineteen

WITH A FLAP OF DAVIEN'S WINGS, WE BREAK AWAY FROM THE HOLD THE EARTH HAS ON US AND SOAR THROUGH THE SKIES ABOVE DREAMSONG. My heart is in my throat once more, stomach doing flips. But not with terror.

I feel safe in his arms, I realize. He holds me with easy security. As if, even with my broad shoulders and strong hands, I'm no trouble to him.

My fingers tease his hair at the nape of his neck lightly. The long strands are raked by the wind, away from his sculpted face. The wind shifts and his gaze turns from the horizon to where he'll put his foot next. He catches me admiring him and a flush covers my chest and cheeks.

Davien chuckles, but says nothing about my staring. His foot hits the pointed spire of a building, like a feather balancing on a needle, and he pushes off once more. We start our ascent back to the cotton clouds drifting as effortlessly through the blue sky as us.

"May I ask you something?"

"I believe you just did."

I roll my eyes and he chuckles.

"Yes, Katria, what is it?"

"Why is your flying more like jumping than the other winged fae?" I look around us. Davien soars higher than most of the others. But only at the crest of his arc. Then he comes back to earth as others sustain their altitude.

"*Ah*," he says with a soft sigh. "That…"

"Is it because of your wings?" I ask.

"Do you want to hear me answer your question? Or should I just let you speculate?" Davien laughs and I give a sly smile. We touch down, this time on the railing of a balcony, and shoot up once more. The rooftops of Dreamsong glisten with the sunlight. Gilded gutters and glass shingles catch the early dawn. "Yes, it's because of my wings. And they are weak because of my being forced to grow up in exile. I was far from this land—my homeland—and all its magic. Think of our power as a muscle. It languishes from lack of use. And I had precious little magic to use in the Natural World to train myself."

"So your wings were tattered from not being used?" I glance over his shoulder at the beat of his wings. Even though they are frayed and thinned at the edges, holes punched through as though he was shot down once by archers, they flap with power and force. They seem stronger than the first time we flew. Perhaps I'm not the only one becoming more luminescent in this world.

"Among other flaws in my magic," he admits. It sounds painful for him to do so. Which makes it all the more meaningful when he continues. "It's why I could never let you see me." His grip tightens slightly. "I couldn't even so much as glamour myself when we first met, or dismiss my wings when I wished. You would've known exactly what I was from the first moment. I was a pathetic, weak creature."

"That's not true."

"It is."

"You fended off a Butcher to save me."

His eyes dart toward mine, lips parted slightly. I have never paid more attention to a man's lips before. And he seems to be just as keen on mine. I imagine him staring at my mouth as I spoke, blindfolded. The thought nearly has me squirming in his arms.

"Oren did, technically. I could only flee."

"You charged in and saved me."

He seems frustrated and embarrassed by my trying to pay him a compliment. I can relate to that discomfort. "I should have been able to do more…"

"That was another thing you wanted the power of the old kings for, wasn't it? To restore you to the fae you would have been if you'd grown up in Midscape?"

"Yes." He glances at me with longing. Once more, he's looking *through* me, not at me. He's looking at the power that's his.

"I'm going to do my best to give it to you," I say softly. "I promise I am."

"I know."

Before anything else can be said, he descends. This movement has a bit of finality to it and I tighten my grip slightly around his neck, bracing myself against him for when we meet the ground. Of course, our landing is as delicate as the rest of his flight has been.

We've landed on a vacant plot on the far edge of the city, at the edge of the mountains where the forest is encroaching on the valley. All of the houses of Dreamsong are packed together, right on top of each other. It didn't fully strike me how closely until I saw this empty lot. Giles and Oren stand together, engaged in a heated debate over a book that they don't so much as glance up from as we approach.

"I see you've made a lot of progress while I was gone," Davien says, that deep voice of his silencing the argument and bringing all eyes—mine included—to him.

"We just started for the day," Giles says with a dramatic sigh. "We're trying to decipher the instructions Vena sent us out with."

"Show me? I'm certain I can help." Davien steps forward.

Oren turns the book, holding it out so Davien can flip through the pages. I look around his side. There are pictures of houses and their various parts on the left-hand pages and instructions on the right. Whoever made the drawings had a meticulous attention to detail. Every joist and joining has been carefully labeled and marked. The instructions detail everything from supplies, to timing, to words that need to be said and actions that need to be performed.

"Is this a spell book?" I ask.

"It's a record of rituals, yes." Davien continues flipping to the pages marked with silken bookmarks.

"It was passed down in my court," Giles says fondly. "Rituals from a different age, when the Court of Pillars were the best builders in all of Aviness."

"So if I do this—" I point a finger at the instructions on a random right page "—then I get this?" I move my finger to the left page, where there's a detail of an awning over a door.

"Simplified, yes." He nods.

"Though *you* likely won't be doing anything. These are for fae." Giles chuckles.

"You speak too quickly about things you don't know, Giles. Always a shortcoming for you," Davien says plainly.

"Pardon?"

"I brought Katria here because I thought she might be of critical use to us."

"You're going to have her help with a ritual?" Giles balks.

"I'm going to have her perform one. If she's up for it."

"Excuse me?" It's now my turn to share in looking at Davien in disbelief. "I've never—I don't know—you saw how it went earlier."

"How it went earlier is exactly why I brought you here." Davien looks at me. "You don't do well in confined spaces. You struggle with instruction and rules." I suppose that's not *entirely* untrue. "And you clearly were uncomfortable around Allor." That's definitely true. "None of that makes for a positive environment to use magic in. I thought this would be a project you could be enthusiastic about— you like working with your hands. You enjoy building things. And you prefer to have a purpose stemming from a clear goal. We're working on something important for all of Dreamsong."

I force myself to ignore just how much detail he has gathered about me and my personality, instead asking, "Which is?"

"A tunnel into the mountain," Giles says eagerly. Oren gives him a sharp nudge. "What?"

"It's supposed to be a *secret*."

"Who is she going to tell?" Giles throws his hands in the air. "We're basically her only friends here!" I blink several times and my chest tightens. He catches the expression and hastily adds, "Sorry, I mean, that came out harsh—"

"You think you're my friend?" I whisper.

All three of them look at me now with strange, unintelligible stares.

"Well...yes. Unless that bothers you?"

I shake my head quickly. "Not at all. I'm not familiar with friends. Never really met many people. My family kept me inside. A lot." I force laughter, trying to ease the awkward atmosphere but no doubt making it worse.

Davien gently grips my shoulder and squeezes lightly. "You have friends here, Katria."

"I finally make friends and they're a world away." I'm still laughing. So why does it hurt? Pain flashes through Davien's eyes, as though it's his chest tightening and not mine.

"Just a Fade away," Oren reminds me. "One we're fairly well versed in crossing."

"Right. So, this project is a tunnel into the mountains?" I quickly try and divert the topic away from me.

"Yes, just in case Boltov attacks. At least some of Dreamsong will have a place to escape to," Giles says solemnly.

"How many?" I can't help but ask.

"Not enough. Though we'll do our best."

"Why don't you two start?" Davien suggests. "Katria and I will watch for a bit so she can get a sense of it." Davien retreats back to the beaten path that lines the front of the lot, motioning for me to follow.

I look back out over Dreamsong. I can see the entire city from this vantage as it slopes down around Vena's main hall. Hundreds of displaced people and families, living in danger...struggling and fighting to reclaim a homeland that they might never see again and, even if they could, might not be the same when they return.

That feeling is so foreign to me that I have to struggle to comprehend it. I've never felt that drawn to anywhere. I've never had somewhere I would fight at all costs to get back to.

Davien's manor? I suppose? I'm fighting to get back there. But even that...it's just a house. It's not my home. Maybe I could turn it into my home someday. But for now, it's just a place to lay my head. Is *that* what I'm struggling to get back to? Is *that* the best I have to hope for in life?

"Your thoughts are heavy," Davien interrupts my contemplations.

"What?"

"Your shoulders hunch slightly when you're thinking about something sad." He runs his finger along the ridge of my shoulder from my neck to the edge, where it hovers.

"Do you really think we'll be able to defeat Boltov?" I ask softly, avoiding the truth of what I was thinking.

"I do. We have to. I refuse to entertain any other option." Davien turns his gaze over Dreamsong as well with purpose. "And you know what?"

"What?"

"Even though none of this is happening how I intended, I can't shake the feeling that you're meant to be here, with me, while I do this." He finishes his sweep of the city and his attention lands on me.

"I'm holding you back."

"You're helping me learn. Forcing me to take time to become acclimated to Midscape before I have full use of my powers. Teaching me to be still and patient—that I can't charge ahead and defeat Boltov overnight. I shudder to think of what might have happened if you weren't here to force me to slow down."

His mouth tugs into a smirk at one corner. The look is a bit sultry, in an entirely unintentional way that makes it all the more irresistible. Davien doesn't realize just how attractive he is, I realize. His appeal is like his magic. It was unused in the human world. A muscle that went unflexed for such a long time that he doesn't even realize the strength he has. Soon enough, he'll realize that power, too. And then women will be fawning over him left and right. A handsome prince returned from exile to claim the throne... I bet there are a hundred fae like Laura who will trip over themselves to be with him.

And where will that leave me?

Forgotten, back in the Natural World.

You never had a place here to begin with, a nasty voice seethes in the back of my mind. *You were never even* meant *to be here. Or with him.*

"I'm doing all that?" I arch my eyebrows skeptically, keeping my reservations to myself.

"And more." Davien reaches for my hand and then thinks better of it, as if he can read my mind. "Oh, look, they're going to begin." I do as he commands, relieved for the distraction.

There's a small pile of supplies off to the side that Oren and Giles are moving—materials I would and would not expect to find for building. It's everything from lumber, to blocks, to geodes—cracked like eggs, their shimmering, crystal yolks catching the sunlight. There are buckets of paint and brushes, one of which Giles picks up.

He begins to dribble paint along the ground, murmuring as he goes. Meanwhile, Oren is taking some of the smaller tree limbs and placing them at the four corners of the outline Giles is making. At the top of each of the rough posts he places a crystal, the branch magically weaving around it to hold the stone like a jewel at the top of a scepter.

Giles goes back to the foot of the mountain to paint swirls, dots, and lines across one of the stones there. He does the same on the wood off to the side. Oren and Giles square off against each other on opposite ends of the outline they've made. They each crouch down, pressing their fingers into the wet paint that's pooled unevenly in the divots of the hard-packed earth.

In my periphery, I see Davien move. His lips brush lightly against the shell of my ear as he whispers, "Watch closely. Feel their magic. Feel their connection to the earth—to everything around us—all that was and could be."

I want to do as he instructs, but I don't think he realizes just how painfully distracting he is when he speaks like that.

Giles and Oren's chanting becomes fast and low. The air around them pops with small sparks of light in increasing frequency. I hear a rumble off to my side. The giant tree trunk groans with unseen pressure. A crack splits the air and the wood. Simultaneously, the mountainside comes to life like a sleeping golem waking. The stones behind Giles begin to levitate as the marking he placed on the large boulder glows.

It's a maelstrom of shimmering magic, stone, and wood. Invisible builders saw, hammer, and nail. They fit the joints with careful precision as a hole is bored into the mountainside. The magic does the work of several craftsmen in a blink. Before I know it, a tunnel has begun. Clay seeps up through the ground, beading and joining along the path. Support beams shore up the overhead.

I stare in awe…and frustration. The latter must show on my face because Davien asks, "What's wrong?"

"It's so…so simple."

"I assure you it only has the appearance of simplicity. In actuality, to perform magic like this takes years of practice to understand both rituals and your power."

I thrust my hand toward the start of a tunnel. "In mere minutes, two men bored into a mountainside with *thoughts*. They accomplished something that would take years. If I had this power—if I had even a fraction of it—my family's home would've been different. I could've done more. I could've been free of them long ago because I could support myself."

My eyes are burning unbidden. Why does this frustrate me so much? Why do I feel so wounded? Davien just stares at me in that inspecting way of his, making me feel more vulnerable than anyone or anything has before. I look away and shake my head. I'm about to say that it's all right and dismiss my feelings when his hand lands on my shoulder.

"If you want to do it so badly, then do it," he says softly. That draws my attention straight back to him and I stare into his emerald eyes. "Right now, you have this power and so much more. If you even drew on a fraction of the power of kings, you would be able to finish the tunnel and its main hall in a blink."

"But I…" I think of my attempt with Vena and shake my head. I didn't learn how to repair plaster or mend a roof overnight. I won't learn how to use magic overnight either. It'll take practice. "What should I do?"

Davien smiles, genuine, big, and bright. His whole face lights up with excitement. "You're going to start small. Some lanterns, perhaps?"

"All right." I follow him toward the front of the tunnel. Oren and Giles are leaning against stones, catching their breath.

"Well done, you two," Davien says as he picks up the book.

"We're done for the day now, right?" Giles pants softly. He

looks like he just worked an entire day in a quarry. Which quells my frustrations about the "ease" of their building some.

"A bit more." Davien hands the book to me. "We're going to do it together, you and I."

"You could just do it in an instant," Giles says to Davien.

"This isn't about me," Davien says curtly.

"Rare of our lost prince to recognize that not everything is about him." Giles grins. Davien ignores him.

"Come with me, Katria," he says. I follow him to the now significantly smaller pile of wood. Davien lays the book out on the ground. "The first thing you need to remember about rituals is that they all require base components. This can be anything from time, to location, to physical objects, to actions you take. The components can be consumed—like the book I used that night in the woods. Or, they can be reused, like those crystals." He points to the crystals still on posts in the ritual workspace Giles drew on the ground.

"I understand," I force myself to say, ignoring the reminder of the loss of my mother's book. But I can't. "My m—" I almost say *my mother's*, but the promise I made to my father to never tell anyone whose book it was sticks. He wanted no one speaking of that book. It was only for us. Unsurprising he never gave it to Davien for so many reasons. "My family's book, the one you used in the woods, why did you need it?"

He looks uncomfortable. Guilty, even. I wish it made me feel better about him destroying it. But his guilt won't return what I've lost. "It had special magic woven in its bindings. The components of a ritual can sometimes be strange, and not always make sense. But when they come together, the magic is unleashed, and that's what's important. If I'd had any other option save for destroying the book, I would've done that instead."

"I see." Silence passes between us and I push the memories aside. I don't want to think of the book any longer. It's gone. What good can come of lingering on it? And, in a way, if burning that book could save an entire people, I'd like to think it's what Mother would've wanted. Davien waits to see what I say next. Determined, I return us to the topic of hand, pointing to the top of the page. "Up here?"

"Yes, these are the components of the ritual." Davien points to what looks like the ingredient list of a recipe. "Next is preparation. Sometimes, before the ritual even begins, you have to do something to yourself or the components. That's blank here because this is fairly simple."

I nod and he continues.

"Then there's the instruction of how to perform the ritual itself. And that's it. Fairly simple."

"In theory, I suppose," I say, still somewhat uncertain about the prospect of all of this.

"In execution, too. First things first, you need to make these markings on the stone you want to use."

"What do the markings do?" I ask as I take the paint he hands me and begin copying from the book.

"They attune your magic to the item you're trying to manipulate. It helps give you control—or connection—with the person or thing."

"Person, too?" I think of the lines that Vena drew on our faces and how connected I felt to him in that moment.

"Yes. Now, next step is to visualize what you're going to make. This is why they included the picture with the ritual." He points to the lantern in the book. "As you visualize, you're going to say these words and then, when you're ready, unleash your magic."

I stare at the picture, thinking about how I would build this lantern... I take a breath and close my eyes. *Unleash.* I think the command to the magic within me. *Make the lantern.* My brow furrows. Nothing happens and I feel the same. "Come on," I murmur.

"Say the words," Davien whispers at my side.

My eyes shoot open. *Oh, right, words.* I look down at the page.

"Broken little pieces. Joined back together. Make something anew. That can withstand time and weather," I say. But still nothing happens. "I don't think—"

Davien shifts and kneels behind me. His hands settle on my shoulders, running down my arms, pulling the thin fabric of my borrowed shirt in unintentionally teasing ways. His hands layered on mine, he laces his fingers around my palms.

"Stop trying to force it. Take a breath. Let it happen," he says in that husky voice of his. I feel something stir in me that is not entirely magic related. "Feel the magic in me. Feel it as I let it go. Feel my breaths and the power I draw from the earth itself. Think of your magic like a dance. You are leading a partner with their own will."

Like a dance...steps I have to take with the magic, not forcing it. I close my eyes once more and envision the lantern. The words I need to say come to the forefront of my brain. I feel power ripple through the muscles of his forearms atop mine.

"Broken little pieces," I start softly. I try and give myself to the words. Relinquish the control I so crave to a part of me that has never been there before. "Joined back together. Make something anew. That can withstand time and weather."

Cracking of stone has my eyes jolting open. I see the pieces dance through the air. My shock makes them falter, shuddering, nearly falling to the ground.

No, I think calmly. *Carry on, we're still dancing.*

Davien's magic merges with mine. He's helping, but not by much. His power more runs alongside mine, walling it in, channeling it. Almost like he's guiding me with the lightest invisible touch.

In an instant, a lantern is now on the ground before me. I'm left breathless and I slump. Davien catches me with a hand across my shoulders. He pulls me back to him and I lean against him for support.

"It's natural to feel exhausted after your first time," he says softly.

"Exhausted? I feel...I feel..." I stare at the lantern in awe. "I feel *alive*."

twenty

WE SPEND THE REST OF THE AFTERNOON WORKING ON THE TUNNEL. I can still barely muster even the simplest of rituals on my own. But, by the end of it, I have nearly completed an entire lantern by myself. While the rest of them carved out the entire tunnel and the rough hollow of what will be the escape hall.

In all, Oren, Giles, Davien, and I leave triumphant. We walk back through the city since Giles cannot fly. Which gives me more time to drink in the sights and sounds of Dreamsong.

"It really is magnificent," I say thoughtfully. I've only spent a few days here, and yet I feel like I've known this place for a century. Time feels as though it passes differently in Midscape, slower. Though I think I only feel that way because every hour of every day has been life changing.

"What is?" Davien asks. Oren and Giles are still behind us, debating over the contents of the ritual book and what else they absolutely must complete before they have to return it to the crafter they borrowed it from tomorrow.

"Everything in this world. How every home is tailor-made, unique, crafted by the hands of those who live there. The smells of fae food, how it singes the nose with spice and citrus. Even your sunsets are more beautiful…until the mountains cut them off."

Davien chuckles. "Yes…it's good to finally be home." A

frown briefly crosses my lips. He misreads the expression. "You'll be home soon enough, too. Especially with the rate you're managing to manipulate the king's magic. Soon enough you'll be able to abdicate it to me without issue."

"That's not what..." I quickly abandon the objection. I wasn't envious of him. I was sad at the idea that he would be here and I would have to return to that cold and so painfully normal world on the other side of the Fade. How do I communicate that to him when I barely am willing to admit it to myself? "Yes. That'll be for the best. And when that happens, I'll go back to the human world and live in that manor, alone."

The silence is heavy and surprisingly awkward. "It doesn't have to be alone," he says finally, and so tenderly I nearly break. I look up at him, my heart tripping over what I hope he'll say next: *I could come with you*, my mind tries to fill in for him. But, instead, he says, "You would be considered a widow by your laws. No one will know what's happened. Say I was lost in the woods, I made the letter ambiguous enough. You could find a proper human companion to spend your days with and no one would question."

"I find I can't stand most humans," I mumble.

He hears me and laughs. "And fae are better?"

"Surprisingly, yes. I seem to have a better track record of getting along with fae." I think back to our conversation about friends, earlier.

"You just think that because you're forced to be with us." He grins.

"No. I'm perfectly capable of still hating you while being forced to be with you. In fact, forcing me to be with someone usually means I end up hating the person more." I think of Joyce and Helen. They might have been my family, but that didn't stop them from being the wardens of my prison. I had no trouble hating them while loving Laura. "I was prepared to hate you when you first bought my hand in marriage."

He laughs. "I have to admit I was afraid of that happening. I had told myself it didn't matter, that you were a means to an end...but I was very glad when you didn't. I never wanted you to or relished in putting you in that position."

There's not a bit of smoke. He's telling the truth, as always. I inhale the fresh air and exhale all the lingering ill will from our rocky start—both in the Natural World and here in Midscape. He did offer much by way of my dowry, and even tried to look after me how he could when he thought he was leaving without me.

"I was thrilled by the idea that you didn't hate me, too. For whatever a human's opinion is worth."

"A human's opinion? Not much," he says casually. Then Davien turns those eyes toward me and I know in that moment he's going to break my heart before this is all over. Whatever pieces are still left to be broken. "But *your* opinion, Katria...I'm finding your opinion is worth more and more by the minute. Worth more than all the lost magics of the vampir in the southeast and all the ancient powers swirling in the mer waters of the north."

Is it just my imagination, or are our steps slowing? Are we walking a bit closer together? Our shoulders are brushing when they weren't before? I swallow thickly. A thousand questions burn on my tongue.

What I want to ask is, *Will you hurt me like the rest of them?* What I ask instead is, "Why did you bequeath that manor to me? Oren and the others said it was your family's lost estate. Why wouldn't you keep it for yourself?" I have to know if he was as well-intentioned as I am giving him credit for.

"I'll have a whole castle in the High Court and all the land of the fae wilds. The least I could do is give something to the woman who helped me reclaim my birthright." He glances in my direction. "Granted, that decision was made *before* you messed up the ritual."

"Lucky for me I have that letter in your handwriting back at the manor, I guess," I tease lightly and nudge my shoulder with his. He chuckles again, leaning back toward me. "Will you come and visit me?" The words escape as a whisper. I think he doesn't hear me and I'm ready to abandon the question. I shouldn't have asked. It was foolish. I open my mouth to change the topic when, to my surprise, he answers.

"If I'm able."

Fae can't lie. He *would* come and see me. Even after he's the fae king. Though…it also wasn't a resounding yes. Was the sentiment another one of those half-truths of the fae?

Our conversation is cut short by the sounds of music and singing. I look ahead along the cobblestone road. "What's that?"

"Oh, I suppose that starts tonight," Davien murmurs with a small smile.

"What does?"

"The first feast celebrating the coming end of autumn and the arrival of winter. It's been so long since I observed any fae holidays."

"Feasts for autumn?" I ask.

"Yes, we relish in all the changes of our earth, especially after the long winters during the Human Queen's absence. Come, Katria, let me show you more of my world." He holds out a hand, expectant. I hesitate, but only for a second, and then I take it. His warm fingers close around mine and I follow the line of his arm to a broad shoulder, and then to the sharp cut of his jaw—the delicate curve of his lips. What would it be like to kiss them?

No! The protective part of my mind objects. I can't think that way. That's how you end up hurt. That's how you end up in love. That's how your world gets taken over by another.

But that voice is weaker by the moment. Maybe I can go into this with both eyes open. Maybe, if I accept that if this is nothing more than a casual infatuation, I'll keep my head and my heart. I won't get hurt.

It sounds like lies in my mind, but his hand is so soft. His smile is so infectious. The way he looks at me, as though I am the only woman alive, is a thrill greater than any I have ever known, and together we rush toward the large square in front of the main hall of Dreamsong.

Merchants have moved their usual stalls from the markets to line the square. All manner of food and drink has been spread upon them. Some still have wares laid out, but I see no money changing hands.

In the center of the square there's a platform where a band plays. Dancers covered in billowing silks move like the wind, carried along by the thrumming of the drum. Fae mingle, laughing, singing, and dancing. Some dance overhead, twirling in gravity-defying waltzes, the shimmering magic of their wings cascading down toward the earth like the tails of dying fireworks.

"This way." Davien leads me through the mass of people.

"Davien, why don't they part for you?" I take a step closer to him to whisper.

"Part for me?"

"I thought people would show more deference to a king."

Comprehension flashes across his face. "Yes, usually...but I've been gone for so long, only a handful of Vena's most loyal assistants know who I am. My identity has largely been kept a secret to help keep us safe—especially since I am still more vulnerable without my magics."

Us, not "me." My chest tightens. The doubts that plagued me grow weaker and weaker in the face of this wild fantasy I'm starting to indulge with him in this magic place.

"Does it bother you?" I ask.

"Should it?"

"That's not an answer," I point out.

"You're growing accustomed to the fae phrasings faster than I would've liked." He chuckles.

"Such hardship for you." I smirk. "You struck me as wanting to be king. So I would think that them not showing you proper respect would upset you."

A thoughtful expression relaxes his brow. His lips part for a soft sigh and fall into an easy smile. He runs a hand through his hair. I watch as every silken strand cascades back into place, the braids he's woven through it snagging slightly on his fingers.

"I think there will be years for me to enjoy the trappings of kingship. For now, I want to see this world as an ordinary man— as much as I can be ordinary—to understand the struggles of my people. To feel their needs as I live among them. And even when I am king, I should hope that my subjects see me as a man as much as their king. As someone with his own hopes and dreams and desires." He pauses, brow furrowing slightly. "What is it?"

I hadn't even realized we'd stopped walking. The square has faded away. The squeals of laughter? Gone. All that remains is him and the music in a triumphant symphony.

"I think you'll be a great king." I really do. So why does my chest ache? Why am I already feeling the edges of a hurt I was trying to avoid?

Davien's hand lifts and hovers by my temple. He hesitates. I don't know if I want him to touch me or not. The ground under my feet has changed in more ways than my simply coming to Midscape. Even if I can return to the human world, everything will be different. My world changed irrevocably when I fell into that fire.

He brushes a stray hair behind my ear lightly and whispers, "Why do you look so sad about that?"

"Because…" *When you're king, that means I won't see you again. It means you won't be right here…within arm's reach.*

"Because?" He shifts slightly closer to me. I am his sole focus. He's joined me in this bubble I've made where everything else has fallen away. For once, I know he's looking at me and not the magic within me. If I held my breath, would time stop? Could I use the magic within me to build walls around us to keep everything else out?

I have my answer in the form of Giles and Shaye crashing in on our moment, bringing with them a noisy reality.

"What're you two doing?" Giles asks. Shaye lifts her eyebrows, glancing between us skeptically. I'm distracted by the crown made of glass on Giles's brow.

"I was about to get crowns for Katria and myself," Davien says, lowering his hand and crossing to the stall we'd been headed toward. Shaye hums, narrowing her eyes slightly. Her usually threatening aura is diminished some by the ring of pink roses across her forehead.

Davien returns promptly, handing me a similar crown. But instead of roses, the flower is one I don't recognize.

"What're these?" The flowers are pink and purple, with dozens of thin, long petals.

"Aster," Davien answers as he holds the crown over my head. "May I?"

"Sure." I try and sound casual but my throat is so thick I almost choke on the simple word.

"Women wear the crowns of the last flowers to bloom before winter, men wear replicas of the glass crown to bring strength and leadership needed to endure the coming winter," he says thoughtfully, running his fingertips lightly over the crown's flora. I have never been jealous of a flower before…but here I am.

"Interesting choice of flower and color." Shaye continues her examination of me. I feel as if she's sizing me for a dress. If she was, that'd explain the sensation of not being able to measure up.

"I'm sure it just *happened* to be the one Davien grabbed." Giles takes Shaye's elbow.

"There are many over there." Shaye hangs on the topic, refusing to budge as Giles attempts to guide her away. "Was it a careless choice? Or is there more thought behind it?"

Davien's brow knits slightly and he looks at Shaye from the sides of his eyes. Agitation ripples off of him.

"What does aster mean?" I ask. I know very little about flowers other than some rudimentary knowledge of edible ones. The language of flowers was one my sisters learned. There was never an extra seat at the table during their lessons for me.

"It's—" Davien looks back to me with panic flashing in his eyes. He hangs on the next word a little too long, searching for what to say. For the first time I wonder what it feels like for a fae to try and tell a lie. Does it hurt? Do rocks fall from their lips like in the old stories? Or…does he taste metal, too?

"Oh! I can't believe I found you, miss!" Raph materializes out of nowhere, wedging himself between Davien and me. It's only then that I realize how close we've been standing. As soon as I take a step away, the world sharpens once more. The noise, the people, the celebrations that carried on, oblivious to Davien and I. Raph thrusts a lute into my hands, the motion sets his miniature glass crown crooked across his brow. "Toldja I'd get you one. It's even pretty decent if I do say so myself."

I take the lute as though he's passing me a babe. I cradle its neck, treating it with all the gentle care it deserves. It's not as nice as Mother's, not by half. But it's fine enough make.

"What did you make her give away to get that?" Davien looms over Raph ominously.

"Just a song, and I let her decide all the conditions of it!" Raph holds up his hands, backing into me. I rest a hand on his shoulder protectively, looking up at Davien.

"I made sure I was careful on what I promised."

"And did you get that through upstanding means?" Shaye asks. "Or the kind that Uncle Giles is going to have to bail you out of trouble for?" Giles looks a little too excited about the prospect.

"I got it properly," Raph says defensively. It's not a clear answer, and I smirk. I really hope the lute wasn't stolen. But I don't hope that to the point that I'm going to give it back without playing at least a little. The strap is already over my shoulder, my fingers plucking the strings as I tune. "Are you going to perform now?"

I glance over my shoulder at the platform where the musicians are. "I'm not going to interrupt."

"It's like the tavern," he says. "Anyone can go and play."

"It seems rather full up there…" Part of me is slightly nauseous about performing before all these revelers. The other part longs to be on the stage once more, lute in hand.

"I think you should." Davien's deep voice cuts through my objections with ease. "I'd love to hear you play again when I can gaze upon your face, rather than just the back of your head."

How am I supposed to say no to that? "How many times did you listen to me in the woods?"

He gives me the gentlest smile. "Enough to know that you're better than half the people up there right now." Davien rests his hand on mine over the neck of the instrument. "Go and play, for me. Fill my world with your song."

I give a small nod. My eyes stay trapped with Davien's as my thoughts are tangled up with him to the point that I'm nearly tripping over my feet. The song the band is playing is swelling. Music is glittering in the early night and I tear myself away from that magical man to duck and dash on light feet to the stage.

At the steps that lead up to the platform, I hesitate. The words of Joyce and Helen are still whispering to me. But, day by day, they seem to echo from a place farther and farther away. They're not of this world. They don't know this Katria. A Katria who is bold and plays music for and with fae. I dash up the stairs, jumping the last two steps.

The music catches me and my hands are moving before my feet touch the rumbling boards of the platform. I fall into step with the other musicians as we move and sway, serenading the crowd. There are no words to this song, no familiar melody. Yet the sound is so sweet that I could cry. I twirl with a laugh as my fingers speed over the strings; my heart races in an effort to catch up.

The musicians play around me. I recognize them from the Screaming Goat and we all share conspiratorial smiles. The man who seems to be leading the troupe gives me a nod of approval, raven hair falling over shimmering tattoos inked over his brow.

My turn about the stage reaches an abrupt stop as I lock eyes with Davien. He's right in the front, Raph propped on his shoulders. Both are looking at me, but I only have eyes for Davien the man. He's procured a crown, and even though it's identical to all the other men's... it's different on his brow. He's their prince, hidden in plain sight among them. That crown—the real one—was made for him. The sight of it reminds me of how precious little time I have left with him.

Hear me, a new voice within says, spurred by how fleeting this world is. *Hear my song, this one is for you and only you. Hear it now, because I may never have the courage to play it again.* I don't know whose heart is beating in my chest. But it's stronger than the one I've known my whole life, surer. It has wants and needs all its own and seems to assure me with every feverish beat that it will not be denied.

I will not be denied.

Davien's lips part slightly. His brow softens. His cheeks pull up into a relaxed smile, more sincere and sweet than I've ever seen from him. It lights up his whole face brighter than the fae magic glittering overhead with the flaps of dragonfly and dove-feathered wings.

I play until the song has ended—far longer than I expected. In the lull I sneak off the platform. It's darker on the ground. I didn't realize how deep night had fallen underneath the glowing bell-flowers that magically illuminated the performers.

"You were amazing!" Raph claps his hands as Davien puts him

down. The two have made their way to me. "Thanks for letting me hear."

"Of course."

"You *were* amazing," Davien echoes in a whole different way, one that makes my heart skip a beat.

"But, uh, miss, I'm gonna need it back now." Raph taps the bottom of the lute. "Y'see, I kinda borrowed it. You didn't really say you had to keep it. And... Sorry."

His words become weaker, softer, no doubt because he sees my expression. I can't conceal my longing and regret. I curl and uncurl my fingers around the instrument, convincing myself that I can let it go. It was fun while it lasted, just like this whole world.

"No," Davien says. "Raph, you tell whoever it is that I will personally see they have a new instrument."

"Huh? Really? You can do that?"

"I can."

"It's all right." I hand the lute back to Raph. I don't know the history of this lute. It might be as sentimental to someone else as my mother's lute is to me. A fine instrument like this is meant to be passed down, between family, between friends. "It was worth it just to play. Thank you."

Raph takes the instrument and scurries away. It's wrenching to see it go. But I already have a lute back in the human world. One far finer and far more meaningful than any I could ever find here.

"I suppose it's for the best." Davien encroaches on my space. One hand lands on my hip, gliding around to the small of my back. The other laces fingers with mine. "If you were holding a lute, I couldn't dance with you."

"I'm not much of a dancer."

He tilts his head back, narrowing his eyes skeptically. "I think you are."

"You think wrong."

Davien leans in, placing his lips on the shell of my ear. "I've spent months watching how your body moves." His hand presses lower, gripping my flesh. "You have music in you, and the grace of a dancer."

"I don't—" I don't get to object. He sweeps me off my feet,

drawing forth a soft yelp of surprise. His toes crunch under my heel. "I told you I'm not a good dancer."

"Stop worrying so much. Just move, Katria. Move with me."

His voice, that tone…as sumptuous and slow as a bow drawn across the lowest note on a fiddle. The demand resonates within me like the tumbling of the feet in the square. I press my hips against his. Every shift of his weight moves his thighs against mine. I follow on instinct, not worrying about the fool I must look because—when my eyes meet his—there's only him.

My chest against his. His arm encircling my waist. His tunic, cut low, reveals the firm plane of chest I saw in the moonlight back in the woods. His crown a shimmering reminder of just how *forbidden* he should be to my very human hands. I'm breathless and not just from the dance. I gasp, barely holding back from begging for more—I want everything I've always denied myself.

I want to dare. I want to dance. I want to be someone I have never been even if it's only for one night.

The music stops and cheers erupt. People clear the square as the musicians take a break. But Davien's eyes are only on me, breaths heavy.

"You need to come with me."

"Anywhere," I pant softly.

Everything is left behind as Davien pulls me into the main hall of Dreamsong. There are a few people milling about. The celebration has spilled across the city, painting it with song and joy in the colors of autumn and winter grays. He leads me upstairs and all the way to the door at the end of the hall.

It's his room.

The four-poster bed is boxy, simple, not the ornate furniture I'd expect of a king. It's made of a dark wood, the grains catching the moonlight like currents in a river. Navy, velvet curtains reveal more pillows than I'd expect. He has an armoire, desk, and sitting area that opens to a small balcony overlooking all of Dreamsong.

Davien guides me to the chair positioned before the opening. He sits next to me, our thighs touching. His hand still lingers on mine.

"Sing for me again," he whispers.

"What do you want to hear?" I breathe. I couldn't sing right now if I tried. My throat is too tense. Mind blank.

"Anything." He lifts a hand, cupping my face and dragging his thumb lazily along my lower lip. "As long as I can watch your lips."

"I can't think of a single song." My cheeks are burning.

"This is why I never wanted you to look at me," he says slowly, a smirk curling his mouth dangerously. He looks as if he intends to devour me. "Because I knew if you did you'd be stunned into silence. And I never wanted to see you quiet."

I laugh with more conviction. I've never had anyone tell me they wanted to hear me before. Feeling heard and seen is more intoxicating than too much faerie mead. "I thought it was because if I looked at you, you could never let me go?"

It's his turn to chuckle. "You remember that."

"I remember every single night we spent together in excruciating detail." I shift, our thighs brushing, pressing closer together. "Do you?"

"Yes."

"As do I."

"Davien…" I search his eyes for an answer I know I can't find without asking both him and myself. "What am I doing here? What are *we* doing right now?"

Davien hooks my chin, directing my face upward. He leans a bit closer. "I don't know…but I think I like it. Do you?"

"I—I don't want to be hurt." Anything more than a whisper would feel like a scream now. He's so close. A breath away. A mere quiver and my lips would be on his. A shiver tickles my spine, tempting me to test the theory.

"I would never hurt you."

Truth. My eyes prickle. How can something be both truth and a lie at the same time? How is it possible for him to mean something completely and yet I know it's untrue? "All of this will hurt me though."

"All of what?"

"All these *feelings*. I know how this ends." It ends with a cold house and a one-sided marriage. It ends in emotional warfare with words sharper than any steel.

"Then let's not worry about them," he suggests casually.

That is everything I hoped for. "Can it really be so simple?"

"I told myself when I married you that I could never love a human."

"There is no way I'd ever love you." Or anyone else.

"Good, then we're on the same page." He keeps leaning forward and I keep leaning back. Soon I'll be flat against the armrest and sofa. Soon he'll be on top of me. Heat rushes throughout my body.

"No emotions?" My eyelids are heavy. Every blink is longer than the last. His lips curve like a scythe, and I am ready for harvest.

"No love." It sounds like a promise. "Though, if you let me, I will make you *feel*."

"Feel what?" My voice quivers.

"Everything." The word hangs as he waits for my objection. This is the point of no return I saw coming days ago. Everything about him is forbidden, everything screams of heartache. But I will not be my father's daughter. I can indulge in these physical needs without falling in love and giving all that I am in the process.

Can't I?

Before I have a chance to reexamine, his mouth crashes on mine.

twenty-one

HE TASTES OF SPICED HONEY. His skin smells of wood shavings from our earlier work and of smoke from the fires that lit the square below. His hair tickles my face and cheeks, curtaining around us, protecting this moment from the cruel world that will collapse on us all too soon.

I brush my fingertips up his sides, running them over the expanse of his chest. The shirt he wore today is almost open to the navel. It hangs invitingly and my fingers brush against his hot flesh. A groan escapes me and he inhales sharply, as if trying to consume the pleasure his mere existence elicits in me.

Davien shifts his weight. One hand is beside my head, the other cups my cheek. He guides me with light pressure against my jaw and probing from his tongue. I've kissed before, once, but it was nothing like this. The butler's boy—back when we could afford a butler—was only a year older than I and we were both little more than curious adolescents.

But Davien kisses me as a man. It's better than every teasing dream and indulgent fantasy I could ever concoct. I knew how a man and woman fit together conceptually… but nothing could've prepared me for the actual feeling of it.

His tongue slides against mine and I arch upward. I can feel his lips pull as he smirks once more. My brows knit. I hate that he's getting amusement from my pleasure. I know I'm inexperienced and he has likely had hordes of women throwing themselves at his feet.

But I'm not frustrated enough to break away from his kiss, either. Maybe it's because of fae magic they have yet to tell me about. I'm an utterly willing captive under him. My fingers slide underneath his shirt, following his collarbone. They wrap around his shoulders, holding him to me until the point that we have to force ourselves to separate for air.

His hair continues to partition us from the world. His green eyes hold their own luminescence in the darkness. I trace the outline the sheen from the kiss leaves on his lips with my eyes.

"I'm sorry I'm—"

"What could you possibly have to apologize for?" he interrupts.

A scarlet flush burns my cheeks. "I'm not well versed in these sorts of matters."

"What sorts?" There's a wicked glint in his eye as he traces his fingers down my cheek and neck. He teases the silken collar of my blouse. I've never been more aware of exactly how much fabric is covering me and where.

"You know what sorts," I manage.

"I want to hear you say it." His eyes flick from my chest to my face.

"The sorts of things that a lady of my standing isn't permitted to indulge in until I'm wed."

"Until you're wed..." he repeats thoughtfully. "To think, I could've had you long ago and I never did." Davien leans toward me again. I tilt up my face but he shifts so his lips brush against the shell of my ear as he whispers huskily. "Would you have enjoyed that? Your mysterious husband whose first name you didn't even know coming to you in the night? Would you enjoy feeling my weight atop you in the darkness? Would you keep your eyes open, roving my silhouette for any hint of how I might look? Or would you close them and submit to every caress of my hands and mouth?"

Every inch of skin puckers into gooseflesh. My body responds to his words as if he were physically touching me and not merely describing the things he could do to me. Old gods help me, the things I think I *want* him to do to me.

"I thought of you, then," I admit. I hadn't ever expected to tell him so. But there's nothing keeping me from him right now, not even my vault of secrets. "In the night, I would imagine you coming to me."

"Oh?" He hums in the back of his throat. The sound rumbles though me, turning whatever bones I had left to molten heat. "Tell me what you would imagine."

I suppress a groan. Why am I allowing him to do this to me? I should push him off and walk away. At least, that's what my better sense tells me I should do. But my better sense is no longer in control. All I can think of is heeding his every demand, and I find a dark sensuality to the notion of setting my mind aside and following my instinct instead.

"I imagined you at my door, waking me from sleep…asking if you could stay the night in my bed."

"And, in your fantasies, did you allow me to stay?"

"Every time."

"And what did we do when I spent the night in your bed?"

I haven't thought about these waking dreams since coming to Midscape. How long has it been since I first stepped foot in this strange world? A week? Two? A month? It could be a year for all I know in this moment. Time has become strange and distorted. I'm helpless underneath a fae and all I want is for him to kiss me again. And if it takes my telling him my darkest fantasies, then so be it.

"I felt you," I whisper.

"*How* did you feel me?"

"I felt you on me, touching me. I felt you lavish all of your attention on me—for me, solely, only, completely for me."

"And did it feel good?" His fingertips lazily caress down my chest on the arcs of my curves. I inhale sharply.

"Yes."

"Good." He pulls away, licking his lips. I have never seen anything more sensual. "Because in my every fantasy you felt nothing less than exceptional."

"You…fantasized about *me*?" The thought of him awake and

yearning for me, his large hands caressing every inch of what I now know is his firm body has my brain sputtering.

"Oh yes." He rocks his hips against me and crashes his lips down on mine once more. He kisses me in time to the music as it rises outside. The band has struck up once more and our moans make a harmony to the crescendo in the square below. Davien holds my head in place, fingers tangled with my hair, tongue plundering my mouth. He has me right where he wants me, pulling me further and further away from anything that resembles reason or sense. When he breaks away, it's only to get enough space to speak, lips moving over mine as he growls, "I imagined making you mine as a man should make his wife. I ached to take you to my bed and have you until you screamed my name and your throat was raw. Until my body was the only thing you knew or wanted."

I initiate the kiss this time. His words have wound me up so tight that I'm going to break if I don't have his mouth on mine again. I grab him, pulling myself toward him, abolishing the space between us—forsaking the cold night air for a primal heat that cannot be denied.

We kiss for an obscene amount of time. When he finally breaks away, I pant softly through swollen lips, gazing up at what is easily the most handsome man in existence. The crown still shines on his brow. King, ruler and protector, *my* king. Wordlessly, Davien shifts off of me. Our eyes remain locked, even if our bodies are no longer.

Crouching, he scoops me up, as though he's going to carry us to the skies. But, instead, he takes me to the bed. My soul is soaring as he lays me down. The mattress is firmer than mine, but it still sags under his weight. Davien's fingers curl around the back of my head once more.

"We only do as we desire." He looks me dead in the eyes as he speaks. "Nothing more, nothing less. No expectations."

"And no feelings," I repeat our earlier promise.

He nods and kisses me again. Our hands and fingers explore, till long after the music stops in the square below. There are places on his body that I am still not brave or bold enough to explore yet, no matter how badly I might want to. He seems to take my lead, only going as far as I do. It results in a tug-of-war between passion and sensibility. Lust and reason and the hopeless space between where frustration makes its home.

Eventually, the kisses stop and we lay next to each other wordlessly, staring up at the ceiling framed by the top of the poster bed. I swallow thickly and brave a glance over to him, wondering if he will be upset we didn't do more. There's a slight smile to his lips, his eyelids heavy.

"I should go," I whisper.

"Must you?" He shifts onto his side, propping up his head with his knuckles.

"We did as we desired." The night's events have my cheeks pulling into a sly smile. Even if I want so much more...this was good. It was enough. "No reason for me to stay."

"Unless you don't want to sleep alone?"

I consider the suggestion. I've never thought about how sleeping with another might feel. Would it be too hot under the duvet with the two of us? Would I kick him in the night? Or would his body curl around mine—a perfect fit? He would make me feel protected, safe...*wanted*... I shake my head and push away, sitting.

"Sleeping alone is fine. It's served me well thus far."

"Has it?" He arches a single eyebrow and I stand so he doesn't see the roll of my eyes.

"Besides, sleeping together? That's something actual married couples would do."

"We were an actual married couple and didn't sleep together." He laces his fingers and puts them between his head and the pillow, watching me as I adjust my clothes. They're still on, for the most part. Just a bit tugged askew from his eager hands.

"We were hardly an actual married couple." I shrug. "You married me for a book. And I resented you for it as much as I could."

"How far did that resentment get you?"

I scrunch my nose at him. "I think I liked you better when I was kissing you. You were silent then."

He's a blur of movement, kneeling on the bed before me, taking my hands. "I could resume kissing you if it would encourage you to stay."

"I'm tired." I pull my hands away with a slight laugh.

"Then come back to me tomorrow."

"I'll think about it." I doubt I will. I've succumbed to the urge. I've filled this need. There's no reason to ever do this again.

"My door is unlocked for you whenever you desire, or should you change your mind about tonight."

"I won't change my mind about tonight, and we'll see about tomorrow. I'm not your lover, after all." I still as my eyes snag on the crown of flowers. It must've fallen off the first time when he laid me back. He might be a king, but that will be the only crown he could ever give me. Pointless. Condemned to rot. Discarded by dawn.

I ignore it, going only for the door. It'd be dangerous to accept too many gifts from him. He'd get the wrong idea. The flower crown stays on the floor. His remains on his head, somehow still there even after all our indulgences.

"You could be my lover, if you wanted. It's not uncommon for kings."

I freeze. As if that would be appealing to me. "That's the *last* thing I want."

"Why do you resist all notions of love so fervently?"

The question gives me pause. I stare into a dark corner of the room. Every memory of Joyce rises to the forefront of my mind. Her torture. Her candy-coated words to my father.

My father's weak excuses, time and again. His explanations. *Katria... I was lost in an abyss that she saved me from. You will never understand the wound the death of your mother left...* Oh, I understood. I understood Joyce sold him lies and he bought them up faster than the silver from her mines.

Just like I understood how it became easier for Father with time to be on her side. The older I got, the more I looked like Mother. The harder it was for him to be around me. All the while, my home became a crumbling remnant of bygone days. Lost forever for what?

Ah, *love*.

"Because love is pain," I whisper.

"Love is life."

I glare at him and snap, "What would you know—a runaway prince locked in a tower who buys the only wife he's ever had?"

Davien's eyes widen a fraction, but instead of anger, his brow furrows into something that looks like focus. Sympathy radiates off of him. "What makes you say love is pain?"

I don't answer, focused only on my escape route. With a flap of wings summoned in a blink and a shimmer of magic, he's in front of me, hand holding the door shut just as I go to open it. I glare up at him.

"Let me out."

"Why do you think love, of all things, is pain?"

"I have seen what happens when two people fall in love. One collapses into the other, all sense of self, and worth, and strength crumbling under the boot of the party who ends up on top." Like the statue of my father that I had built in my mind, strong and resolute, turning to dust the moment Joyce entered our lives. "I have heard the bitter fights, the barbs, the hate that is slung and smoothed over in the name of *love*, precious love."

"None of that is love," he whispers.

I roll my eyes. "Love isn't like the storybooks. It's a transaction at best."

"No." Davien takes a step forward, encroaching on my personal space. "Love is the closest thing we have to meaning in this world. The love of a mother for her children, the love between friends, the love of a husband and wife, love for who we are and all those who strove before us to hand us the world we have now—love is why we live, why we fight, why we carry on when things get tough…it is not always easy. But it is our reprieve from true hardship, not the hardship itself."

"You lie," I seethe.

"Katria…" He trails off, eyes searching me. "What happened to you before you came to my home?"

"Let me pass."

"I'm trying to—"

"Let me pass!" My voice raises a fraction and he steps aside quickly.

I yank the door before he can say anything else, storming out and barely resisting the urge to slam it in his face.

I lay in bed well past the sun the next morning. Footsteps echo down the hall as the world wakes around me. I wonder who else stays here—Shaye and Giles seem to. Oren, likely. Hol has his own home. Vena and her advisers, maybe?

My breath catches as a familiar gait traverses the hall. His steps seem to slow at my door, all but coming to a stop. How do I know him by his walk? Can I really smell him from here? Or is my mind dredging up memories of last night? Or, far more likely, does my skin still smell like his?

Davien keeps walking.

I keep replaying the night in my mind, but it doesn't make any more sense the more hours that pass. I toss and turn. Not sleeping. But not feeling like I'm awake either. I'm trapped in those moments we shared. Moments that should have never transpired, but somehow did.

Why did I kiss him? Why did I let him kiss me? How did I end up in his bed?

I groan and roll over, tangling myself in the sheets. I ache from head to toe. I thought kissing him would relieve this tension but it has only made it worse.

When I can no longer bear the heat from stewing in my thoughts, I finally get up. The best thing I can do is confront Davien. The sooner we're together, the sooner things will feel as though we're back to normal. We can shrug off whatever happened last night as the oddity it was and move along.

"It's normal, really. Two people, our age, obviously attracted to each other. These things *happen*. There's no reason to read into it or make matters awkward. The itch was scratched, we're done," I murmur to myself, trying to find my own encouragement as I dress.

The flowing fae fashions are no longer odd to me. I'm more and more accustomed to showing my shoulders and arms than ever before, though I'm still mindful of my back. I wonder what my sisters would think if they could see me now, flowing sleeves and plunging necklines I'd never dare to wear back home. I stop and stare in the mirror. My skin is bright and dewy. My cheeks are rosy and lips full. The longer I stay here, the more and more I look as though I am a part of this world.

I wonder if there could be a way I'd never have to go back. If the king's magic can keep me, a human, alive here, then maybe there's something Davien could do for me that would allow me to stay and live out the rest of my natural life. I frown at myself.

What am I thinking? Live out my life here? In Midscape? Among fae and their magics? What place is there for a human like me? None.

Moreover, that would mean I'd have to live out my days in the same world as Davien. I'd have to watch him become king, watch him marry and sire heirs from afar. Or worse, as a lover relegated to the auxiliary corners of his life. No…a life back in the human world would be far better than that. In fact, being a world away from him might not be enough.

I emerge from my room and head downstairs. To my surprise, Hol, Shaye, Giles, and Oren are all clustered at the usual table. Maps are scattered between them, dotted with scraps of paper that look like memos exchanged by pigeon. They all look at me at once.

"Vena wanted you," Oren says. "Davien is already there."

I hesitate, picking up on a strange feeling in the air. "Is everything all right?"

"Yes. Go on." Oren tries to give me a reassuring smile but there's too much worry twinging his black eyes.

Dread fills me as I stand before Vena's doors. I hesitate just a second, seeing if I can overhear any talking from within. But the doors are too thick. I give a knock.

"Enter," Vena calls.

Sure enough, I find Vena and Davien within. But they're not alone. The Butcher from before, Allor, is there as well. She leans against one of the walls to the side, arms folded.

"What's happened?" I ask as they stare at me. My eyes lock with Davien's. Worry twists his face, scrunching his brow. A terrible silence continues to tighten the muscles in my chest to the point that it hurts to breathe.

"Well if neither of you are going to tell her, I'll—" Allor starts.

"King Boltov is sending an army to Dreamsong." Davien's rumbling voice only makes the words more ominous.

"What?" I inhale sharply.

"Word has finally reached him that I've returned...and that you are with me."

"Does he know of the magic?" I whisper.

"He knows everything."

"There was a spy among us." Vena curses. "He must have slipped through our wards at the beginning of the celebrations to deliver word."

"What does this mean?" I had prepared myself all morning to face Davien, but not like this. While I was dancing last night, a king was plotting my death.

"It means the king knows you have the magic he needs to never be challenged again." Allor wears a wicked smile when she speaks. "So he's coming to kill you for it."

And here I thought the worst of my problems today was facing Davien.

twenty-two

"WHAT DO WE DO NOW?" I look between each of them.

"We've been working on a plan," Davien says. His calmness is unexpectedly grating.

"I hope it's a good one because I've no interest in dying."

"I have no interest in seeing you die." The muscles in his cheeks tense. "Besides, the king doesn't care about *you*, he cares about the magic within you. The sooner we get the magic out, the sooner you'll be safe."

"Then I take it we've made progress on that front?" I look from Vena to Allor and back.

"We have an idea."

I'd like something more secure sounding than "an idea" but if it's the best we have right now... "Which is?"

"To the north of us, right at the edge of the mer folk's borders, is the Lake of Anointing," Vena says. "It is where all the old kings went before their coronation to bathe in the waters closest to the Ancestral Tree at the world's edge. If there's anything that's going to connect you enough with the king's power to pass it to Davien, it's those waters."

Ancestral Trees, world's edge. I gloss over the elements that don't seem to matter critically to keeping me alive. "Doesn't Boltov think we'll be heading there?"

"He won't if I tell him you're hunkering down here." Allor shrugs.

"You have so much sway over the king." I press my lips together to keep from scowling.

"I do what I can. He has no reason not to trust me."

"Will you tell him that Davien and I are bracing for attack here?" Her earlier remark could've been some clever fae side-stepping.

"Of course I will." She smiles wider. "Do you have any reason to doubt me?"

"Enough, both of you." Davien sounds agitated.

I shoot him a glare. But he's right. We have other, pressing matters. And even if Allor isn't a real ally, there's very little I'm going to be able to do about it to prove to them differently. That much has been made clear to me.

"Will Boltov be guarding the Lake?" I ask.

"It wouldn't be worth the manpower to him. The path there isn't easy. It was part of the trials of aspiring kings to traverse the haunted fogs—a rite of passage."

"Oh, there's also *haunted fogs* to get to the magic lake without dying at the hands of Butchers. Lovely." I fold my arms.

"If you have a better plan I'd love to hear it." Davien crosses his arms as well, head cocked to the side, staring down at me. Why does his smugness somehow make him both more frustrating and attractive in equal measure?

"You know I don't."

"Then it's settled. You go and tell Boltov that we've been alerted to the movements of his armies and are bracing ourselves here for the attack, fortifying Dreamsong's barriers," he says to Allor. Then, he faces Vena. "Please prepare everything we might need for our journey, and then focus on readying Dreamsong for whatever Boltov might bring on our doorstep."

Vena rests her hand on Davien's bicep. "What our people need to protect us is a king—a true king, reunited with the trio of Aviness's powers. Worry not for Dreamsong and focus on regaining your birthright, Davien. Return to us a conqueror."

"I shall." Davien stands a little taller.

"When do we leave?" I ask.

"As soon as we can." Davien makes his way toward me. To my surprise, he takes my hand in his. I can't stop the flush that rises to my cheeks at the unexpected touch. Him doing so publicly somehow feels even more intimate and desperate. "There's not a moment to spare."

Within the hour, four horses have been tacked. Their saddlebags are full of supplies that are only just finished being loaded as we emerge into the square. Hol and Oren have opted to stay behind and help defend Dreamsong—Oren will focus on finishing the evacuation tunnel and Hol will help the city guard. So it is just Shaye, Giles, Davien, and myself on the road.

The afternoon sun shines happily on the oblivious city. People are still going about their daily affairs as though nothing is amiss. The square is still set up for celebrations. There's no sign of the impending battle.

"When will Vena tell them?" I ask Davien as we descend the short stair to where the horses are waiting.

"When the time is right." Davien swings up into his saddle somewhat clumsily and it takes four adjustments until he's found a comfortable seat. His horse is a speckled gray stallion. A strong boy whose muscles speak of good breeding and even better stable hands. Were it not for the intensity the horse exudes, he would remind me of Misty.

"And when will that be?" I ask, trying to push thoughts of my long-lost mount from my mind. I hope with all the money my family gained they found enough to spare to take care of her. Maybe when I return I could take some of the coin Davien left me in that house and go and purchase my horse from them.

Maybe when I return I'll just steal Misty in the night. No one knows the stables and grounds better than I. And after spending weeks surviving in the fae wilds…the thought of confronting my family, or thieving from under their noses, is far less frightening than it might have been months ago. Old gods, maybe I'll be brave enough to just tell them I'm taking Misty and say to Laura, *come with me.*

"That's not for us to worry about." He motions to the all-white mare at his side. "We just need to focus on getting to the Lake of Anointing as fast as possible. It'll be a hard ride for two days to make it there. Do you need help getting up on your horse?"

I snort. Did he mistake my checking the horse's saddle and bridle for uncertainty about riding? He'll certainly be in for a surprise today. "I think I'll be fine."

I put my foot in the stirrup with confidence and swing up. The saddle is broken in and well-worn in all the right places, but still strong and of quality make. I give the horse a pat on the neck then take the reins with an easy grip. I don't know this mount as well as Misty. For all my confidence, I should also still be careful. Last thing I want is to spook the girl, or push her too hard, and be thrown.

"Are we ready?" Shaye asks. "Daylight is burning."

"Lead on." Davien nods.

Shaye clicks her tongue and charges into the city with Giles close beside her. Davien hesitates when I don't. As I pass him, I can't stop myself from flashing him the smallest of smirks. He catches it. His eyes widen slightly and his mouth purses. He snaps the reins, causing his horse to startle and whinny.

I turn ahead with a laugh. He'll figure it out. He's a prince, after all.

The rogue thought catches me off guard. *He's a prince*, my mind repeats. I've always known that he is. But the closer we become, somehow the harder it is to imagine. I glance back over my shoulder. His hair is tousled by the wind, catching the sunlight with almost liquid shine. To think that a few hours ago I ran my fingers through that hair…that I kissed those lips.

I look ahead again, tearing my eyes from him before my stomach can do so many flips that it becomes uneasy. I let Dreamsong blur around me, not focusing on the houses or their incredible construction for the first time as I traverse the streets. "Last night was nothing," I repeat only to myself.

No feelings. That's what we promised. Last night was nothing more than a release of the tension that has been building between us for weeks. There's no need to overthink it. No need to complicate it. No need to feel guilty now. It can be just that—a fun escape, an indulgence. It was so much nothing that it's not even worth talking about.

If I feel anything, it's only that I won't be able to indulge in that escape for much longer. Soon, if Vena is right, the magic will be out of me. After that happens, I'll need to leave Midscape as quickly as possible before the withering begins.

Davien and I were never meant to be. He's the fae king and I won't let myself fall in love. The fact that I found even a brief enjoyment with him is enough. *It's enough*, I repeat to myself, more insistently than before. Yet for some reason, the thought can't seem to settle in my mind. It keeps chasing me and I ride faster and faster, as if I'm trying to outrun it.

We break away from the city, cresting the peak of the valley that Dreamsong is nestled within. We're back into the forests now, magic fluttering in the air around us. I can go even faster here; I'm not constrained by the streets or the people on them. I weave between trees as I grow more and more comfortable with my horse.

"Are you trying to lead the way?" Giles calls with a laugh.

"Certainly not," I shout back.

"You seem like you're trying to race us."

"If I knew where we were going, I would be inclined to race." I slow my pace to hold a conversation, trotting over to where Shaye and Giles are still riding together. Davien has mostly caught up since we left the city.

"You're fairly comfortable on a horse for a noble lady," Shaye observes.

"I don't know if I would call myself noble," I say with a small smile. "My father was the first lord in our family tree. He only attained it because of his luck trading." My smile falls and I stare across the golden and red expanse of the forest. "And when that luck ran out...so did everything that came with lordship except for the title."

Shaye stares at me for a long minute. There's a deep understanding in her eyes—a thoughtfulness that most people lack. I don't feel seen in the same way that I feel with Davien. It isn't as though she's peering into my deepest thoughts and darkest corners. No... There's almost a subtle acknowledgment with Shaye. As though she sees and recognizes pain, just as I can see and recognize it in her, even though our pain is different and unique.

"Did you take riding lessons before the luck ran out?"

"No, though I did manage to get a horse as a gift. One of the only things my father gave me. I had to take care of her, see to all of her needs. But the stable hand we had was kind enough to teach me the basics of riding. After that, I taught myself by escaping early in the morning." I stare intently at the point where the faintly glowing motes begin to obscure the trees in the distance. "I would ride, and ride until I was at the very edge of my small world...and at that point, I fantasized about keeping on. About riding to a place far out of reach from them."

"I suppose you succeeded." Giles laughs. He's a lighthearted one and seems oblivious to the pain lingering underneath my words that Shaye so clearly picks up on. "After all, you're riding pretty far from them now, in a place that they will never get you."

I laugh softly. *If only I could stay here.* The thought crosses my mind so naturally that it takes me a full three seconds to be caught off guard by it. It's not the first time I've had this sort of musing. So it's not surprise that's alarming me. It's how natural the want has become.

"Is that the horse you wanted to keep?" Davien asks. I don't recall when he got so close. He's now on the other side of me, and I'm sandwiched between him and Shaye. "Oren told me that there was a point of contention the day you left about a horse."

"Her name is Misty," I say. "My father only ever gave me two things—my mother's lute, which was more of an inheritance from her than a gift from him, and Misty. My sisters don't even ride." Though, Laura did say she'll do her best. "She'll be wasted there."

"Maybe when you go back you can retrieve her."

I laugh. "Funny enough, I was thinking the same thing just earlier. I thought that if I can have magic within me, if I can cross the Fade, and dine with fae, then what do I have to fear from my family?" Yet even as I say those words, there's still a scared little girl within me, fearful of whatever punishment Joyce might concoct next.

"Very little, I would think." Giles chuckles.

Davien continues to regard me thoughtfully. With him on one

side and Shaye on the other, I've nowhere to hide my thoughts or emotions.

"Perhaps, once this is all over, and the dust has settled, I can make a trip back to the Natural World and help you reclaim Misty. Having the magic of the Fae King would prove valuable in any sort of caper." He grins slightly. I can't stop my face from splitting into a smile. The thought of the two of us, sneaking through the night, breaking into my family's old home, and taking something from them after they took so much from me is a sweeter fantasy than I could've ever imagined previously.

"Or, His Majesty might want to send his loyal vassals to assist her," Shaye says formally, giving Davien a pointed look. "After all, you will be busy enough settling into the throne and making sure no one wants to take it from you. It wouldn't be wise to leave."

"The fae aren't accustomed to keeping their leader long, after all." Giles sighs. "It's been ages since our land has known stability."

"All that will change with me," Davien vows. "And I believe I will have enough time, power, and energy to help both my people *and* Katria."

The image of a scale appears in my mind. All of the fae—his entire kingdom—is on one side, and I'm on the other. Yet somehow, those scales are not so far out of balance that I am tipped into oblivion. Davien is still considering me and my well-being. Perhaps he spoke true when he said that he would make an effort to come and visit me. Maybe that wasn't a careful dance of fae words.

"I suppose time will tell." Shaye's words are as uncomfortable as she suddenly looks in her saddle. She keeps casting sidelong glances in Davien's direction. There's something on her mind and I have no inclination of being here whenever she gets it off her chest.

"What's our plan?" I ask, trying to change the topic.

"There's a safe house right at the northern edge of our borders— due north of here. We'll ride there today and rest. It's still within the barriers of the Acolytes of the Wild Wood, so we can spend the night in relative safety. Then tomorrow we'll wake with the dawn and ride hard into the northern forests, through the fogs, until we reach the Lake of Anointing at the northernmost point of the fae wilds."

"Understood." I lean forward, looking at Giles around Shaye.

"Then I think it sounds like we have time for a race. What do you think?"

Giles bites. "I think my horse is larger than yours and of better breeding."

"Too bad that's not going to make up for me being the superior rider," I taunt. "I'll race you to the safe house. Last one to get there is in charge of dinner."

Giles roars with laughter. "Either way you're going to lose because I'm a wretched cook. But you have a deal. Shaye, will you count us off?"

Shaye sighs, as though she is indulging two children. But she counts anyway. "Three. Two. One!"

Giles and I are off. I leave Shaye and Davien behind me, along with all of the uncomfortable thoughts that they inadvertently dredged up. I let my mind go blank as the wind pulls at my hair and clothes, pricking tears in the corners of my eyes. Giles was wrong. No matter what, I win. Because I get to ride as fast as I want through the magic woods of the fae.

Even when those thoughts are trying to weigh me down…when I ride like this, I feel like I am the one with wings. I feel as if I am soaring.

As Davien explained when we first set out, the trip is going to take two days. So our race ends up being more of an endurance challenge. Our initial pace slows to a good trot and we end up side by side.

"This isn't much of a race," he chuckles.

"Most races are won at the start, or very end. The middle is just keeping pace." I wink.

"I'm not sure that's how racing works."

I laugh. "You're probably right. I've never raced someone before." These are exciting and new perks of having genuine friends.

"A pity, because you are a very good rider."

"Thank you." I preen a little, allowing myself to savor the compliment. "I think all of you are the first people to ever see me ride."

"Not even your family?"

"They might have seen me toward the end of my morning rides, or at a distance... I had to have their breakfast ready not long after dawn. So they were usually asleep when I went out in the mornings and still when I returned."

Giles is silent for a long stretch. I can almost hear his thoughts. I sigh. "Go ahead, ask whatever it is you're debating."

"I'm not—"

"I can feel it." Much in the same way I could feel Helen's thoughts as she mused over what the best way to torture me next was.

"Davien didn't tell us much about your circumstances. In fact, we knew very little about you before you came into our world."

"That makes sense." Especially given how they treated me when I first arrived—with such skepticism, almost outright anger. After having some time to see Davien and his loyal companions, it's clearer to me now. I was a loose end, a liability. I barged into his life in a way that he never wanted and they had no idea that I felt very much the same. Then I "stole" his magic. I had very few things that would've encouraged them to like me.

"But he did tell us that you were a noble lady." Giles chuckles softly. "Hol was very concerned about the idea of our future king marrying a common-born woman."

I grin bitterly. "I was common born...and whatever title or esteem I do possess I'm certain is not high enough to merit my marrying of a king. Not that it matters, since we're not considered married in your world." As has been made so abundantly clear to me.

"Yes, that did ease Hol some."

"But that's not what you wanted to ask me, is it?"

"No." Giles purses his lips, thinking to himself, before finally asking, "you don't have a very good relationship with your family, do you?"

"What gave it away?" I laugh. "The fact that they sold my hand in marriage off to pay debts and fund their parties once more? The fact that I have not had one good thing to say about them since arriving?"

"The fact that you tense up, your voice changes, and your eyes lose focus on the present, whenever they're mentioned."

I stare at him, gaping. I can feel my lips are parted, but it takes me a moment to gain my composure enough to close them. "And here I thought I was good at concealing my emotions and thoughts."

"You are, I think at least. Shaye was the one to notice. Davien as well. But he always seemed to know you better from the time you spent together before you came here."

I suppose I wasn't the only one listening those nights we spent together, paying attention to what the other said. "What's your point?"

"If you're worried about them hurting you, Davien has made it clear that no one will ever bring harm to you—not as long as he draws breath."

"What?" I whisper.

"He's already charged us with the responsibility of guarding you."

"Because I am the vessel that carries his magic."

"No, even after the magic is removed. He made his wishes *very* clear. When you return to the human world, we will come and check in on you regularly. For the rest of your days, or as long as you want it, you will have his protection."

I shift uncomfortably in my saddle. The afternoon is suddenly too hot, even though winter is trying to slip under my riding cloak. He wants to protect me—not just the magic in me. He wants to protect *me*. I don't know how to process this feeling. Why is it easier to handle the thought of him seeing me only as a vessel than of him seeing me as a person?

"What is it?" Giles asks softly.

"Nothing." I shake my head but the thoughts stick to the inside of my skull. I can't escape them.

He levels his eyes with mine. "You're crying."

I raise a trembling hand to my cheek, touching its swell lightly. Sure enough, there's moisture there. My breath quivers, snagging on emotions that threaten to strangle me.

"Why is it that it is so much easier for me to process being treated like a thing than a person? How is it that the latter hurts more?" I blurt.

Giles blinks several times over. His brows arch upward, knitting together in the middle. I can't stand his pity already.

"Because now you know this is how you should have been treated all along. Because you know that if one person sees you, respects you as they should, then there's no excuse for anyone else not to. The fault does not lie—has never lain—with *you*, but rather the shortcomings of those you have been surrounded by. You were always worthy."

"I—" I choke on my words. I shake my head and stare forward. "We've forgotten we're racing. I'm not going to let you distract me so I go easy on you."

"I wasn't trying to distract you. Katria—"

I don't hear whatever he says. With a kick and shift of my weight I'm off again through the woods, running like I did every morning at my home from all the thoughts that threaten to smother me.

twenty-three

UNSURPRISINGLY, I'M THE FIRST TO ARRIVE AT THE SAFE HOUSE.
At least, I presume it's the safe house. I haven't seen any
other structures for hours since we left Dreamsong.

The "house" is more of a hut that's one large room.
There's a small firepit in the center, black coals resting on
a bed of sand. A pot hangs from the ceiling over it, several
other rudimentary cooking elements and supplies racked
around. Bunk beds line the walls to the right and left.

There are no mattresses on the beds, just solid wooden
boards. It's odd to see anything less than supremely lavish
for the fae. An investigation of the trunks at the foot of one
of the bunks reveals a stash of blankets. Another trunk has
an assortment of various supplies from preserved rations
to what I can only presume are medical supplies and ritual
resources.

I see no point in sitting around while I wait for everyone
to arrive, so I head behind the house to a well I saw when
I entered. With two buckets of water, I fill a large, tapped
keg for drinking. A third bucket is split between the pot that
hangs over the firepit and a small basin for washing up.

As suspected, there are fire-starting tools among the
cookery supplies. It takes two tries, but I manage to get the
coals to ignite. It's not a very large fire, but it's warm, and the
coals don't put off much smoke.

The door opens and reveals Giles, interrupting my peace.

"I thought I was supposed to be the one cooking? I lost the race after all."

"Unless we're eating boiled water for dinner, there's still plenty of cooking for you to do."

"Mmm, boiled water, my favorite." He rubs his stomach. I laugh. "It's good to hear you laugh. Earlier I—"

"Don't worry about it."

"No, I do, I upset you—and I certainly didn't intend to—so I want to apologize."

"I said don't worry about it." I poke at the coals.

"But—"

I'm saved by the arrival of Davien and Shaye. The whinny of their horses distracts Giles from whatever was he was going to say next. I stand and return my poker to its peg.

"As far as I'm concerned, that conversation was left far behind us in the woods. Leave it there, Giles," I say lightly enough, but with a note of caution. Giles and I are fine and I hope he allows us to remain that way by not insisting on lingering.

He regards me thoughtfully but doesn't have a chance to respond before Davien and Shaye enter.

"Thank goodness you started a fire, the air was already getting a brutal chill to it," Davien says.

"Which means we should go and figure out food," Giles says to Shaye.

"*We?*" She lifts her eyebrows.

"Yes, we. I lost the race against Katria."

"I fail to see how your poor gamble results in me also having to cook," Shaye balks.

"Because you don't want to eat anything I cook unsupervised." Giles grabs her elbow and heads toward the door. Shaye's feet move begrudgingly. "Come on, let's do some scavenging and hunting before the sun is completely down."

"Fine, fine," Shaye agrees.

Davien chuckles as the door closes behind them. "Those two are such an unlikely match. Yet whenever I see them together, I can't help but smile."

"So they are together then?" I'd had a growing suspicion.

"They try and hide it." Davien shrugs. "But yes, Giles has only had eyes for her since he first came to Dreamsong. At least that's what Hol tells me...and what I saw whenever the two of them were together in the Natural World."

"And Shaye? Does she return these feelings?" There must be some reason that they generally keep themselves at a distance in public, or are modest about their affections.

"She does, though she's taking her own time with it all. Shaye..." Davien crosses over to the fire and sits next to it, clearly debating his words. I sit once more. I can't bring myself to sit on the opposite side of the fire from him even though I know it would be for the best. I can feel his radiant warmth across the narrow gap between us. He finally finds his words. "Shaye has lived a difficult life."

"She told me some... that she was born to be a Butcher."

"Like all Butchers, she was trained to fight from the moment she could walk. For the first fifteen years of her life, she never knew a scrap of kindness. She never knew people could be gentle or trusted. When she first arrived in Dreamsong, she didn't even know what love looked like." The smoldering coals illuminate Davien's face more than the fading light of the sun as it quickly disappears on the other side of the mountains. "Giles was patient with her; he still is. He's told me that he's in no hurry and the best are always worth the wait."

"He seems like a good man." I draw my knees to my chest, hugging them. He meant well in the woods. He just...doesn't understand.

"He is. But then again, I try and only keep the company of good men and women."

"So how did you end up married to me?" I ask with a laugh.

"Because I think you are the best woman of them all." Davien looks me directly in the eyes as he says it. There's no hiding from him. His truths are relentless and catch me off guard at every turn.

"Then I guess you don't know me very well," I say softly.

"I think I know you better than you want me to."

"How?"

"How does anyone learn anything? I paid attention. I listened while you sang. I heard the melodies you played from the heart. I watched your movements with more attention than I ever gave to the studies that would help me assume the crown."

"You lie." My voice is a whisper now, incapable of anything stronger.

"I wish I could." He grins, lips highlighted in red by the coals. "But you know I can't." Davien leans forward, shifting onto his knees. He almost prowls toward me, erasing the gap between us with slow, deliberate movements. I lean backward, palms splayed on the wooden floor behind me. He's hunting me, like a beast of shadow and firelight. He kills the space between us. With a glance he strikes me between the ribs. I'm helpless. "My every thought returns to you. You are like a whirlwind, down and down I spin, every time, until I'm caught in your center. Now, I know there is only one way to escape."

"And how is that?" I'm framed by his arms as he supports himself above me. One knee is between my legs, shifting as he moves forward.

"To give in, to stop fighting, and see where you take me."

His lips crash on mine with a force that pushes me back in a mirror of how he had me the night before. My arms fly up and wrap around his neck for stability. He holds me to him with one hand, the other supporting both of us. I feel the strength of him above me, around me, protecting me. I groan softly as my body arches toward him without command.

How did we end up here? Wasn't I thinking earlier about how I could never allow this to happen again and that it was nothing more than an itch? Why is he kissing me now? Why do I want it all so badly?

They're questions I can't answer because my mind is blank, yet for the first time my heart feels full.

Slowly, he eases me down to the floor, never breaking the kiss. His tongue runs along my lips and I grant him entry. The second I do he probes in gentle exploration. I further deepen the kiss, acting in kind.

In these moments, there are no thoughts. I no longer worry about what is and what might be, what could or couldn't be. I don't fear for the future and what it might hold for me in that lonely house back in the Natural World, protected from everything, separate from everyone.

There's only him, his heat, his life. He exhales, I inhale, and we breathe in tandem. My world narrows to consist only of him—his one hand in my hair, the other on my breast.

I dig my hands into the folds of his shirt, tugging. All of our clothes are suddenly tight and ill fitting. There's more to the want that drives me. I haven't had enough of him yet. I want to expose him. I want to kiss until we are broken and breathless and glorious in the night.

His mouth leaves mine, heaving breaths ragged. "We should stop, love."

The word is a bucket of ice water crashing over me. I stare up at him, grip weakening on his clothes. He must see the horror in my face because there is a flash of panic in his eyes.

"You said—"

"It is a mere expression," he murmurs, leaning forward to slide his lips over mine once more, as though he intends to silence my already racing thoughts with a mere kiss. "Don't read into it."

Did you mean it, though?

The question doesn't escape me. It fills me with too much panic. I push him off, scrambling to collect myself.

"Katria…"

I can't face him. I wrap my arms around me and hold myself tightly, nails digging into my triceps. "We made a deal," I finally whisper.

"Nothing but entertainment. I remember."

"No feelings."

"I remember," he repeats.

"Are you keeping up your end of the deal?" I finally face him.

Davien's lips part slightly. "I am trying."

Trying? But are you succeeding? Yet another question I can't bring myself to ask. Not when he must tell the truth.

I push off the ground and sway as I stand. Yet again, I'm leaving him while sorting my clothes and feeling a mixture of confused and terribly unsatisfied. How many times must I indulge in this urge before it's satiated? This need he fills me with is a relentless beast, charging through my thoughts, consuming me with one giant bite after the next.

"Katria." He murmurs my name and rests his hands on my shoulders, running them down my arms. His fingertips on my bare forearms shoot tingles through me that go straight to my head. I almost tip my head back to expose my neck so that he may bite it.

"Davien…" I sigh his name like a soft prayer. I've never believed in the old gods the elderly in town pay homage to. But if I'd paid more attention to them I'd bet they'd have a name like him.

"You think too much." Sure enough, he kisses the exposed skin of my neck.

"One of us has to."

"Let yourself go; give yourself to me."

I shiver and he pulls me back to him with a tug. I'm enveloped once more. His hands sliding over me. His mouth on the soft flesh of my neck. That is, until the door latch is undone.

Davien releases me in a second, pushing me away lightly. He's collected and composed as I'm scrambling to re-sort my clothes again. Luckily, we didn't manage to get too far this time.

"What did you find?" Davien asks casually.

"Hare, nettle, some wild mushrooms." Giles holds up a hare and a plump bag.

"We're not interrupting anything, are we?" Shaye misses nothing.

"I love wild mushrooms," I say quickly.

"Good, then you can cook them." Giles grins, but it falls quickly when Shaye gives him a jab with her elbow.

"You lost your bet; you're cooking. It's time you refined some skills. A bachelor like you can't survive forever on the charity of others."

"Maybe I'll find myself a lovely wife to cook for me?" Giles waggles his eyebrows.

"Good luck with that." Shaye crosses to the fire pit, but her eyes keep darting between Davien and me.

"I'm going to go and check on the horses. Make sure they're sorted for the night." I make my escape before a red flush creeps up my neck and gives me away.

Alone, I take a breath, allowing the night's chill to brace me as the door shuts. I head back to the well, drawing up a bucket for our steeds. My reflection stares back at me in the water.

"What are you doing?" I ask the rippling woman. This is a magical place. Maybe she'll answer? Maybe she'll have better luck sorting through these feelings than I. My reflection is silent. "A lot of help you are."

I sigh and make my way to the posts the horses are tied to. They're lazily grazing the tall grasses that poke through the moss without a care in the world. One by one, I let them drink from the bucket and, when they've had their fill, I return to the well and draw one more to leave out for them. By now, the smell of roasting hare and wild mushrooms sauteing in drippings is becoming almost unbearable.

Hushed conversation within has me pausing at the door.

"...answer my question," Shaye says curtly.

"I already have." Davien's tone is lazy and almost hides the agitation beneath his words.

"You've dodged it at every turn."

"I have not."

"What do you feel for Katria?" Shaye demands plainly, making my heart jolt.

"I made a promise that I would not feel anything."

"I don't care about a promise you made with yourself when she came to live under your roof, or one you made to us." Shaye sounds exasperated.

"Leave him be." Giles sighs over the clanking of cooking tools. "He can feel what he wants for our human friend; I rather like her."

"And I want to know if that feeling is love." Shaye is a dog with a bone, there's no way she's giving this up. "Do you love her?"

I lean into the door slightly, pressing my ear against the cool wood, and hold my breath. *No*, I want to scream, *say no*. If he doesn't love me, things remain uncomplicated. It means I haven't made a mistake. If he doesn't love me then—

"I do," Davien says. I slowly slide down the door to my knees. Covering my mouth, I wheeze. My stomach clenches. I feel like my body is trying to turn itself inside out. I am my father's daughter after all my attempts to avoid his fate.

No, I will not make the same mistakes as him. Just because love is brewing for Davien doesn't mean anything for me. I will not be taken in by these affections. I will not indulge my desires with him any longer. I will give him the magic and be gone before he traps me into a life of misery like Joyce trapped my father.

"You know—"

"I know." Davien cuts off Shaye curtly. "I know that she and I could never be together. However I might care for her makes no difference. I will get the magic from her and I will send her away."

"Your Majesty…" Giles says softly, almost sadly, even though Davien is talking the most sense he possibly could be. There's nothing to be sad about. He clearly knows the lines.

"In time, I'm sure she will mean nothing to me and this will be little more than an infatuation. I will find a proper queen. And I will be free of this hold Katria has placed upon me." Davien's words become more forceful with every sentence. "She will become nothing to me."

There's not a whiff of smoke. Every word he said is the truth.

twenty-four

Dawn filters through the windows of the safe house. Giles stokes the coals in the pit, bringing them to a low fire once more. But the sound of him clanking is distant and dulled. All I can seem to focus on is Davien's soft breathing in the bunk above me.

My eyes open and close slowly, each time shorter than the last as I slowly wake in a dream-like haze. The fae used their magic to turn blankets and weeds into plush bedding that has transformed the wooden bunks into a bed as comfortable as what I had back in Dreamsong.

But I'm not distracted with wonder of their magic. That has become normal. What is definitely not normal are Davien's words still echoing in my mind. They bounce off the memories of my parents that I've tried to pack away into neat little boxes that I never want to open.

Do you love her?

I do.

He loves me. I close my eyes with a wince. This is the pain I've been trying to shield myself from my whole life. It's the start of the agony I watched my father endure for his love. Luckily, Davien is still working to spare us both. The sooner I'm gone, the sooner we're both free.

When Shaye bounces from her bunk, I know it's time to get moving. Davien has the same idea and he descends as I sit. At some point in the night he lost his shirt. Every bulging muscle I felt underneath his clothes is now on display. The gray dawn highlights them in streaks of light and shadow.

Our eyes meet as my gaze trails up his body. His lips part slightly. I wonder if he's thinking of kissing me again. I wonder if his confession to Shaye has cast me in a new light, because I certainly see him differently. I've never been more painfully aware of his sheer presence—he assaults my senses, forcing them into submission to the point that he is all I'm able to focus on.

"Good morning." His voice is husky from the night.

"Morning." I break away while I can and swing my legs off the bed. "I'm going to check on the horses, make sure they're good for the day."

"You're so dutiful. Thank you." Giles smiles.

"It's no problem." I make my escape as fast as I did last night. I can't look at Davien when he's only half-dressed.

The forest is quiet. The motes of light that are usually fluttering about during the day are still bedded down. They drift upward with each step I take, some still hovering in the air, others returning to the mossy ground for what I presume is a few more hours of sleep.

I check the horses' saddles and fetch them some fresh water. There's a hard day's ride again today. They should get hydrated while they can.

"I think I'm going to get a whole bunch of you when I go back to the human world," I say to my mount, giving her a pat on the nose while Davien's stallion drinks. "You're much simpler than people, or fae."

"But are they better conversation?"

The familiar voice has me frozen. I slowly turn to face the speaker. Sure enough, Allor is standing mere steps away from me, her shadowed form cut against the mist of morning.

"Depends on who I'm speaking to." The curtness of my tone does little to hide my discomfort at her presence.

A smug, cat-like grin spreads across her mouth, as if my displeasure is supremely satisfying. "I hope you enjoy speaking to me. I bring good tidings."

"Do you?"

"Yes, of course. I'm here to let you know that the king is collecting his forces for the attack on Dreamsong."

"And how is that good?"

"His focus is on Dreamsong and not on you." She sighs dramatically. "I really didn't think I'd have to spell this out."

Oh, she doesn't. I've already picked up on what she's trying to say. If King Boltov is drawing all his forces for an attack on Dreamsong, then what I think she wants me to assume is that he doesn't have people who would come after us. But why wouldn't she say as much outright if it were true?

"Do you think he will come and attack us?" I try and phrase my question as carefully as possible.

"I can't presume to know what the king will do."

"Guess."

Allor tips her head to the side slightly. It's a subtle quirk, one most might miss. I read it as annoyance.

"I'm just trying to figure out how much danger we might be in." I lay my ruse on thick, trying to look as worried as I'm able to muster.

"The king's focus is still on Dreamsong."

She's not answering. I'm on the cusp of all of my suspicions about her being justified. I can feel it. "Has he given any orders for others to pursue us?"

"I don't know everything he says or does."

"Does he have reason to suspect us?" I set down the bucket.

"I don't know the inner workings of his mind, either." Her hands ball into fists and then relax, as if she's forcing herself to remain calm.

"Will we be attacked when we leave these borders?"

"The world is a dangerous place."

"Why won't you answer me directly?" I demand, voice raising slightly. I don't give her a chance to reply. I go right for the proverbial throat with my questioning. "Yes or no—will the king send people to attack us once we leave the safety of the borders of the Acolytes of the Wild Wood?"

"I don't owe you any answers." Allor has gone quiet, her voice a deadly hush.

"No, you don't. But even if you did, you couldn't give them to me…because you *can't* lie and you *won't* tell the truth."

She smiles, her lips splitting to show her teeth. They're like Giles's—a little *too* sharp. "You don't trust me, do you, little human?"

"I don't think I have many good reasons to trust you. I don't think anyone should trust you."

"Careful about making threats you can't back up." Her eyes flash. Power seems to shimmer off of her shoulders, collecting around the shadowy cowl she wears.

This is the moment I would back off. If Allor was Joyce, I would cower. I would give up here and now because I had no power, no strength. Instead, I boldly take a step forward.

"I have the power of the kings of Aviness in me." I take another step. "I have power Boltov would—*has* killed thousands for." Another step, and another. Soon enough we're mere inches apart and my blood is boiling. There's a swell rolling. A tide that's about to crash down on both of us. "You wouldn't be the first fae who tried to end me. You might not be the last I kill for it, either."

"Do you think you can kill me?" Allor straightens slightly to look down at me. I gather my height as well. She tilts her head back and points at the vein bulging in her neck. "If you do, I'd recommend you strike here. Go right for the throat. Don't give me a chance to fight back. Because if you do…that'll be your last mistake."

"How dare—" I'm cut off by Davien emerging.

"Allor? What're you doing here?"

"I came to wish you luck on your passage today." Allor eases away from me with a smile. "All other messages I've left with Katria. I really should be going now." She jumps back into one of the long shadows cast by the trees and vanishes like smoke on the breeze.

"What was that about?" I didn't even hear Davien approach, but he's at my side. His hand is suddenly on the small of my back. I jump at the touch. "Katria? What's wrong?"

A lot. But I focus on the most important. "We should go back to Dreamsong."

A scowl crosses his lips. "You know we can't."

"I have a bad feeling about this." I grab Davien's shirt, ignoring how natural it feels to reach for him. My voice falls to a whisper. Allor could be anywhere. For all I know, she could have magic that allows her to listen to us from afar. Nowhere but Dreamsong feels safe and she can get to us even there. "We need to go back, circle the wagons, and stand together against Boltov. I'm certain that we can figure out a ritual there with a little more time." A ritual that Allor has no hand in.

"We have to keep going." He grabs my hands. "The sooner the magic is transferred from you to me, the sooner I'll be able to effectively use it to protect everyone."

"Don't you see? She's sending us away, beyond the wards, dividing us from the pack. I don't trust her." My grip tightens. "She's playing a game with us and she's going to win if we don't stay one step ahead."

"That's just the way Allor is. She has that air about her."

"Then she's 'just' someone we shouldn't be working with."

"We don't have a choice in that." He frowns. "I know you haven't liked her from the start but—"

"I think we're going to be attacked," I blurt.

"Why do you say that?" His eyes search mine, as if he's looking for a reason to believe me, as though he wants to…but wanting doesn't seem like it's enough and I feel my ribs crumble in on my heart at the realization.

"She couldn't give me a straight answer to my questions."

Davien chuckles. "That's just fae mannerisms."

"No." I hold him as he tries to step away, jerking him back toward me. "You weren't here to hear what I was asking. *How* I was asking." I wonder if Allor left without saying very much to Davien to sow this very doubt that's taking root. "I think she's a double agent and I think we're going to walk right where they want us. I asked her if the king was going to attack us—yes or no—and she wouldn't answer."

"That's Allor."

"Stop making excuses for her." My grip finally goes slack. I search his face, desperate for him to believe me. "Davien, who do you believe more? Her or me?"

He inhales but no words come. I stare up at him, expectant. I wait until I ache, until his silence is a weight that wounds me with slow, crushing force. He said he loved me, but he won't believe me. So what good is love? This is just further proof of what I've always known—love is good for nothing.

"I need the magic. Everything can be put right once I have it," he says, finally. "That is what Vena and all of Dreamsong wish for."

"And I want to give it to you but—"

"No buts. If you are truly on my side then you will help me. Now what did she say?"

"Just that the king's focus is on Dreamsong." I open my mouth to continue speaking but he ignores it, stepping away.

"We ride within the hour."

My hands ball into fists and that same feeling of magic overtaking my better sense returns. I breathe in through my nose and out through my mouth. Davien will never forgive me if I turn his magic on him.

One last attempt. "Davien, can we at least wait until tomorrow? Delay a little? Maybe by changing our schedule we can throw them off."

"There is nothing to throw off because there is no attack coming on us. Though we have all the more reasons to hurry."

"But—"

"I need my magic to protect Dreamsong and the more we delay the greater the risk. I have spoken on this and I am your *king*." His voice raises at the end to a near shout. Davien points at the ground, as though he is trying to stake the very earth as his own.

"No…" I shake my head. "You are not *my* king. You are the Fae King. And I am clearly nothing but a lowly human vessel housing your magic. So fine, we ride, Your Majesty. But if there is blood today then know it is on your hands."

I turn back to the horses and ignore him as he storms back into the safe house.

The border of the Acolyte's territory on the north is nothing more than a break in the trees. As the sun hits my shoulders, the same crawling feeling as the last time I crossed through the great barriers that surrounded the forests of Dreamsong inches up my back, causing shivers. On the other side, I am exposed and more alert than ever.

But there is just more forest ahead of us, at least until we reach a glassy lake. The trees on the other side are sparse, with moss hanging off their skeletal arms. The ground looks lower, wetter. More like a marsh than the firm earth we've been riding on for the past day and a half.

However, what is most notable is the wall of swirling fog that obscures even the sun. It's impossible to see more than one tree deep. *Anything* could hide in that milky mist.

"That's it, isn't it?" Davien says softly.

"The fog of histories, fog of kings, the rite of passage kings of lore traversed to be blessed in the ancient waters of the Lake of Anointing," Giles says as if reading from a storybook.

"So this isn't the Lake of Anointing?" I whisper to Giles. He shakes his head.

"I find rumors of haunted places to be greatly exaggerated." Shaye nudges her horse, guiding it around the lake. We three share a look and follow behind her. "Usually, it's just places someone wants to keep others from and doesn't know how to do it better than some silly story."

"It's not a silly story." Giles catches up to her. "Why do you think King Boltov never came to anoint himself?"

"Because he anointed himself in the blood of his enemies and didn't need a lake to validate his claim to the throne after that?" Shaye's words are dry and peppered with bitterness. I swallow thickly at the thought. My eyes are already scanning the mists for Allor. She could be *anywhere* in that murk. And she is just as bloodthirsty as the king I know she serves most faithfully.

"Because he knew that the fog would refuse to let him pass since he wasn't a legitimate heir of Aviness. He would be lost forever."

"We will have no such trouble," Davien proclaims.

"I hope we have no trouble at all," I say under my breath. None of them hear me. My mare whinnies and shakes her head. I pat her neck and give a soft shushing noise. "We might find it to be slow going through here."

"They'll calm once we get in the fog," Davien says confidently.

"I doubt that, unless horses are different in your world than mine."

"We don't have time to coddle them."

"I wasn't suggesting to coddle them," I mutter. There's something about this place that has me on edge too.

"We'll ride nose to tail so we keep visibility," Shaye suggests.

"And hopefully we don't encounter anything in the fog that would separate us." I see Giles's throat tighten as he swallows nervously. I wonder just what he thinks lies in wait for us on the other side of this magic mist.

"Just in case, take these." Shaye hands out compasses to each of us. "As long as you keep heading north, you'll either intersect with the old road that heads toward the Aviness keep by the lake, or the lake itself. Should we get separated in the fog, we'll meet there as soon as we're able."

I'm familiar with compasses; as the daughter of a trader lord I've seen many. But this is unlike any compass my father ever owned. Instead of the spinning needle underneath a panel of glass, the compass is completely flat and made of wedges of crystal fused together by magic. The normal indicators of North, South, East, and West have been etched into the stone. The direction and facing is indicated by one of the wedges illuminating a ghostly green color. As I turn in my saddle, wedges fade and illuminate depending on where I'm facing.

"Are the cardinal directions the same in Midscape as they are in the natural world?" I know this isn't the time or place for a lesson on Midscape's geography, but I'm too curious not to ask.

"As far as we can tell," Giles answers. "Which, make sense, given that the Natural World and Midscape were once one." He looks to Shaye. "How do we know these will work in the fog? Isn't it supposed to confound anyone not of Aviness blood?"

"There's one way to find out." Davien starts ahead. For once, I can't read him. I don't know if the fog is playing tricks with him, putting him on edge just like the rest of us—or if he's merely eager to get to the lake, that way he can get the magic from me and we can be done with this whole affair.

"I'll lead," Shaye declares, riding in front of him.

"Shouldn't I?" Davien sits a little taller in his saddle.

"My king, if they're going to attack, I would rather they attack me first. That way I can buy you time to escape if need be." It gives me some relief to think Shaye is planning for the possibility of an attack. "You'll be after me, then Katria, and Giles will take up the rear."

"Very well. If it is what the head of my future armies thinks is most strategic, then I will listen to you." Davien falls into place behind Shaye.

At least he listens to someone, I think bitterly as I get my horse behind Davien, Giles taking up the rear, just as Shaye instructed. There's a single moment of quiet hesitation. There's no wind, no birds chirping, or crickets singing. Everything is still, with the exception of my thunderously beating heart. It's so quiet I'm surprised they can't all hear it.

"Here we go," Shaye says softly. The silence breaking sounds like a scream. She moves forward.

Her horse struggles the second she tries to enter the fog. It shakes its head and stomps. Shaye forces it to carry on. It looks as though the beast is trudging through deep water, or sand, or tar. It's obliging her, but every step is more difficult than the last.

Davien begins to have trouble as well, but it goes away as he crosses the wall of fog. The mist parts for him, curling like ghostly tentacles around him. I'm close enough that I can trail in his aura. Giles only seems to get the tail end of it, and his horse struggles too.

"Further proof that the real reason why Boltov never tried to take, or dismantle, the keep at the Lake of Anointing was because there's no way he would be able to get an army through this fog. What's the point of protecting something no one can get to?" Giles says. Even though he's right behind me, his voice is distant and muffled. Space is stretched around us. What was once a condensed forest is now uncomfortable expanses of nothing. The ground beneath the horses' hooves is muddy and rocky. Very little grows here.

"I suspect you're right." Davien appraises how the fog is parting for him.

"Let's hope it's not parting so you can embark on one of the horrible trials of lore," Giles says.

"I told you not to worry about those tales." Shaye's tone betrays an eye roll. "I assure you that they were just invented to keep people away." Even though she says that, it's clear there's magic in the air here. Even I can feel it.

It's as if a thousand invisible hands are running over my shoulders and arms. I can almost see my clothes being pushed by forces I cannot comprehend. The air remains perfectly still, so I know it is not some rogue breeze that's rippling the fabric.

"How do you explain the mist parting for our king then?" Giles asks.

"It's likely a barrier, yes. But haunted ghosts keeping the Lake of Anointing safe? I doubt it." Shaye's steely bravery is unyielding. I wonder what would frighten the woman. I don't think I ever want to meet it. "However, if you're scared, you can certainly turn back," she taunts.

Davien snorts. "We shouldn't separate."

"There's no way either of us would really abandon you, Your Majesty. Isn't that right, Giles?" Shaye twists in her saddle, looking back. I can see her face clearly as her expression goes from mischievous teasing, to wide-eyed shock, to panicked horror. "Giles?" she repeats with a whisper.

I look behind me. It's only mist.

Giles is nowhere to be seen.

twenty-five

"GILES?" I call out.

"Shh," Shaye hisses. "Don't make any noise."

"But—"

"Ride next to Davien," she commands, leaving no room for questioning. I do as I'm told.

"Shouldn't we look for him?" I whisper.

"No. He knows what he needs to do. Just like we have to press on. We came here on a mission; one we can't deviate from."

I look back over my shoulder. My stomach knots at the idea of leaving him behind. Shouldn't Shaye want to charge after him? Doesn't she care about him? Her love for him is just like all the love I've ever known—it's dependent entirely on his use to her. When he is no longer useful, or would be a detriment to her, he's cast aside.

"We should pick up the pace," Davien suggests. He turns to face me. "Stay close to me, all right?"

I nod. "You don't have to worry about me, I can keep up."

"Good."

Whatever pleasure I would've gained from his confidence in my skill on a horse is quickly gobbled up by the worry that's consuming me. It's as if Giles was never there. I look behind us and the wet earth has completely filled in the hoof prints. We're not even leaving a trail he could follow. I hold onto my compass tighter; it might be the only thing that keeps me from wandering these woods until the day I die.

Shaye charges ahead, and Davien and I stay close behind. The skeletal trees that whiz past us have me jumping in my saddle. They come out of nowhere, a shadowy blur, and then they're gone. My stomach knots. I hold onto the reins and the compass for dear life. I scan the mist for a sign of anyone or anything.

In the blur of shadowed trees, I see a humanlike form.

"Did you see that?" I ask them both.

"See what?" Davien contorts himself to look at where I'm pointing.

"There was a person there."

"It was probably a tree."

"I swear there was someone," I insist.

"Keep riding," Shaye snaps back at us. "Only focus on that."

I check my compass. We're still headed due north. "How much longer do we think this will be?"

"At least another hour of riding," Davien answers grimly.

Another hour in the soupy fog. Another hour to give whatever took Giles a chance to get us too. Maybe Giles merely got separated. Maybe. But even as I try and think that way, I know that's not the case. There's no way he could've separated by accident.

There's something out there, stealthy, silent, hunting us. Somehow managing to track us even through all the fog.

I shudder. If only I could use the magic that was within me. If only I were able to learn how to hone it, focus it, fight with it. Instead, all I can do is run and try and put that magic in Davien's hands as fast as possible so we can save this land.

A blur of motion startles me. I pull hard on the reins and tilt, causing my horse to protest loudly, rearing and stomping. We slam into Davien and his mount, knocking them off course. But luckily, his feet stay in the stirrups.

"What the—"

Before he can be mad at me, a breeze follows the slash of a weapon as it cuts through the air in the space Davien and I just occupied. Black hair, like the shadows that radiate off the Butcher's cowl, streaked with white that almost matches the pallor of her skin. My eyes meet Allor's.

I *hate* that I was right.

Allor plunges into the mist at our left, completely obscured in an instant.

"We're under attack!" Davien gets Shaye's attention. No sooner does he say it than Allor plunges from the mist once more.

I thrust my palm into him, pushing him from his saddle. It's sheer luck that the blade of shadow Allor is wielding only nicks my side. The sharp pain startles me; I lose my balance and come tumbling down between the horses. Allor vaults over me.

The stomping feet of the startled mounts rumbles the earth. I roll, covering my head with both my hands, trying to make myself as small of a target as possible. One of the horses lets out a scream as Allor plunges her blade into its haunch. I scramble away before the mount comes crashing down. As I find my feet, I grab the other horse's reins. She's not going to take our escape if I have anything to say about it.

"No you don't," Allor snarls. I hold out my hand, willing magic to come to my aid. But nothing happens as the woman lunges. Davien tries to move in my periphery, but Shaye is faster. She leaps off of her saddle, twists in the air, and tackles Allor to the ground. The women roll as the remaining two horses stomp around them.

"You traitor," Shaye snarls. Allor is already trying to fight against the pin Shaye has her in.

"Shaye—" Davien sprints over to Shaye, but the woman stops him in his tracks with a sharp glance.

"You two go! Leave her to me."

Allor breaks free and thrusts upward with a dagger made of shadow. Shaye ducks and knocks Allor's arm away, forearm to forearm. Allor reaches across to grab Shaye's shoulder, and her leg frees and wraps around Shaye's body. They grapple.

"Go!" Shaye locks eyes with me. The command isn't to Davien. It's instantly clear she's charging me with the care of her king while she stays behind. I'm stuck in place, too stunned to move. "Go!"

I move, swinging up onto the stallion that was Davien's. The man is already moving for Shaye as she grapples with Allor. I pull my foot from the stirrup closest to him and hold out my hand. "Davien!"

"You're not escaping!" Allor shouts, launching Shaye from her. The Butcher regains her footing in a blur, using the momentum to hurl a projectile toward us. I kick the horse, maneuvering it deftly out of the way as Davien dodges.

Shaye lunges from the fog, clawed gloves made of shadow covering her hands. She goes for Allor's throat, misses, and connects with her shoulder. My stomach churns at the gore.

"Davien," I repeat, loudly, getting his attention. His gaze darts between Shaye and me.

"Damn. You. Go!" Shaye snarls, barely managing words between Allor's relentless attacks while still partly focusing on us.

Davien finally is moved to action. But he doesn't move for Shaye. He sprints to me as I round the horse to meet him, the fog continuing to part as I turn.

"Move," he says.

"I'm the better rider, get behind me," I snap back. I can't believe he'd even think otherwise. Luckily, Davien is only startled for a moment, and then he obliges. He throws his foot in the stirrup and swings into the saddle behind me. "Hold on tight."

With a shout and a kick, I push the horse into the fog. The skirmish turned me around, but my compass is in my pocket. We'll figure it out later. All that matters right now is that we get away.

Get away, and leave Shaye behind. My stomach churns. *She can take care of herself,* part of me wants to say. Yet I'm already sick with worry. *She's just a fae.* But she's not. In the time we've spent together, she's become more than that to me. She's Shaye, the woman with a darker past than my own. The woman whom I wanted to see aid in the killing of Boltov and liberation of the fae wilds.

She's... Giles was right; she's a friend.

Davien shifts behind me. He's looking back. But all I'm focused on is forward—dodging the skeletal trees that emerge like new enemies from the mist.

"Shaye," he murmurs.

I slow the horse at the sound of conflict and longing that's so present in her name. "We could go back."

"No... You did the right thing. We have to keep on. She's fulfilling her duty and her oaths to me by giving us a chance to escape." He speaks like a king, but the words are clearly forced, each more difficult than the last. "Moreover, there's no way we'll find them again. And hopefully no way Allor can find us."

I twist the reins in my fingers, and we continue on at a trot. It's quieter than a gallop. Hopefully we've lost Allor for good. She must have tracked us all the way into the fog. I curse inwardly; I hope she's dead.

"You did the right thing," he says softly, his breath moving the small hairs on the back of my neck. There's no space in the saddle for two. It's uncomfortable and leaves nothing to the imagination as his body is pressed against mine. His hands are on my hips, lacking anywhere else to be.

"Leaving Shaye and Giles behind doesn't feel like it."

"We have to keep going. Everything is riding on you and me. The sacrifices of Shaye and Giles, Vena, of all of Dreamsong are riding on this one shot. As long as we get to the lake and transfer the magic from you to me, all of the sacrifices are worth it. No matter what the cost was."

I have no response to that. What could I say? That I disagree? It's not my place to even if I did... I don't know if I do. I don't envy the choices that he has to make, the position he's putting himself in, the responsibility he bears.

My hand leaves the reins and rests lightly over his. I want him to hold me and tell me everything will be all right. I want to hold him and reassure him he's making the best decisions he could. Even though we're running for our lives, even in a situation like this, I want to comfort and be comforted by him.

These sentiments might well get me killed. *This* is why you don't dare let yourself love. All I have to look to is Giles. He was left behind by the woman he loved. Shaye had no problem pressing on without him. And if it weren't for the magic in me, I doubt Davien would have a hard time leaving me behind either.

I try and shake away the thoughts by reaching for my compass. "Oh no," I breathe.

"What is it?" Davien asks. Though I know he can see over my shoulder what the problem is.

"Do you—" As I'm about to ask, I feel him move. I glance back and he's already pulled out his own compass. Sure enough, it's doing the same as mine.

The glowing light spins, brightening and fading each of the wedges of crystal one after the other. No wedge is illuminated for more than a second. Even when I bring us to a complete stop, the compass continues to show no stable direction.

"What's happening?" I glance behind us nervously. Everything is still so quiet, so still. Allor could be half a world away, or right behind us. I want to keep going, but doing so without a heading seems almost more terrifying than facing Allor.

"It must be something with the old barriers that surround this place." He curses under his breath. "Hopefully whatever is trying to throw us off course will be twice as bad for Allor or any of her allies that might be lurking."

"What do we do, my king?" I ask, looking back. His eyes widen slightly. He realizes before I do what I said. *My king*, as if I am part of this world. One attack from Allor and my tone has shifted since the morning.

"We keep going straight," he says after clearing his throat.

I purse my lips. We were utterly turned around in the scuffle. And even if I somehow guessed north correctly, I know from my father's sailors that it's impossible to make any kind of accurate heading without a compass or other bearings. But I also know, at this point, it would be worse to try and turn around. Hopefully we get lucky and the lake is just beyond our field of view.

"Eventually we'll hit the road," he says reassuringly.

"Or, even better, the lake." I try and be optimistic. I'm pretty sure I fail. "Do you think Shaye and Giles are all right?"

"I hope so." He sighs heavily. "I was afraid of them coming, afraid of something like this happening."

"You thought we would be attacked?" He could've fooled me. His grip tightens on me for a second. "I knew it was possible."

"Yet you treated me as if I were crazy when I shared my suspicions of Allor with you." My words are a little sharper than I wanted them to be. I'm sure he can hear between them, *I told you so.*

"I didn't see it." He sighs and holds me a little tighter. I can feel his fingertips against my hip bones. His body as he leans into me. "You were right, and I was wrong. Somehow, a human knew more about my people and my world than I did."

"I don't think that's the case." I scan the fog, trying to focus on anything but him. The things this man does to me...the way he makes me feel...it's all going to be my undoing. "You trusted the people underneath you to keep you safe—to be skeptical for you. I was naturally hesitant, doubtful, ready to assume that fae were the dangerous creatures from the tales my father told me as a girl that I couldn't trust I needed to look out for."

He chuckles under his breath. It warms my neck. I pointedly ignore the heat that shoots through me at the feeling of it.

"Doubting everyone is no way to be a leader." I force myself to continue speaking. "Real leaders have faith in those underneath them."

"You speak as if you have experience with leadership."

"When I was younger, my father had many people looking up to him in the trading company. I saw how he managed them. I also knew many of his captains and I could always tell the good captains from the bad ones—I could see if someone had the traits of a good leader or not." *Except for my father.* He was the one person my best judgments failed me on. The one person I gave the benefit of the doubt to for far too long. He was never the leader I saw him as. If he was, he would've managed our household better. He would've curbed Joyce and Helen's worst tendencies, not allowed them to be cruel as they were to me.

"So what do you think about *me*, then?" His question makes me glance over my shoulder. I scan the fog to make sure no one is coming up behind us, using it as an excuse to not meet his eyes. "Do you think I will be a good leader?"

"I think your kingdom is lucky that you've returned to them. Anyone is lucky just to be in your presence." The words are as surprising to me as they are to him. His gaze softens, posture relaxes.

"That means a lot to me."

"Even from a human?" I stare forward once more, reminding myself of what I am to him—of everything we can never be. I can't love him. Even if I was oblivious to the poison that was love, I couldn't love *him* of all people. In the next day, the magic will be gone from me, and we will be nothing. He even said as much himself.

"How many times must I say it? *Especially* from a human, so long as that human is you. Katria, I—" A noise from the right startles me. I jerk, nearly falling from the saddle. He holds onto me, keeping me in place. "What is it?"

"Did you hear that?" I whisper.

"Hear what?"

There it is again—the sharp sound of a high note being played on a lone fiddle.

"It sounds...like music." I continue to stare into the fog where the sound seems to be coming from.

"Music?" Davien hesitates. "Perhaps this is the haunting that everyone speaks of."

I shift in the saddle and tug on the reins lightly, changing our course to the direction of the music.

"What are you doing?"

"I don't know," I confess.

"We should move away from it. We're not far from the border of mer folk territory. It could be some kind of siren call."

I don't think it is, but I don't know how to explain to him why I think that. As we move through the fog, a lute joins the fiddle. There's the soft thrumming of hands on drums, and I hear the chiming bells in the rattle of tambourines. I'm just about to make out the melody when Davien speaks again.

"Katria—" he places his hands over mine on the reins "—we should head in the opposite direction."

"No." I shake my head and glance back at him. "I don't think we should."

"This might be some kind of magic to lure those that aren't heirs of Aviness away from the keep. I don't hear anything."

I can recognize the song now. It's one my mother played. I can almost hear her voice on the edges of my memory, hazy, echoing back to me from a distant time. A song of safety, a song of home—that was what she had called this melody. It had no words but she would always hum along as her fingers danced on the lute. I heard this song recently, didn't I? When? I search within myself but find nothing.

"You need to trust me," I say firmly to Davien. "You didn't with Allor. Do it now. My gut tells me that this is the right direction."

He purses his lips. I think he's going to say no. But, then, to my surprise, "All right, we ride for no more than an hour. If nothing changes by then, I get to decide our new course. And we flee at the first sign of danger."

"Deal." I bring the horse's pace up to a trot. "Thank you for trusting me. I know you had a lot of reasons not to." I think back to our time together at the manor and that fateful night that set us both on this path.

"You've also given me a lot of reasons why I should trust you." He lightly caresses my hips, fingers trailing down my thighs, almost absentmindedly. I wonder if he realizes he's doing it. I don't point it out because, dangerously, I don't think I want him to stop. "You saved my life back there. You risked yours for mine."

"I acted without thinking."

"And your instinct was to save me."

"We shouldn't speak. We don't want to give away our position and I need to listen to the music."

He sighs softly. He knows I'm cutting him off—that I'm avoiding this conversation at all costs. "Very well. We can speak tonight at the keep."

I hope not. I hope to never speak about what I did. Because if I do, then I might be forced to unpack all these complex feelings that I've been trying so desperately to ignore. But, even ignoring them, I almost gave my life for him.

I push the thoughts from my mind and focus on the music. After a little bit, I begin to hum along. Davien sits a little straighter, body tensing.

"Is that the song you hear?"

"Yes." Well, in all honesty, what he heard me humming was the harmonies my mother would sing to the melody. Wordless sounds that are more music and emotion than anything coherent.

Davien chuckles and shakes his head in disbelief. "Then yet again, you were right."

"What are you talking about?"

"That's the melody of the Aviness family. It was played at all of their coronations. It's one of the oldest songs of the fae. If you're hearing it here and now then the barriers that protect this place must be calling out to the magic in you."

I can't fight the swell of pride I feel at being right. "See, it pays to listen to me." I toss my head back to shoot him a grin. His grip tightens and pulls me back in the saddle, and my head lands on his shoulder.

"If you smirk like that at me again, I won't be able to stop myself from kissing that smug expression off your lips." His breath is hot on my neck, the words deep and gravelly. "Consider this your warning."

He releases me and I straighten in the saddle once more, but there's nowhere I can go. There's no escaping him as we ride together. For a while now, we've been pressed against each other with nothing left to the imagination. I was able to ignore it while I was focusing on the music, but now he's made that nearly impossible.

Blessedly, he doesn't distract me further. The music guides us to the road, only getting louder as we continue down the cobblestones. Without warning, the fog dissipates. We break through into a golden sunset, shining down on a sheltered lake, and a long-forgotten castle.

twenty-six

THE KEEP REMINDS ME OF DAVIEN'S MANOR BACK IN THE
NATURAL WORLD. The architecture is incredibly similar
even if it is significantly more dilapidated. This place has
clearly been forgotten by man, though not by nature.

The small, crumbling castle overlooks a perfectly clear
lake. I've never seen water so brilliantly blue in my life.
Even underneath the orange sunset it gives off an almost
cerulean glow.

The oak trees of the forest we left are gone. In their place
are massive, ancient sentries of wood and perseverance.
Their trunks fan out at their base, looking as if they wear
flowing skirts beneath their bark. The mountains have also
vanished.

I stare at the western horizon, blinking into the sunset.
"I've never seen the sky so large and unbroken."

"Me neither." Davien's voice is low with reverence. "And
I've never seen anything so beautiful."

I guide the horse over to the entrance of the keep. The
doors have long since rotted off and vines trellis around the
opening in their place. We dismount and Davien walks right
to the water's edge where it meets the castle wall.

"So, what do we do now?"

"Let's go inside," he decides and returns to me. "It's
getting late and there are some matters involving the ritual
to finalize."

"Finalize?" I ask.

"Vena was able to work out most of the ritual…but she admitted that we might be forced to adjust once we are in this space. Ritual is an art and we didn't know what our canvas would look like."

My heart sinks into the cold water of the lake and I shiver. The fae have made it clear how important ritual is for their magic to work properly…and how difficult rituals can be to make and perfect.

"How long do you think the adjustments will take?"

"I hope no more than a day, at the absolute most." Davien begins unhooking the saddlebags. I lend assistance. "Fortunately, my horse was the one we carried on with, so I didn't lose any of the supplies that Vena sent."

"I can only imagine how much bloodier that scuffle would have become if we were also trying to get the saddlebags off my horse… Poor girl." I sigh, wishing I could go back and find the horse to give it a proper burial. I only knew her for a short time, but she served me well.

"Speaking of bloody, are you all right?" Davien's hand touches my side. "I didn't see this when we were riding."

I look at my side where Allor nicked me with her blade. "It was small and it's already healed." I press my fingers through the hole in my shirt to confirm what I already suspected. The skin is already knitted; there's not even the slightest sign of any trauma. "I have to admit, fast healing is one really nice thing about your fae king powers. I'm going to miss having it."

He chuckles. "If I could let you keep a fraction of this power, I would."

"Well, if I get to choose, then please give me the magic healing." I focus on the saddlebags in an effort to hide my shock at the admission.

He shifts a little closer to me. "You have a deal, but only after I defeat the most bloodthirsty fae to have ever walked this earth."

"I think that sounds fair." I look up at him with a sly smile. I hate how much just his face makes me happy. Even when the world is tough, even when death and danger lurks around every corner, there's a lightness that only his presence exudes. I tear my eyes away from him, before I'm lost in the heady emotions. "We should go inside…see if our friends are waiting." *Hopefully not our enemies.* "I'll keep the stallion saddled, just in case we need to make a fast escape. One night with a saddle on shouldn't hurt him."

"Good thinking." His expression becomes serious as he looks up at the crumbling walls, scanning the dark windows. If Shaye or Giles had made it here before us, they would've most certainly come to greet us by now. It's far more likely that if anyone is waiting, it's an enemy. "I'll go first. Stay right at my side." He holds out his hand and I take it.

We enter at the top of an L-shaped hallway. At our left is an antechamber that is completely overgrown by the vines and other greenery that was creeping up the front facade. Rounding the L reveals the main hall of the keep.

There's a staircase at our right that heads up to the second floor and a gigantic hearth at our left. A rectangular, stone table positioned before the hearth is the only piece of furniture that persists. Opposite the hearth are three large windows, cut into the wall, that overlook the lake. Miraculously, the stained glass is still intact.

"It's almost like the designs at your house." I keep my voice to a whisper as I cross over to one of the windows, yet my words still manage to echo around the pillars and into the giant rafters that support this cavernous room. I run my finger lightly along the dark outlines of the images. Every other panel is a portrait of a man or woman wearing a shimmering crown made of glass almost identical to the one Davien wore on the night of the festival in Dreamsong.

"My home and this place were both made by and for the Aviness family." Davien examines the glass as well. I can feel the warmth radiating off of him as the castle becomes colder with the setting sun.

"There are women wearing the crown."

"There were a few times in our history where in lieu of a male heir, a woman took the throne." Davien shrugs. "The last heir of the direct bloodline would have been a woman."

"Everyone makes it sound like there have only been kings."

"That has been the predominant way of it. And the Boltovs only pass down the crown among the men of their family. I think some forget that there were queens long ago."

I come to a pause before one man holding the crown rather than wearing it. "Why isn't it on his brow?"

"He must be one of those who abdicated." Davien strokes his chin thoughtfully. "The glass crown can only be worn by a true heir. It's part of the ritual placed on it long ago by the Aviness family. When the original fae courts banded together to fight against the early elves and named Aviness their king, they swore fealty in a ritual that still binds all fae to this day to the crown. I hear Boltov began to wear the crown on his brow through some illusion or dark ritual in his attempt to claim I was not legitimate. Though any fae would know the truth by sense alone."

"Sounds powerful," I murmur, staring up at the man in the glass and trying to imagine myself pictured in a window someday, abdicating to Davien.

"It is, immensely. And the Boltovs can only tap into a fraction of it. I've no doubt Boltov thinks if he can get the magic of the ancient kings…he could do far more regardless of whether I'm alive or dead."

"Which is why we can never let him get it." I look up at Davien and he gives a small nod that feels conspiratorial. Even though I know I am only playing a small and accidental part of this great story of Aviness, for the first time, I feel as though I am truly a part of it rather than a spectator.

"Indeed." He starts back for the fireplace behind us. "We should set up our camp here tonight. We'll do a quick search of the keep, and then barricade this room. Whenever Shaye and Giles arrive, they won't be able to miss us."

My chest tightens as I stare at his back. I don't know if Shaye and Giles are coming. The thought nearly makes me sick. They were with us mere hours ago. To think that right now they could be… I shudder and force the thought from my mind. They're strong. And if Davien has faith that they will come walking through that door, then so will I. At the very least, I choose to believe they've turned back to Dreamsong to help protect it.

"I'll make the fire," I offer.

"You?" He seems startled. It elicits a laugh from me.

"I assure you I'm perfectly capable of making a fire. I did for my family most mornings. I did in the safe house yesterday." I cross over to the hearth and begin to check the flue. From what I can see, it doesn't look like there are any obstructions. Even if there were, the ceiling is high enough in here and there are enough holes in the roof that I doubt we're going to get smoked out.

"I can use magic," he offers.

"Or you can begin your search. Unless you'd rather I search the rooms and corridors?"

Davien frowns. "I'd rather you stay at my side. But I can see the benefit of dividing and conquering."

"I'll shout if there's any trouble."

"Be sure you do. I would never forgive myself if something happened to you." He gives my shoulder a squeeze and heads up the stairs. Leaving me to remind myself to breathe for a moment after a remark like that.

I rummage through the saddlebags, assessing our supplies. There's not a great deal, but there's enough to be comfortable at least for tonight. Luckily, among all the other supplies are some flint and steel. I retreat back through the entry hallway to an antechamber and collect dead brush and twigs for kindling. Shockingly, I find some split logs stacked and dry on the side of the fireplace. I wonder if there's some kind of old ritual on the closet they're stored in, given that there's no sign of rot.

Practical fae rituals to make my life easier when I return to the human world. Those will be a must. I chuckle as I collect the wood, imagining the Fae King in my home, charming a closet so my firewood is always dry and ready. It's certainly a nice image.

Ferrying the supplies back, I stack my wood atop the kindling and proceed with striking the flint until I get spark to catch. Davien hasn't returned by the time I'm done stoking the flames, so I turn to focusing on food. There are some rations at the bottom of the saddlebags that I lay out on the table. I spend way too much time making sure they're as aesthetically pleasing as possible, given that it's only a small loaf of bread, a jar of blackberry jam, and salted meat.

"You eat with your eyes first," I mutter, thinking of all the times Joyce chided me for the table not being set just right.

"What was that?" Davien startles me. He comes in through one of the other side doors of the main hall.

"I don't suppose you found a larder miraculously stocked with food, did you?" I ask instead of repeating myself.

"Unless you consider moss food, no." He approaches. "I think this will be enough."

"I do too, I just wish it was more substantial."

"It's a dinner fit for a king." He helps himself to a hunk of bread, popping open the jar and slathering his piece with jam.

I laugh out loud. "It is not."

"I am a king, and I am eating it, therefore it is." His eyes shimmer with amusement. He could kill me with a smile.

"Very well, *Your Majesty.*" I dip low into a bow.

"If you're that concerned, why don't we make it fit for a king?" The sun is setting outside and he's cast in a warm glow from the fading light of the stained glass and the fire.

"How would I do that?"

"A small ritual should suffice." He begins rummaging through the saddlebags, glancing back at the food. "What would you have in mind? Perhaps some kind of pasta? Or meat pie?"

"If those are my options, meat pie." I watch with keen fascination as he takes a piece of chalk and marks a series of triangles and circles in a grid-like pattern on the table. His movements are strong and confident.

"Food rituals are fairly simple. You need some basic requirements of the ingredients, some heat." He gives a nod to the fire. "And then the rest is magic."

"All right." Excitement rushes through me at the idea of getting to use magic again. I'm about to lose these powers, so I might as well enjoy them as I can, in whatever way I can.

"Stand here." He maneuvers me in front of the table, standing behind me. I've never been more aware of the strong length of his body or the way his breath cuts straight through my clothing to hit the nape of my neck. "Put your hands like this."

His voice is soft and low as he runs his fingertips down my arms. They land lightly on the backs of my hands, taking them with a gentle grip. He guides my palms onto the table, resting lightly at two points on the grid.

"Now, just like we did with the lantern, think about what you're trying to make." How can instructions be so...sensual? I try not to squirm. "Will the magic to bend to you, to do your bidding as its master. You control it. It doesn't control you."

"What does it feel like for you?" I ask, fighting to stay focused. "I've been trying to feel the magic within me, but I can't. Every time I want to summon it, there's nothing there."

He draws small circles on the back of my hand with his fingertips as he considers my question. I don't even think he's aware of what he's doing and I don't point it out to him. The sensation is too delicious to stop.

"Magic... I wouldn't say it's a thing that I feel, not consciously at least. It's more of a state of being. An awareness of the world and all its mysteries—the ones you know, the ones you don't, what you can control, and the forces you are helpless to do anything but to submit to. Magic is one of the greatest things we will ever know and never be able to explain. To know magic is to touch the old gods that brought this earth from primordial chaos. It is to embrace the glimpse of greatness that we all possess within us—to boldly reach for what could be and not what is, both in ourselves and the world around us."

Davien's words are thoughtful and poetic. If not for his pauses and breathy stillness I would think he had practiced the speech. But every word is as sincere as the last.

I laugh softly, trying to free up some of the restless energy his speech filled me with. "You realize none of that is very helpful for me, right?"

"I suppose it's not." I don't even have to turn around to know that there's a grin on his face. "Why not treat it as you would a dance? That seemed to work for you during the tunnel construction."

"It did, but..." I trail off with a sigh. "I wish I could feel it, is all. I struggle to conjure something that I don't know is there half the time."

"Knowing magic is like trying to tell you what the color red sounds like. Once you hear it, you know. But until then it's madness to try and explain."

That gives me genuine pause. I run my fingertips across his chalk lines thoughtfully. "I think I know what you're trying to say."

"You do?" The question is a mix of delight and surprise.

"I know what the color red sounds like." I begin to think of magic in an all-new way. "Just like I know the harmonies of the pollinators in summer, or the soft requiem of winter. The world has a sound to it, a song, if you're able to listen." Magic must be the same. Once you hear it, you'll be able to sing along. It is not a dance. It is the music itself.

What is the song my magic sings?

The question rattles my core. It isn't *my* magic. This isn't my power, my destiny. My fingers curl as I lift them from the table.

"What is it?"

I step away from him with a shake of my head. Wrapping my arms around myself, I cross over to the windows. The lake is a bright cerulean in the late twilight. Just as I first suspected, it really is glowing.

"Katria?"

I hear his footsteps approaching. I speak without looking at him. "It doesn't matter. There's no point in me learning any of this."

"Did I say something that upset you?" He comes to a halt just behind me once more. I don't turn to face him.

"No." I'm clearly perfectly capable of upsetting myself.

"What's wrong?"

"Nothing."

"Don't lie to me, please." In the face of my silence, he continues with his incorrect assumptions. "There's no reason to be frustrated with magic. Even though we fae work on honing and perfecting our skills, our knowledge of magic is somewhat innate. We know it from birth. You don't have that benefit, so it's only natural that you struggle and—"

"I'm not upset that I don't know how to use magic." I hang my head. "I just don't see the point in learning it. Doing so will only end in disappointment."

"You'll be able to master it," he assures me.

"With what time?" I round on him. "Tomorrow, if everything goes correctly—and I know I don't need to tell you what rides on tomorrow, that it *must* go correctly—then the magic will be out of me. This power was never mine, it's yours. There's no point in my learning it now or ever. I'm just a bystander, an accident, a thief. I am a brief note in your symphony, and it hurts too much to pretend to be anything else."

His gaze softens, his brows turning up slightly in the center. "I don't want you to hurt," he says softly.

"I'm used to being hurt. I can survive being hurt." It's all of these *other* feelings that are difficult. It's the happy feelings that I don't know what to do with; the ones that highlight just how deep all my other wounds are.

"That's not a way to live. You should have never had to live that way."

"Well I have, and I've done just fine."

"You *survived*, and that's commendable given that I only know the tip of the iceberg of your suffering. But merely surviving isn't any way to *live*. I want you to thrive—you deserve to thrive." He takes a small step forward. I take a wide step back.

"You shouldn't concern yourself with me." I shake my head.

"But I do."

"But you won't." My words are as cold and icy as the air seeping through the window at my back. "Soon enough, I'll be nothing to you. All of this, whatever this is, will be nothing. You'll be king and I'll just be a human living on your land across the Fade."

"It's *your* land now," he insists.

"Stop being kind to me." My voice raises a fraction. "Stop pretending like any of this is real."

He staggers, almost as though I've struck him. Davien shakes his head slowly. "Every minute of this has been real for me. More real than I ever wanted or asked for it to be."

"It's not." Maybe if I say it enough times, it will be true for both of us. "It can't be. Not just because of what our futures hold. But because we never were even supposed to have met."

"But we did. And despite all odds—"

"Don't say it." I know it's coming. There is the same tone in his voice as there was when he was speaking to Shaye. "If we stop this now, we can pretend none of it has happened."

"We are beyond pretending."

I know what he says is true, but I continue anyway. I can't stand idly by as he condemns us both. "Neither of us will have to be hurt more than we already will be, already are. We can—"

"Despite all odds, I love you, Katria."

I can't do anything but stare at him. I burn with anger, with frustration, with passion. No three words have ever made me happier, or cut me deeper. Nothing has ever meant more to me while simultaneously having to mean nothing at all.

"No you don't," I whisper.

"I do." He takes a step forward. "I love you in a way that I never expected to love anyone. I have always been destined to be thrown into a marriage of convenience. I never expected to love."

"And I don't want it." I shake my head. My eyes are burning, tears pricking at their edges. "I don't want your love."

His expression crumples. I've wounded him more with those words than I've ever seen him before. He hovers in limbo, mouth opening and closing, clearly unable to figure out what he wants to say next. I allow him to stew in the silence. I've made myself clear.

"Why?"

I shake my head at his question, glancing askance.

"Will you not even give me the kindness of knowing what I have done to wrong you? Was I just not the man for you? I will accept whatever it is you say, even if it is nothing more than that you simply don't feel the same. But please, take pity on me, and tell me clearly, just this once, because I thought... I thought that you might—"

"It's not you," I confess, knowing that silence would be easier— better. But I don't have it in me to wound him in the way I should. "I will never love *anyone*."

"What?"

"I made that vow to myself long ago. I made it before you even bought my hand. The belief that I would not fall in love with you had nothing to do with you."

"Why do you refuse love?" The question is earnest and filled with naivety.

I bark laughter, incredulous that he doesn't know better. "To love is pain. Just look at us, here and now, only at the start of this infatuation—" I won't dare call it love "—and it is already boring holes in us that can never be filled. And this is just the beginning. Soon it will be honeyed words that are poison in disguise. It will be obliviousness to the wounds we inflict on each other. It will be children, forgotten, locked in closets, and used like weapons against each other. And it will be that way until the day we die, driven into an early grave by the other, no doubt."

He disrupts my tirade with another step forward; he's now encroaching on my personal space. I should flee, but nervous energy has me frozen in place. I'm trembling all over but I don't know why.

"None of that is love," Davien says simply, sadly.

"My father loved Joyce. She loved him in return. And I watched as that love consumed him day after day, blinded him. I watched as my father became the husk of the man I knew. He stood by as Joyce and Helen abu—" The word sticks in my throat.

"As they what?" His voice is low, teeming with what I would dare say is anger. I shake my head. "As they what?" he repeats more firmly.

"As they abused me." I'm truly trembling now. But I don't think it's fear. It is as if every year of my life I was ratcheted tighter and tighter by an unseen hand. By the world's worst torture device that I never even realized was on me. There wasn't a moment of relief. Wrenching. *Tighter and tighter.* Constant. Yet with that one word, the bonds that held me are fraying. It is if by acknowledging it, I can finally begin to find release. "My father loved me…but what good was that love in the wake of that woman?"

"None of that is love." He scoops my face with both his hands. His thumbs run across my cheeks as angry tears spill over my lower lids. "To call it love is an insult to the greatest thing we have on this world—love, true love, is the only thing more powerful than magic itself."

"Then why?" I ask even though there is no possible way he would know the answer. "Why would my father stand by, if not because he loved Joyce?"

Yet even as I ask I can hear the remnants of a conversation I tried to forget. One I was too young to have and that was too brief to seem important until now. *We need her, Katria, she has the mines. The company is struggling…and she is the first thing to alleviate the darkness of your mother's death.* I draw a shuddering breath.

"I don't know," Davien admits.

"I wish I could ask him," I whisper.

"I wish you could as well. But even if you had the time to ask all the questions you need answers to…only you will be able to come to terms with all you have endured. Only you can grant yourself peace now." He presses his forehead lightly against mine. "And that peace will come from love—loving yourself."

I push him away. "Enough with love!"

"What you've known has never been love."

"You're lying." I shake my head.

"I'm not. You just want me to be because it's been easier to explain away the horrors you've endured." He sees right through me. My tears fall more freely, pain escaping as sobs. Davien closes the rest of the gap between us. I don't push him away again. One hand cradles the back of my head as he presses my cheek to his chest. The other hand wraps around my waist, holding me firmly.

"Why?" I don't know what I'm asking. There's so much wrapped up in that single why. Why was my family the way it was? Why was I never good enough for tenderness?

"There's no reason for cruelty, no excuse." He shakes his head and kisses my hair. I've never felt more protected than in this moment and it only makes me cry harder. "But I swear to you, Katria, with all I am and all I will be…as long as I draw breath, I will never let them, or anyone, hurt you again. You will *never* have to go back to that house. And should you ever wish to, because you feel that confronting them in the cruelty they have wrought will bring you some peace, I swear I will stand by your side if you need me."

His words are sweeter than a song. I've never heard anything so lovely. There's not even the slightest hint of smoke in the air around him. I pull my face away from his body to look up at him, tilting my head back as far as it will go to meet his eyes. His hair curtains around me like it did the first night I fell into his bed.

"Why would you do all that for me?" I whisper.

"You know why." A sly smile plays at the corners of his mouth. "Because *I love you*, truly. I love you in a way that makes me want to sacrifice for you. That makes me want to move the mountains, or oceans, or stars, to merely see you smile." He strokes my cheek again, looking down at me with all the wonder in the world. "*That* is what love is, Katria—what it should be. You are worthy of that love, from me, from others, and from yourself."

I open my mouth, but words don't come. I want to tell him I love him. I want to so badly that my entire chest gets so tight that I can't breathe. Yet wanting to tell him isn't enough. There is still a block that I can't overcome with words.

But maybe…

Maybe I can *show* him.

My hands slide up his sides, his chest, and wrap around his neck. I know his movements by now. I know the look of admiration and lust that he gives me as he stares through his lashes. It is always accompanied by kisses that taste of promises yet to be fulfilled.

Tonight, I will make good on those promises.

For one night, I will stop worrying about tomorrow. I will put aside all of the terrible ways that we might be hurt by this. I will ignore the oncoming fall from grace that we are destined for.

And instead, I will kiss him. I will know him. And I will regret nothing.

twenty-seven

HE SEEMS TO KNOW MY MIND AND MY HEART BEFORE I DO. Even as I'm still gathering my resolve and acknowledging my wants he kisses me fiercely. He makes wordless demands with his mouth that my body aches to oblige. I want to forget my pain and let it go. To give in to something for me, solely for me.

I grab his neck with fervent need, fingers knotting in his hair, pulling his mouth closer to mine even when there is no space left between us. Davien follows suit, hands coming alive. His palms and fingers are all over, from my face, to my breasts, to my hips. He draws hard circles with his thumbs, sending me into a frenzy with that movement alone.

We kiss deeper than we ever have before, as if we are trying to consume every last bit of doubt that could still linger between us. His teeth rake against my lower lip; I tilt my head back in tandem and release a moan. It's met with a sharp inhale and a quiver on his breath.

"I want you," I breathe.

"Tell me what you want." He ducks his head, going for my exposed neck. I feel his teeth sink into my muscle, his lips close around.

"I want you," I repeat. The world is spinning and I have to clutch on to him even tighter so my knees don't give out from my light-headedness.

"Tell me what you want," he growls as he pinches my flesh between his teeth.

Something within me breaks. Perhaps it is the last recesses of my self-control. But it feels as though a levy has been torn asunder by his thick and needy words.

"I want you to kiss me all over until there is not a part of my body that you don't know. I want you to explore me with your tongue and fingers. I want you to make me yours as a man should make his wife. I want you to go slow until I am breathless and begging, and then I want you to go hard. I want to shatter together and fall like the silvery arcs of shooting stars as we descend from heaven of our making."

He exhales a moan and retreats from my neck to return to my lips. He kisses me with rising intensity, each shift of his mouth messier and more sensual than the last. Without warning, Davien pulls away and presses his forehead into mine.

"I will do all of it...and then some," he rasps. "And when I am done, when you are left aching, blissful, and yet still filled with desire, I will do it again. I will show you as best I am able just how loved you are."

He holds me to him with a crushing grip and takes a step backwards. My knees nearly give out, forcing me to cling to him as the only stable thing in my world right now. Somewhere between the window and the table, his shirt is lost. I run my hands over the vast plane of his chest, bare to my touch, exposed only for me.

His skin is so hot in the cool night I'm surprised it doesn't burn me. His hands bunch up my shirt, reaching for the hem. He pulls it over my head and I don't stop him. Yet, as winter's touch runs up my spine, sending a shiver through my body that has nothing to do with the tides of pleasure he's already stirring within me, I pause.

Davien senses my hesitation, pulling away slightly. "Are you cold? Is it too much?"

"It's not that. And no." I want to cover my increasingly exposed flesh, but that want competes against my desire to continue running my hands up and down his arms. "I've never—"

"I haven't either." His mouth quirks into a relieved smile. "We will be each other's teacher tonight, and eager student." He bends down to brush his lips against mine.

"What if you don't like me once you really see me?" I ask between quivering lips. I have yet to show him the scar on my back. He has only caught glimpses of the wounds I still carry with me.

"I really saw you in the first moment you walked in my door. I have seen your soul, and I have fallen in love with it. So there's nothing about the mortal casing it's housed within that could make me love you less." He is so sure, so confident, the grip I have on myself relaxes. My hands return to his hips. "Trust in my love, in me. I will never break that trust."

The next kiss he gives me is deeper than any of the others, slower and more confident. He inhales as I exhale, stealing my breath and my doubts with it. I give myself further to him.

I want him. I want all of him. If tonight is the last real night that we have with each other then I'm determined to set aside my doubts and enjoy him while I have him.

Davien's hands leave my body. I let out a low whine. He chuckles. "I don't want you to be colder than you already are." He rummages in the saddlebags, pulling out a blanket and tossing it across the table.

"I am on fire," I whisper.

He grabs my hips, pushing me up onto the table. My legs wrap around him on instinct. The feeling is glorious. My heart is a pulsing beat that begins to guide the melody that only we can sing.

He's on top of me, his presence demanding every inch of my attention, as if he did not already have it. I shift as I lie back, allowing him space on the large stone table with me. Davien snakes his fingers through my hair, brushing it away, looking down at me between kisses as though I am a goddess incarnate.

Then, with a look that promises a thousand desires—the kind that are unspeakable in the light of day—he moves down my body, removing the remaining garments that keep us apart one by one and replacing them with kisses. Propping myself up on my elbows, I stare down at him as he nips lightly at each of my hip bones. He looks up at me with glassy eyes and heavy lids. Then slowly, deliberately, he works himself between my legs.

Before I can speak a word of shy protest, he reminds me that the time for modesty has long gone with a kiss that takes my breath away and I inhale it back as a moan. My toes curl. He holds me in a limbo of ecstasy that I have never felt before. Hot. Building. It can only escape with cries of pleasure.

This is what I wanted. This was the release I was looking for. This is why all of our other stolen kisses were never enough. Could never be enough.

I arch off the table, fists knotted in the blanket. At once, I come crashing down with a cry. I break in a way I never thought possible, and I land in a bliss so consuming that it seems as if it is the first real thing I've ever felt.

Davien straightens away, licking his lips with a grin. He moves to hover back over me. Positioned between my thighs. Our eyes meet. I see excitement, hesitation, nervousness—all emotions that I share.

"Are you sure?" he asks. "If you have any doubts we will stop."

"I have many doubts…about everything *but* this moment. I want you, Davien," I echo myself from earlier.

He presses himself forward. There's tension, aching, a sudden snap of pain. I wince and he freezes.

"Are you all right?"

"I'm fine," I reassure him.

Luckily he takes my word and does not stop. We inhale in tandem as his hips are flush against mine. My breath is thin and shallow as I grow accustomed to the feeling of him. And, when I am ready, he moves. I have never been more aware of his strong, sure presence than in those first few movements. Neither was I aware of just how hot the rolling core in the pit of my stomach could become.

We move together, breathlessly building our desire as one. This time, when the crash comes, we fall together. He lands in my arms and we are a tangle of ecstasy and delight. Pure joy escapes as laughter as he pulls away and we share a smile—an intimate understanding that is only possible for lovers to comprehend.

"That was… That was…" I struggle to form words.

A sensual smirk slowly spreads across his lips. "That was merely round one."

Davien claims my mouth once more and we tumble back into the throes of bliss.

twenty-eight

I AM AWAKE WELL BEFORE THE DAWN, SO I GET TO WATCH SUNLIGHT CREEP ACROSS THE ROOM AND WARM DAVIEN'S CHEEKS. We're bundled tightly in the blankets and each other's arms, warded against the chill. I slept harder than I have in a long time and woke with the thin sheen of bliss still coating me from last night's affairs.

But rather than going back into that deep and dreamless rest, I chose to stay awake so that I could imprint this image of him onto my memory. This is our first and only morning together. It is likely the only morning I will ever wake up in a man's arms. Even if Davien is right and love is not the wicked poison that was fed to me by Joyce, I still don't think I will ever seek it out.

Partly because I'm still afraid of falling in love. But now, also, because I will never find a man who knows me as Davien has come to know me. Who sees me for all I am and wants me despite my scars. Who makes me smile with his sheer existence in an utterly illogical, impossible, and yet wonderful way.

He stirs and I can feel the peaceful spell that had been woven over us unraveling. Soon, we will get up. There'll be clothes, and breakfast, and planning of rituals. I will give the magic that I've been carrying to him. And then the only way I will exist in this world is in the memory of a fae king.

Davien's eyes crack open. He blinks sleepily, and then

turns his head to face me. "Good morning," he mumbles, rubbing his nose against mine before giving me a peck on the lips.

"Good morning," I echo with a smile.

"How did you sleep?"

"Fantastic, and you?"

"Best sleep of my life." I feel his muscles tense as he stretches. The sensation fills my hollow and aching core with a desire that I'm still far too spent to indulge again. "I'm beginning to think that the old folk tales about the fae were more accurate than I previously assumed."

"Oh?"

"If I had known that stealing a human and spiriting her away to my world would fill me with such joy and give me the best sleep of my life, I would've done it much sooner."

My laughter echoes off the rafters above us. "If you had stolen away any other human she would've been dead."

He purses his lips. "Then perhaps I am finding myself more grateful than I previously thought possible that you stole my magic."

"And now I need to give it back." I begin to untangle myself from him but as I go to sit up, his arms circle me. He latches on, pulling me back to him. He curls around me, my back against his chest. We fit together perfectly in every way imaginable.

"A little bit longer," he whispers. "I want to remember everything about this morning."

"I am helpless to deny you," I murmur. The notion still terrifies me. But I suppose I don't have to come to terms too much with this love since we will be in different worlds soon enough. That's certainly one way to protect myself from becoming too involved.

"Good, then I have you right where I want—What's this? I didn't notice it in the darkness last night." His thought turns into a whisper and I feel his finger press into my back. I wince and draw a shuddering breath. "Katria?"

"I... It was a long time ago."

"If you don't want to tell me, you don't have to." He must hear the pain in my voice.

I am well and truly hopeless for this man, because I say, "I want to. It was a long time ago...before Laura, my youngest sister, was born. Helen had been relentless that day and I fled to the rooftop." In my mind, I'm six years old. Joyce and Helen have just come into my life. "Helen chased me to the edge of the rooftop. She kept pushing and pushing. She wouldn't stop. The edge of the roof came so fast and we both went over. I remember seeing her falling ahead of me. Then, somehow, I caught up to her. My arms around her, we landed hard on the walkway that stretched around the manor. My back to the stone, her on top of me."

The scent of burning flesh fills my nose and I cringe. "Everything after that was a blur. I was in shock, I think... But my back was so damaged the wound had to be cauterized. Joyce did it with an iron shovel from a set of fireplace tools."

That day was the closest I ever saw her to being worried for me. The entire time, she looked horrified, scared even. And yet, over and over, I can still hear her whispers, *monster, monstrous creature*, as my father looked on helplessly. *You are lucky you have me,* she told him, *lucky I can handle this.*

"After I healed, I was never allowed on the roof, or anywhere high up, again. Joyce hated me more after that. I think she resented me for almost getting Helen killed." She began her long process of sending my father away more and more not long after...and I became relegated to the servant's quarters like the *monster* I was.

"It wasn't your fault." He sighs, running his fingers over the scars. "I wish I had magic enough to take every pain you have endured so that you would never have to suffer them again."

"Well, if my family loved me more—properly—they wouldn't have sold me off to be with you so easily." I lace my fingers with his.

"That isn't an excuse in the slightest."

"I know. But I'm finding it makes me feel better that you are my silver lining."

"Then I'm happy I can help," he murmurs and shifts closer.

We lie together for as long as we can. But the dawn is as relentless as our duty to all of the fae folk. Eventually, his arms relax, and we both know that we have procrastinated long enough.

"Hopefully Shaye and Giles show up today," he says as he tugs on his pants.

"Agreed. Though, I must say, for as much as I want to see

them all right, I'm glad they didn't show up last night." My grin is reflected on his face. Davien's eyes shine mischievously. He wants to kiss me; I know what that expression means now. I almost take a step forward so that he can.

"Don't tell them, but I feel the same."

"So, what do we need to do for this ritual?" I ask, now clothed.

"Here, I'll show you what Vena sent me with." Davien retrieves a folio with several loose pages. He lays them out across the table where our blanket just was. The last thing he retrieves is the glass necklace that I tried to put the powers in weeks ago. "The idea is still the same—you'll abdicate and in doing so fill the necklace with the king's magic, then you'll bestow it on me. The lake will offer a catalyst to help draw out those powers. We will anoint you as an heir to the throne would be. That way the magic will hopefully be less dormant and more controllable."

As I scan the pages intently I begin to find some sense in them. It's a pattern, a rhythm. Maybe some of what he said last night during our short-lived magic lesson sank in.

"May I make a suggestion?" I ask.

"Always." He regards me curiously. No doubt wondering what would make me speak up.

"Here...I think that I should be the one to say this line, not you." I point at a part of the script Vena has written out for us.

"Why is that?"

"I'm not sure... I—" I hum, trying to find words. "It'll flow better, I think. The ritual will just work. It's a gut feeling. But I... How to explain—"

"You don't have to." He stops my fumbling. "Your instincts have proven themselves right time and again. Be it the magic within you guiding, or just some innate ability you possess, I trust in you."

"Good, because I have some other changes." I give him a sly smile and he chuckles.

"Tell me."

We discuss all throughout breakfast, debating Vena's rituals and making adjustments. It's a bit awkward at first. No matter what he says, I still worry about overstepping. He is the Fae King. Who am I to question?

But he had said some, like Vena, were so in tune with their magic that they could see rituals. Perhaps it is the magic within me guiding the path forward. I put my faith in it.

The sun is high when we finally head outside. The fog still encircles this place as a living wall. It feels as if we are encased in clouds, floating somewhere high in the sky.

"Are you ready?" he asks.

"No reason not to be." I clutch the necklace with a white-knuckled grip. I stripped down to my small clothes and am already almost shivering even though the sun is on my shoulders. I made it a point to stoke the fire before we left the keep. No matter what happens, I am promptly returning to the warmth of the hearth after this is over.

"At your leisure then."

Sucking in a bracing breath, I step into the water. It's ice in liquid form. I exhale through chattering teeth, forcing myself to keep walking over the smooth pebbles that make up the bottom of the lake. As I move, the ripples in the water shimmer like the cosmos I saw on my first night in Midscape. I can feel the magic radiating all around me, calling to me. The faint song I heard in the fog resonates once more, as though its source lies deep within the lake's center.

I pause as the water hits my lower stomach. Shaking, I wrap my arms around myself, trying to conserve the last scraps of warmth I have. Davien stepping into the water behind me is what forces me to keep going. I inhale sharply as the water reaches my rib cage.

Davien comes to a stop behind me. He looks just as cold as I am. "Are you ready?"

"I am."

"Very well." The air around him shifts as his tone becomes serious, his eyes focused. He's back to staring at the magic within me, magic he's determined to draw out here and now. "Heir of Aviness, rightful ruler of these wilds, keeper of the power of the old kings, you've entered these waters as a woman, but you shall emerge as a queen." He lifts a hand, drawing lines from my neck, to my shoulders, collarbone, and breast. "I, as loyal subject, anoint you with the sacred water."

"I receive your blessing." With the tip of my finger, I draw the shining outlines of shapes on him as well, swirls and dots that have no coherent meaning and yet all seem to say, *I see you, I am one with you.* "I am the vessel of Aviness."

All at once, I take a deep breath and plunge under.

The moment my head crosses beneath the surface, warmth surrounds me. I open my eyes and see dozens of silvery figures waiting beneath the water. They all wear crowns of glass that I recognize from the stained glass of the keep. I surface, coughing up the water I inhaled in shock, swimming backward. Davien's hands close around my shoulders.

This was *not* part of our plan.

"What is it?"

"I saw—I saw—people underneath the water," I stammer, teeth clacking no longer from the cold. The warmth that I felt from the moment I was submerged still coats me just like the shimmering water. It turns my skin to a pale gray color, iridescent and flecked with rainbow spots. "What?" Words are failing me now as I hold up my forearms.

"This is what we came here for," Davien says reassuringly. "Don't be afraid. Don't hesitate. Accept the anointing as a queen would."

I think of what Shaye told me weeks ago—*walk with your head held high, for you have the power of kings.* I've been pretending this entire time to try and live up to the expectations of the magic in me. I can pretend a little longer. I straighten away from Davien. Even though I'm making every best effort, I still regard the water warily. I can't see those ghostly figures from above. But I know, if I opened my eyes underneath the surface, I would see them once more.

Closing my eyes, I choose to focus on the sound of music still thrumming. The more I focus, the louder it becomes. The sound gives me strength, makes me think of my birth mother. I imagine her looking fondly at me from the great Beyond, proud of her daughter for all she could accomplish.

I clutch the necklace with both hands to my breast and let my consciousness detach from my body. Somewhere, between his words and the music, I will find the magic. And once I can hold that power as tightly as I hold this pendant of glass, I will be able to hand it to the man I have given everything else to.

"I am ready for my oath." Somehow, my voice no longer sounds like my own. It's smoother, more confident than I have ever heard it before.

"Do you swear to guard and guide your people? To protect them with the ancient magic that has been bestowed on you by fate and family? Will you rule with righteousness and justice as your weapons? To strengthen our borders, and defend our cause?" Davien repeats the words from the pages Vena gave us. He finishes with one of my additions: "Do you take these oaths with reverence and severity?"

"I do."

"Will you forsake all temptation that could lead you astray?"

"I will."

"And will you use every last recess of your power to further, uphold, and revere the way of our people forevermore?"

"All this and more, I swear to you." My eyes flutter open and I meet his emerald gaze. Davien's lips part slightly. He can feel it too. I wonder if he can even hear the music that is reaching its crescendo. It fills my ears like the water; it fills my soul like the magic of fae kings. "I take these oaths freely and sincerely."

"Then draw your last breath as the woman you are, and arise as a queen." He leans forward and places both his hands on my shoulders. I suck in a breath and Davien pushes me back. This time I'm ready for what awaits me.

Underneath the water I hear cheering, a joyous symphony soaring around me as though it is playing in a hall three times as magnificent as the keep we slept in last night. The applause of kings and queens from long ago bolsters me and the magic that I can feel crackling from my every pore.

I am pulled back above the water by Davien. I take in a greedy gulp of the crisp air. I blink up at the sky and relish in this feeling of immeasurable power.

If I wanted, if I dared, I could change this world.

And then, my eyes fall from the heavens and land on him. The first and only thing I do with this power is pour it into the necklace still clutched in my hands. I stand and Davien kneels. Now is the part we wrote together.

I move to the sounds of music—of the magic that lives within me. I step around him, making mirrors of the shapes he drew on my body with the water earlier. I come back to a stop before him and hold out the necklace.

Davien stares in wonder and anticipation. He slowly lifts his hand. Everything he ever wanted is within his grasp.

The magic begins to drain from my body. I feel heavier by the second and wonder if I'll have the strength to say what needs to be said next. But we are so close. "I abd—"

Out of nowhere, a shadowy arrow knocks the necklace from my palm and the power the ritual had been building breaks with an almost audible *snap*.

twenty-nine

FOR A SECOND, I'M TOO STUNNED TO DO ANYTHING. Davien stares at my outstretched hand where the necklace just was, blinking as though our eyes have deceived us. Then, simultaneously, we react.

Davien jumps from the water, spinning toward where the arrow came from. I lunge for where the necklace has sunk beneath the lake's glassy surface. The song I heard earlier has come to a halt. The water is cooling, frigid once more. Even though I open my eyes underwater, I don't see any of the ghostly figures. It's as though not just the magic that was within me was placed in the necklace, but the magic of the lake itself, of this entire place.

My horrible theory is confirmed when I resurface, pendant in hand.

The mist that surrounded and protected the keep is evaporating in the sunlight. Like a shroud being pulled off, it reveals the sparse, skeletal forest we rode through with pristine clarity. Lining those trees are ten Butchers, their cowls radiating angry shadows around their necks and shoulders.

I had intended to gather the power of Aviness…but I hadn't dreamed or wanted to be *this* successful.

Davien is in motion toward the nearest Butcher. Two others break away from the line, disappearing in the shadow of one of the nearby trees. Motion at my right distracts me from Davien. The two Butchers have reappeared in the shade of the keep, racing toward me.

I scramble, looking frantically between Davien and the necklace. Three Butchers have descended on him now. Davien is strong and has become more powerful during his time in Midscape. But without the power of kings I know that he's too outnumbered. I look back to the two that are nearly upon me, stepping hastily away into the deeper water.

"Don't come any closer," I say. "I have the power of kings."

"That's exactly what we came here for." The man approaching me smiles thinly.

"Don't force me to use it." I'd sound far more threatening if my voice wasn't quivering.

"As if you could. You already separated the magic from your body. You're nothing more than a pathetic human now."

"Katria, run!" Davien booms at the top of his lungs. Without warning, a flash of light radiates out from him. I look away at the last possible second. The Butchers are blinded. I sprint for the horse, kicking up water in my haste. It's slow going until I hit the shallows. But by then, the Butchers are already recovering. I hear the sounds of struggle coming from Davien.

I glance over, seeing him dodging attack after attack. He rears back and claws—long and deadly—protrude from his fingers. He sinks them into the side of one of the attackers. But I don't get to see the woman go down because in my periphery the two men are charging for me with the speed of angry boars.

The horse is our best chance. We can't fight. We have to run. Luckily, they haven't thought to kill the stallion yet. I thank my past self for thinking of keeping the mount saddled.

Using the steps that lead up into the keep, I grip the vines that grow around the open doorway, and use them to help hoist myself up as I jump. I land awkwardly on the horse's back, scrambling to get my feet astride and in the stirrups. I manage to just as the Butchers are on me. Between their lunges startling the horse, and my shout, he shoots off faster than the arrow that caught Davien and me by surprise.

I clutch on, staying low and swerving as more arrows *whiz* past me. "Davien!" I scream. He glances over his shoulder, seeing me coming right for him.

Davien brings his hands together once more, clapping them with a boom of light. Once more, I shield my eyes at the last second. The horse is not so lucky; he startles, rearing back. I hold on for dear life, soothing the beast as best I can while still spurring him onward. *Trust me*, I plead silently with the stallion.

He's truly a well-trained mount, fitting for a king, as he presses on even though I'm sure he's still partially blinded. I hold out my hand for Davien. Three of the Butchers are hot on his heels. His flash of light trick is less effective than last time, and I doubt it'll work a third.

We clasp each other's forearms and I let out a grunt as I help swing him up. Davien gives a mighty leap and lands as awkwardly as I did—nearly knocking me off in the process. The horse swerves as I lose control while I readjust my balance.

"Do you have it?" The question is filled with desperation.

"I do." The pendant is clutched in my right hand. I don't dare unfurl my fingers from it or the horse's reins to show him.

"Ride like the wind," he urges, clutching me tightly. Still in our small clothes, soaking wet, we begin to flee.

Seven of the ten are far behind us, but the three that managed to shield their eyes from Davien's last burst of light dart between the shadows of the trees we sprint through. They launch projectiles with shouts and cries of maniacal laughter.

I swerve the horse right and left, trying to avoid as many shadows as I can. The last thing I want is for one of them to pop up right in front of us. Our only hope is my skill in riding against their luck in hurling things at us.

"You can do this," Davien encourages. No sooner does he say it than a Butcher appears in a nearby tree, vaulting themselves from the upper branches. I look up on instinct. "Focus ahead," he snaps. I don't see the Butcher's body as it meets Davien's claws, but I hear the crunching of bone, the shrill scream, and the thud it makes as she hits the ground behind us.

Is that one down? Or two? Or did he fell even more that I didn't see back by the lake? I hope that's the case.

"The horse can't keep this pace forever." I glance back at him.

"The ritual on their cowls will run out soon enough. It draws more power to be used in broad daylight like this. We can outpace them," he reassures me.

Sure enough, two of the remaining Butchers are no longer giving chase. I turn my focus back ahead so I can weave through the trees. Another one lunges for us from a treetop and completely misses.

There are only three now who are keeping pace with the horse. Davien is right. We can outrun them. *We can do this.*

Yet no sooner do I think that than an arrow whizzes past our horse's snout, causing the stallion to rear back. I manage to hold on, but Davien doesn't have as good grip on the beast as I do. As he tilts off balance, I feel him pulling me with him, until he releases his hold so we aren't both unseated.

"Davien, no!" I scream as the stallion rights himself.

"Go!" he booms. "Don't stop!" Davien jumps to his feet, claws unsheathed, facing the remaining Butchers.

"I—"

"Go!" he speaks over me, hearing my objection before I can say it. "I won't let them get you or the necklace."

A sticky, hot, sickening feeling overtakes me, chasing away the cool air on my clammy skin. If I leave him behind, here and now, they're going to kill him. I can't... I must.

"Katria, *go!*" he shouts a final time.

With all the pain of ripping open a wound, I give the horse a kick and we begin sprinting once more. Even as I'm riding away, my neck is craned back toward him. I watch as two of the three remaining Butchers descend on him, only one chasing me now.

I have to go back.

I can't go back.

If I don't go back, they'll kill him.

I can't let them kill him. I love him. I have to go back.

No, the voice of reason is quiet and calm, *because you love him, you can't go back.* Going back would be the wrong kind of love, the reckless kind that disregards his most earnest wishes. It would be a selfish love, where I put what I want above what he does. Going back would mean handing over the magic that countless fae—that Giles and Shaye—gave their lives to protect.

Is this choice love?

I press my eyes closed and let out a scream of frustration and agony that harmonizes in the most horrible way with a cry of pain from Davien in the distance.

Don't kill him, I plead with fate, with luck, with whatever old god might be listening. Maybe Boltov wants him alive. My stomach clenches. No, if they take him to the High Court, he'll face a fate worse than death.

No matter what, he's going to die, and I never had a chance to outright tell him I loved him.

I dodge another arrow, pushing the horse onward. I continue at our relentless pace, avoiding the shadows, and running as though our life depends on it. I don't relent even after the final Butcher has fallen out of sight, the magic of their cowl expended.

Davien's cries of agony chase me far longer than any of Boltov's men and women.

thirty

NUMB. Inside and out. I feel nothing.

My skin is so cold that I'm surprised it hasn't cracked and started bleeding. Its healthy hue is gone, replaced with a shade as ghostly as the barren earth beneath me. Every muscle has seized from shivering for so long.

Even my mind has frozen over. My thoughts are still, encased in frost. The only thing I seem to be able to comprehend is forward. *Ride forward.* Keep going.

So when I see a shadow emerge at the edge of my vision, I can hardly react in time. The Butchers have finally caught up to me. They have me now, and the magic, and I left Davien behind for nothing.

"Katria!"

"No!" I scream back and try to spur the horse onward. The mount is exhausted from riding hard all morning. He's got nothing more to give.

"Katria." The man approaches.

"I won't let you take me. I won't—" I finally turn and realize who it is coming toward me. "Giles?" I rasp.

"I thought it was you." He rushes over. I can only imagine how I look to him—still in nothing more than my small clothes, my wet hair hanging in knotted clumps, my lips blue, my body covered in mud and rock and blood. "What's happened?"

I shake my head and choke on the words. Moving my

head back and forth sets my whole body in motion. I'm shuddering, violently. I rasp incomplete breaths, wheezing them out only halfway before I inhale again. I stare at the necklace in my hand.

"I— I— Davien— He."

Giles frowns. He knows what I've done. He knows I've left his king behind for the Butchers. Will he believe me that it was Davien's wish? Will it even matter? I left Davien—the heir of Aviness— behind.

What have I done?

"Let me take this." Giles slowly reaches for the reins of the horse.

"We have to keep going. We can't go back there."

"Obviously. There's a tree not far from here that I holed up in last night. I was making my way north when the fog lifted and my compass worked again." As he speaks, he shrugs off his coat, and it's then that I notice his shirt is covered in blood.

"You're hurt."

"I was. It's why I didn't meet you both at the keep. Instead, I found shelter and healed myself. I'm fine now." He says it in a way that betrays his true meaning—*I'm fine, you don't need to worry about me, worry about yourself.* Giles drapes his coat over my shoulders. "We'll go there now."

"We have to keep moving, it's not safe."

"It's not far and you're going to die of exposure if you keep on like this," Giles says firmly. "We need to get you warm and dry."

I'm too tired to argue anymore. I let him take the horse's reins and he leads us diagonally away from the course I had been charting. Fortunately, it's still in a somewhat southerly direction, and away from the main road.

But nowhere feels safe as long as the Butchers know I have this necklace. Boltov has the crown, the hill, and now the heir that was standing in his way. All he needs is this power to be the unquestioned ruler of the fae.

Soon enough, we arrive at one of the larger trees of the skeletal woods. We're definitely closer to the forests of Dreamsong. The trees here are larger and well-nourished. They still lack life, like the rest of the once foggy forest. But they're large enough that two people can fit inside, albeit tightly, which is just what we do.

We squeeze into a split in the trunk. Giles suggested we tie up the horse at a distance, still in our field of view, but far enough that if someone attacked it they wouldn't immediately see us. I don't want to watch another horse die...but *I* want to die even less.

"Pass me back my coat. I only need it for a second."

I oblige him. Giles places it on the ground just outside the tree. He peels off his socks, belt, and riding gloves. After drawing some lines and circles in the soft earth, he piles them up. With a soft incantation and a touch of his hands there's new clothes—a long tunic, leggings, and a simple pair of ankle boots.

He hands them to me and says somewhat apologetically, "They're not my best work. I don't have much in the way of materials out here right now. But it'll be better than nothing."

That much is certainly true. No sooner have I pulled the tunic over my head than I feel it trapping in what meager warmth my body is still producing. When I'm dressed, Giles shifts closer, wrapping an arm around me.

"Don't get the wrong idea," he says, not meeting my eyes. "I'm just trying to warm you up as quickly as possible so we can get moving again."

"I don't have the wrong idea," I say softly. "I know you only have eyes for Shaye."

"What happened to her? And to Davien?" he finally asks.

My lower lip quivers, but not from the cold. I fight for every word. I made my choice when I left Davien behind. I have to stand by it now even in the face of—no, especially in the face of—his staunchest allies.

"We made it to the keep last night." I shake my head and backtrack a little bit. "We were attacked not long after you vanished. It was Allor."

"I knew it." He curses under his breath. "She got me first."

"How'd you escape?"

"She wasn't after me, so she didn't pursue when I disengaged, but I was hoping to lead her away from the three of you." He shook his head. "It looked like she had a glass shard of some kind. Perhaps an old Aviness relic she was using to navigate the fog."

I look at the necklace. Allor said she was the one to find it. I'd bet she found it while looking for a way through the fog for Boltov. All along she'd been playing us…and we let her. Rage warms me more than clothes or Giles ever could.

"I saw her go after you and couldn't follow. She caught up to you, then?"

"Yes. Shaye engaged with her; she fought so that Davien and I could get away. My horse was killed in the fight. Then we made it to the keep…"

The memories of last night flood me. It seems impossible to think that just a few hours ago I woke up in Davien's arms. That this is the same reality as was then. It should be impossible for one person to feel so full and warm then feel so cold and bitter in the same day.

"We made the ritual work." I finally uncurl my fingers from around the necklace. I have to physically move one or two with my other hand because my grip has locked up. "All the magic is out of me now, and in this necklace. But then, right as I went to bestow it on Davien, there were more Butchers. We fought. We were going to get away… And then… Giles, it happened so fast. He was there with me on the horse, and then he wasn't. They surrounded him. He told me to go." I meet Giles's sad eyes. "What was I supposed to do? I know how much this means to him—to all of your people. I couldn't let the Boltovs get it… But that meant… That meant…"

"It's all right," he whispers. His arm tightens around my shoulders, pulling me closer. The embrace is warm and secure in a wholly different way than Davien's. "You did the right thing."

"Why do I feel like I betrayed him?" My voice cracks. "Why do I feel like I've condemned him to death?"

"We won't let him die." Giles has strength that I could only dream of possessing right now. It's the strength of a man who didn't see multiple Butchers descending on a lone fae.

"Won't Boltov kill him?"

"Oh, most certainly." A shadow crosses Giles's face. "But not before he makes a mockery of Davien. Boltov won't give him the honor of a clean death. Davien has eluded him too long for that. Boltov will make a statement before killing him—he'll want to make killing the last Aviness heir public. He wants people to know the deed is done so none will ever dare speak out against him again.

And that'll be his mistake as it will be what gives us the time to infiltrate the High Court."

"Do you really think all that's true?" It fills me with a glimmer of hope that almost feels dangerous to possess.

"I do. But first, how do you feel?"

"What?" How I feel is hardly a problem.

"You don't have the magic anymore. Have you begun withering?"

"I am exhausted," I admit. "But I think that's to be expected."

"True…"

I shake my head. "I feel fine. Well enough to continue on."

I have to. I won't let him tell me no. The realization that I am willing to give my life for the fae hits me harder than expected. I swallow down the initial rush of fear and steady my breathing. I'm going to see this through to the end. I'm going to see Davien on the fae throne with the glass crown. Or I will die trying.

Giles gives me a skeptical look.

"I don't think I'm withering yet. I still have time here," I insist.

"All right. But keep an eye on it," he relents. "Either way, we need to head back to Dreamsong. It's the closest path across the Fade if we need to bring you back. Moreover, the supplies and allies we need are there. Hopefully we'll run into Shaye on the way, or meet her there. But if not, then we'll save her too."

"Would Boltov also let her live?"

"For a time, and for a similar reason as Davien—he would want to make an example of her, of the horrors that befall a Butcher who would dare break rank. I imagine her torture would be less public, but no less severe." Emotions are straining the edges of Giles's face, causing his mouth and brow to contort. His usual levity has been crushed under immense weight. I know exactly what he's feeling.

Both of our loves have been taken by Boltov.

"We should keep moving," I say, pushing myself up. As I step out of the protection of the tree and Giles's warmth, a breeze whips through me and I fight a shiver.

"Are you warm enough?" He must have seen it. "Is it the withering?"

"I'm *fine*," I insist again. "We don't have time to waste." I put the pendant around my neck, tucking it under the tunic. "The faster we get to Dreamsong, the faster we save Shaye and Davien."

The ride to Dreamsong is a cold, silent, and tense affair. The stallion is too tired to support both of our weights, so I still ride alone. Giles insisted I be astride, that way I can flee faster if need be.

I can feel my face crumple the moment the demarcation line of the territory of the Acolytes of the Wild Wood comes into view. We're so close to safety. It's now late in the afternoon and I know that if we're forced to take a rest, the safe house isn't far.

"Are we going to press on through the night?" I ask.

"I can carry on." Giles eyes the mount. "What do you think about him?"

"We've kept things easy; I think he can manage. And if he begins to struggle I'll dismount and walk too."

"All right, then—" Giles stills as we cross over the bare strip of earth that marks the Acolyte's territory.

I feel it too. Or rather, I *don't* feel anything. There is no tingle of the barrier that surrounded the territory before. The earth is the same here as it was on the other side of the line.

"Something is wrong." He gives sound to my thoughts. Giles looks to me. "Change of plans. We'll go to the safe house and you'll stay there. I'll go on ahead and scout Dreamsong and then come back."

"No." I shoot the idea down quickly. "Our plan remains the same. We're just more cautious."

"But—"

"I'm not sitting somewhere alone, defenseless. Moreover, if you leave and something does happen to me—if Boltov gets this necklace—then no one will know until it's too late. Our best course of action is to stay together."

He purses his lips, clearly debating this, but ultimately relents. "Fine. But if we do encounter a struggle, you flee with the necklace.

Head for Dreamsong, and keep your eyes open. No matter what happens, Boltov can't get that power."

"Understood." I didn't come this far and sacrifice so much to hand over the magic now.

We press on in silence for the rest of the day. Neither of us are in the mood for small talk. Shortly after the sun has gone down, we pause at a stream and give the horse a chance to drink.

"Are you still strong enough to continue?" Giles asks. Hearing his voice after hours of silence seems shockingly loud.

"I am, but I'm not the one who's been walking this whole time. How are you?"

"I'm tougher than I look."

"You look pretty tough." I give him a weary smile; one he weakly returns.

"Let's keep going, then."

The stars are out and the moon is high when we smell smoke. We exchange a wary look and a frown, but we don't alter course. However, when an orange haze appears through the trees, Giles holds out his arm.

"This isn't good," he whispers. "You should stay here."

"No, we go on together."

"I'm trying to protect you." The edge of weary frustration is present in his voice. It's well intended, even if it's misplaced.

"I know," I say as calmly as possible. "But I've come this far. I'm not going to back away now. No matter what happens. I'm seeing this through to the end."

Giles regards me thoughtfully and then resigns with a sigh. "Very well. But if anyone asks, I thought you should stay back."

"Your objection is noted."

"Stay close and follow me, then, we don't want to go on the main road." He begins leading us to the side, away from the well-worn trail we've been traveling on for the past hour.

It's the feeling of sneaking that fills me with dread. It underscores that this place I once thought of as truly safe is no longer. I touch the necklace at my throat, thinking of Davien. I have to be strong for him. I can't be afraid. I am still the keeper of the magic of the old kings. And until I can give it back to the person who can really use it to save these lands, I have to do what I can to help save the fae from Boltov.

The sound of fire crackling in the distance grows louder. I dismount, leaving the stallion tied loosely around a low-hanging branch, and we continue on foot, both agreeing that it will be less noticeable this way. We stay low and hunched in the brush as we approach the upper rim of Dreamsong.

Smoke is thick in my lungs and the orange glow is even brighter now; it's almost like the dawn is breaking through the trees. I pull up my tunic over my nose and mouth but it does little good. My eyes are watering and lungs burning, but I don't stop. I have to see what's on the other side of those trees. I have to see Dreamsong even though something tells me that this pursuit is one I will regret. That what I'm about to witness can never be unseen.

As we break through the brush and stand above the smoldering remains of the brilliant city I danced in the streets of not more than three days ago, I'm proved right.

thirty-one

DREAMSONG IS NOTHING MORE THAN A CHARRED HUSK. I'm reminded of the smoldering embers of a fireplace, shining like angry stars, glowing with vengeful heat, sparking flames to consume whatever fuel still remains. I think I've left my body for a second, because I don't realize that Giles is shaking me until the third time he calls my name. "Katria."

"They burned it, all of it." All that magnificent craftsmanship, gone up in flames. Even if the fae can make things quickly with rituals, it's still a tragedy. Then my thoughts go to the people and my mind comes to a screeching halt. I spin toward Giles and grab him by both shoulders. "The people—"

"I know." He knocks my hands away. The smoldering remains of the city are alight in his eyes. The city...*his home*. "But I don't see very many bodies in the streets."

We clearly have different definitions of "very many bodies" but I say nothing.

"Which means that our plan worked."

"Plan?" I repeat, still staring over the wreckage. The Natural World has known nothing but peace for centuries. Sure, on occasion, squabbles arise. But nothing major. Nothing like *this*.

The fae had told me from the start of the horrors the Boltovs could wreak. But I'd failed to comprehend it.

I never thought anyone capable of this level of destruction and disregard for life...even with magic at their disposal.

"Yes, remember the tunnel?"

My thoughts begin to coalesce again. "The tunnel...but we didn't finish it."

"Vena saw it was completed when all were distracted by the autumnal celebrations. She was worried about the increasing probability of an attack ever since Davien and the magic returned." Giles begins to head back into the forest, eyes darting around warily. "The plan was that the soldiers and guards would stay to defend the city, holding off whatever Boltov threw at us for as long as possible, while the civilians escaped to the mountain."

I can no longer see Dreamsong, but the sight of the streets, red with fire and blood, is seared on my mind. I think of those people, staying behind so that others might have a chance at life. The sight, the thought, will likely haunt me for years in ways that I can't possibly comprehend now, not when my focus remains on my own survival.

Giles heads left toward the mountains, bypassing the horse.

"We're leaving the stallion?"

"It risks too much attention, and we can't bring it under the mountain," he says.

"Right. How many people knew about the tunnel?" We hadn't exactly been keeping it a secret while working on it.

"I'm not sure. I wasn't that high up in the ranks."

"But...everyone had to know, right? So they knew what to do in case of an attack?" I bite my lip, unable to shake a clammy, sickening sensation that's wrapping my spine.

"Unless they were informed only when the attack was happening, instructed to follow orders and nothing more." Giles glances at me as he leads us around Dreamsong toward the mountains. I get glimpses of their frosted peaks through the dark canopy, reflecting the angry fires below. "What are you getting at?"

"What if Allor knew?" I whisper.

He spins in place, staring at me with wide eyes. "You don't think..." he breathes. "But she... Shaye would have come back and warned them."

"I don't know," I say weakly. "I never saw what happened with them and she wasn't among the Butchers who attacked Davien and me at the lake. I don't know what happened to Shaye."

Without another word, Giles sprints toward the mountains. I follow behind through the dense forest. The usual motes of light that bed down on the mosses are gone, casting everything in menacing shadow. It is as if life is slowly being sucked out of the world wherever Boltov touches.

"Giles," I hiss as my ears pick up on the sounds of distant fighting. He keeps running. He's going to run headfirst into what's surely a trap. I grab his wrist, digging my heels into the soft earth. Giles turns his panicked eyes to me. "*Listen.*"

His eyes only grow wider as he hears what I have been—shouting, laughter, grunting, and crying. Not the sounds of people enjoying a reprieve.

"No," he breathes. I watch as the hope leaves his eyes, darkening his expression further.

"We go slow. We have to stay hidden," I whisper.

He nods.

Firelight begins to glint through the trees, the dancing flames shimmering on the sheer faces of the mountain not far from where Giles, Oren, Davien and I were working on the tunnel. As we grow nearer, the voices grow clearer.

"Your king wants you alive. So no one put up a fight," a man sneers.

"Of course, accidents do happen." *That's Allor.* I meet Giles's eyes—he has the same realization as I do.

"I'm going to kill her," he says under his breath.

"You're going to have to fight me for that honor."

He gives a conspiratorial nod and motions for me to follow as he starts for a nearby tree. "Are you good at climbing?"

I stare up at the tree, thinking back to the roof. *No climbing,* Joyce had ingrained in me. *No heights. Stay close to the ground...* where I belonged.

"I'm actually really good at climbing," I admit to myself and him. Because I still did even despite her, to repair the outer walls of the manor, or clean the molding that ran along the ceilings. Even after the fall, I never became afraid of heights. They always felt natural. Strange, how some of those skills are coming in handy when I least expect them.

"We can get a good look from up there, I think." Giles points to one of the far-reaching branches of the oak tree and I follow him up. Sure enough, we can see the Butchers and the survivors of Dreamsong below while being shielded by the wide branches we now lie on and the leafy bough of the oak.

There are the remnants of a struggle on the ground—more bodies and blood. The survivors have been corralled into three different groups, each of them facing a small army of Butchers. Most of them stare at their feet or at nothing in particular with vacant, hollow eyes.

"Are they going to take them all back to the High Court?" I whisper.

"I can only assume so."

"How many examples does one king need?" My question has the edge of a growl at its end. This is too much. Boltov is going too far. And yet, based on everything I've been told, this all is still just the tip of the horrors that this king has brought to the fae wilds.

"We're going to move in groups," the man who I presume is the lead Butcher says. "I strongly recommend that you listen to the instructions we give you, as failure to do so might resolve in further unpleasantness."

The Butchers pass around small tokens made of what appears to be glass.

"What are those?" I glanced toward Giles. "More relics?"

"No. Those are shards of the crown—summonses from the king. It's one of the many powers of the glass crown. Any fae who receives a summons must respond within the day or they'll die."

I wince. For as beautiful as this world is, it certainly has vicious undertones that I had overlooked for weeks. But now I see them. Now I see the darkness as clearly as I saw every glittering spark of magic light.

The head Butcher walks over to a group that's mostly obscured by the trees. "As the leader of this rebellious group, you'll show them how to return to our king's loving embrace."

"*Loving.*" Vena snorts. She's alive. Relief floods through me. If

Vena is alive then there's hope. I'm not quite sure why I feel that way, perched in a tree, helpless to do anything to assist... But if anyone can concoct a way out of the situation she now finds herself in, I believe it to be Vena.

"We have shown you mercy." The Butcher stalks closer to her and out of my view. "It is up to you to decide if that mercy continues, or if we exact our king's vengeance here and now."

There's a long pause. I wonder what's going through her mind. What if she's thinking of Davien coming in to save the day? Maybe that's what makes her say, "I heed my king's summons."

There's a small flash of light. Some men and women in the other groups begin to weep quietly. They just watched their leader, their hope, go into the arms of the enemy. I see others bringing the tokens to their chest and repeating the same, vanishing with small sparks.

As I'm watching the group closest to the mountain, I see a thin trickle of rocks bouncing down the boulders at the mountain's foot. I lean to get a better view of where those rocks came from—what might have knocked them loose. I had been hoping to see a horde of Acolytes ready to rain terror down from above on the Butchers. But instead, my eyes lock with a familiar lilac pair. I see the curve of horns I recognize attached to a small face peeking out from behind one of the high-up ledges.

Raph's eyes widen slightly. I bring a finger to my lips. He nods and we both lean back into our hiding places.

Unfortunately, I don't think I'm the only one who might have seen the rocks Raph knocked loose. As the groups of survivors slowly disappear one by one, the main Butcher barks an order. "Search the area, make sure there are no stragglers."

"If we find any, what are your orders?" Allor asks.

"Kill them on sight. The king has enough executions on his hands already. We can have a bit of fun."

The Butchers fan out with excited rumblings. Giles and I pull in our arms and legs as much as possible while still keeping our balance. I hold my breath, watching as two Butchers pass beneath us, searching. We wait for what feels like nearly an hour. An hour of tense muscles, shallow breathing, and the creeping dread that at any second I'm going to hear a shout that marks my death.

But it never comes. And instead the next thing I hear is a new order.

"Head back," the man commands.

Giles and I remain in the tree for at least ten more minutes, not moving. We stare at each other, as if we're waiting to see who's going to take the responsibility of being the first one to speak. I surprise myself by rising to the occasion.

"Do you think it's safe?" My voice is so soft that I'm sure he reads my lips more than hears my words.

"I don't think anywhere is safe for us anymore," he says solemnly. "But I think all the Butchers are gone."

"Good. Follow me."

"And just where do you think you're going?" he asks as we slowly climb down the tree.

"I'm not sure yet." Even though I think all the Butchers are gone, I still slink through the dark forest, clinging to trees and trying to make myself as small as possible. We come to the edge of the clearing where the Butchers caught the survivors.

"We should give them a proper burial," Giles says softly.

"There's no time."

"No time? All we have now is time…while we wait for them to come and kill us." Anger creeps into his voice. I know I'm just a convenient outlet for it. He's not actually angry at me. Yet another thing that my family prepared me for—allowing vicious tirades and wounding words to be nothing more than glancing blows that rarely meet the mark.

"I'm not going to wait for anyone to come and kill me." I scan the mountains, trying to figure out where Raph might have climbed from. "I spent my whole life at the whim of others, waiting to see what they'll do to me next; I'm not waiting anymore."

The hiss of my name nearly startles Giles out of his skin.

"Katria! Over here."

Raph stands between a boulder and the mountain, at the edge of the carnage. Giles is a step behind me and rushing over to him, dumbstruck as he lays eyes on Hol's son. Raph's gaze is distant. Shock has hollowed out his usually precocious demeanor. He stares up at us, blinking several times, looking for the first time like the child he very much is.

"I thought we were the only ones who survived." His lower lip quivers as he fights back tears. "I saw them rounding everyone else up. I didn't know what to do."

"Who else is with you?" Giles asks.

"I'll show you." Raph leads us through nooks and crannies created by boulders and rocks removed when the tunnel was made. It's nearly impossible for us to squeeze through in some places; no wonder the Butchers didn't think to even try. But for Raph's lithe, little frame, it's no trouble at all. He saw a path where no one else did. A hideaway not even Allor would know. "When it happened, my father told me what to do. I was gonna be where he told me to. Swear. But...I was worried, you know, since not all of Dreamsong coulda been told... I went to see how Ralsha was. And well, then she had a friend, who had a friend. We were just tryin' to look out for each other and by the time we got here, they were already...you know. I had this hiding spot and shared it."

The pathway enters the mountain. On the other side of the brief, naturally formed tunnel is a sheltered glade. Two dozen fae children huddle together. Some weep openly, others consoling them. Most just clutch themselves, or each other, staring blankly with eyes much like Raph's.

"I didn't mean to break the rules and not go with the rest, I swear." Raph wipes his nose with the back of his hand and shakes his head. "D'ya think my dad'll be upset?"

"No." Giles breaks then and there. He falls to his knees and clutches the small boy tightly. I can only imagine that Giles has watched this child—maybe all of these children—grow up in the city that he swore to protect. The city that is still burning. "You did amazing, Raph."

"You really did," I echo. "How did you manage to evade the Butchers when no one else could?"

Raph looks up at me. "Told you already, the best guide there is. No one knows—" he gulps down a burst of emotion "—*knew* Dreamsong like me. No one can get into places like I can to make deliveries. Especially not those Butchers. And specially not if my 'delivery' is my friends."

I kneel down as Giles finally releases him. I place my hand on Raph's shoulder and lock eyes with him. "Raph, what I'm about to ask you is entirely unfair. It is a burden that not even the most skilled adults could shoulder, and I'm going to ask if you're willing to do it."

The spark of fire in his eyes reassures me. Underneath the shock and sadness is anger and determination. Even though his city is still smoldering, he wants revenge. We all do.

"I have something very important I need you to deliver. And I swear, if you do this, it's the last delivery I'm going to ever ask of you."

"Katria?" Giles asks worriedly, as if he can somehow sense what all of this is building up to. I wonder if he can see the plan that's forming in my head even though I'm making it up as I go. Raph just continues to stare in determined silence.

"I need you to deliver *me* into the heart of the High Court."

thirty-two

"No," Giles says instantly.

Yet nearly at the same time, Raph says, "I'll do it."

"Raph, you cannot." Giles turns to me, pointing his finger. "And you cannot ask this of him."

"Getting the powers to Davien is the best chance we have now. And Raph is clearly the most qualified person to see this through," I say calmly.

"You risked your life to take these powers out of Boltov's hands. You left the last remaining member of the Aviness bloodline behind to keep this power out of Boltov's hands." Giles stands with purpose, grinding out the words. His fingers ball into fists; the anger I sensed earlier continues to rise in him. And now I've given it a reasonable excuse to be directed at me.

Still, I remain calm. "Things were different then. When I left Davien behind, I thought there was a city that was safe to bring the power back to. I thought there was a small army ready to take on the High Court and free him. None of that is the case any longer.

"Boltov has the last heir, and once he kills him, the ritual preventing anyone but an Aviness from wearing the glass crown will be broken—it will be free. He will be able to wear the crown then and command its power. He has the people that would stand up against him in shackles." Or worse. "He sits on the hill and all he needs now for his

role to be cemented for hundreds of years to come is this necklace."
I touch the pendant on my throat for emphasis. "How long do you
think we can keep it from him?"

Giles eases back some.

He's no doubt beginning to see my logic. So I double down.

"He's going to throw every resource he has at hunting this
necklace down. And there's nothing you and I can do to stop him.
The one chance we had to keep it from him has gone up in flames."
I take a stabilizing breath. "Except Davien. He's our last hope. If
you're right and Boltov hasn't killed him right away, then I can get
to him with this necklace, I can finish abdicating. I can give him the
power within and he can take on Boltov."

"You might die trying," Giles whispers.

I shrug, thinking I look braver than I feel. "I think I'm going to
die no matter what." I try and wear a bold smile. I'm sure it comes
off a little wild. I must be for suggesting this. "Either from the
withering, or because Allor knows my face. She knows there is a
human who helped—who likely has the necklace. I don't think I'll
be safe even in my world. Even if we manage to keep it from her,
she'll hunt me down."

"You could go far from the edge of the Fade. Folk of Midscape
never go far in the Natural World. We're not made for it. Being there
breaks us down." Giles takes my hand with both of his. "You can
still go. This isn't your fight."

"But it is," I say softly. "I took an oath to protect the people of
this land."

"What?"

I'm back underneath the waters of the lake. All the past kings and
queens watch me. I feel their eyes even now. "I swore I would keep
this power safe and protect the fae, to Davien, to the Aviness family
who came before."

Clarity dawns on him. "That was merely part of the abdication
ritual, wasn't it?"

"The words still meant something to me." They're seared on my
memory. I said those words with every past ruler bearing witness.
They weren't just words. "Maybe you're right. Maybe it shouldn't

have meant anything. I am just a human. But I'm invested in this fight." I grip the necklace tightly. "I want to see Davien win."

No... I just want to see him alive. I can't stand the thought of him being locked away, captive to Boltov's whims. If nothing else, as tragic as it is to even think, I can't let him die without telling him that I love him. That even though I swore never to love, he burrowed deep within my heart, underneath all the walls. I won't let myself die before I do that much.

Giles turns to Raph. "Do you really think you could do it? Sneak us into the High Court?"

Raph has only a moment of hesitation before he's gathered enough resolve to give a firm nod. "I know I can. I can get anywhere I set my mind to and—and they have my parents."

"You can stay here," I suggest to Giles. "Look after the children."

"There's no way I'm letting you go alone. Hol is already going to kill me for this plan. He would kill me a second time if I let his son out of my sight to go on this insane mission alone with a human."

"All right." I don't fight. "We take the rest of the night to gather our strength and then at dawn we head for the High Court."

Raph leaves Ralsha in charge when we depart. There's a tearful goodbye between them where he swears to get back her mother, too. Davien's affections have even made me see their young love in a new light. Maybe there is goodness out there to be gained from the act of loving. Benefits of love I'm only just beginning to understand. It'll take me time, but I'm at least open to seeing it now, which is a start.

After we leave the children's stronghold, Giles leads the way. In the daylight, the remnants of Dreamsong are somehow even worse. The sun hides nothing. Boltov's brutality is on shameless display. I wonder if the king intends to leave this earth singed and blackened for the rest of eternity—a reminder to anyone who would ever dare rise up against his family in the future of what happens to usurpers.

It takes two days to reach the outskirts of the High Court. The trek is long, but the hardest part about it is constantly looking over our shoulders, expecting to see a Butcher lunging from a nearby shadow. However, Boltov must be feeling secure in his victory, because no one prowls the forests looking for survivors. I wonder if he has them back by the Lake of Anointing looking for me, arrogant in thinking there would be no way a human could make it this far.

The first Butcher we see is from a distance, walking along the ramparts of the large stone wall that surrounds the High Court. The three of us are perched at the top of a hill, lying down among the tall grasses to make ourselves nearly invisible to the guards below. We survey the terrain, debating our next move.

"The wall is only about two hundred years old," Giles says. "The last Boltov king built it to try and cement his perceived legitimacy to the Council of Kings. I'm pretty sure the winter after it was finished, his son assassinated him so he could ascend to the throne."

"Tell me, has a fae king ever died of natural causes? Or do you just kill each other before such a thing can happen?"

"It's been rare for a king to make it to the end of his natural life since the fall of the Aviness family." Giles glances to Raph. "I don't want you to feel pressured, not even now. If you don't think there's a way that we can safely get in then—"

"There's a hole in every wall," Raph says with a small grin. "We just gotta find it."

After half a day of walking, we finally do. Sure enough, there's one segment of wall where the forest has encroached on the stone. Of course, Raph is the one to notice it.

"See that?" He points. "The big bushy section, like there's a small tree poking through. Well, actually, I think there *is* a small tree poking through. You know what that means, right?" He rolls his eyes at our oblivious expressions. "It means that the wall isn't quite so sound right there. So I just gotta go down there tonight, take a peek, and if I'm right then you two will come and join me. And just like that, we'll be in." He snaps his fingers.

Into the deadliest area of the fae wilds. I have the rest of the afternoon to contemplate the decision. I spend it munching on some mushrooms we found a day ago during our long trek and watching the patrol patterns of Boltov's Butchers on the walls.

As night falls, Raph moves during a break in patrol. The boy is nimble and small; in a blink, he disappears through the foliage protruding from the wall. Giles and I share a nervous glance. But then Raph pokes his head back out and waves us down the hill.

The wall is much larger than it seemed from a distance. The wicked-looking spikes that protrude from the top are far sharper than I imagined them to be. Ignoring the creeping sense of dread working to smother me, I press through the foliage, pushing against the jagged, crumbling rock, and emerge on the other side. I hear a soft chime in the back of my mind and an invisible hand wraps itself around my throat, disappearing on the wind before I can choke.

"We need to move quickly to the forest up there," Giles whispers as he breaks free of the wall with a rustling of leaves. "The faster we can get away from the wall and under cover the better."

"What was that?" I ask as we retreat from the moonlight for the cover of the trees. I rub my neck for emphasis.

"That was Boltov's ward. He knows someone has trespassed in his territory now. It's only a matter of time until they're looking for us."

"Do they know it's *us*?" I ask, picking up my pace to match Giles's. "Will they know it's us on sight? Can they track us?"

"Tracking, I don't know. On sight? Well, at a glance, Raph and I might be able to blend in with the other fae of the High Court, you less so. But they have rituals they can perform to expose us."

"Then we have to move quickly."

"Already working on it," Raph mumbles.

The city looms ahead, perched at the top of the hill. Another wall surrounds it with more guards at the entrance. We slink through the forest, straying away from the main gate.

"Do you know anything about the city inside?" I ask Giles.

"Not a bit. I'm as oblivious as you are."

"Don't look at me." Raph shrugs. "I've never been this far from Dreamsong."

"We'll just keep making it up as we go then."

We're almost through the forest to the edge of the city wall when there's a rustling in the trees behind us. I turn. I've been hunted by Butchers now too many times not to know the way they move, the way they sound, as they ride on the shadows. My hand is on the pendant and I'm not sure whether I'm about to put up a fight, or submit in the hopes that maybe I can get close to Davien one last time.

The woman is a blur. She's on me in a second, faster and more deadly than any Butcher I've ever seen so far. Yet, rather than killing me, her hand clamps over my mouth. Her other hand is on Giles's. Raph is in too much of a stunned silence to do anything other than blubber.

"You're going to get yourselves killed," Shaye says with a crazed grin.

thirty-three

THE MOMENT SHE REMOVES HER HANDS FROM OUR MOUTHS, GILES EXHALES A SIGH OF RELIEF THAT ENDS WITH HER NAME. "Shaye."

There's no chance for her to react before his arms are around her, clutching her, holding her as though she's the last woman on earth. Shaye is clearly startled. Her eyes dart from Raph to myself. I give a small and knowing smile before turning to Raph.

"Why don't we give them a moment?"

"We don't need a moment," Shaye says defensively.

"Shaye." Giles pulls away with a hard look.

Shaye rolls her eyes, but the small smile at the corner of her mouth betrays her true emotions. "All right, *one* minute."

I pat Raph's shoulder and guide him over to a nearby tree that we stand on the other side of. I lean against it, crossing my arms, and stare out over the sloping forest. My gaze is soon brought up to the High Court, glittering against the night sky, looming above us.

"He likes her a lot." Raph startles me from my thoughts.

"He does," I agree.

"She likes him, too, even if she doesn't want to show it."

"That's astute for a kid." I ruffle his hair. He scowls and combs it back into place. I've learned that Raph doesn't like things that remind him of his age. I must be the worst, because it only makes me want to remind him more.

"One, not a 'kid,'" he says firmly. "And two, I know a thing'r two about love."

I snort. "What do you know about love?"

"I know it when I see it." He puffs out his chest. "Like, that night when you and Prince Davien danced. You two are in love. Anyone could see it."

A knot in my chest eases as a different one forms in my stomach. I wonder if he's right and how many people could see it. I wonder how many recognized what was happening well before I did, or even Davien. I wonder if that night, even when he swore to me that there would be no feelings between us, he knew he already loved me and that I loved him.

"Well? Am I right?" Raph presses relentlessly.

"Yes," I confess with a soft laugh. "You are right."

"Knew it! And that's why you're going to save him."

"It's one of the reasons. Saving your kingdom is also a pretty big motivator." I look back to that tall city looming up on the hill and the sheer wall that encapsulates it. For every one Butcher I see prowling, I'm sure there's at least five more, hidden away. A whole army of killers, trained from their very first breath. Do we really stand a chance against them?

"Sorry for the delay." Shaye rejoins us with Giles at her side.

"No apologies necessary." I push away from the tree.

"Were you two kissing?" Raph waggles his eyebrows.

Shaye leans forward, sticking her nose right near his. "You know, your father and mother aren't here right now to protect you. You really want to try me, little man?"

Raph's spine goes rigid as he stands up tall. "No, not in the slightest, sorry, Lady Shaye."

Shaye hums and straightens away. "I'm watching you, kid." Funny enough, he doesn't object to being called "kid" when Shaye is the one to say it. She does have that intimidating aura—one that only grows more intense when she looks up toward the city. "So, you came here with the intent to break into the High Court?"

"Giles tell you?" I ask.

"He didn't need to, it's obvious. Why else would you come? Especially with Dreamsong destroyed." Shaye's mouth twists into a frown. Her eyes flash with a rage unlike any I have ever seen. This battle has always been personal for her, and Boltov only compounds the reasons she has to fight with his attack on Davien and Dreamsong.

"How did you survive Allor?" I ask.

"Tell you on the way." Shaye starts up the hillside. "I think I know the best place for us to make our way in."

As we walk around the circular city, Shaye tells her tale. She engaged with Allor for as long as she could, taking blows so that Davien and I could escape. Once Shaye had reached her limit, she activated a magic that she calls "the dreamless sleep."

"And what does that do?" I ask.

"It's a ritual of my own inventing—it's how I escaped Boltov the first time. Think of it like wrapping myself up in the shroud of death. I can cocoon in it for a short period of time. Doing so stills my breathing and slows my heart to the point that it's nearly impossible to tell that it's still beating; it's a sort of stasis. But if I stay there too long, I actually will perish."

"So you made Allor believe she killed you and revived yourself after she left."

"Yes. Butchers are always too eager to believe that they bested their kill. That no one can compare to their skill or ruthlessness. They don't stay around to give burials or double check their finishing blows." Shaye shrugs. "It worked once before, it worked again. Then I tried to find you and Davien. When I saw the remnants of a struggle at the keep, I went for Dreamsong." All that time, Shaye was on her way just several steps behind us. "And, on seeing the ruins, I came straight here. I came to make good on my promise. I had no idea who else survived."

"You came to kill Boltov," I finish for her.

"I always said that I would…or, I will at least help the man who does." Shaye's gaze falls to my neck. "I take it he didn't get the powers and that's why we're in this mess?"

"No, he didn't get them. And it was my fault. If I had moved faster—"

"It was the fault of the Butchers that attacked you and Boltov for sending them," Giles interrupts. "Don't take blame when it's not deserved."

"Bloody Butchers." Shaye curses under her breath. "Never miss a chance to ruin something, do they?"

We come to stop at a low-lying point in the hillside. A small stream rushes past iron bars set in the wall.

"It's one of the water sources for the city," Shaye explains.

"This will work nicely." Raph scampers over, inspecting the bars.

"Move aside, kid." Giles approaches. "Leave this to the man with the history of building."

As I watch Giles begin to set up a small ritual on either side of the narrow riverbank, I feel hopeful for the first time. Giles and his knowledge of construction will help us get into doors, and out of tight situations. Raph is small and nimble. He's also proved himself to be creative and resourceful—things we're definitely going to need on the inside. And Shaye, she has the most valuable information out of all of us. She's lived in the High Court before. If anyone is going to know where they're holding Davien and how to get to him, it will be her.

I glance over at her, prepared to tell her how grateful I am that she's here with us. But her solemn expression takes the wind from my sails.

"What is it?" I ask softly, so as not to draw Giles or Raph's attention. Shaye stares silently up at the city, her chest rising and falling slowly as she breathes deeply—in through her nose and out through her mouth. "Shaye?"

"I can't believe I'm finally back here," she admits, bringing her eyes to mine. There's a searching quality to her gaze, tinged with a frantic worry that I know I can't calm. "I can't believe I'm going back in. Willingly."

"It's all right if you don't want to." Boldly, I rest my hand on her shoulder, trying to offer some amount of comfort. In a small way, I think I can relate to the fringe of what she's feeling. I imagine what emotions might smother me if I ever stand before my family's home again. I would be terrified to say the least.

Shaye laughs softly and shakes her head. "I'm not upset. I'm proud of myself for coming back—for being strong enough to make good on my promise."

"I admire you," I say softly.

Shaye brings her eyes to mine. "And I admire you. Throughout all this you've remained resilient, more than I expected. You're not so bad...for a human."

A small pop interrupts our conversation. We both look back to see Giles lifting a section of the grate away. He rests it off to the side. Raph scrambles to try and help, but I can imagine the boy is not doing much in the way of heavy lifting.

"You both ready?" Giles asks, though his eyes are mostly on Shaye.

"Yes." She strides forward with confidence, grace, and murderous intent. I watch as the woman willingly marches back into the den of her tormentor without the slightest trace of fear. No... That's not quite true. I saw her eyes. She is afraid. But she's not letting that fear win—she's not giving him power over her anymore by allowing him to frighten or intimidate her.

I hope that someday I can be half as strong as Shaye. That I live long enough to try. As I cross beneath the wall of the High Court, I make a silent vow to myself:

I *will* go back to my family's home, confront them for what they did. I will tell Laura to leave and to be her own woman—with me or on her own—and then I will leave them behind me forever. I will never be afraid of them again. I will never let them intimidate me again. I will not let the fears they have entrenched in the dark corners of my mind rule me.

Halfway through the tunnel, Shaye pauses, motioning for us to do the same. When she speaks, her voice is nothing more than a whisper. "This is going to drop us right in a busy area. Even at this time of night, there's going to be people out on the streets—heading to or from taverns, or conducting business."

"And with the water, there's no way we can glamour." Raph stares at his feet.

"Which means there's no hiding." Shaye nods.

"No wonder it was left with such meager protections." Giles strokes his chin in thought. "So what's the plan?"

"I'm going to make a distraction," Shaye says.

"No," Giles tries to interject.

She continues speaking over him. "I have a few more rituals charged. I can make enough chaos that you three can slip into the crowd."

"I'm not leaving you." Giles grabs her hand.

"And we're lost without you," I say. "You're the only one who knows the way through the High Court."

"It's not hard. And with his keen sense of direction, you'll have no trouble at all." Shaye gives a nod toward Raph. "You can do it, right?"

"I…"

"I know you can." Shaye blows over his hesitation with her fierce determination. "And just because I'm going to make a distraction, doesn't mean they're going to catch me. I think I proved by now that I can be pretty slippery, especially when it comes to Boltov's clutches."

"I don't want you to use yourself as bait." Giles still clings to her. "There's another way."

"Maybe there is, maybe there isn't. We can't risk spending all night debating it. The autumn's end celebrations are coming to a finale, and if I know Boltov at all, he's going to use their culmination as his platform to show everyone that the last Aviness has finally died under his grasp." Shaye shakes her head. "We don't have time to look for better plans, or second-guess ourselves. We have to just move forward with what the world has given us, and make it up as we go."

"You're sounding like me, and I don't think I like it," Raph says.

Shaye grins. "You're not the only one who knows how to make trouble."

"Fine." Giles resigns himself to the idea, running a hand through his golden hair on the side of his horns. "But I'm going to help you make the distraction."

"You should stay with them," Shaye insists. "If they run into more trouble along the way, you might be needed to combat it."

"Or, Raph and I will be able to move faster with one less person," I speak up. "The two of us look pretty nonthreatening."

"Are you saying I look intimidating? No one has ever called me intimidating before." Giles seems oddly pleased.

"I was pretty intimidated by you when I first met you." I grin. The expression quickly falls from my face as my tone turns serious once more. "With two of you making the distraction, it'll be better than one. And you can look after each other. So hopefully, you can meet up with Raph and me again."

Shaye locks eyes with Giles. I get the sense that there are unspoken conversations happening between them. She frowns. He nods. She shakes her head; he sticks out his tongue; she rolls her eyes.

"*Fine*," Shaye says finally. "Can't exactly go against my own advice and spend too long debating this. Now, you two, listen up, it's not hard to get to the castle from anywhere in the High Court..." She tells us the best route to take as we finish our walk through the tunnel, the water masking our words. When she's finished she doesn't even bother looking my way. "Did you get all that?"

Raph gives a confident nod. "Leave it to me."

"How do we get *into* the castle?" As the light at the end of the tunnel draws nearer, the reality of our plan dawns on me. I'm about to go into enemy fae territory without magic, with a child as my only ally.

"Unfortunately, that's not something I can help you with." Shaye frowns. "It's been so long since I was in the High Court. And I left before I was high enough in the Butchers to know the ins and outs of Boltov's personal guards. Besides, even if I had, I'm sure he's changed it by now. You're just going to have to adapt to whatever you run into."

"I'll do my best. One last thing, do you have any idea where they might be holding Davien?"

"If I had to guess, it'd be somewhere deep within the castle, and hard to get to. The power of the hill becomes stronger—making all fae but the king weaker—the deeper you go." Shaye comes to stop. Raph stays behind as well while Giles slinks toward the bars that cover the entrance of the city. I see him moving around, readying whatever ritual he's going to use. "Listen to me, Katria, you're only going to have one shot at this. As soon as Boltov knows that *you* are in the city, he's going to do everything he can to hunt you. They already know that there's some kind of trespasser via the wards on the outer wall. Once he knows it's the human who's thwarting him, nothing will stop him from exacting vengeance on you.

"As hard as it will be to stomach, don't take the first opportunity you have, not unless it's the right one. If you're clever and careful you'll both be able to hide in plain sight. But the second you're identified, well, you'd better move very quickly from then on. Treat every action as though it might be your last, because it very well could be."

"I understand." I nod and grab the necklace around my neck.

"Good." Shaye claps my shoulder once. "I don't know if you humans believe in the great Beyond across the Veil, but, if this should all end badly, I hope to see you there."

"I hope so too, assuming the old gods, or whatever the rulers of that world are, let humans in."

Shaye chuckles. "For all you've done for the fae, I'll make sure they make an exception for you."

A smile crosses my lips.

Giles returns. "All right, I'm ready. You three?"

I look to Raph, who says, "Ready. Stay close to me, Katria."

"I will."

"You sure you want to do this?" Shaye asks Giles. "You could go with them."

"You're not the only one who wants to cause Boltov a little bit of pain." Giles smirks. "I've been waiting for this moment since he murdered my whole court. Don't deny me my opportunity to wreak havoc now."

"Never would dream of it." In the most bold, outward display of affection I've seen from her so far, Shaye takes his hand and brings it to her lips. Her eyes flutter closed and she kisses each of his knuckles. "It has been my honor to be by your side."

"You shall always have a place there." Giles looks back to the exit. "On the count of three then. One."

"Two," Raph says. I see him sink low in his stance. I do the same after I shuffle off to the side to have a clear path to run.

"Three," Shaye finishes for all of us.

Giles slams his palm against the tunnel and a rumble vibrates from the heart of the wall itself. The ground beneath the exit falls out, and I watch as the grate and half the wall crumbles with it. Shaye doesn't waste a second. She bolts out into the city beyond and waves a hand. Dark shadows pour from her fingertips, clotting in the air. I hear shouts.

"That's our cue," Raph says with a glance toward me. I nod. He sprints ahead and I'm close on his heels as we emerge into the High Court.

thirty-four

RAPH SETS A BREAKNECK SPEED. He's so much more nimble than I that I'm scrambling to keep up. He bounces down the rubble as though it were skipping stones, landing on a cobbled river walk below as I'm just climbing down the first boulder.

I bite back shouting his name. I don't want to draw attention to ourselves. I just have to keep up. So I jump. I land hard, falling forward and scraping one knee so I don't roll my ankle. I push off with both hands and run in the direction that Raph disappeared, praying I haven't already lost him.

Citizenry of the High Court are only adding to the confusion. They're silhouettes, darting around frantically. It's utter chaos. Yet miraculously, I manage to spot Raph among the fray.

He glances behind him and catches my eye; I nod and we keep running.

A sudden, icy wind whips through the area, dissipating the smoke. As it does, I grab Raph by the collar, and yank him into a small alcove where others are huddling. I push to the back, holding him close with both hands. Raph glares up at me.

"We should—"

I *shush* him, looking back over the square. None of the other people around us seem to pay us any mind. We're just two other citizens of the High Court, afraid of and darkly fascinated by whatever wrath the Butchers are about to reap on the intruders.

Shaye stands alone on a bridge that spans the river in the center of the square. Her shoulders are relaxed, hands on her hips, as she looks up at the four Butchers that are perched on the nearby rooftop. One of them lazily flips a dagger.

"Impressive you made it this far, traitor," one of the Butchers says blandly. "Maybe that means you won't be totally boring while we kill you."

"Why don't you come down here and find out?" Shaye cocks her head to the side.

"She's confident," the Butcher flipping the dagger says. "We should see if she has such a bold tongue in a few minutes."

I scan for any sign of Giles. He's nowhere to be seen. That can only mean he's taken up some kind of strategic position to help Shaye. After his insistence on staying with her, I know he's not going to abandon her now.

"Oh, if she does, can I cut it out?" One of the Butchers laughs. "I find that's sometimes the only way to deal with smart talkers like her."

"Well, if you're too intimidated to stop me, I think I'm going to go and have a word with the king." Shaye shrugs, and starts down the bridge in our direction.

No sooner has she moved than the Butchers launch themselves from their perch. Shaye doesn't so much as look their way. A giant wall is erected out of nowhere—no doubt Giles's doing. Shaye puts her back to the initial three Butchers to fling daggers at two others who jump from hidden vantages.

As the fight picks up, the citizenry begins to scatter.

"We should go now," Raph whispers. I nod, yet I can't seem to bring myself to move. My eyes are glued to the battle that's only just beginning. Though I already know how it will end. For as strong as Shaye is, and as clever as Giles can be with his magic...there are only two of them, and a seemingly infinite number of Butchers. All I can hope for is that they're taken alive and put with the rest of the survivors of Dreamsong.

We'll save them with the rest. I have to believe it to be true.

Raph tugs on my hand and I can finally force myself to move. We fall into step between two couples rushing away from the combat. We keep our heads down, and miraculously, no one stops us.

We walk until the sounds of battle have faded. I don't know if they faded because the struggle has ended…or if we are too far to hear it anymore. That's when I finally gain the courage to look around.

I'm instantly overwhelmed by how…*normal* it all seems—well, normal by Midscape standards. I had been expecting the High Court to be a place with blood running through the streets and screams hanging in the air. I expected to see people living under a vicious ruler, the threat of bodily harm hiding behind every corner.

But the men and women seem no different than the people of Dreamsong. Away from the chaos and the nightlife of the section of town we entered in on, the streets are quiet. People keep to themselves, heads down and shoulders high, as they march toward wherever it is they're going this late at night.

The buildings are made with the same style construction as many I saw in Dreamsong. There's stained glass, and iron lampposts. Most are two or three stories tall and far more condensed than Dreamsong was.

It's in the comparisons that I slowly draw that I begin to see the darker undercurrents. The construction is *so* similar that it can't be by chance. I think of what Giles told me of his people—that the courts of crafters and tradesmen were slowly rounded up by Boltov and assimilated or killed. Or perhaps the houses are even older and date all the way back to Aviness. They are a part of stolen history; their occupants are captives. Even though they're going about their business, the normality is a shroud—a lie to cover up the constant fear they must live in.

"I don't like this place," Raph whispers.

"I don't either. We'll do what we came here to do as quickly as possible." Yet even as I say that, I think of Shaye's warning. I only have one chance to make it into the castle. I have to wait for the right moment.

We move up the streets, heading for the highest point of the High Court—the castle. As we near I can hear faint music. It makes me all the more aware of how quiet things have been. We emerge onto a main street. Down in one direction, far in the distance, is the main gate of the High Court. In the opposite direction is a large portcullis that protects the opening of the castle.

"So that's it," Raph murmurs.

"I hate how pretty it is," I say under my breath. Spires made of silver are edged with crystal that almost looks like frost. Motes of light drift through the air, circling up the high points, and then out over the city—as if all the magic I saw throughout the fae wilds stems from this one source. Every window is embellished with a frame of carved stone in the shape of lilies and stars. Every balcony railing is adorned with scrollwork. It's the castle I always saw in my dreams after listening to the storybooks Joyce would read through the door.

"It's pretty 'cause Boltov didn't build it."

"I figured as much."

"Mom would tell me stories of Aviness when I was little. She'd say the castle, the hill, the glass crown, and the fae people are all one. As long as one stands tall, so do the others. And that's why the glass crown can control the fae, and why it can't leave the High Court."

I crouch down and lean against a wall, listening to him. We perch ourselves at the edge of where the narrow road meets the main one, the castle in view.

"Did your mom's stories have any tips for how we might get inside?" I ask, trying to keep my focus on him and our mission rather than the music drifting through the portcullis.

"Of course not. Stories don't really tell you that."

"Yeah, they're pretty useless," I mutter. "The stories of the fae from my world haven't really done me much good here." I close my eyes and listen to the tune as it reaches its end. At first, I thought I was so focused on it because it had been a few days since I last heard music—that wasn't the magical sort. But the more I hear, the more I begin to think I recognize it. "That song... I know it."

"Do you?" Raph arches his eyebrows.

I push off the wall. "I'm pretty sure I do."

"It's coming from inside the castle, right?"

"I think so." I bring my thumb to my mouth and bite on the nail lightly. "I want to wait here for a bit."

"What are we waiting for?"

"I want to see if we can figure out who's playing that music." I keep my eyes focused on the portcullis, ignoring the four Butchers lined up on either side.

"Do you want to get closer?" Raph shifts from foot to foot, as if already restless.

"No, we stay here until it seems unsafe or unwise to do so." I make sure my words are firm and leave no room to be contradicted. One shot. That's all we have. I have to be patient and take it when the time is right.

The music plays on through the night. The longer I listen, the more certain I am that I've heard it before. It's not just the tune, or the melody, or even the unique harmonies—what I cling to is a unique rendering of those notes. Music is like painting. Artists can use the same medium, but no two people will create in the same way.

As dawn begins to streak across the sky, the portcullis finally opens. I stand. Raph pushes away from the wall as well. He grabs for my hand, clutching it tightly as we watch people stream from the castle.

They stagger into the early morning, clinging to each other and swaying. I watch the macabre parade stroll down the main street, fanning out into alleyways, and disappearing into the lavish homes that line the main run of the High Court.

These fae aren't like the others we saw in the lower rungs of the city. They're dressed in sumptuous clothes—silks and scandalously transparent chiffons with cuts that leave very little to the imagination.

Gold and jewels weigh them down, circling every finger and neck. The finery is even draped from their horns and wings, tied with ribbons and small chimes that sing as they move. These people float through the world as though they own it, as though they don't have care.

"Look," Raph whispers. "Their feet…"

Their gilded presentation is merely a distraction, I realize. Their hems and boots are bloody. I see crimson splatter on men's waistcoats.

"You don't think that's from—"

"Don't even think it." I pull Raph a little closer to me. "We're going to help them, and stop all this forever, I swear to you, Raph. I will stop this." I look back to the portcullis in time to see the music troupe emerging. Sure enough, I recognize them. "Those are the players from Dreamsong," I breathe.

"What?" Raph looks as well. "*Those traitors*," he snarls. "How dare they—"

"Stop." I clutch him tighter before he can run off in a just rage. Kneeling down, I look him right in the eyes. "You have to keep your wits about you now and think through every action. Will you do that for me?" Raph swallows hard and nods several times. "Good. Now, tell me, can you play any instruments?"

"The drums, a little."

"The drums it is. Come with me."

"What are we doing?" He stays at my side even though he is clearly uncertain about what has prompted me to march along the main street.

"I'm going to talk to them."

"I don't like this; I don't like any of it." He folds his arms.

That's certainly an understatement. None of this is going as I would've hoped. I'm exhausted, pushing my limits; my brain is running out of good ideas. Maybe it ran out a while ago. I guess we'll find out if Raph is right and this is a terrible idea in the making.

We trail the performers to an inn not far from the castle. As soon as they go inside, I hear the band strike up again and I breathe a sigh of relief. At least they didn't immediately retreat to their rooms. It will be easier to catch a word with them this way.

I stop Raph. "You're going to stay here, okay?"

"What?" He blinks several times in shock as he watches me remove the glass pendant from my neck. "You can't— What're you—"

"If I don't come back out, you find a safe way out of here and you *go*. You take this as far away as you can, you hide it somewhere no one will ever find it." Guilt and sorrow are companions of desperation as I stare down at the small boy, watching the fate of his people rest on his little shoulders. "Wherever you hide it, you take that secret to your grave. Anyone who could know you have it would do the same—I will do the same. Keep yourself and the magic of Aviness safe."

"I can't…" He grabs my hand with both of his. "I can't do this without you."

"I hope you won't have to." I pat his hands with my other one. "But if things go badly in there, this is the safest way. So promise me you understand what you must do."

He reluctantly nods. "I understand."

"Good." I turn to face off against the inn. Sucking in a deep breath, I march across the narrow street on the exhale. Before I inhale again, I've opened the door. There's no turning back now.

The troupe isn't so much performing as sitting and strumming together. The first floor of the inn is a tavern, empty at this time of day. I can smell the herbaceous aroma of something slow cooking in the back—the owners no doubt getting a head start on the dinner rush before the sun is even up.

Because it's so empty, all eyes are on me as soon as I enter. Instruments fall silent. I cross straight for them, weaving around the vacant tables. My eyes meet the man who I assume is the head of the troupe. The man with the raven hair and markings on his brow whom I played with in Dreamsong.

We simply stare at each other for several long seconds. I can tell he recognizes me instantly—I can tell they all do by their demeanor. We're silently sizing each other up, waiting to see who's going to act first. The muscles in my legs are tense and ready to run.

"You look weary, traveler." The leader hooks a chair with his toes and kicks it toward me. "Take a load off."

"I've come a long way." I sit. "I heard the king has something truly special planned for the end of the autumnal celebrations."

"Can't speak for the king, but we've heard whispers of the like." As their leader speaks, the troupe exchanges wary glances. I see the flash of steel as one of them moves. Bards who live on the road would be armed to the teeth.

"Must be nice, having the opportunity to see those celebrations inside the king's halls."

"It's certainly something." The fact that he doesn't agree—that none of them have immediately called the Butchers at the sight of me—gives me hope.

"Do you play for royalty often?" I have to be absolutely certain where their loyalties lie. How they can go from playing for the people of Dreamsong to Boltov's inner circle in a few short days is beyond me. But if I'm to work with them, I need to understand.

"Only when we're summoned. The king has a good ear for music; he appreciates quality."

That must be why they've been afforded some freedoms. They must've cut a deal with the king—or at least reached an understanding. Is what I have to offer enough to sway them from the security they've managed to procure?

"Do you think he would appreciate the quality of my playing?"

"As I said, I can't speak for the king."

That's not a no. "It would be an honor to play for the Fae King."

"Would it now?" He arches his eyebrows.

"I *desperately* want to get inside the castle."

"And why is that?"

I bite my lower lip, weighing my next words carefully. "There is something—someone—within his walls that I would very much like to see. But alas, the Butchers keep the place well-guarded and I'm not of high enough standing to gain entry otherwise, so there's no way I'll be able to get in on my own."

"You want to play your way in, is that it?" His directness gives me hope.

"If that's what it takes."

The man holds out a hand to one of his fellow performers. She hands him her lute without question. The leader then passes it to me.

"Play for it."

"Pardon?" As I take the lute, he picks up his own from where it leans against the chair.

"A duel of the strings." His fingers pluck up the neck of his fiddle. "I play, then you play, then I play, then you, until one of us is bested."

"And how do we know when one of us is bested?" I'm already tuning the lute.

"We'll know; that's never a problem."

The other minstrels are settling into their chairs. They wear smiles, as if this is all an amusing game to them—as if the fate of the fae wilds doesn't hang in the balance. Maybe it is just another amusement. Maybe the life of these bards is looking for one burst of inspiration, or entertainment, after the next. They have no loyalty, no fidelity, but to the muse of music.

Perhaps it's their lack of loyalty to anyone that means I can trust them. It makes them simple and straightforward. I'll always know where they stand—for themselves.

"If I win, you let me and my friend join your troupe for the next performance inside the castle, yes?" I ask carefully, knowing I need to be mindful when cutting a bargain with fae.

"You *and* your friend?"

"He can play the drums." I consider this, knowing the musical aptitude of the people I'm speaking to. "Or, he can be like a jester, dancing about. He's small and can be quite silly."

The leader exchanges glances with another woman. She chuckles. "I think I'd like to see her little assistant."

"Very well then. You've a deal."

No sooner does the man say it than his fingers start to move. He starts off slow, dancing around single notes, plucking one string after the next, before they evolve into chords. It's a shrill, short little ditty, almost like a wordless limerick in music form.

The second he stops, I begin to play. I take the same line he laid with his notes and turn it into full chords. When he plays next, he harmonizes those chords, bow in hand this time and blazing across the strings.

I'm in as much awe watching him play now as the very first time. Inspiration makes my fingertips itch. The music soothes away my troubles. It puts the world on hold. I can't stop myself. I don't wait for my turn.

I begin playing in harmony, and then, in creative dissonance to him. The leader gives me a glance, and a smirk, but he doesn't tell me to stop. I grin slyly at him as well and begin to play faster. We egg each other on with glances and clever notes. The troupe begins to stomp and clap. And as we reach our crescendo, we both finish with a flourish. Breathless.

We share a smile, as only two musicians can.

"All right. You should get some rest. Because tonight, you come with us to play for Boltov."

thirty-five

I SLEEP FOR MOST OF THE DAY. When I wake, it's because the other troupe members I'm sharing my room with are beginning to stir. I feel like I could've slept for eternity. Raph is curled up at my side, snoring softly. His face is relaxed and he looks so vulnerable, so peaceful. I've never been more aware of just how young he is. Guilt cuts me deep at what I've thrust him into. I gently stroke hair from his eyes.

One of the musicians crosses over, holding out a small bundle of clothes. I take it with quiet thanks. They have three whole trunks of costumes that they all source their attire from. What they gave to me is a ruffled blouse with billowing sleeves and a plunging neckline. It's paired with tight, black, leather pants. I fuss over the pendant, eventually deciding to twist it around and hang it between my shoulder blades. Like this, it looks almost like a choker, as long as my hair covers my shoulders.

I rouse Raph to give him his clothes. He sleepily dresses in the brightly colored tunic and spotted leggings. He's awake enough by the end to frown at the ensemble.

"I look like a clown."

I chuckle softly and don't tell him about my jester comment the night before. "You look like a *performer*."

"You got the good clothes." He pouts.

"I look like a pirate."

"Pirates are fabulous."

I laugh and shake my head. "Let's get breakfast."

Raph and I keep to ourselves as we eat. The troupe isn't unkind, but they don't seem to be interested in engaging with us more than they have to. I suppose it's for the best. The less they know, the safer we all are. Moreover, no matter what happens tonight, I get the keen sense that we won't be leaving the castle together. This is strictly business.

I'm halfway through my meal when it strikes me that the food *still* has taste. Raph notices the sudden shift in my demeanor and tries to inquire as to the reason. But I brush him off.

We have enough to worry about. Adding concern for me withering away as a human in the world of the fae is something we don't need. And I still don't *think* I'm withering. It must be because I still have the necklace on my person—the power of kings is still with me even if it's no longer in me. Fortunately, it seems to be enough to sustain me in this world.

The lamps are being lit as we emerge from the inn. The leader guides the troupe in a merry jig as we walk and dance down the road. I try and throw myself into the music. My fingers move on instinct, sure. But it's impossible for me to get lost in the melody the way I usually do, the way I did last night, not with the castle looming over me and the portcullis drawing ever closer.

"Hold it." One of the Butchers stops us just before we can enter. Her eyes shift to me and Raph. "Those two weren't with you yesterday."

"Ah, yes, they were late in getting to the High Court. They joined us last night. But we'd be remiss to perform again without their skill," the leader says. All technically true.

The Butcher still seems wary. "I don't recall any new people entering the city."

I clutch my lute a little bit tighter, trying to keep my face as calm as possible. When we crossed through the barriers, did they know how many people entered? Or did they just get a sense of the wall being breached? Did they think that by capturing Shaye and Giles, they got everyone? Even if they don't...I can only hope that they would assume that anyone who is foolish enough to sneak into the High Court will stay far away from the castle.

"Do you recall everything that happens in the High Court?" The leader tilts his head.

"Do you often lose members of your troupe?"

"I lose many things." The man chuckles and plucks his fiddle.

The Butcher looks to me, narrowing her eyes. "Going to ask you a very simple question. You can only answer yes, or no. If you say any other words then I will kill you without a second's hesitation. Do you understand?"

"Yes." This is going to be too easy. She's treating me like a fae and thinking I can't lie. Even though I have no horns, or wings, they have no reason to expect a human to be here.

"Did you and him—" she points to Raph "—infiltrate the High Court, yes or no?"

"No." I smile widely and can't help but add, "Everything he said is completely true. They came out and got me."

One of the women of the troupe laughs. "Do you think something is funny?" the Butcher snaps.

"I think the world is one big joke, and the only tragedy is the people who can't seem to laugh at it," she says with a smile.

"Get out of my sight," the Butcher snarls and waves us along.

As we pass under the portcullis, the leader of the troupe looks back at me with a sly smile. He slows his pace to fall beside me. "I thought you were a bit different...a bit boring...but now I realize you are most interesting indeed. For it is what you lack that makes you special."

"I'm unique in my own way, as we all are," I agree, sharing in what might be the only smile I have of the night. "And you're right in that I don't need horns or wings to be special."

"You certainly don't." He dips his head and raises his catlike eyes to meet mine. "I want you to know that it has been my supreme honor playing with you."

"Likewise."

"No matter what happens tonight, I think I shall compose an epic ballad inspired by your tale."

I chuckle softly. I begin to suspect that's why he let me come along. "Hopefully, that song is not cut short and has a happy ending."

Our conversation comes to an end as we emerge on the other side of the portcullis. There is an antechamber where people mill about in their finery. A few clap and smile as we enter. A grand, gilded staircase winds around the room, but we head for the double doors that open into the main hall of the castle.

All breath leaves my body and I'm suddenly torn between awe and horror. Buttresses support a ceiling that feels as if it could touch the sky. Holes in the roof have been punched out with circular panes of glass, giving the stars and moon a view of the revelries below. Fae dance to unheard music, spinning around the floor, laughing. Some linger off to the side, eating and scheming.

It would be a normal enough celebration were it not for the men and women suspended in cages between each of the buttresses. I see Hol in one of the cages and instantly grab for Raph. The child looks to me and I meet his eyes.

Be strong, I mouth silently and stare at him with an intense gaze. Then, I lift my eyes back to Hol. Raph must follow my stare because I can feel him trip; I hear the choked whimper that almost escapes. I clutch on to him with white knuckles, so tightly that I know it hurts. He would've seen his father eventually. It's better for him to not be caught off guard. But, yet again, I'm overwhelmed by the guilt of bringing him here.

All of this will be worth it so long as our plan works. Raph and I went over the details multiple times last night before we slept. He knows why he's here. He knows why I need him. And he won't back down...not even when he sees his father on the menu of tonight's entertainment for these demented people. This is his only chance of *saving* his mother and father.

At the far end of the hall, perched high atop a dais, is the throne and the man that I can only presume is King Boltov. From this distance, it's hard to make out the details of him. I can gather only the broad strokes—like his fiery red hair, or how tall he must be to still dominate a chair while so hunched and sullen. I'm taken aback by how wiry and frail he looks. This is the man that has kept the Boltov legacy alive and the fae kingdom on its knees? This is the king who has committed all of the atrocities I've seen and imagined? He looks like the one withering, not me.

No, I can't let his appearance fool me; I must stay on guard.

As we cross the room to ultimately stand before the king, I search for any sign of Davien or Vena. The people in the cages are certainly captives from the sacking of Dreamsong, but I can't see any of the leaders. I'm not sure if that makes me feel better or worse.

"Your Majesty." The leader of the troupe dips into a low bow. "Thank you for bringing us back tonight to serenade your great hall."

King Boltov nods his head ever so slightly. The glass crown that sits heavily on his brow picks up the light of the massive chandeliers and breaks it into a thousand pieces. It puts the replicas from the night in Dreamsong, and those on the brows of the men in this hall, to shame. Its craftsmanship is more refined and it oozes staggering power. A thousand rainbows cage in a cosmos within it.

It also appears that Davien was right—he's performed some dark ritual to allow him to wear the crown. Seeing it on his head churns my stomach. I am enraged, as if seeing him with that crown is an affront to *my* history—an insult to me.

"My favorite minstrels have returned."

"We would not dare object to your summons, Your Majesty." The troupe leader has yet to straighten. He still stares at the floor. The rest of us have followed suit, bowing our heads. Though I look up through my lashes.

This close, I get more details of the bloody king.

His face is weathered, like leather that has been over-tanned, thinned in the process, and stretched taut over jagged stones. His eyes are sharp blue, piercing, threatening to expose even the slightest hint of deceit. The man's fingers are more bone than flesh or muscle, and gnarly yellow claws extend out in place of nails. Two crescent horns, as black as pitch, curl up from his brow around the glass crown. There is nothing about him that is soft, or warm, or inviting. Everything is brutal angles.

"I look forward to what you perform for me tonight as we are at the end of our celebrations. Play well and I'll let you keep all your fingers and feet. Play poorly and you'll be forced to dance on nubs."

I'm beginning to figure out why the troupe was so willing to allow me to join them. Even if they're not strictly loyal or disloyal to anyone but themselves, Boltov is an easy enemy to all.

"It will be our pleasure to play for you. We will not let you down, sire."

"Good. But do know when to stop; I have a special surprise planned for the culmination of the autumnal celebrations that I do not want interrupted."

The words "special surprise" fill me with dread—anything that this man feels is special is surely something I won't like. But I move with the troupe off to the side of the dais. The leader lays down the initial melody. The rest of us follow. Raph taps along on his comically small drum, bravely putting on a smile.

Two hours and my fingers are aching. I've never played this long or this hard. But I continue forcing myself to do so even when my hands are threatening to cramp. I'm playing for my life.

And then, the music suddenly stops. I look from the leader of the troupe to the king. Boltov has lifted a hand. Like a dark omen, he slowly unfurls himself from the throne, standing at full height and towering above everyone else.

"Good subjects, today is the last day of fall and the first of winter. It is the day when the living gives way to the dead. When one world passes to the next. And the Veil between us and the great Beyond is at its most thin."

There's excited murmuring throughout the hall. I see courtiers grabbing up goblets and taking hearty sips. They can't wait to see what their king has planned, and it makes me sick.

"I know many of you are expecting entertainment tonight similar to that of last night, especially given my décor." Boltov lifts his hands and motions to the cages around the room. "However, tonight's special. Tonight is for *me*, and for a history that began hundreds of years ago with the death of King Aviness the Sixth." The gathered fae hiss at the mention of the former king. He slowly begins to descend the staircase that wraps around the dais. "As you know, there are some who still think that the Aviness line can be restored. That the *true king* to the throne is out there, even though it is *I* who wear the crown." He taps on the glass circling his brow for emphasis. Chuckles ripple through the hall. "So tonight it is my pleasure to see that the last of that line is finally cut off—henceforth, there will never be a question about who is most fit to rule."

Boltov curls his fingers and doors at the side of the hall open. A small legion of Butchers led by the leader I saw in the woods manhandles in Davien. He's chained up, shackled, helpless. The courtiers jeer and spit on him as he is paraded through the hall to ultimately be brought before the king.

"Kneel before the true king of the fae," the Butcher sneers, and strikes him behind his knees. Davien falls to the ground.

"This man-child is the last hope of the 'mighty' Aviness bloodline? This is the man who was to threaten me? Who was guarded for decades in the Natural World?" Boltov laughs, and the court laughs with him. "This pathetic creature thought he would be ordained by the ghosts of the old kings in the Lake of Anointing but lacks any true power."

Boltov gives Davien a sharp kick underneath his jaw. One that would've sent Davien reeling were it not for the Butcher holding him in place by both of his arms. Blood dribbles from Davien's mouth as he glares up at the king. He hasn't seen me yet, which I suppose is a blessing.

"I suppose it must take a lack of true power in oneself to notice it in others," Davien growls and spits in the king's face.

"You uncultured cur," Boltov almost purrs, running his claw down Davien's cheek. "I will enjoy dismantling you, piece by piece." Boltov glances over his shoulder. "Music, fitting for blood."

The lead minstrel picks up his fiddle and hesitates, only for a breath. He draws a shrill note from the strings reminiscent of a distant scream. The drummer begins thumping a pulsing beat, unhasty, but determined. Horrible in how slow it is.

This is it. My chance. I lock eyes with Raph and nod as I pull the necklace from my throat, palming it in the hand I strum my lute with.

As the music picks up, I step forward. Eyes are on me as I approach. Enough that it draws Boltov and Davien's attentions. Davien's eyes widen slightly. I force a crazed grin across my lips so well that he's startled.

Laughing, I twirl as I begin to strum my lute, frantic, mad. I stomp and look on eagerly. The chords I play are minor, intentionally dissonant on the off-beat to the fiddle. It's not music, it's horrid sound. Fitting of the look in Boltov's eyes.

"Yes, yes!" Boltov laughs, rearing back a clawed hand. "We shall dance for his death!" The rest of the fae begin to laugh and spin as well as Boltov strikes Davien in the face. Blood spatters the floor.

My stomach churns and I keep playing. Davien is no longer looking at me. He's hunched in the arms of the men holding him. Does he know what I'm doing? Can he see my feet? *Please let him notice*, I pray. In my periphery, I see Raph step forward, nerves causing the beating of his little drum to become frantic.

Everything is rising to a boiling point. Boltov's attacks become more brutal. I keep spinning, drawing invisible shapes on the floor with my feet. They're the same shapes I was making in the lake. The same symbols Davien and I reviewed for the abdication ritual. Hopefully, the charged start of that ritual is still within us. Waiting to be finished.

"Look upon him!" Boltov shouts. Everyone slows. I finish my movements, the necklace hot in my palm. "There is nothing special about this man. He is—"

"There might be nothing special about him, yet, but there certainly is about me," I interrupt. Boltov spins in place. I hold up the necklace. *Look at me*, I say with my actions, *look only at me. You failed to notice everything else I'm doing.* I snarl at him, as if I, too, have wings and fangs. As if I can be as monstrous as any fae. "You want this, don't you? This is what you need to become the true king of the fae, and not some pretend sovereign who lives in a castle stolen by his ancestors, ruling with nothing more than fractured power and fear."

Boltov's eyes widen slightly, and his mouth splits into a grin that exposes sharklike teeth. "*You* are the human."

"And you are the last Boltov the fae will ever suffer."

He takes my bait and lunges for me. I wait until he's in motion; he's too committed to change course when I release the necklace, allowing it to drop. A blur at my side whizzes past me before the pendant can hit the floor. Boltov can't catch it, not when he's already stretching his clawed hands toward me. Raph is so nimble and small, he's faster than even the Butchers caught flat-footed.

I hear Hol shout. I'm focused only on Raph and Davien. The boy tosses the pendant. Davien reaches out as far as his chains will allow. His fingers close around the glass even as the Butchers are lunging for it.

"I abdicate!" I scream at the top of my lungs for all to hear. I scream so that it echoes in every recess of this ancient castle. So that my voice rattles the very foundation of this hill upon which the first fae was crowned. So that the rulers who still have their eyes on me might know my intention. "Rule in my stead; the kingdom is yours; the crown is yours; and the strength of the ancient kings is yours; rise King Davien Aviness."

My words reverberate unnaturally in my ears. There's a strange echo, a delay, as the world trembles beneath me. The invisible lines I drew on the floor glow in tandem with the pendant. The light becomes so bright that the floor cracks and the pendant shatters in Davien's hands. The shackles turn to dust on him and he stands straighter than I've ever seen. His wounds are healed and his wings are complete, no longer in tatters. His eyes are the most brilliant shade of green that ever existed.

And they're the last thing I see before Boltov finishes his swing for my throat.

thirty-six

I'M GOING TO DIE, THAT'S MY FIRST THOUGHT. And my second thought is, *fight*.

I fall backwards, not even caring how I might land, as long as I dodge his attack. But Boltov has fae speed and power. When his first swipe misses, he follows through on his momentum, spinning and dropping down to the ground over me. I roll, amazed his claws don't find their mark a second time. Then I look up and see why.

Davien looms over us, still glowing and holding Boltov by his wrist. Chaos abounds in the hall; some people are running for the portcullis; some step out of the way and pour themselves fresh glasses of wine to watch the entertainment they were promised.

"For even trying to touch her, I condemn you to death," Davien snarls. Boltov struggles to break free of his grasp, but can't.

Butchers are charging from every corner of the hall. "Davien, Butchers!" I shout.

He glances over his shoulder to assess the threat. With his free hand, Davien grabs the glass crown on Boltov's brow. Boltov screams. There's a horrible ripping as the crown is freed. I watch as his flesh is sheared from bone in chunks that cling to the crown, as though it had been cemented to Boltov's head. Davien looks at it in surprise and disgust, before throwing Boltov back into the dais with unnatural force. Boltov's head cracks against the stone, leaving a trail of blood, and his eyes are dazed. His lids slowly droop closed. Without the crown, he looks like the frail, little man I first saw him as.

"I'll hold them off." Davien looks between Raph and I. "You two, find a way to free the others."

"With pleasure." I push myself off the ground. Davien doesn't have time to place the crown on his brow before the Butchers are on him. The head Butcher knocks it from his grasp.

"Davien—"

"Go!" He snarls and lunges for the man who rounded up Dreamsong.

I curse, fighting the urge to stay and help him. "Follow me, Raph."

Raph is at my side as I begin to run to the doors that Davien was escorted in from. "Where are we going? What about the people above?" I know without seeing that he's looking up to his father.

"I'm not sure about them yet." I push a startled courtier aside and right in the way of a lunging Butcher. "They were keeping Davien through these doors, so I can only assume that's where they're keeping the stronger, or more dangerous people. We need them."

"Do we want more dangerous people?" Raph spins out of a Butcher's grasp. He reaches into his pockets and holds up what looks to be shimmering sand. He blows it out of his palm and it ignites in the air, exploding into millions of tiny sparks—harmless but effective in concealing us escaping through the doors.

"We want dangerous people if they're *our* dangerous people," I whisper. Even though the main hall has erupted into chaos, these passages are quiet and I would be a fool to think that Boltov would leave his prisoners unguarded.

"Oh." Raph gets it. "Like Vena and Shaye?"

"We can only hope." The hall continues away, lined by doors that look far too nice to hold prisoners. "Raph, if you were keeping prisoners, where would you put them?"

"In the heart of the hill," he answers without missing a beat. "Closer to the center where all powers are weak except for the king's."

"Then we head down."

"Wait." Raph takes my hand. "I doubt this will work, but it's better than nothing." He closes his eyes and a look of extreme focus overcomes him. I watch as an image overlays on top of him, slowly condensing into place like water solidifying into ice until it appears solid. Where Raph once stood is one of the Butchers who stopped us by the castle's portcullis.

"Did you just make us both look like Butchers?"

The illusion laid on top of him nods its head. I have no idea where to look, because I know Raph only came up to my hip. "Again, I doubt it'll work. Most fae can see past others' glamours."

"But it's better than nothing. You're brilliant."

"Just hold my hand. I have an easier time glamouring you as long as I can touch you."

"Fine with me."

We start down the hall. At the end it opens into a room. Fortunately, it's empty, and there's a staircase that heads both up and down. We take the downward path into another room. It's in the fourth hall that we see a group of Butchers racing past in the distance. We wait, clinging to the wall and holding our breath. Only one glances our way but doesn't seem to register us as out of place. Raph's glamour works.

Down another staircase, the finery of the castle is beginning to disappear and be replaced by what I would expect of the Boltovs. There are rooms designed solely for unsavory delights—the sort that makes me cringe and pass through as quickly as possible. I hold Raph's hand a little tighter. It's going to take him some time to process all this once we're done. But if we succeed, he'll be able to have that time with both of his parents still alive.

As we're passing by a door, I hear faint mutterings inside. I halt and press my ear against it, confirming my suspicions.

"What is it?" Raph asks.

"I think they're in here." My hand lands on the door handle. "Are you ready?"

"After what happened in the hall, I'm ready for anything."

"Yes you are." I try and turn the latch, but it won't move. I bite back a loud groan of frustration.

"It's all right, I can take care of this one." Raph releases my hand and the glamour disappears. His nimble fingers pick at the door and he mutters to himself. I hear the soft click of the latch coming undone. He smiles up at me sheepishly. "Don't...tell my parents about that particular ritual, okay?"

"Your brilliant secret is safe with me." No wonder he can get anywhere and into anything. I grab the latch again and debate how I want to proceed. Do I open the door and go in ready for a fight? Or do I try and sneak in? Unsure, I crack the door slowly. A sliver of light cuts through the doorjamb and I can hear the words more clearly.

"...you hear the echoes of screams, don't you? Those are cheers of delight, as your fake king gets torn apart by the courtiers he would try and rule," Allor sneers.

I open the door a little farther, poking my nose in. There's a bloodied table in the center of the room, and all manner of wicked-looking instruments on the walls. In the back are several cages, all full of people whom I recognize from Dreamsong—namely Shaye, Giles, and Vena.

Allor paces in front of the cages, as though the bars are designed for her—to keep her out—rather than keep her prisoners in. Because if she had access to them, well, her threats make it clear what she would do.

I open the door a little bit more, the hinges are silent, and I ease myself in, staying against the back wall. Vena's eyes dart over to me only for a second. Giles is slumped against the wall, not moving. I'm sure Shaye notices me as well, but neither her words nor demeanor betray anything.

"You would hope those are cheers of delight," Shaye says loudly to Allor, as if trying to keep the attention on her. "Because if they're not, it's going to be disastrous for you, isn't it? What do you think our new king will do to the Butchers who served Boltov so faithfully? He seems like he's a generous man but—"

"I don't want generosity from the likes of him." Allor scoffs.

"No? And here I thought you wanted the generosity of kings. You don't seem to have any problem kissing Boltov's boots." Shaye leans into the bars. "Maybe that's because you realize that without him you're absolutely nothing."

"How dare you!" Allor rages, lunging for the cage. As she rattles the door, I slowly take a bulky steel mallet off the wall. It's so heavy my muscles tremble just holding it up. "*You* are the one that is nothing. You are the one in the cage, not me."

"I escaped the cage he put around me long ago." Shaye smiles, keeping Allor's focus on her and her alone. "But I do feel sorry for you, that you're not strong enough to escape. Weak body, weak mind. It's so very sad."

"I'll show you who's weak." Allor fishes in her pockets. As she produces a key, she sees me in her periphery, now only a step away. "What the—"

I don't hesitate. I swing. The hammer meets the side of her head with so much force it flies from my hands and slams on the floor with a *clang* so loud I'm certain it's alerted half the castle. Allor falls to the floor, motionless. I stand over her, panting softly. With one strike my pulse is racing even faster than when Boltov attacked me. Every inch of my body is aflame, panicked, ready to fight.

"Nice hit." Shaye whistles.

"I—Do you think she's dead?" I ask uncertainly. I didn't expect to make good on my threat to Allor in the woods that day. I guess she was the next fae I killed.

"I hope so? I think it would be very poetic if one of their lead Butchers was killed by a human."

As Shaye speaks, Raph picks up the key that Allor dropped and begins to unlock all the cages. Shaye is freed while I'm still staring down at Allor. She rests a hand on my shoulder. "I don't think she's dead. Which is also good, because I'd like the honor of killing her if it's all the same to you?"

"By all means," I murmur.

"What's happening?" Vena asks, emerging like she had been sitting in there by choice and not force. "I take it that the fact that you're here is a good sign?"

"Davien has the magic of the old kings. The abdication ritual was finished. He's up in the main hall fighting off the Butchers but he needs help," I say quickly.

"Reinforcements are coming." Vena looks to Shaye, who's dragging Allor into the cage she was just trapped in. "You know where the others are being held?"

"I don't know anything about the castle; I told you that already." Shaye rolls her eyes. "But I can make an educated guess."

"Do that," Vena commands as Shaye locks the door to the cell on Allor. "The rest of you who are able to fight, come with me."

"I can lead you back to the main hall!" Raph says excitedly.

"That is no place for you." Vena frowns. Raph deflates some and frustration reddens his cheeks.

"Raph, I need you," Shaye says. "I need your little fingers to get into any locked doors there might be standing between me and the rest of our friends. Plus, after we free everyone, we're going to need a guide back to the main hall."

"All right." Raph looks up at Vena. "You'll free my father, right? He's in a cage in the main hall."

"I will," Vena swears.

"I can show you the way," I say.

Vena shakes her head. "That's no place for a human, either. You should stay here."

"I'm going to lead you."

"Vena is right," Shaye says as she tends to Giles's wounds. He groans softly. "You should stay here; it will be safer."

"Let's go," I say firmly to Vena.

"This isn't your fight," Vena says.

"This is my fight." I point to the ground, as if I'm making my stand, as though I'm swearing on the rock on which the first fae king was crowned. "This has been my fight from the moment the magic of the old kings entered my body—from the moment I married Davien back in the Natural World. And then I made an oath to your people. I followed through on my promises. I want to see this to the end." I want to see the first moment Davien sits on the fae throne.

"Very well," Vena relents with a glint in her eyes that almost looks like approval. "Lead on."

We race back through the corridors and rooms. There's not a sign of a single Butcher on the way. But as we grow near, I can hear why.

The fighting in the main hall has reached a fever pitch. Screams and explosions of magic rattle the doors that Raph and I escaped through. *Hold on*, I plead from the deepest recesses of my heart to Davien, hoping that somehow he can hear me. *Hold on just a little bit longer, I have things I need to tell you.*

I hang back, and let the fae charge around me. Even if this is my fight, they're better warriors than I am. Especially since I lack all magic now.

Doors burst open to reveal a hall scarred by magic. Wispy weapons fling through the air as Butchers leap from shadow to shadow. Davien is in the center of it all. He is alight, power still rippling off of him as cold flames that deflect most of the attacks. With a mighty flap of his wings, he launches into the air, catches a Butcher by the throat, and throws them to the ground, landing atop their chest before engaging with another.

The fae from Dreamsong flood into the room and further level the playing field. With this many hands, they're able to free those that were still trapped in the cages hanging from the ceiling and they join the fight as well.

As the tides turn, I look to the dais. The smear of blood from Boltov's head is still there, but Boltov himself is not. I thought he was killed, or knocked out at worst.

Where is he? I don't see him in the fray, and the fact spurs me to action. I begin to run along the wall, jumping over debris and dodging deflected attacks that dig pockmarks into the brightly colored frescoes at my side. Crouching low to make myself small, I inspect the blood trail that leads away from the dais and around the back. Following it, I find a small door, hidden from view of the main room. It's ajar.

I glance back to the hall. No one seems to have noticed me. They're all too busy. Before I can think better, I cross the threshold.

Behind the door is a tunnel that I have to crawl through. It widens to open up to a spiral stair. Up and up, I spin until I'm spit out into what appears to be a closet. Dozens of coats and pants, all stained with blood and left on the floor to stink up the room, cushion my feet as I push through the curtain of hung clothes.

Shuffling in the other room has me halting. Boltov mutters to himself. Footsteps grow near and I crouch, sinking back into the passage before he can see me.

The hanging clothes obscure most of my vision, but I can see him rummaging around in glimpses. He grabs things frantically, as blood is still streaming from his forehead, painting his face a haunting shade of crimson. He opens a cabinet, revealing daggers, but instead goes for the jewels that are laid out beneath them.

When he leaves, I slink back out and take one of the weapons for myself, silently lifting it off of its pegs. He's trying to run and I'm not going to let him escape. One bloodline will end tonight, but it's not Aviness.

I emerge into the king's bedchambers. He's in an attached office, framed by bookshelves on either side, illuminated by a window-filled wall that overlooks the city and stars. Sure enough, he has an open bag on a desk he's trying desperately to stuff too many yards of fabric into. He curses, frustrated, and sends clothes scattering with a grunt.

I silently pad up behind him. This is the king that has held the fae kingdom at its knees? No, he's just a watered-down version of the first usurper, clinging to prestige that no longer exists.

Boltov reaches down for one of the jewels he dropped. He's far too frantic to notice me. When he's on his knees, I slip the dagger in front of his throat.

"Don't move," I say softly. He looks up at the window that dominates the wall behind his desk. Our eyes meet in the reflection on the dark glass.

"You." He rasps laughter. "A human girl has come to kill me."

"I'm not going to kill you." Though I certainly considered it.

"You're going to show me mercy? I doubt your friends will like that." His upper lip curls as he sneers.

"I'm going to let the new and rightful king decide what to do with you." Is there a better coronation gift to give Davien than Boltov's head?

"The new king...that squalling bastard won't last a year."

"A bold statement to make with a knife in your throat." I pull in the dagger just a little for emphasis. Boltov leans his head all the way back to look up at me. His expression is mad glee.

"Davien Aviness—except he's not *really*, is he? He wasn't born with that name. He's stealing the power of the old kings just as much as I would be. There's not a drop of Aviness blood in him. That crown won't heed him any more than it heeded me."

"If you don't think he could wear the crown, why try and kill him?" I'm not going to allow him to sway me.

"Because anyone who dares utter that they are part of that family is put to death. That name alone spurs rebellions. So long as people think there's hope of an Aviness returning, they fight me." He hisses and exposes all his sharp teeth.

"If Davien wasn't the heir, then why couldn't you wear the crown?"

"I'm sure there's some squalling babe, or boy, a distant offshoot that has *just enough* blood in their veins to keep the ritual alive, likely from the last true Aviness who escaped my clutches. But who that babe is?" He chuckles darkly. "Not even I know. And killing every possible Aviness prevents anyone from even thinking to seek their heritage. So the true heir will never know either and the glass crown will never be worn again. The fae will be at an eternal stalemate."

"Davien *will* wear the crown," I snarl and jerk the blade even closer. It nicks his neck. Boltov merely smiles wider. "He is the heir."

All this fighting. All this blood. To think Boltov is right...that all this time he was dissuading anyone from ever seeking out the discovery of the true bloodline...that killing Davien was a means to shatter the resolve of the Acolytes and he never was chosen for the crown...I can't bear it. He's lying, he must be.

"No, he won't. The glass crown will only ever grace the brow of the true heir, and that is not Davien." Boltov suddenly grips my wrist with strength I didn't know he still possessed. I was a fool for thinking that just because he didn't have the crown any longer, he would be helpless. He's still a fae.

The world spins as I'm flung through the air. Boltov tosses me as though I am a rag-doll. But I grab onto him with my other hand at the last second and the momentum pulls us both toward the window. Glass shatters, raining down over the High Court.

Wind whips my hair and I feel my stomach sucked out of me

as solid ground disappears beneath me. Boltov clings to me, scrambling. It's just like the day I fell from the roof. I stare up at the sky, just like I did then, the moon a silent observer.

Never climb again.

Monster child.

The smell of the burning flesh on my back singes my nose.

For a moment, everything is clear. What really happened that day returns to me. The world seems to fracture because none of the pieces fit together for me any longer.

"I will not lose to you!" Boltov shouts. It brings me back to life. I have to catch myself. I reach for one of the ornate carvings of the windows and catch myself on a lily. "You will not—"

I silence him by plunging the bejeweled dagger into his neck. Boltov gurgles blood and his grip goes slack. He slips from me, falling, farther and farther, until he is nothing more than a speck swallowed by the shadows of the streets of the High Court far below.

thirty-seven

I'M TOO SHOCKED TO MOVE FOR SEVERAL SECONDS. I keep staring down, waiting for him to sprout wings and fly back up, waiting to see a Butcher dodging to the shadows to save their king. Or, waiting to see a man resembling Boltov somehow magically run off in the distance.

But nothing happens and my grip is going to give out if I wait any longer. I reach for the next window ledge, climbing until I pull myself over the broken glass and back into the room. Panting, I wrap my arms all the way around myself, reaching for my back.

That memory.

My memory?

I squeeze my eyes shut, trying to expunge it from my mind. *No, no no no*, a scared girl who still lives in me screams, *don't think about it. Push it down.* It makes no sense. I'm tired. I was near death. I'm in a world that my human mind can barely comprehend. The memories retreat, slinking back into the depths they tried to surface from. That day was one of the worst days of my life, but it wasn't *that* bad. *It's all in my head*, as Joyce would say.

I push myself up off the ground and head back down through the passage and emerge into a much quieter main hall. The fighting has ended. The remaining Butchers have been rounded up and are ringed by familiar fae like captives of war.

Davien is with Vena in the center of the room. The fiery magic has faded from around him, but he still has a faintly glowing aura. His eyes meet mine.

"Katria." My name sounds like pure bliss on his lips as he heaves a sigh of relief. He rushes over and scoops my face up with both his hands and, without warning, in front of everyone, kisses me square on the mouth. Just like that, the world vanishes for a blissful moment. There is only him, the feeling of his lips on mine, the way his breath tickles the hair by my ear—it's all more perfect than I remember it. When he finally pulls away, I'm left stunned and wanting.

"Davien," I whisper softly, my eyes darting around the room. "Everyone…"

"I don't care." He presses his forehead into mine. "Let them see. Let them all see that their king loves the woman who saved his kingdom."

I shut my eyes as tightly as possible, wishing that this moment would never end. That the world was uncomplicated and I could remain by his side. But things are not simple. My soul is as murky as the shadows that usually surround the Butcher's necks.

"That was not the fate we were dealt though," I whisper only for him. "And your kingdom still needs to be saved."

"We have won." Davien pulls away and looks to the dais. His eyes widen as he no doubt realizes that Boltov isn't where he was left. "What the—"

"Boltov is dead. I killed him."

"You?" he breathes.

I tell him what transpired while they were fighting off the Butchers in the main hall. "…and then he fell."

Davien releases me and looks over his shoulder. "Shaye, to me." Shaye sprints over and Davien quickly summarizes what I just told him.

"I will lead a search party, Your Majesty. I will not rest until I have brought you his body." She races out of the main hall.

"Before there are any more distractions, I think there is an important matter for you to attend to, Your Majesty," Vena says, holding out the crown.

Davien turns to me. "I would like you to do it."

"What? Me?" I glance between him and Vena. Boltov's words about the crown are still fresh in my mind. "I don't think—"

"There's no one else I want to do this. The fae are saved because of you." Davien takes my hands. "Please, if nothing else, for me."

"All right," I say weakly. Vena hands me the crown. I've never seen anything more beautiful. Even though it is made of glass, it's warm to the touch and the most jagged-looking edges feel smooth. I see light shimmering from within, a similar haze to what was underneath the waters of the Lake of Anointing.

Davien kneels before me, looking up expectantly. I swallow thickly. Boltov was lying, surely. He was in a desperate position. Yet... *This* feels *wrong; something's not right.* I push the thoughts from my mind. I hold the crown out over Davien's waiting head.

"At long last," Vena says softly. I lower the crown to Davien's brow and release. "All hail—" Vena's words catch in her throat as the crown careens off of Davien's head, bouncing to the floor as we all stare in shock.

"What does this mean?" I hear Oren ask.

Davien is too stunned to say anything right away. He stares at the crown in disbelief, as though it has somehow betrayed him. I want to wrap him up, hide and console him. I want to scream at the crown for daring to make the man who has stolen my heart hurt in this way. I want to kill Boltov a second time for being right.

"It means...I am not the true heir," Davien finally says.

"But the bloodlines...you were the last. By marriage, but..." Vena mumbles, hardly coherent. "We were certain...there is no other. And *you* have the power."

"But there is someone else out there who is more fitting for the throne than I. There must be an Aviness by blood and not just marriage." Davien stands, looking older and wearier than I have ever seen him. Yet, somehow, he still manages to hold his head high. "So I will lead, until this person can be found and assume their rightful throne. The search begins tomorrow."

Night has turned to day, and yet I am somehow still awake. I feel like it has been a century since I last had a good night's rest. Davien stands before the dais, Vena on one side of him and me on the other, as he begins to organize the fae under his new regime. There are countless matters that must be attended to, and they all blur together as the hours drag on.

The hall before me has been transformed thanks to the hands of the people of Dreamsong, and the courtiers who returned to the castle, all too glad to be rid of the Boltovs. Pennons bearing the Aviness seal have been hung throughout the hall—a star atop the silhouetted image of the glass crown done in silver and set on a navy background, circled by white lilies.

I stare up at them, bleary-eyed. I think I've seen that symbol somewhere before. But I have no idea where. I shake my head and rub my temples. It was probably in Dreamsong. Or I'm just so tired that my mind is playing tricks on me, like it did when I nearly fell to my death.

That's the most likely explanation.

"Katria," Davien says softly. I blink, wondering when he moved in front of me. "You should go rest."

"I'm all right."

"You don't have to be strong for me." He tilts his head and gives me a smile. "You've done more than enough."

"I was hoping that I might..." I trail off. He's so busy. He's the king now—at least the temporary one until the real blood heir of Aviness can be found. And I'm no one. Even though he kissed me in front of everyone. Even if I helped him save the fae...I'll be no one soon enough. I'll have to go back to the Natural World and at best I will be a line in a bard's epic.

"You might?"

I open my mouth to speak but Oren approaches. "Your Majesty, we found the remaining banners deep in the vaults. Would you like them hung up along the main road of the High Court?"

"Yes." Davien stays focused on me. "What are you hoping for?"

"It's nothing."

"Whatever you desire is not 'nothing' to me."

"I just wanted a moment with you...alone." So much has

happened over the past few days since we were parted, that it doesn't feel real that he's here with me now—that he's safe. He went from chains, to battle, to ruling in a whirlwind. And other than a kiss, we haven't had a moment to ourselves. His brow softens slightly, mouth relaxing from the hard line of a king and into a smile I know. "It is not important."

"Vena, I'm going to retire for a few hours. Bring anything urgent to me. But for minor matters, I authorize you to act in my stead while I'm gone."

"You really don't have to do this," I protest, though not with conviction. I desperately want him to do this. So badly I feel a touch guilty.

He ignores me and takes my hand. "Oren, is there a room that I and the Lady Katria might rest in?"

"Certainly." Oren smiles and bows his head. "I think I know of an unused guest room that was spotted as we were looking for the old relics of Aviness. I can lead you to it."

"Please do."

"Davien, they need you. I can just go lie down for an hour and—"

In the midst of my objection, he hoists me up with both his hands and cradles me in his arms. I don't miss the curious glances of the courtiers who have been lingering in the main hall, watching their new king settle into his rule. I wonder what they think of me. If I am already the king's human concubine in their gossip.

"Perhaps you're not the only one who wants to steal a moment for just the two of us." He gives me a sly smile, oblivious to my insecurities, and follows Oren out of the main hall.

We're led in a different direction than I went the last time I explored the castle. Instead of to the right of the hall, we head left. There are bare patches on the walls where I assume Boltov tapestries were once hung. Some have already been filled with new pieces of artwork, others are still waiting.

Oren opens a door to reveal a comfortable-looking bedroom. "Will this do?"

"Wonderfully. See that we're not disturbed unless it's urgent."

"Most certainly." Oren bows his head and closes the door.

I'm instantly aware of how alone we suddenly are. Just like I am aware of every beat of his heart through the tattered shirt he wears. We hover in the center of the room, him holding me, and me just looking up into his eyes. Wordlessly, he takes me to the bed and lays me down.

There is no need for words between us. If we spoke we would have to talk about the complex circumstances that we have found ourselves in—all the uncomfortable truths that surround us. Namely that he is now the Fae King and I will have to leave all too soon.

Yet as he moves over me, he makes me feel...magical. Even though my back is against the bed, I feel as if I am soaring. Our bodies move together in a dance that only we know—that we invented. Our delighted sighs, gasps, and moans sing a chorus made for only our ears.

We put aside everything else and focus only on each other, once, twice, three times, until we are left sweaty and satiated in a breathless tangle of ecstasy. I run my fingers down his chest, tracing the curves of the muscle. He catches my hand and brings it to his lips, kissing my fingertips lovingly.

"I wish I could stay in this bed forever," he murmurs.

"You have a whole kingdom to run."

"A kingdom that isn't mine," he says sadly.

"If there is an heir more true out there, how could the Boltovs not find them?" I ignore what Boltov told me before he died. "Maybe that heir doesn't *want* to be found. Maybe they don't want the responsibility. Or maybe they have no idea who they are."

"It is not about what we want, it is about our duty to our people. Only the true heir can wear the crown and control all the parts of the great Aviness power."

I give him a tired smile. "Do what you must, but know that my confidence is with you and you alone."

"And your confidence is the only thing that matters to me." He kisses my fingertips again and pauses, refusing to meet my eyes. "Tell me, Katria, how do you feel?"

"Tired, but I think that's unsurprising."

"The magic is out of you now. We'll have to return you to your world before you wither away to nothing."

I knew this was coming, but hearing him say it makes it no easier. "The world is cruel."

"I will still come and visit you whenever I am able, I swear it." For a brief moment, I indulge in that fantasy. I think of summers in the forest clearing when I sit on the stump and play my lute for him. I imagine winters huddled by the fire, planning what we will plant in the garden next spring. I think of him coming to me in that manor, as though he lived up the road and we were torn apart by a minor inconvenience—like him needing to live closer to town for his work—rather than the reality of us existing in different worlds.

"I would like that, but you must also act as the king of the fae for however long you are. And that might mean you need to take a strategic wife."

"If I am the king of the fae I will do what I want," he insists. I resist pointing out how much his tune has changed on the matter and keep the thought as a personal delight. "Or, perhaps I will find the true heir soon. And when they are established on the throne, I will come and live with you in the Natural World forevermore."

It is a lovely fantasy. But I know better. This love, however meaningful it was, was not meant to last.

There is a knock on the door followed by Oren saying, "My lord—I mean, Your Majesty—fae have begun to arrive claiming they are heirs to the Aviness line and are demanding to try on the crown. How would you like us to proceed?"

Davien heaves a mighty sigh. "I thought I would have more time."

"Duty calls," I needlessly remind him with a coy smile.

"I will return as soon as I am able, my love." He kisses both of my hands and then shouts to the door, "I'll be there in just a moment."

Davien stands and begins to dress. With every article of clothing that covers his pristine flesh, my chest grows tighter and tighter. I wonder if this is the last time I will touch him, will kiss him. I'm so lost in my own thoughts that his hand is on the door handle when I blurt, "I love you."

"What?" Davien blinks at me several times over.

I sit up, clutching the blankets to my chest, although modesty seems like such a foolish notion between us now. "*I love you, Davien,*" I repeat, enunciating each word. I had hoped to say it at a more meaningful moment. But our time is fleeting, and every second that passes without my saying it is a tragedy.

"I thought you swore you would never fall in love?"

"A wise man taught me that I didn't know what love was when I made that promise," I say coyly. "And besides, I think that when I made that promise to myself, I was thinking about *human* men... You're not in that category. So I'm not breaking any of my old rules."

He grins and is back at the bed in an instant, cradling my face with both hands, and bringing his lips to mine again and again. "And I love you; I will always love you."

We breathe in tandem, relishing in the swell of emotions that those three words can bring. But all too soon, he releases me. Davien gives me a smile. There's a spark of yearning to his eyes, like he wants to stay. Yet he leaves...and I know this will be my life for the rest of my days.

I will yearn for a man I can never have. A man who will always walk out of the room, and out of my life, to a world that I'm not a part of. And I will live alone, in an empty manor, with the knowledge of a world that no other human has or would believe.

Part of me is grateful, even still, to know this love, this completeness.

And the other part of me is slowly withering for a reason completely unrelated to magic...already crushed by the incomprehensible loneliness that awaits me.

thirty-eight

I THOUGHT I WOULD DEPART FOR THE HUMAN WORLD IMMEDIATELY. But Davien has been so busy that it's been logistically untenable for that to happen. He's insisted that he will be the one to escort me when we ultimately return. For that reason, neither Shaye, nor Oren, nor Giles, nor Hol has been given permission to take me across the Fade, causing the delay.

Miraculously, I'm still doing fine in Midscape. They ask me regularly how I'm feeling. But after a good night's rest, the weariness from recapturing the High Court has vanished from my bones. Food still has taste, too. All this fascinates Vena. She eats with me at almost every meal now, asking relentless questions about every single flavor. Once, she even tried to test me by serving me food that was laced with an intense spice. I passed that test, much to my annoyance.

The current theory is that the ancient kings' magic was in me for so long that a bit wore off on me. It gives Davien unexpected hope that perhaps I could stay. Vena tries to curb that, but to no avail. Davien still seems to think that he'll find a way to grant me the ability to live in Midscape with the power of ancient kings reigniting the old human magics, hidden within me, languished from living in the Natural World.

Yet despite all this, I know the truth. I know what's

going to ultimately happen. And I've been bracing myself for it every day. If anything, my time here is becoming more torturous than fantasy. It is growing harder and harder to wake up next to him in the mornings, knowing that I will have to leave him. Returning to the Natural World will be a kindness when it finally happens.

During the day, Davien is busy with the relentless parade of fae coming to try on the crown. Each claim is more ridiculous than the last. Initially, I stand in the main hall as part of the audience. Watching each man and woman come up to explain how they were somehow, tangentially, possibly related to the Aviness bloodline. The tenuous relations are almost as ridiculous as their stories about how they were "lost to history" and "came to remember their calling."

Davien listens dutifully—more patient than I could ever be—and then invites them up onto the dais with him. The man or woman sits on the throne, and Davien lowers the crown onto their brow. Time after time, it falls to the floor. Naturally, I quickly grow bored of watching this farce, and begin to explore the castle instead. I'm not going to wait around as he places the glass crown on every fae in the kingdom.

But distaste for their disrespect of the glass crown and all Davien suffered to finally achieve it isn't the sole reason that I begin to wander.

Something is haunting me, chasing me. It has been in my darkest dreams. It is a memory that fades more and more with each passing day, as though it wants to be forgotten again. Part of me wants to forget. But the other part of me remembers that second of clarity I gained during the fall.

That's how I ended up back in the king's chambers—the one place that has yet to be changed from how Boltov left it.

That's how I ended up here, staring out the shattered window, heart pounding. Shaye found Boltov's body later that night. He has crossed the Veil and into the Beyond. But the ghost of him remains. The memories he forced me to confront seared in my mind.

I bite my thumbnail, worrying it with my teeth. I don't want to remember. *But I have to.* This night has haunted me for years and I am on the cusp of recalling something that feels so incredibly important. My back aches again as I stare out and into the sky.

"Remember *what*?" I curse and storm away from the window. How can my memories become distorted like this? What happened that was so bad my own mind refuses to allow me to recall the details? Why is this truth just out of my grasp?

I pace the room, frustration rising with every turn until I end up punching one of the bookcases with a grunt. As I massage my stinging knuckles, my eyes turn up to the books. I run a finger over the spines, catching in an empty hole where a tome is missing.

On each of the spines the symbol of Aviness is emblazoned. The eight-pointed star over the glass crown ringed in lilies. I run my finger lightly down the stretched leather, coming to a pause on the crown. Like this, the upmost spears of the glass crown's outline look almost like a mountain.

"*No*, it can't be..." I breathe.

"What can't be?" I jump, spinning to see Davien. He approaches, hands folded behind his back. Even without the crown, he has the trimmings of a king. His movements become more regal by the day.

"I... You're done early," I manage to say.

"I can't stand another person coming into these hallowed halls, spewing their half-truths and half-baked claims of legitimacy." He runs a hand through his hair as he comes to a stop beside me. "I waited for decades for the opportunity to assume that throne. I trained, and I struggled, and I fought, for the chance to bring peace and prosperity to our people. To see these individuals come out of the woodwork with no comprehension of what it is that they're trying to assume—"

I rest a hand on his shoulder gently, stopping him before he can get too worked up. "You could always stop the search," I needlessly remind him. "And rule as you were meant to."

"Eventually, the Aviness heir would be found. Eventually, some son or daughter would learn of their bloodline and come to claim the throne. It is better to find them now, when I can teach them, when I hold the respect of the people and can give the throne graciously to ensure a smooth transition of power. I will find them no matter what it takes."

I shake my head. "And that is why you are the king that they don't deserve."

"The bar was set fairly low when I assumed this position."

"And whenever you leave, it will be set far higher."

"What would I do without your encouragement?" He gives me a loving smile. Before I can answer he asks, "Now, what 'can't be'? And why have you come here?" Davien sniffs as if the air offends him. "It still reeks of usurpers."

"I…" I run my fingers along the journals. My fingers catch in the grooves of the embossing on the spine. I remember my mother's book, its worn-away title and fraying binding. "When I fell with Boltov…I had a memory of that day."

"What day?"

"The last time I fell," I whisper.

"The day you and Helen fell off the roof?" Davien rests a palm between my shoulder blades, over the scar.

"Yes." The word is gummy.

"What did you remember?"

"I thought I remembered *flying*," I whisper. That idea has been what's haunted me through these halls.

"I'm sure, to a child, falling from a great height must have felt like flying."

"No, I—I think I actually flew. Clumsily. Not well. But…there's no way Helen and I could've survived a fall from that height. No way I should've been able to catch up to her." I continue staring at the bookshelf. My finger is still wedged in the missing spot between the journals. At the pieces falling into place that I wish desperately I could ignore. "Sometimes, ever since I came to Midscape, I've had these strange sensations of knowing, of belonging—"

"The ancient magic of kings."

I give him a small glare in frustration. He's not taking me seriously. Then again, I did just talk about flying. I haven't been taking myself seriously for the past few days, either, with thoughts like that. But this damned bookshelf is forcing me out of my blissful ignorance. These things can no longer be ignored. "It's more than just that memory though. Like these books. This one is missing… the book you used in the ritual that night came from here, didn't it?"

"I believe so." He sighs softly. "That book was one of the few to have ever escaped the High Court."

"What *are* these books?" I dare to ask.

"Long ago there was a Court of Stars, seers of the fae. For every Aviness, they would record their destiny upon these pages with an ancient magic that could be read only by the individual. Every book on this shelf represents an Aviness lost... recorded by a magic that the Boltovs stamped out."

I swallow thickly. I'm wrong. I have to be wrong. This is insanity.

"Do you know how my father got that book?" *Please have a simple, logical explanation,* I silently beg.

He shakes his head. "No one in the Acolytes could figure out how the book made it to your father's estate. The last known person with Aviness blood was said to have escaped with it. She took it and ran, disappearing into the night." I think of what Boltov said: *the last true Aviness to escape my clutches.* "It took ages for Vena to track the tome down to your father. At least the book got as far away from Boltov as possible. I'm sure it would've been reclaimed or destroyed otherwise. I tried for years to get your father to sell it to me but he would always refuse."

What do I say? How can I explain this to him? Fear that Davien will see this secret I've kept as a great betrayal coats me. "That book..."

"It would've been impossible for you to know what it was as a human. Don't feel bad." He has no idea why my skin has gone clammy. "And your father, as a merchant, I'm sure he came across it at some point in his dealings. How it made its way across the Fade is a mystery, but I'm sure the last of the Aviness bloodline was just trying to keep it safe before Boltov got his hands on her. Stranger things have happened and—"

"That book was my mother's," I interrupt him. I'm unable to face Davien. Instead I stare at the place on the bookshelf where that tome should have been slotted. I pantomime fitting a book into the slot, my fingers sliding down the shelf to fall at my side.

That was it. The piece that was missing for everything to make sense. My gut wrenches and I'm not sure if I'm going to be sick or cry.

"*What?*"

"I told you, my birth mother wasn't Joyce. My mother died

when I was very young. She was the one who taught me all my songs. After she passed, my father forbade me from the woods, just like he forbade me to ever tell others who the book belonged to." I face Davien. "I thought he was just being cautious, overprotective because Joyce destroyed everything of my mother's. Or, I thought he wanted me to know how sentimental it was so I never gave it away."

"And that's why, when you saw me throw it into the fire—"

"I lunged after it. It was one of the two things that I had left of my mother."

He grabs my shoulders, shaking me. Davien is beginning to see it, too. "The other thing of hers—you said it was your lute, right?"

"Yes."

"The woman who should have been Queen Talahani Aviness was rumored to be an excellent musician. The songs you know, always knew, *fae* songs..." Davien's grip goes slack. "No, no, it's not possible." He shakes his head, staggering away. "And yet, the songs, the secrecy, the scars on your back... Your memory of flying...Queen Talahani's book being found at your father's estate."

"Wait, you don't think—" It's not possible. This can't be possible.

"You summoned wings the day you fell. Your father didn't let that woman burn you out of callousness. He let her burn you in a misguided and draconian human attempt to keep you safe—to keep you 'normal' by their standards. You sprouted wings and they clipped them."

A shudder rips through me as the memories return in full. The memories I tried to repress but can no longer ignore. The memories of that day that made no sense to me as a girl and even less as an adult.

"My father knew too much about the fae," I whisper. "I always thought it was chance. Or his proximity to the woods. Or the stories he'd encountered on his travels. No...he knew so much about the fae because he fell in love with one. He always said my mother wasn't made for that world," I echo my father's sad lament. "He meant it because she was made for Midscape."

"You're half fae." Davien steps back and leans against the bookcase as though he needs to catch his breath. "Queen Talahani was always rumored to have fled in an effort to save the bloodline. The Boltovs claimed they killed her, but her body was never found. Then the book the Boltovs were searching for—the one that Vena knew to look for through Allor—was discovered in the possession of your father. Talahani must have escaped to the Natural World. She must've fallen in love with your father, and given birth to you."

"No, I can't—I might be half fae, *maybe*, but I'm not—if I am, I'm sure my mother was some random fae. No one important." I begin to laugh, slightly crazed, wholly overwhelmed. "You're making no sense."

"I'm making *every* sense. You thrive, even still, in Midscape. You can eat our food and live here without withering. The magic of the ancient kings went to you—not me—because you are the heir; *you are the true heir*. And you could not give me the power, without first formally being anointed, and then abdicating, because the crown should have been yours to begin with. I was wrong. So wrong. You weren't a thief ever. You were claiming your birthright." Davien runs his hands through his hair, shaking his head. He vibrates with disbelieving laughter. "For the past few days, I've been thinking that I would never find the heir. That our people would have to *compromise* with me and be condemned to uncertainty on my death. All along I've been thinking that I have to let you go but it's not true. None of it is true!" He runs over to me and sweeps me up into his arms. "Katria, you were born to be the queen of the fae."

I blurt more laughter. "You're too tired. You can't possibly believe what you're saying."

"You know what I'm saying is true," he whispers into my ear. "You know it deep within you."

I ignore the nagging feeling that he's right. The feeling I've been desperately trying to ignore for days. "You're desperate."

"Fine then." He pulls away. "If you don't believe me, come and put on the crown. If you're right, and I'm wrong, then you have nothing to fear. It will fall from your brow like any other's." Davien starts for the doorway but I'm frozen in place.

"And, what if you're right?" I ask in a very small voice.

He glances over his shoulder with a small smile. "Then you will rule, as your birthright intended."

"But you still have the magic." I rush over to him. "I abdicated."

"These things can be undone. Remember, abdication was only ever meant as a placeholder until the true heir was ready. You are ready and I will give you back your power gladly." He grabs my hands. "Come with me."

"I can't."

"No matter what, Katria, I will be by your side. If you are the lost heir, then I will be with you as your most faithful servant. If you are not, then you are still half fae and we will spend our lives together in bliss. There is nothing but joy before us, I promise you."

I drift through the castle, led by Davien. My mind is still churning through his words, trying to make sense of them. And yet I feel like my logical thoughts are trying to catch up with what my heart has already known, has maybe known for a long time.

I never belonged to the world I was born into. I never fit in there. And yet here, ever since I came to Midscape, I found purpose—I found love.

The second we cross the threshold of the main hall, Oren is upon us. "Your Majesty, there are more here who would—"

Davien waves him off. Wordlessly, before all that have gathered, he guides me to the throne at the top of the dais as though he is guiding me to the bed. He motions for the seat and I hear whispering erupt around the hall.

"Your Majesty?" Vena steps forward. "What are you—"

"Many years ago, we lost the woman we believed to be the last *true* heir of the Aviness bloodline. Though she never held the throne, she was rumored to have lived in the High Court right underneath Boltov's nose, keeping the relics of her ancestors safe. It was the pursuit of a book she stole when Boltov finally discovered her that led me to meet Katria." Davien addresses the room. "The book was found across the Fade and in the Natural World. And when I used it in a ritual to regain the power of the ancient kings, that power did not flow to me, but to *her*." He motions to me. More whispering and glances are exchanged. "It did so, because she is a child of two worlds. Talahani fled and made a new life far from where Boltov could find her. She fell in love with a human and gave birth to a daughter."

Davien comes to stand before me. He looks down at me with eyes full of love and admiration. It's enough to make me feel brave. To make me, well, honestly, a little foolish.

"Sit, Princess Katria, on the throne that you saved, that is rightfully yours."

I oblige him. The throne doesn't feel any different from any other chair. But I'm keenly aware of the moment that the glass crown hovers above my head. I glance up at Davien, stealing whatever bravery I can from his loving gaze. He lowers the crown to my brow.

It stays.

A perfect fit.

"All hail, Queen Katria, true blood heir to the fae throne, last of the Aviness bloodline," Davien intones and the hall echoes. He gives me a small smile, love glittering in his brilliant eyes. "Long may you reign."

thirty-nine

"You know, we could still wait and go in the dead of night like two thieves." Davien sits across the carriage from me, looking rather pleased by the notion.

I laugh easily, louder, brighter than I ever have before. Laughter becomes more natural by the day. Even though it has been nearly three months since I was formally crowned as the new fae queen and my responsibilities have increased beyond my imagination, I feel lighter. For the first time in my life, I know where I belong. Granted, knowing where I belong doesn't mean it's always easier to be there. It just means that the hard work is more palatable because I know it means something.

"I'm not going in the night. I'm getting Misty myself. *And* I'm confronting them once and for all." I made a vow when I entered the High Court, one I'm determined to make good on. But I don't tell him that.

Davien smiles. He knows what this means to me. He knows why I need it. But even still, he wouldn't make me feel like a coward if I needed to run.

"I'll be with you the entire time, or not, if you prefer the latter."

"I think I want to try and do this on my own." I reach over and pat his knee. "But I so appreciate that you came with me to do this. Knowing you're here makes all the difference." He's usually my second whenever I'm unable to rule—

which is often, as I'm still spending many hours a day learning how to use my magic and studying the nuances of Midscape. There's so much for me to learn. So much history I'm now a part of and need to remember…especially since the Elf King and Human Queen requested an unexpected audience with me shortly before we left. As soon as we return, we'll move right into final preparations for their arrival. Which are many, since we only just wrapped up our Springtime Rites—so many festivals in Midscape to observe. Vena is overseeing things in our absence along with Shaye, Giles, Oren, and Hol assisting her. I couldn't dream of better people to be at my side as I settle into ruling.

"Whatever you need, I'm always here."

"Knowing that is what's giving me strength." I look him in the eyes as I speak so, hopefully, he knows how sincere I am.

But Davien must mistake my gaze, because he leans forward to kiss me fiercely. It's a kiss that promises more later, should I be inclined. And I am always inclined when it comes to him.

"I would go to the ends of the earth for you."

"I would traverse worlds for you." I laugh and he echoes the sound, rubbing his nose against mine. Both are true. I lean back in my seat, looking out the window. The Natural World is so plain compared to the magic of Midscape. These streets seem so little, the houses that once intimidated me so unimportant. "I remember the last time I rode in this carriage…I was nervous to meet my husband."

"Oh, that's right…" Davien trails off with small smile. "We're back in the Natural World. That means we're married again." I snort laughter. "Perhaps we should consummate that marriage tonight. We never did in this realm."

I smirk. "You would like that, wouldn't you?"

"You know I would like it very much."

We both heard the whispers at court. People are expecting us to be betrothed within the year. Davien and I have only given the topic passing discussions. There are more important things for us to worry about than formalizing our love in Midscape. Moreover, I'm not ready. I'm still learning how to love and how to be a queen. I want to master both of those before I think of getting married again. Davien has been more than patient on the matter, and has insisted that the next time we wed, it will be on *my* terms.

The carriage turns up the drive to my family's manor. I inhale sharply as the familiar lawn comes into view. It's far lusher than I have ever seen it. Gardeners are out tending hedges. I suppose Joyce didn't totally squander the money, at least not yet, if there's still coin to pay such a staff.

Davien squeezes my knee. "You'll do great."

"I know," I say softly. And yet my stomach is in knots as the carriage comes to a stop at the top of the drive.

Unsurprisingly, Laura is the first to greet us. She races out of the house, skidding in the gravel next to where the carriage comes to a stop. I open the door and see her eyes widen slightly as she catches her first look at Davien. Now that he has spent proper time in Midscape, he can hide his wings and glamour his more unnatural beauty to appear as nothing more than a human. In my periphery I see him give her a wink.

Laura's breath hitches. "Katria, I, you—you weren't lying, he's *very* handsome."

I laugh and wrap her up in my arms, squeezing her tightly. "It's good to see you, sister."

"I've missed you so much."

I can hear the pain and longing in her voice. It resonates deep within me, cementing my resolve. I had been unsure of what I intended to say next. But now that I'm here, I know what I have to do. *No hesitation, Katria.*

"I've missed you too." I pull away. I know Helen and Joyce are coming. I must be quick while it's still just the two of us. Hands on my sister's shoulders, I look her right in the eyes. "Your mother is not a good woman."

"Katria…"

"I know you might think me biased. And that might be true. But I know you also see it," I continue, voice level and determined. "Do not let her corrupt your kindness, Laura. Leave this place as soon as you can. You can come with me. You can marry your own handsome man. You can strike out on your own and forge your own path—I will support you, if need be. Whatever pleases you. But leave while you can and while you still have the heart I adore."

Laura doesn't get a chance to respond.

"Katria?" Helen is the first to emerge.

"I believe it is Lady Fenwood," I say loftily as I smooth my loose-fitting tunic of fae silk and step away from our younger sister.

"What are you doing here?" Helen manages to say through her shock.

"I've come to collect my horse." I start toward the stables.

"But—that's—you can't—"

I pause to give her a sharp look. "I assure you, I can." I continue to the stables, to finish what I should have done months ago.

"I'm going to tell Mother!" She runs inside. Laura still stands alone in the drive, too stunned to speak.

"Go and tell Mother, that's the only thing you've been able to do for your entire life," I mutter under my breath.

Cordella is outside of the barn, to my pleasant surprise. She nearly drops the rake she was using to collect hay for the horses at the sight of me.

"Well, old gods be resurrected. I never expected to see you around here again."

"I didn't expect it myself. But I won't be here for long. And I assure you, this will be the last time I ever step foot in this place. But it's good to see you, old friend," I say sincerely. Cordella always did her best for me. Sometimes her best didn't feel like enough, but I've had the distance now that I can recognize all her help for what was. "How is Misty?"

"She needs her legs stretched a bit. But I do what I can to keep her in top shape." Cordella wears a knowing smile. "You finally come to collect her?"

"I have." I pause as I start into the stable. "You knew I would come back?"

"I had a feeling." Cordella looks at me from the top of my head to the bottom of my toes and back. She gives me a nod of approval. "You look good, Katria. You wear yourself better than I last saw you."

"I know who I am now," I answer easily. I am the heir of the last of the Aviness bloodline. I am the queen of the fae. But I am also the daughter of a merchant lord, who grew up in an abusive home, with parents who modeled all the wrong kinds of love. I am whole and broken and mending. I am all of those things, and more. I am Katria Applegate Aviness, and I will never feel small again.

"Katria?" Joyce's shrill voice interrupts our conversation.

"Please tack up Misty," I say to Cordella. "And I will make sure that they know to not *dare* punish you for doing so."

"With pleasure, Your Ladyship." Cordella bows her head and heads into the barn.

"Yes?" I stare at Joyce as she tries to lord over me from the veranda that circles the manor. I had been dreading this moment. But, now that it's here, I find myself fearless. She holds no power over me any longer. The final knot in my chest unfurls and I can breathe again.

Joyce means *nothing* to me now.

"We did not expect you to come back so soon." The words are fake etiquette.

"I'm only here for a moment." And it has been months since I left. *So soon?* I can only assume she never wanted me to come back at all. "I'm collecting the last thing I made the mistake of leaving behind. Don't worry, once I leave this time I'll be gone for good."

"There is nothing here for you."

"There won't be soon."

"Misty is ready, Your Ladyship," Cordella calls from the stables.

"Thank you." I take Misty's reins.

"What do you think you're doing?" Joyce demands.

"I'm taking what is mine." I mount Misty and sit tall. "I'm taking the last of me that is in this house and I'm leaving for good. You will never see me again. You will never hear from me again. You will never be welcome in any house or lands that belong to me. Because I have found a family who celebrates me." I think of Oren, Giles, Hol, Raph, Shaye, Vena, and all of Dreamsong who have supported me in the first months of my reign. "I have found meaning, purpose, and *true love*. You have no power over me anymore. No matter how hard you tried to make me afraid of you for the rest of my life, it didn't work. I am free of you; and I'm going to take Misty with me to my new world. This is farewell forever." I pause, leveling my eyes with Joyce's. "And if you dare think to punish Cordella for this, I will find out and you will know my wrath."

"You—You—stop right there!" Joyce blubbers.

"No." With a light kick from me, Misty springs into a trot. I can tell she remembers me. The feeling of her gait brings a smile to my lips. Fae horses are good, but they were never mine. I round the front of the manor faster than Joyce can keep up. Helen is still in front of the main doors, gaping down at the drive. I can tell why: Davien is leaning against the carriage, talking with Laura.

"I see you got your horse." He pushes away from the carriage.

"I did," I say proudly. "My business here is done."

"Katria," Laura interjects. "When you said…I could go with you…" She looks between Davien and I.

Davien is clearly uncertain, but even now, he defers to me. I have the power of Aviness, after all. If anyone can find a way to give Laura a place in Midscape, it would be me. At the very least, I can give her the manor on this side of the Fade for as long as she needs or wants it…until she's ready to strike out on her own grand adventure, whatever that might be.

"You will always have a place with me, sister."

Laura's face crumples with relief. I wonder if she's been harboring guilt for Joyce and Helen's actions. I wonder if she thought I hated her as I hated them. There are many discussions to be had between us, but we will now have time for them.

"You're sure?" she whispers.

"I decree it." I smirk slightly. I'm looking forward to her reaction when she learns that my husband did indeed have magic, and he taught it to me—in a way. Laura will do just fine mingling with fae, I think. "Ride in the carriage."

"But my things?"

"If we don't go now, Joyce might never let you leave," I say solemnly. "I swear I will give you anything you need and more." Laura's gaze drifts back to the house as Joyce rounds the veranda to stand by Helen. She must know it to be as true as I do because she begins to climb in behind Davien.

"What are you doing?" Joyce flies down the stairs, shrieking.

I position Misty between her and my sister. "She is doing what she wants."

"That is my daughter, you—you're kidnapping her!"

"I'm leaving, Mother," Laura says, a little shaky, but braver than I could've ever hoped. I've never been more proud. She was always the strong one between us. "I'll write to you."

"How dare you!" Joyce says as the door closes. Helen continues to stand, expression changing between dumbstruck and angry. "You cannot—"

"Laura and I will do as we please. Goodbye, Joyce." Further conversation is pointless. I spur Misty into a trot and give a nod to Oren as I pass. I hear the carriage come to life with the clopping of hooves behind me.

Joyce gives chase, screaming halfway down the drive. What a pitiable creature. She might never realize that this pain is what her actions have wrought. But maybe Helen will. Maybe there's some good left in her and this will be the catalyst for her change. I can only hope so, for her sake.

But they are no longer my problem. I look ahead, leaving them and the manor behind me.

As a lone rider, I'm faster than a carriage ever could be. I know my way back to my home—my kingdom. This time, I will ride down the hillsides of my family's estate, through the hazy dawn, and into the forbidden woods. I will keep riding until I find the old markers that Giles and Hol taught me to navigate to find my way through the dark mist that separates Midscape from the human world.

My heart races in tandem with Misty's thunderous gallop.

The torturous dirge Joyce had conducted for my life has come to an end. But a new song is only just beginning. One with my sister, with the man who will be my husband in *both* worlds, and with my kingdom.

How about a bonus scene?

Not ready to say goodbye to Katria and Davien? Want a glimpse of the arrival of the Elf King and Human Queen at the fae court? Head over to my webiste to learn how you can get a special bonus scene from Davien's perspective that takes place after the end of the book. It also has some hints about what you can expect from the next books in the Married to Magic universe.

Learn how you can get the bonus scene for FREE at:

https://elisekova.com/a-dance-with-the-fae-prince/

Do you want more?

Married to Magic is not a series, but a world. Each stand alone novel set in this universe will be championed by its own heroine who encounters magic, romance, and marriage before reaching her ultimate happy ending. If you enjoyed *A Dance with the Fae Prince* and want more, then check out the other novels in the **Married to Magic** world on the next pages...

a DEAL with the ELF KING

a MARRIED TO MAGIC novel

Learn more at

https://elisekova.com/a-deal-with-the-elf-king/

NINETEEN-YEAR-OLD LUELLA HAD PREPARED ALL HER
LIFE TO BE HER TOWN'S HEALER. Becoming the Elf King's
bride wasn't anywhere in her plans. Taken to a land filled
with wild magic, Luella learns how to control powers she
never expected to save a dying world. The magical land of
Midscape pulls on one corner of her heart, her home and
people tug on another... but what will truly break her is a
passion she never wanted.

a DUEL with the VAMPIRE LORD

a MARRIED TO MAGIC novel

Learn more at

http://elisekova.com/a-duel-with-the-vampire-lord/

ON THE NIGHT OF THE BLOOD MOON, THE VAMPIRE LORD MUST DIE. But when it's up to a forge maiden to deal the killing blow, her strike misses the mark. Now, bloodsworn to the Vampire Lord, she must survive by helping end an ancient curse. Loyalties are tested and the line between truth and lie is blurred. When her dagger is at his chest, will she be able to take the heart of the man who has claimed hers?

About the Author

ELISE KOVA has always had a profound love of fantastical worlds. Somehow, she managed to focus on the real world long enough to graduate with a Master's in Business Administration before crawling back under her favorite writing blanket to conceptualize her next magic system. She currently lives in St. Petersburg, Florida, and when she is not writing can be found playing video games, watching anime, or talking with readers on social media.

She invites readers to get first looks, giveaways, and more by subscribing to her newsletter at:
http://elisekova.com/subscribe

Visit her on the web at:
http://elisekova.com/
https://twitter.com/EliseKova
https://www.facebook.com/AuthorEliseKova/
https://www.instagram.com/elise.kova/

See all of Elise's titles on her Amazon page:
http://author.to/EliseKova

More books by Elise...

THE
AIR AWAKENS
SERIES

A young adult, high-fantasy filled with romance and elemental magic

A library apprentice, a sorcerer prince, and an unbreakable magic bond. . .

The Solaris Empire is one conquest away from uniting the continent, and the rare elemental magic sleeping in seventeen-year-old library apprentice Vhalla Yarl could shift the tides of war.

Vhalla has always been taught to fear the Tower of Sorcerers, a mysterious magic society, and has been happy in her quiet

world of books. But after she unknowingly saves the life of one of the most powerful sorcerers of them all—the Crown Prince Aldrik--she finds herself enticed into his world. Now she must decide her future: Embrace her sorcery and leave the life she's known, or eradicate her magic and remain as she's always been. And with powerful forces lurking in the shadows, Vhalla's indecision could cost her more than she ever imagined.

Learn more at:

http://elisekova.com/air-awakens-book-one/

AIR AWAKENS:

VORTEX CHRONICLES
THE COMPLETE SERIES

A sweeping magical adventure, filled with royals, romance, family bonds, and sacrifice. Perfect for fans of Sarah J. Maas and Holly Black!

Vi Solaris is expected to rule an Empire she's barely seen... but her biggest problem is the dangerous magic that's awakening within her.

Now, alongside her royal studies, she's training in secret with a sorcerer from another land. From his pointed ears to enchanting eyes, he's nothing like anyone she's ever met before. She should fear him. But he is the only one who knows what's happening to her.

As Vi fights to get her magic under control, the Empire falters from political infighting and a deadly plague. The Empire needs a ruler, and all eyes are on her as Vi must make the hardest choice of her life: Play by the rules and claim her throne. Or, break them and save the world.

This coming of age, epic fantasy is a story of family, sacrifice, sorcerers, slow-burn romance, wrapped up in a magical adventure that will ultimately take readers to places they never imagined.

Learn more at:

http://elisekova.com/vortex-visions-air-awakens-vortex-chronicles-1/

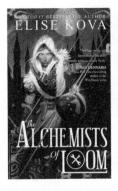

Acknowledgements

The Man—thank you for every time you cleaned the house, took care of the lawn, dinner, laundry, or any other errand so I could focus on bringing my books into the world. Thank you for your insights and support in every arena of my life. I can confidently escape the real world knowing you're holding down the fort.

My turtles—authoring would be so much harder without all of you. You are my support. My safe space. My masterminds. And my humor. You get me and I'm so lucky to have all of you. Thank you to each and every one of you for all you've done for me.

Teal—thank you for being such a good friend and for helping me with A DEAL WITH THE ELF KING. Yes, you should have been in the acknowledgments of that book, but this author friend of yours can be scatter-brained at times... Better late than never?

Mary—to the best fae I know, thanks for being such an uplifting friend. Also, thanks for making sure my body doesn't break from writing all the words I have to write.

Danielle Jensen—I hope you know how amazing you are. Thank you for everything you do for me, both related to books and not.

Marcela Medeiros—you continue to be a dream to work with. I couldn't imagine anyone else capturing the whimsy and magic of these worlds that I'm trying to make.

Merwild—my stories are richer for your art. Thank you for continuing to work with me on bringing my characters to life.

Amanda—I wish I could give you a big hug, but a line in the acknowledgments will have to suffice. THANK YOU for everything you've done to support me as both a friend and author.

The Book of Matches Media Team—you are all incredible and have been a delight to work with to help spread the word about my stories.

Rebecca Heyman—another manuscript down and onto the next one. Thank you, as always, for your continued help. I write with confidence knowing that you'll be there to give me input.

Melissa Frain—thank you for cutting, splicing, chopping, and helping me put this manuscript back together. It is stronger for all your help and my motivation was always spurred on by your delightful comments.

My Dear Tower Guard — every one of you is brilliant, supportive, and a whole lot of fun. Thank you for all your insights and just being willing to be kind and have a good time in our little corner of the bookish world. Let's keep looking after our own.

Every Instagrammer, Facebook Expert, BookTok'er, Blogger, and other influencer who helped spread the word on any platform — you are my heroes. I am so lucky that you're willing to work with me and will be forever grateful. I hope that there are many more books in the future for us.

My Patrons — Andra P., Melisa K., Serenity87HUN, Liz A., Amé van der V., Nichelle G., Sarah P., Janis H., disnerdallie, Giuliana T., Carmen D., Alli H., Malou7, Becky T., Jordan H., Siera, Matthea F., Caitlyn, Stephanie Y., Catarina G., Bri B., Stephanie T., Heather E., Mani R., Lori, Elise G., Traci F., Beth Anne C., Jasmin B., Maria D., Ashley S., Shirin, Samantha C., Lindsay B., Lex, Katrina S., Sassy_Sas, Veronica R., Karin B., Eri, Sam van V., Ashley D., Amber V., Amy P., Michael P., Kate M., Aanja C., Aemaeth, Alexa A., Alexis P., Ambermoon86, Amy B., Angela G., Asami, Axel R., AzFlyGirl, Betsy H., Bookish Connoisseur, Cassidy T., Cassondra A., Dana A, Elly M., Emily C., Emily R., Emmie S., Jennifer B., Justine B., Kassie P., Kelley, Kira M., Lauren G., Lauren S., Lindsay W., Meagan R., Michelle S., NaiculS, Reva, Rhianne R., riyensong, Sarah P., Sheryl K B., Tamashi T., Tarryn G., Tiffany L., Allie D., Chelsea S. — thank you all for your support, feedback, thoughts, and time. I have deeply enjoyed our moments together and I hope there are many more to come with every book I release. You all are with me at the start of this new adventure in my publishing world, and I couldn't imagine better people to spend it with!